TAKE YOUR LAST
THE WORLD YOU
YOU KNOW

A calm June day. A cloudless blue sky. The sun beaming down on the rolling South Dakota cornfields. **In one minute, a Soviet satellite will zero in on this piece of American heartland. Underground, a U.S. atomic missile will arm itself to rise to meet it.**

But this hideous confrontation is only the opening shock wave of an exquisitely orchestrated global master plan. A plan that will make helpless puppets of the most powerful figures on earth. A plan that will dangle the lives of millions over the horror that no world leader believes can happen, and that just one desperate, hunted man can head off. A plan that will teach you the ultimate meaning of treachery and terror as the final seconds tick away. . . .

"A THRILLER FROM BEGINNING TO END . . . moves with the speed and punch of an ICBM. . . . You cannot put it down and dare not miss a page!" —*Booklist*

"EXPLOSIVE . . . with a grim prediction about our future that well may be valid!"
—NEW YORK TIMES

Big Bestsellers from SIGNET

LAUNCH!

by
Edward Stewart

A SIGNET BOOK
NEW AMERICAN LIBRARY
TIMES MIRROR

Library of Congress Catalog Card Number: 76-3130

This is an authorized reprint of a hardcover edition published
by Doubleday and Company, Inc.

 SIGNET TRADEMARK REG. U.S. PAT. OFF. AND FOREIGN COUNTRIES
REGISTERED TRADEMARK—MARCA REGISTRADA
HECHO EN CHICAGO, U.S.A.

SIGNET, SIGNET CLASSICS, MENTOR, PLUME AND MERIDIAN BOOKS
are published by The New American Library, Inc.,
1301 Avenue of the Americas, New York, New York 10019

FIRST SIGNET PRINTING, NOVEMBER, 1977

1 2 3 4 5 6 7 8 9

PRINTED IN THE UNITED STATES OF AMERICA

*To Bunny Dexter,
who asks for it;
and to David Behrend,
who made it possible.*

Neither the U.S.S.R. nor the United States
has, or can hope to have, a capability
to launch a disarming first strike against
the other . . .
  —James R. Schlesinger, Secretary of
    Defense, in Report to the U. S. Congress
    on the Defense Program for Fiscal
    Years 1975–79

. . . since each of us possesses, and will
possess for the foreseeable future, a
devastating second-strike capability against
the other.
  —Alexei Kh. Gorchakov, Director of
    Defense Research and Design, in
    Interim Report to the U.S.S.R. Presidium
    on the Five-Year Defense Plan, 1976–80

When patience has begotten false estimates
of its motives, when wrongs are pressed
because it is believed they will be borne,
resistance becomes morality.
  —Thomas Jefferson, in letter to Madame
    de Staël-Holstein, July 16, 1807

The First Monday

They plant more than crops in South Dakota. At Ellsworth Air Force Base, on the Meade and Pennington county line, they've buried 150 missile silos beneath the soil. Each silo houses an updated ready-to-go Minuteman, and each Minuteman carries enough payload to take out forty Hiroshimas.

The first Monday in June, in Control Center 3 at Ellsworth, a fifty-two-year-old solid-state physicist saw a white dot appear in the lower left-hand quadrant of a radar screen. The time was 11:46 P.M., and the Soviet satellite Akula-3 had just shot through the lower fan of perimeter acquisition radar beams. Akula-3 had been launched in transiting orbit from the central Siberian plateau fifty-one days earlier. The Russians called it a weather monitor. Like many American weather monitors, it was a spy and it was exactly on schedule. The physicist had not slept in seventy-two hours. He had been waiting and preparing for Akula-3.

It was 11:46 P.M. when a young mother in a mobile home eight miles northwest of Control Center 3 heard her six-month-old baby crying. She slipped out of bed. Her bare feet skirted the aluminum ring of a flip top soda-pop can glittering on the floor. Her hip narrowly missed bumping the wooden rocker where her husband had dozed off in front of a late TV movie. She went to the two-burner stove and, still half asleep, began heating milk for the baby's formula.

It was 11:46 P.M. when a seventy-year-old farmer stepped onto a porch thirteen miles southeast of Control Center 3. He lit a cigarette and gave his eyes time to adjust to the dark. He had heard noises, and he strolled to the barn and glanced inside to make sure the three cows and the mare were all right. He took three puffs of his cigarette, tamped it out on the drainpipe, and tossed it to the ground.

It was almost four seconds later when Akula-3's sensors became aware of radiation seeping up from beneath an empty field. An alert flashed to its compact three-pound brain. It bent its gaze twelve seconds of arc toward the infrared

1

source. Two doors in the earth had begun to part, spewing up energy. Akula-3 gazed down into Silo 29 at Ellsworth Air Force Base and feasted on the heat pattern of a Minuteman IV ICBM.

A shortness of breath: that was how it happened to the farmer. He was looking up at a strangely rapid star and wondering if it had a name. A shadow flickered across the sky like a wrinkle on water, and his vision narrowed, exactly like a TV image shrinking during a power brownout. *Damn,* he thought, *it's my retina going again.* A sound of rushing water drowned out the crickets and the crackle of the mare pawing straw. He couldn't breathe. He pitched forward against the rain barrel, and his last thought was that something was the matter with his left arm.

For the solid-state physicist it ended with a buzz. He heard the IBM 360 computer signal. Suddenly he had no strength to hold his head up. His nose was flat against the green radar screen, and in that last surprised instant he realized he had omitted something from his calculations.

For the young mother it was a premonition, a certainty of danger as unmistakable as a footstep at the window. She dropped the pan of milk and spun, fully awake. Ignoring the scalding burn, she stumbled toward her husband and child. She never reached them.

At 11:47 P.M. on the first Monday in June a farmer, a housewife, and a solid-state physicist were dead, and a Russian spy satellite dropped silently toward the northwestern horizon. In Silo 29, a Minuteman IV missile stared paralyzed at a crack of night sky, and in Control Center 3 an IBM 360 computer vomited an incoherent, non-terminating scream for help into the printout basket.

Till that moment, Jack O'Brien had never given a thought to telepathy or clairvoyance.

He was sitting with two associates at a perfectly routine business dinner in a Seattle restaurant. The waiter had just served coffee. They were discussing Hornet, the Navy fighter plane. O'Brien mentioned that his company had modified the craft to accommodate four of those new 2500-mile nuclear cruise missiles.

And then, for no reason he could fathom, there flashed into his head the words from the Burial of the Dead, *In the midst of life we are in death.*

Jack O'Brien was not a religious man and he was far too

busy to brood about mortality. But the thought would not let go of him. His eyes circled the guests at the table. Tate Erlandsen was a dark-haired man in his late forties and he'd kept himself in good shape. Melvin Culligan was in his mid-sixties, but he had a new Bahamas tan and he still had a firm chin and most of his hair. O'Brien himself was fifty-three, and only last week his doctor had certified him 100 per cent fit, and not even a word about watching his weight.

And then Melvin Culligan reached for his wallet. He took out a check and laid it face up on the table. The check was drawn on the account of Rebus International at a Fifth Avenue branch of Citibank of New York. It was certified.

None of the three men at the table moved. The chatter of the other diners seemed very far away.

The check was for ninety million dollars.

"Mel," O'Brien sighed, "we'd be breaking the law."

"So?" Melvin Culligan said.

"You represent a foreign government. We can't sell your people U. S. Navy fighter planes before we sell them to the Navy, for God's sake. And we can't sell them to the Navy before Congress okays the procurement."

Melvin Culligan's manicured fingertips stroked the edge of the check. "Who says this pays for planes? Call it an unsecured loan."

It was Tate Erlandsen who broke the silence. "Why buy trouble, Mel?" His voice managed to suggest that he was used to seeing all sorts of things written on Citibank checks. "We've been negotiating with your people for I don't know how many years. The State Department has copies of every document. Congress could subpoena the whole file. If we touched five cents of your money, it'd be a commitment to deliver those planes. You know it and the State Department knows it and Congress knows it. And if we make a commitment like that before we have a commitment with the Navy, every America-first diehard in the Pentagon is going to scream that we're arming the Shah instead of our own boys."

Melvin Culligan suddenly looked pale and old. "Those Pentagon patriots are the same four-star ignoramuses who warn America about Jewish take-overs."

O'Brien was not happy to hear Melvin Culligan talking like that in a public place. "They happen to be our biggest customer," he said.

The check stayed on the table. O'Brien sensed that more

than anything else in the world Melvin Culligan wanted him to reach out and touch that piece of paper.

"My people have been waiting a long time," Melvin Culligan said. There was an edge of threat in his voice.

O'Brien calculated that the check must be costing Rebus close to thirty thousand a day in short-term interest. He couldn't see the point. "Mel, we're doing our damnedest. Don't you think we're as anxious to sell the plane as you are to buy?"

There were several ways of viewing Hornet. If you were the Navy, the sixteen-ton two-engine fighter was another step in your continuing attempt to whittle away at the missions of the other services. If you were Iran, it was an updated bid to maintain tactical air supremacy over the Persian Gulf. If you were Pacific Aero, Hornet was two billion dollars, and the company had fought for the contract.

"We had to sink forty-three million of our own money into the prototype," O'Brien said. "We set up five hundred million in debentures to get our assembly lines ready. We're paying a hundred twenty-one thousand in interest a day—and we're floating another ten million in paper next Monday." Of course Melvin Culligan had sat on the board of directors of Pacific Aero for twelve years and if he'd bothered reading the company reports he'd have known all that. "What more could your people want in the way of assurance?"

"Look," Tate Erlandsen interrupted, "before we say something that gets us hauled up in front of a congressional committee, why don't you put that check away, Mel?"

O'Brien had noticed that good ex-generals had two things in common: a gift for staying cool under fire, and a gift for being obeyed. Tate Erlandsen was frozen carbon dioxide among the ice cubes. When he'd served in the Canal Zone, Panamanian guerrillas had snatched his teen-aged son and demanded the release of seventeen political prisoners. He had refused to allow the exchange. That refusal had won him two more stars and a reputation as a man who'd never back down from his principles. The nation remembered, and he had had no trouble steering Pacific Aero's procurements through the bureaucratic sargassos of the Pentagon and Congress. At eighty-five thousand a year plus forty in untaxed benefits, he was one of the best deals Pacific Aero had ever closed.

Melvin Culligan slipped the check back into his wallet. It came almost as a relief to O'Brien when the Pageboy strapped to his belt began squawking.

"Excuse me, gentlemen." O'Brien pushed a button to kill the squawk. He went to the pay phone by the hat check. There was a message to call his secretary at her home number. She sounded calm, which was not necessarily a good sign. She said the Air Force wanted to talk to him on the scrambler, and she'd meet him at the office right away.

O'Brien apologized to his guests and hurried from the restaurant. He told his chauffeur to take Interstate 5, the superhighway. He rolled down the car window and stared at the distant mountains. It took twenty-five minutes to cover the fifteen rain-misted miles to the Pacific Aero plant. In the dimness, the executive building had the blunt sparkle of a glass fist. O'Brien missed the hustle of employees. Riding up in the elevator, he felt like the last survivor of a nuclear all-out.

When he got to his office, Miss Kelly was standing by the glass wall, staring out at the starless sky as though she could see something there. "They're waiting for you," she said. "The scrambler's on hold."

O'Brien crossed the room to the little red box, incongruously opaque on the glass-and-chrome desk. He lifted the receiver and said, "O'Brien here."

The phone call took three and a half minutes. When he hung up, O'Brien realized he was very close to being a dead man.

It took four minutes to phone the restaurant and get hold of Tate Erlandsen and it was another thirty-five before Erlandsen stepped into the office.

"Sorry to drag you away from Mel Culligan," O'Brien said. "Drink?"

"Scotch on the rocks."

The bar was unobtrusively integrated with the bookshelves twenty feet across the room. Miss Kelly brought two ice cubes floating in a company glass on three ounces of Chivas Regal. Erlandsen thanked her and she smiled. Miss Kelly always smiled. She seemed to make a point of looking just plain enough so no wife need ever worry, but she had damned fine legs and O'Brien found himself wondering what else she used them for.

Erlandsen settled himself into a leather-and-chrome easy chair and sipped his scotch and asked what was up.

"Half an hour ago," O'Brien said, "the Air Force ran a routine ready-to-launch check on the missile in Silo 29 at Ellsworth. The missile went haywire."

Erlandsen set down his glass. "God almighty—what did it do, launch?"

They were alone. O'Brien had not even heard Miss Kelly shut the door. "We'd be better off if it had. From what I can piece together, they were into countdown. The computer hit a malfunction in terminal guidance. It was a new TG—one of ours. The computer called off the test. In an attack situation, it would have killed the launch."

"What kind of malfunction?"

"No one's talking. As soon as we get notification through channels, we're sending a maintenance team down to find out what the hell happened."

Erlandsen frowned. "That terminal guidance has been tested and retested and it's as close to bugproof as you can get."

"Whatever caused the shutdown," O'Brien said, "the Air Force is suspending the modification program. They may even want to scrub the TG's we've already installed. Which means we shut down an assembly line. Which leaves us with upwards of four hundred useless TG's."

Tate Erlandsen got up. He took the carpet in relaxed strides. It was wall-to-wall, forty-five-dollars-a-yard mocha that stretched through the closed door into Miss Kelly's anteroom and not an inch further. "Could a computer be causing the problem? Computers can foul up. Diners Club has one that keeps dunning me with another man's tabs."

"It's our own software in the computer. We still look like goddamned idiots. When do you testify on Hornet?"

"Tomorrow afternoon." Erlandsen looked surprised. "Don't tell me you're worried about Lasting's committee."

"Can you think of a single snag in any defense program that hasn't leaked to that goddamned committee?"

"Senator Lasting is up for re-election next year and the Navy has three bases and two factories in his home state."

"That bastard will point to Silo 29 and ask if a band of dolts like Pacific Aero should be let anywhere near any kind of defense contract. Tate, this could cost us the TG follow-on procurement and the Hornet procurement and the Iranian buy-in. We can't afford to lose them. We can't even afford a congressional delay. We're in hock up to our . . ."

O'Brien's eye went to the platinum-framed photograph above the bar. An enlargement of a quarter-century-old snapshot, it showed seventeen young men in grease-stained overalls grouped grinning and champagne-drunk outside the converted shoe factory that had been Pacific Aero's second home. The picture had been taken the day the company had won its first government contract. Whatever it took to parlay a spare-parts operation into one of the top ten defense contractors—vision, luck, or just plain perseverance—Jack O'Brien had once had it like a disease. But tonight he was scared.

"The Air Force wants you to talk with a man called Lee Armstrong," O'Brien said. "He's a friend of yours, isn't he?"

"We were together in the Canal Zone."

O'Brien thought of Tate Erlandsen's dead son who had been kidnapped in the Canal Zone, but if Erlandsen was thinking of the boy his face didn't show it. O'Brien said that the Air Force seemed to feel Lee Armstrong might have some ideas how to keep Lasting at bay. "Lee Armstrong apparently specializes in things like that."

Erlandsen's nod suggested he agreed without quite approving. "My plane is due in Washington at 10 P.M. I'll try to talk to Armstrong tomorrow night."

"Tate, if it's not asking too much, I'd just as soon you got home a little earlier. Maybe you could have dinner with this man Armstrong. Handle him informally. Get him drunk."

"Okay, I'll take the early flight." Tate Erlandsen shrugged and held out his empty glass.

O'Brien fixed them both scotches. He told himself to relax. He was a millionaire two and a half times over. He had a nice wife, a fourteen-room house, two beautiful kids. He had a Jackson Pollock hanging in his office. It had taken him close to thirty years to get from grease monkey to here, but he'd made it to the top and he was going to stay at the top.

"Jack," Tate Erlandsen said, watching him, "a terminal guidance is not worth an ulcer."

"Wasn't thinking about that," O'Brien said. That line had popped into his head again: *In the midst of life . . .* and his stomach felt like ice.

Tuesday

Tate Erlandsen's wife sat in the room that would have been her son's. The drawers were empty: the clothes had been given to charity six years ago. There was nothing in the closet but hangers. All that remained was a shelf of college textbooks and a baseball trophy on the chest of drawers. They no longer made her unbearably sad.

Sitting in the room was her own idea, not a doctor's. She stayed up to five minutes at a time, alone, just to prove to herself she could do it.

She had opened the window so she could stare down at the street. Afternoon was crumbling into shadow. The whine of a distant jet bored into the hushed, humid air. Two women were walking grim-faced figure-eights on the sidewalk. They carried signs: *Mothers for Life.*

As she reached a hand to lower a window, a yellow taxi swung onto Dumbarton Street and slowed in front of the house. She saw her husband get out. She went to her bedroom and lay down. The front door slammed and she heard Tate talking to Martta and Heikki, the Finnish couple. His footsteps came up the curved staircase, soft but unmistakably his, and the bedroom door made a whispering sound as he opened it. "Barbara, are you sleeping?"

"Welcome home, soldier." She smiled.

He kissed her and handed her a cone of florist's paper. "Careful of the thorns." He sounded tired, but his face was set in a valiantly cheerful expression.

She peeked into the paper. A dozen yellow roses. "Why, General, you must be feeling guilty about something."

"I feel guilty about sitting next to a pretty girl on the plane."

"You always over-atone. These are lovely." She went to her dressing table and moved a bottle of iodine and laid the bouquet down. She saw him in the mirror. He was watching her; looking for danger signs, she knew. He seemed to worry she would relapse while he was away on business. She turned

8

and smiled to show she wasn't about to relapse. "You should sit next to pretty girls more often."

His eye went to the white scar of a Band-Aid on her elbow. "How did you get the cut?"

"One of those mothers-for-life and I were fighting for the same square foot of sidewalk."

"Those women out front? If they laid a hand on you, I'll wring their necks."

"She called me a name and I lost my temper and swung. It's only a scratch."

"Why the hell are they picketing?"

"Dudley Mayhew's been foaming about Pacific Aero and the Hornet the whole week you were away."

A nerve in Tate's cheek twitched. She could tell that the very mention of the name irked him. Dudley Mayhew, a nationally syndicated columnist, was a nonpartisan asp whose venom could as unpredictably sting right as left, high as low. Every year, when budget hearings rolled around, he cranked out articles screaming that defense costs were devouring the nation's health, education, housing, and welfare. He had millions of loyal readers.

"Yesterday," she said, "he called Tate Erlandsen an overpaid apologist for the most overpriced and least necessary aircraft since the F-111. He published your address and he said it's time to call a halt."

"Some freedom of the press. A columnist turns moms into killers. Did it ever occur to that nitwit that if we *didn't* have a few planes we might all wind up in a Soviet prison—including him and his typewriter?"

"You're his greatest ally, Tate. I'm sure it galls him and that's the reason he picks on you." The remark made him laugh and suddenly he didn't look quite so tired. "Now tell me why you're back so early," she said.

"The company ordered me onto an early plane." He sat on the edge of the bed and took off his shoes. "I've had three hours' sleep and I feel lousy."

"Three hours? What do you *do* out in Seattle?"

"Nothing I don't do at home."

"That's not quite so reassuring as I hope it was meant to be. Why the earlier plane?"

"Because we have to take some people out to dinner."

She shook her head. "Can't. I didn't expect you home, and I've invited my sister. I know you can't stand Janey, and it seemed a good night to get her out of the way. Martta is making a dessert soufflé. Finnish specialty. Cloudberry liqueur. It would break too many hearts to cancel. Your guests will have to rough it and eat in. Who are they?"

"Lee and Thelma Armstrong."

"Why them?"

"Because I invited them."

"What's our motive, silly?"

"Our motive is that the Armstrongs are joining us to discuss national security affairs."

"Bull. Why do you always lie about national security?"

"Because it wouldn't be security if I told the truth."

"Does that mean you never tell the truth?"

"The only truths I tell are the unimportant ones."

His furrowed forehead and troubled blue eyes gave the lie to his smile. She reached a hand to neaten his hair. "Then tell me why there's shaving cream behind your ear."

"There isn't shaving cream behind my ear."

She touched a finger to his ear and showed the tip, white with shaving foam that had traveled first-class all the way across America. They burst out laughing. He kissed her. Without thinking or really meaning to she kissed him back, and for an instant they were like teen-agers and their mouths were gulping at one another. He pulled her toward the bed and they made love without even turning down the silk bedspread.

It was unpremeditated and silly and far better than planned sex, and afterwards she felt irresponsible and peaceful and lucky, at least lucky for the time being and you couldn't hope for more than that.

He put his hands on her neck and clasped, a gesture of gentleness and possession and reassurance. Their gazes interlocked and something horribly embarrassing occurred to her.

"Do you know what you made me forget?" she said.

"What did I make you forget?"

"You have a visitor. A funny little man who's very insistent and very patient. His name is Leon Asher, and he's been waiting down in your study for over an hour."

"I know all about the funny little man." He kissed her on the tip of her nose. "Martta told me."

"Then why in the world did you come up here and—"

"Because I was very horny and you're more fun than a funny old man. He told Martta he's from Pacific Aero, and I've given the company enough overtime in the last twenty-four hours. Don't worry, I'll go see him in a minute."

"Tate Erlandsen, you are dreadful!" Dreadful and she thanked God for it. "You go talk to poor Mr. Asher this minute."

"Tell me, General: you take vitamin K, yes?"

Tate detected a German accent, as slight as the old man himself, and he could not imagine what in the world his visitor was talking about. "The normal amount."

"Good." Leon Asher wore a rumpled polo shirt and a rumpled cloth jacket that could once have been the upper half of a suit. "So long as you take adequate vitamin K, you'll never have a mental depression or breakdown."

Tate knew a little about depression from the years that Barbara had spent in the clinic in Kansas, and he knew that vitamin K had nothing to do with it. He kept his expression politely neutral.

"We share an employer: Pacific Aero." The old man coddled a manila envelope on his lap. His eyes, groping through inch thicknesses of prescription glass, scanned the bookshelves. They paused at the Britannica that had belonged to Tate's son and wandered on to the set of Harvard Classics that had belonged to Tate's father. If you didn't look closely the room had a nice stuffy feel. Tate usually found it relaxing. This evening he did not. It was stifling, even with the air conditioner crooning full-blast.

"I used to work full-time for the aerospace companies," the old man said. "They're the whorehouses of physics, but any roof in a storm, right? At the moment I teach freshman physics at Georgetown University. Pacific Aero keeps me on a consultant's retainer. It's small, but it's a help. I followed your testimony at the televised hearing last spring. We agree, you and I," Asher stared in a friendly, unchallenging way. "I'm going into Bethesda Naval Hospital this evening. I hope I'm right in feeling I can trust you." He rose from the sofa and laid the envelope on the desk blotter.

"What's this?" Tate asked.

"I call it the Theta Device. Alpha or Omega would have been tooting my horn, yes? Theta stands in the middle of the alphabet and it also stands for *thanatos*—death: but a very special sort of death. The Theta Device cannot kill any living thing. It can only kill other weapons. Revolutionary, no? I drew up the plans twelve years ago. The Department of Defense was polite, but they didn't want it. Which is ironic, because now they have an energy-relay system very much like Theta. I could have saved them five years of research."

Tate did not touch the envelope. To touch might have implied some sort of commitment.

"The envelope contains two sets of work notes," the old man said. "They're in German. I do all my scribbling in German. An old habit."

"I don't read German," Tate apologized, glad that he did not.

"The Pentagon reads German."

"What does the Pentagon have to do with it?"

"You have friends there, General. Give them my work notes."

"Why should I do that?"

The old man passed fingers through white hair that even indoors was windblown. "This morning I had a phone call from Pacific Aero. The director of maintenance wanted me to go to Silo 29 at Ellsworth Air Force Base. I take it you know what happened there—or what failed to happen?"

Tate was careful to make no sound or movement that might confirm or deny. His visitor was a stranger, and for all he knew the visit was a trick. The military were capable of some extraordinarily transparent security probes.

"It would have to be a tiny malfunction," the old man said. "Imagine: a ninety-eight-million-dollar Minuteman grounded because of a hundredth of a cent's worth of Nichrome on the alumina substrate of a micromodule. I suppose you could call that one of the risks of sophistication." The old man moved to the edge of the sofa. "What do you think of computers, General? The role they play in our weapons systems?"

"I think they play a considerable role."

"They play the essential role, General. Paralyze the computer, and you paralyze the missile."

Military experience had taught Tate to be suspicious of the obvious. The old man was obviously nuts but Tate was wondering if that was all there could be to it. "Doctor," Tate said, "if you've got anything to say about Silo 29, I wish you'd say it. I'm expecting dinner guests."

The old man blinked and smiled. "Consider the missile in its silo or submarine. From countdown to launch, it's in microwave radio contact with a computer. If you interrupt the radio signal, you ground the missile. This is precisely what happened at Silo 29."

"What makes you so sure?"

The old man's smile was childishly eager. "Because it was my idea."

It was an amazing assertion and Tate decided he'd better not let it pass. "Do you mind if I smoke?"

"Not at all."

Tate opened the lower left-hand drawer of his desk. He pressed the start button on the tape recorder. Then he took out his pipe.

"I wanted to get out of the missile-versus-missile spiral. So I aimed Theta at the weak link in missile systems: microwave communication between computer and missile."

Tate was alone in his study. He had set the tape recorder on top of the desk and was watching the wheels turn.

"The principle is simple. You aim a blast of microwave radiation at the silo or the submarine, powerful enough to override communication. The missile thinks it's getting crazy orders from the computer, and the computer thinks it's getting crazy feedback from the missile. Both accuse the other of malfunction. The system shuts down automatically and won't start again till the bug has been found and corrected. Of course, there is no bug."

Tate had phoned Pacific Aero, and the old man had been telling the truth about once working for them.

"Essentially, Theta is a satellite-borne maser powered by solar energy. A satellite is the easiest, least detectable, and least vulnerable way to get to the target. Solar energy is cheap, plentiful, and inexhaustible. A maser transmits a powerful, coherent signal in the required wave band. More important, its effects cannot be distinguished from breakdown within the system itself. Theta has the bonus effect of destroying the enemy's belief in his own deterrent."

Which, Tate reflected, could provoke your enemy to a desperate pre-emptive first strike. Yet the weapon made an imbecilic sort of sense. Theta was nothing more than a radio jammer, turning the missile's own sophistication back against it. All it needed was a satellite, a maser that met the power requirement, and a sensing and targeting technology on a par with any spy-in-the-sky.

Tate had heard of no maser efficient enough to do the job, but that didn't mean one might not exist or be found. The irony appealed to him. The maser—microwave amplification by stimulated emission of radiation—had been the granddaddy of laser technology. Someone had tried stimulated emission in the higher frequencies and discovered light amplification—lasers. Lasers were glamorous, masers weren't. Everyone had rushed into lasers and forgotten old granddaddy maser. It would be funny if the old granddad were getting his revenge now.

"I've kept my work notes in a drawer for over ten years," Asher's voice was saying. "But now that the Russians have got hold of the idea, I've got to speak up."

"What makes you think the Russians have it?" Tate heard himself ask, his skepticism very poorly disguised.

"Silo 29. The computer reported an unspecified malfunction in the missile. The missile reported incoherent signals from the computer. The test launch aborted. Examination of the computer and the missile reveals no error or malfunction. It's Theta down to the letter."

"But why would the Russians test this device at Ellsworth?"

"Exactly as you say: it's a test."

There were two knocks. The study door opened and Barbara peeked in. Tate slammed a fist onto the stop button. Barbara tilted her head and hair spilled in immaculate swirls the color of bleached pine.

"Your guests just arrived," she said. Her eyes were very violet and her nose very tiny and her cheeks seemed to smile even when her mouth did not.

"In a minute." Tate realized he sounded bad-tempered.

She looked curiously at the recorder, then at him, then shut the door again.

Through the glass walls of his foreman's cubicle, Mort Dubrovsky could see most of what was going on. In 810—semiskilled—they were back at their stands: three men and two women in white smocks and gloves and caps and masks bent over their microscopes, playing Tensor beams across eight-by-five-inch printed circuits, sorting the boards into okay, repair, or scrap. An awful lot of scrap these days. It made Mort sick.

At the near counter of 811—semiskilled again—two women were stacking the little printed boards in chassis. No trouble there.

In 809—unskilled—they were just filtering back from the coffee break that had ended at four-thirty, three minutes ago. The violation bell in the air lock went off again, must have been the fortieth time that day. A Mexican with a strand of blond wig sticking out of her cap straggled through. Mort glanced down at the personnel list: *Revueltas, Gabriela.* One of the new ones. He wondered how the hell Mexicans got as far north as Washington State. He leaned on the intercom button.

"Revueltas—you're supposed to stand in the air lock for thirty seconds."

She gave him a simpering look and waddled back into the lock.

Mort sipped his lukewarm coffee. He caught a glimpse of his reflection, heavyset and gray, hovering like a ghost in the glass wall. He sagged all over: his face, his arms, his stomach. After twenty-seven years, the job was getting to him.

Mort's three low-ceilinged, windowless rooms on the eighth floor of Building C had been designed for electronic subassemblies. They could accommodate a maximum of twelve workers each. The company piped in the essentials: water, air, light, music. For Mort, it was like traveling steerage on a spaceship to nowhere.

In the last quarter century, the industry had changed almost beyond recognition. Computers now designed the product. Computers worked out the staging of the assemblies and assigned them to workers scattered through thirty buildings in six states. In more and more weapons systems, the computer was an actual on-board element. It seemed to Mort, as the computer took over all the brainwork, that the people turning out the product got dumber by the year. With the government's fair-hiring decrees, Pacific Aero had had to take on blacks, Mexicans, American Indians, even women. Workmanship had plummeted.

Take 809, for example. Four blacks, a Mexican, three white women. Not a Caucasian male in the room. The job was printed circuits. Circuit boards had to be dipped in a vat of photosensitive solution, placed under glass sheets carrying the circuit designs, exposed to light for ten seconds, baked for sixty seconds, then broken up along perforated lines into separate circuits.

809 was doing well to turn out one usable circuit in eighty.

Four years ago, before the compensatory program had hit its stride, the company average had been one in twelve.

809 was shaping up to be Mort Dubrovsky's first late assembly in over a quarter century with the company. It made him helplessly sad.

He sipped his coffee—tasted lousy, and he'd already had five cups more today than the doctor advised—and he watched the Mexican in the blond wig working the A printer. She was more interested in hee-hawing at jokes with her black neighbors than in laying the board on straight, and she reacted to the ten-second bell as though it were a phone ringing next door.

Mort had been going to some of the company's Thursday-night race-relations raps, thinking maybe it was his prejudices that made him see thumbprints on circuit boards. But when he looked at the Mexican, he knew the problem wasn't just in his head.

The Mexican placed a new circuit board on the printer, leaned forward, and vomited.

Mort leaped to his feet and strode through the air lock. He ignored the clanging violation bell. He grabbed a fistful of the Mexican's smock, the only part of her clean enough to touch, and yanked her into a sitting position. Her head had cracked the glass. It was the fourth A glass they'd lost this week.

He sniffed. Her breath reeked.

"Revueltas!" he shouted. "You don't come to my assembly drunk!"

The wig slipped sideways, freeing knots of oily hair. Her eyes opened halfway in a drugged stare. There was puke on Mort's fingers. He let her drop. He was so angry he didn't hear the violation bell ring again and he didn't see the shop stewardess's twisted face till it was three inches from him.

"You racist fuckhead," the woman screamed at him, "take your dirty hands off her!"

"She's cut bad," someone cried.

"Don't touch her," the shop stewardess snapped. "You." She picked out one of the black men. "Go get the doctor."

"Hey, Stokes," Mort shouted. "I give the orders here."

"I don't give a shit what you give. This is the last sister you're going to cut." Davidine Stokes hissed her words through razor-thin lips, and her eyes jabbed like a lawyer's finger. She had an Afro the size of a beehive and she called herself black. If that was black, so was a skinned almond.

"I didn't cut anyone," Mort said. "She fell."

The violation alarm spat a protest as a black man and the Building C doctor came hurrying through the air lock. The doctor cupped a hand under Revueltas' chin and eased her head back.

The Mexican looked as though someone had put all the extras on a chili burger and busted it open with a concrete wall. Mort felt sick.

The doctor said, "Someone give me a hand with her feet."

They had reached dessert. The dining room was cool and cavernous by candlelight, and Barbara was thinking that it had been a safe, dull dinner: no silences, no laughter either.

"I flew all the way to Spain to see my husband," Barbara's sister Janey was saying. She wore a black ankle-length gown with a slit that ran a little too far up the left leg. She had pinned a cluster of diamonds the size of a champaign button over her right breast. "I was practically thrown into the stockade till they could hustle me onto a flight home. The base commander grilled me for forty-five minutes. Why had I come, what did I know about the *Intrepid*'s movements, who had told me it was expected in port."

"Who *did* tell you?" Tate asked.

"My husband."

"He shouldn't betray sub movements like that."

"What the hell did he betray? They'd obviously changed the orders."

Lee Armstrong had hunched down on his elbows to listen. Sometimes he gave Barbara the impression of monitoring people's statements, gathering them into dossiers. He was a slender, wiry man in his early fifties. Tiny lines radiated from his eyes and his temples had gone halfway to gray. He had a sort of lean and scarred sexiness that Barbara sensed appealed to her sister. "Why do you say the orders were changed?" Colonel Armstrong asked.

"Atomic subs don't go drifting around the Atlantic without someone's issuing an order. Or do they?" Barbara's sister Janey took a long swallow of champagne. "All right, I'm gossiping about sub movements. I'm as bad as a Soviet spy."

"This soufflé's just delicious," Thelma Armstrong said before her husband could reply. She was toying with her necklace of shellacked legumes. Her hair was dyed a flat blond, not cheap but not convincing either, and it gave her face a doll-like look. "What have you put in it? I can't recognize the taste."

"A little cloudberry liqueur," Barbara said. She had worn a dress of deep violet: an old dress but one of her favorites. Out of consideration for Thelma Armstrong, she had put on no jewelry but a single jade pin. "It comes from Finland."

Barbara's sister Janey took a cigarette from her gold-mesh

purse and leaned into the candle to light it. She remarked that the European devaluations must have lowered the price of exported liqueurs, but of course American tariffs more than ate up any savings to the consumer; she wondered whether this had anything to do with the skyrocketing defense budget and asked Lee Armstrong's opinion.

"The defense budget strikes me as pretty reasonable," Lee Armstrong said.

"But the whole Russian-American issue is so phony. Both sides have stockpiled enough to blow one another off the globe twenty times over. Yet things are so relaxed an American doesn't even need a visa to go to Leningrad."

"Are you sure?" Thelma Armstrong said. "I thought the Russians were still paranoid about visas."

"Barbara's servants can tell you. They did it last summer, didn't they, Barbara? Went back to Finland and signed up on a tour to Leningrad. They're American citizens now, and the Russians didn't even require a visa. Now to me that's insane. The Russians want to bomb us *and* they want our dollars."

"Naturally," Lee Armstrong said. "Our dollars help pay for their bombs."

"American dollars help build Russian bombs?" Barbara's sister Janey smiled as though he couldn't possibly mean it.

"You need computers to guide your missiles." Lee Armstrong hunched forward again: the dead-serious, explanatory posture. "The Russians' computer technology is at the level of Univac 1—1948 stuff. They haven't got a glimmer of solid-state logic technology. So they have four choices: develop it; buy it; borrow it; steal it. Since Russians are Russians, they start with the fourth option. The KGB infiltrates agents into West German IBM."

"Do they actually do that?" Barbara's sister Janey managed to sound surprised and rather interested.

"The Germans arrested nine Soviet agents in 1975. They'd been Xeroxing IBM computer-maintenance manuals. That's not your home-grown industrial espionage. It's military theft. Very few people in the West realize that the weapons gap between the U.S.S.R. and the U.S. is a computer gap. Most people don't realize that the computer is a weapon. And it's just about the last weapon we've got. To classify computer technology as nonmilitary is insane. And to trade it off to the Russians in the name of détente—with loans from the Chase Manhattan Bank—is suicide."

"Then why do we do it?" Barbara's sister Janey had settled

back into her chair. Most of her thigh showed through the slit and she looked very comfortable now that Lee Armstrong's eyes were on her legs.

"Because we believe in free enterprise. Because we're an open society. That's the big problem: we're open, they're closed."

"Doesn't sound like a problem to me," Thelma Armstrong said. "Sounds darned lucky for us." With the curio-counter unpredictability of her remarks, Thelma sometimes amazed Barbara. She had bought heavily into Peruvian blouses and African earrings and she dressed like a Third World exposition. With her third after-dinner stinger she was apt to hint that she favored arms reduction. She made sense, but it was State Department sense, suicide for a Pentagon wife.

"I wouldn't call it lucky," Lee Armstrong said. "If the U.S. military wants a weapon, they have to go to Congress to ask for the money. Congress doesn't give away a penny without knowing the reason why. The hearings are published, and so's your technology."

Barbara's sister Janey smoothed her skirt, and Thelma Armstrong stared at her champagne glass as though she would rather not see what her husband was staring at.

"It sounds grim." Barbara's sister Janey smiled. "We've handed the Russians our weapons and now we're rushing to sell them our computers. How do we keep from committing suicide, Colonel?"

"Treat computer technology like atomic energy. Set up a federal commission and pass strict laws to regulate it." Lee Armstrong shrugged as though it was a hopeless dream and he was tired of holding up the world. "Until then, every time a Russian-American trade bill comes up in Congress, we're going to have to tie it to freedom for Soviet Jews."

Lee Armstrong talked weapons and cold war and human misery with a detachment that made Barbara wonder about him. She had heard him called a hardheaded professional, one of the best. No one had called Tate that since he'd left the service, and she was glad.

The Finnish maid began clearing dessert plates. Barbara suggested that the women might have coffee in the living room, and if the men had anything to talk over they might like to have coffee in Tate's study. Tate said he and Lee might have a five-minute chat, and Barbara's sister Janey excused herself. Barbara and Thelma Armstrong went to the living room, and Thelma sat on the edge of the sofa with an anxious, unhappy smile.

"I admire you, Barbara," she said. "Do you mind my saying it?"

"Of course not." Barbara poured a demitasse with two lumps and left room for Thelma Armstrong to add her own cream.

"Considering what the service can do to a marriage, you and Tate have certainly come through winners."

"But we're not military any more. Just plain old civilians."

"That's what I mean." Thelma Armstrong wore the look of someone who had had a few drinks and who was flirting with the idea of being honest. "Tate got to the top fast, and he got out fast. The perfect military operation. If that sounds petty of me, I'm sorry. I meant it to be a compliment."

"Is Lee unhappy with the Army?" Barbara asked.

"Lee's nowhere, and it's my fault." Thelma Armstrong did not wait for a denial. "I'm not a four-star wife. I'm not even a one-star wife, obviously. I'd give anything to be like you, Barbara."

It was an awful moment; Barbara could think of nothing to answer.

Thelma Armstrong shook her head. "You like people and it makes them like you. I can hardly handle a weenie roast for the kids' birthday. I get nervous in groups and I drink and people wonder how Lee can put up with me. I try so damned hard to say the right things, and the right things just won't come out."

"That isn't so. You're one of the few people in this town who has anything bright to say."

"Bright? I should be helping Lee and instead I get sloshed and rant to four-star generals about starving Angolans. It's like stage fright."

"What are you frightened of?"

"The Army—Lee—you."

"Me?" Barbara leaned forward and squeezed Thelma Armstrong's hand. "But we're friends, aren't we?"

"Haven't you ever been frightened of a friend?" At that moment Thelma Armstrong looked very frightened.

"I suppose I have been," Barbara admitted. "A little."

"I love that Miró litho in the john." Barbara's sister Janey stood in the living-room doorway, looking triumphant about something. "Is it new?"

"Jack O'Brien is concerned," Tate said. "If the Lasting Committee gets hold of Silo 29, they'll make Pacific Aero look so incompetent we'll never be trusted with another defense procurement."

Lee Armstrong looked at him in a cool, appraising way. "Senator Lasting will try anything. And there are leaks galore these days." He poured himself a generous refill of brandy. "By the way, we found Lasting's source. File clerk in records. Summer replacement."

"Hell, isn't there any security in the Pentagon?"

"Apparently they waive it if the applicant is blond, female, and eighteen—and a senator's niece."

Tate was glad Lee Armstrong was smiling at last. In aerospace defense, a billion dollars could hang on a smile.

"But," Lee Armstrong went on, "if I do say so myself, we've snatched victory from the jaws. We're keeping her in place, as they say in spy talk, and we've been feeding her a subtle trickle of unadulterated crap and misinformation. Senator Lasting is now in possession of a file of weapons-systems fuck-ups, cover-ups, and mark-ups that would turn even you into a militant dove, General. And knowing that fradulent old vote catcher, he's going to grandstand tomorrow and spring them on you and the American public." Lee Armstrong was grinning, and Tate reflected it was sad for a colonel of the United States Army to spend his time behind a desk thinking up intrigues. "You, of course, will be briefed by me on the true state of weapons-systems fuck-ups, cover-ups, and mark-ups, and Senator Lasting will find himself devastatingly refuted."

Tate camouflaged his opinion of the tactic with a smile. "That's ingenious, Lee. Only we're hoping to sell a third of the Hornet run to Iran. What's the Shah going to think when he hears PA can't even screw a wing on right?"

"He's not going to think anything. You're going to blast Lasting to smithereens."

"You know me better than that. I'd never blast a venerable old turd like Lasting. I'd sooner throw shit at a fan."

"I'd never accuse you of anything less than diplomacy. Stop by tomorrow at eight forty-five for some coffee. I'll give you enough to blast your way out in an afternoon. At least I hope you'll get out in an afternoon. I want to wind this up before I leave town Thursday."

"Where are you off to?"

"Oh, the usual: taking two days' vacation leave—going

down to the cabin in the Blue Ridge." Lee Armstrong had gone down there six or seven times in the past year that Tate was aware of, and several of those times he had left Thelma behind. It had crossed Tate's mind that the retreats might be medical in purpose, prescribed by an Army M.D. The DOD had launched a crash program to cut the rate of alcoholism, depression, breakdown, and suicide among Pentagon personnel, much of it brought on by overwork. Tate sensed that overwork wasn't the whole story: Lee was restless about something, had been for some time. He sat staring into his brandy snifter as though he could read his future in it.

On the other side of the drawn blinds, a car whispered down the street, lonely as a solitary wave in the ocean. Tate asked, "Has anyone got a clue what happened at Silo 29?"

"Looks like a power surge," Lee Armstrong said. "The computer couldn't cope. Could have something to do with that new Canadian grid we're breaking in."

Tate thought how odd it was that his afternoon visitor could have taken a wild guess like that and been almost on target.

"The whole business is weird," Lee Armstrong said. "An Air Force intelligence man was out there. He dropped dead."

"Dropped dead of what?" Tate asked.

"They're not saying. The Air Force was working on something, which is why they're in your corner. No one wants Lasting blowing the whistle on an ongoing intelligence operation."

"Any idea what sort of intelligence operation?"

"A physicist friend of mine was in on it. I might be able to pry something out of him. Matter of fact, I'd like to show him Asher's plans. Get a professional opinion."

Tate had mentioned Asher's plans only because they were amusing and it was best to discuss something light before getting down to business. He stared at Lee Armstrong. "You don't think the Russians have really got a big maser up in the sky."

"Explore the worst possible case. Old Pentagon rule."

Tate opened the middle drawer of the desk and took out the envelope. "They're in German," he warned.

Lee Armstrong riffled through the sheets. "Shucks, looks like the same old formula for converting lead to gold."

"Would you like to hear Asher explain it? In English?" Lee Armstrong said sure, and Tate placed the Sony tape recorder on top of the desk and pressed the start button.

Lee Armstrong listened with his eyes almost shut. "I can see targeting our fixed land-based missiles," Tate's recorded voice said. "Maybe even the mobile land-based missiles. But how the hell can the Russians target our submarine-launched missiles?"

"By homing in on the microwave radiation of the countdown signal," the old man's voice said. "The same way an infrared spy satellite homes in on heat."

"But that launch signal is awfully weak radiation by the time you're a hundred twenty miles up."

Tate watched Lee Armstrong. The military called it "worst possible case" when you assumed the enemy's forces worked 100 per cent and prepared yourself accordingly. A military man had to consider the worst: he was paid for that. Still, it seemed awfully confining to spend your life weighing disasters, and Tate wondered if Lee Armstrong had ever done anything but.

"It doesn't need to be strong," the old man's voice said. "It's the only microwave radiation originating in the ocean."

"How many of these satellites would you need to paralyze the American deterrent?" Tate's voice asked.

"To psychologically paralyze the deterrent, all you'd need would be one."

"What do you mean, psychologically?"

"The way the United States used two atom bombs to convince Japan it had an arsenal of them."

Tate found himself staring at the worn gilt lettering on the spines of the Britannica. He never opened any of the volumes, which still had his son's bookplates in them, he just hid cigarettes behind them. He and Barbara had pledged to give up smoking and he didn't believe in breaking his word openly. The pretense of honor died hard. He'd once been a soldier and he liked to think he'd been an honorable one. Now he was a salesman and it was hard to be an honorable salesman, but he tried, within limits, just as he'd tried within limits to be a father and a husband. He had wound up killing a son and driving a wife mad. A man who had done all that had earned the right to an occasional smoke.

The tape hissed to an automatic stop.

Tate probed a hand behind the encyclopedia and dug out a crumpled packet with three broken-backed cigarettes left in it. Lee Armstrong didn't speak and it troubled Tate that the colonel seemed troubled.

"Wouldn't the CIA know," Tate asked, "if the Russians were developing a weapon like that?"

Lee Armstrong moved his hand in circles, making brandy waves in the snifter. "We develop three hundred tons of useless paper on the Soviet Union every year. The CIA didn't know for sure that Russia had a trade surplus till '76. To dig out the traces of a new weapon would be next to impossible."

Tate stared at the match he had lit, debating whether to touch it to the cigarette. "Theta would have to be a pretty effective weapon," he said. "Even if there are more SALT cutbacks, the Russians couldn't target all the missiles we've got on land and sea. Frankly, the whole thing sounds to me like pure sci-fi."

"You're lighting the filter," Lee Armstrong said.

The two sets of Asher's work notes lay on the leather sofa. The dozen yellowed pages were dry as dead skin, covered in desperate, paraplegic scrawl. Lee Armstrong picked up one set of the papers and aligned the folds and tucked them into his breast pocket.

Asher was insane, of course, but a man in Lee Armstrong's position had to be thorough. Nevertheless, Tate felt very sorry for them both.

"Jack, please. You've been brooding about that silo since one o'clock this morning."

O'Brien started guiltily. He and his wife were alone at the executive table, and his sherbet had melted into a rainbow puddle in the glass. "Sorry, hon. I wasn't brooding, just thinking."

"Don't you think you've done enough thinking? Give it a rest."

O'Brien stared out at the disarray of tables. Men and women crowded toward the dance floor. Red and orange lights played along the accordian folds of the adjustable walls. It was the evening of the Golden League Banquet, the company's annual celebration for employees who had been with Pacific Aero over twenty-five years. The band was playing a slow, old-fashioned waltz, Irving Berlin's "Remember." The cornetist stuck a mute in his horn and made sweet sounds that O'Brien hadn't heard since the days of shellac records and nickel jukeboxes.

Debbie pulled him firmly toward the dance floor.

A heavyset red-faced man lurched between them, hand

thrust out in a pre-emptive howdy. "Mr. O'Brien," he said, "I'm Mort Dubrovsky."

"Hi there, Mort," O'Brien said brightly and automatically.

"And this is my wife Tina."

Tina Dubrovsky hung back. Jack O'Brien tossed her a nod.

"I'm a foreman over in Building C," Mort said. "Electronics subassembly."

"You're doing a great job over there," Jack O'Brien said.

"I just wanted to tell you, that was a beautiful speech you made, sir. About all of us here being the Pacific Aero family."

"Thanks, Mort. Nice meeting you, Tina."

Jack O'Brien made a move to get away, but Mort blocked him. "About us being the backbone, because I agree with you, sir."

"Come on, Mort," Tina Dubrovsky pleaded.

"Like you said in your speech, sir, the times they are changing, but certain things don't change. There are no loafers in this room, sir. Not in the real Pacific Aero family. Mr. O'Brien, there are things I can tell you, from the foreman's point of view, things you don't know."

"I certainly want to hear about it, Mort. Nice talking to you again; you too, Tina."

This time Jack O'Brien got away. Grinning, Mort spun very slowly toward Tina. "He remembered me."

Tina Dubrovsky looked at her husband as though he were plucking her dreams from her one by one. "He didn't remember you."

"He said nice seeing you *again*, and he wants to have that talk with me."

"He just said that to get away from you."

"Cut that out," Mort said. "Quit trying to tear me down. Just knock that off."

Dancing, Debbie pressed so tightly against him that O'Brien could feel a shirt stud digging into his skin like a fingernail. She clung to his shoulder, almost purring. Her body moved with unconscious pride and her eyes were cool green smiles in the tan of her face. He didn't bother to move his feet in time. He was wondering why he hadn't heard from the maintenance team at Silo 29.

Something struck him in the leg.

"Hey, you're supposed to step on her feet, not mine!"

O'Brien glanced at the obstacle. He recognized Elmer Connally, a chief mechanic with the company for over thirty years. Elmer's wife Alma was hanging on to his hand as though someone might try to steal it.

"Hi, Elmer," O'Brien said. Less enthusiastically, "Hi, Alma."

"You better watch it, Debbie." Elmer was too lean and smiling to be an old man. He looked like a schoolboy who had slipped on a white wig and drawn on a few wrinkles for the annual school play. "You dance with bears like him, you're liable to wind up with broken ribs."

"I can handle him." Debbie smiled.

"Animal trainer, hey? Here, let me show you how they do it in the Vienna Woods."

Elmer lifted his arms and Debbie walked into them, and they waltzed away. O'Brien looked at Alma. Her red dress exposed a plump square of upper bosom where moisture had gathered like steam on a bathroom mirror.

There was no choice. They danced.

"Nice of you to give Elmer those nurses," Alma said.

Elmer had gone into the hospital last week for a gall-bladder operation. The minute O'Brien heard about it he had had Elmer transferred from a semi- to a fully private room; he had ordered round-the-clock nurses and a dozen red roses daily and had even managed to go down personally for a fifteen-minute visit. "It wasn't any trouble," O'Brien said.

"Elmer said he lived better in that hospital than we do at home." Alma Connally could pack a lifetime's blame into an inflection or a look.

"Must have done him good," O'Brien said. "He looks spry as all hell."

"We shouldn't have come tonight. He's been real weak."

"I'm sorry to hear that." Elmer and Debbie waltzed back into range. "Say, Elmer," O'Brien said, "can we have a talk—privately?"

"Sure. Just name the date."

"How about right now? Will you ladies excuse us?"

The women's faces were startled blanks. O'Brien took Elmer's elbow and aimed him toward a dim doorway where a busboy had stacked trays of shrimp-cocktail dishes. O'Brien described the business of Silo 29. Elmer angled his head, like a safecracker listening for pins dropping into place.

"Wish I could help, Jack, but I don't know a damned thing about computers."

"Too many people know too damned much about computers. I'm not so sure the breakdown is computer-linked at all. It could be plain mechanical failure or misinstallation. It could be they were sloppy about maintenance. I'd feel one hell of a lot better if someone I trusted looked around that silo for half a day."

Elmer scratched his head. "Tell you what, Jack. If you want to waste the plane fare, I'll be glad for the vacation."

If Jack O'Brien had confidence in two propositions, they were that two plus two will generally equal four, and that Elmer Connally would always have an answer. Elmer had come up with answers where there weren't even questions. Back in the early days, just tinkering for the hell of it, he had designed the welding machine that had turned out to be Pacific Aero's opening wedge into big money rocketry.

Elmer had had the notion of using tungsten arcs, which could create fused welds, on the seam-welding machine. The problem was that in standard seam welding the metal touched the electrodes, while in atomic welding it cannot. Elmer recessed the electrodes into the roller. It was a simple idea, but no one had thought of it before. And it melted high-carbon steel like marshmallow.

The company had taken out the patent and had been leasing Elmer's machine to the other majors for almost a quarter century.

"I'd be obliged to you, Elmer. At least I'd know what was going on."

"One request," Elmer said. "Don't tell Alma. She wants me to sit home and take it easy."

"How are you feeling—any better?"

"Feeling I'll go crazy if I sit around that house another day."

They went looking for Alma and Debbie and found them at a little table under an arbor of plastic grapes, talking with Frances Meredith, the widow of Pacific Aero's co-founder. Frances Meredith was a tall, white-haired woman who had more than held her own against infirmity, the twentieth century, and Pacific Aero's board of directors. Her profile was pure racehorse, but sometimes her stubbornness smacked of mule.

"He studies guitar in New York," Frances Meredith was saying.

"Guitar?" Alma's tone suggested she had heard of men lynched, and rightly so, for less.

"Classical guitar." Frances Meredith had the shrewdly dreaming eyes of a woman who liked to study her oil paintings close up. "He's a very independent boy, devoted to music. He reminds me of his grandfather in that respect."

Alma looked dubious. "I didn't know Mr. Meredith played the guitar."

"In their independence they remind me of one another. His grandfather would have understood him."

"Is that so?" Alma shifted her cotton coat from one arm to the other.

"Sad to say, no one else in the family really understands him. He's had to fight his parents, his cousins and aunts and uncles. He's even had to fight me."

"Nice to have a big family." Alma burrowed a pudgy hand into the arm of her coat.

"It's a big, old-fashioned family. Eight children, twenty-two grandchildren. Unfortunately, life isn't old-fashioned any more. Sometimes I wonder what sort of world my grandchildren and great-grandchildren will inherit. I'm sure I wouldn't want to live in it. That's a problem I won't have to face, luckily."

"Fiddlesticks, Frances," O'Brien cut in. "You're going to outlive us all."

"There you are, Jack." She offered her cheek for him to kiss.

Alma got to her feet. "We'd better be going, Elmer."

"Yes, mother. Good night, all." Elmer waved and Alma led him away under a flurry of farewells. Frances Meredith slid over on the bench to make room for O'Brien.

"The Hornet must be looking good," Frances Meredith said.

The band was playing "I'll Be Seeing You," and O'Brien was thinking of the night he had proposed to Debbie. He glanced at his wife. Her eyes were waiting for him. "We'll know about the Hornet tomorrow," he said.

"Jack, you're much too modest." Frances Meredith turned to Debbie. "Did he tell you how I fought him on that contract?"

A darkness crossed Debbie's smile.

"Jack wanted to sink forty-three million of the company's money into the prototype. I told him he was a crazy gambler."

"Jack's always been a crazy gambler. He just happens to win a lot."

"I practically led a boardroom rebellion," Frances Meredith said. "I'm surprised he's forgiven me."

The boardroom rebellion had failed by one vote, and O'Brien had not forgiven her. She was a tough old bitch. She milked the prerogatives of age and gender and rarely honored the obligations. He knew that the only reason she was even pretending to apologize at this late date was that she must want something from him badly. "There's nothing to forgive," he said. "You had your opinion, I had mine."

"I have all the financial acumen of a nervous grandmother. If I didn't have bankers to invest for me, I swear I'd have everything in cookie jars. Or in AT&T, which is the same thing." Frances Meredith pursed her eyes and narrowed her smile onto a cigarette tip. "More than any other decision, I think it was Jack's going ahead on the Hornet assembly lines that turned the stock around."

"Turned it around?" O'Brien said. "Going up a point isn't much of a turnaround."

"Someone expects it to go up a lot more than that. I was offered thirty-five dollars a share for my common stock." Frances Meredith exhaled twin jets of blue. "I have till next Tuesday to make up my mind."

O'Brien felt as though a fist had punched him in the stomach, but he was careful to show no reaction. She owned 3 per cent of the company: under the right circumstances, enough to swing control to someone else. If the bid expired in a week, that meant it had been made at least two months ago, when the stock had been selling at 32. Now that the shares had gone to 33 and ⅝, she was obviously wondering if she could turn an extra buck by making him an offer: your money or your company. Only a little old lady with a lot of brass could pull that kind of stickup in public.

"Could I ask who made the offer?" O'Brien asked.

"I haven't the foggiest. Cy Hallowell at Chase Manhattan said a client wanted to buy me out. I said to tell my mysterious benefactor I'd consider it."

Debbie was staring in undisguised amazement, but Frances Meredith clearly didn't give a damn what Debbie thought.

"Of course, you know me. I consider everything and I do nothing. I don't feel those shares are really mine. They're a trust for my grandchildren. Selling out would be like selling Tod."

O'Brien's eye fell on the wedding band, thin as a gold incision, that Tod Meredith had slipped onto Frances Meredith's finger forty-three years ago.

"On the other hand, times change. And the industry is—well—troubled." Frances Meredith rose. Her smile was not troubled in the least. "Here I am babbling on like an old granny. It was a terrific speech, Jack; just terrific." She turned a cheek to O'Brien and exacted another kiss. She kissed Debbie and said they must all get together for dinner soon. She moved back into the crowd and caught the arm of a vice-president and laughed at something.

Debbie had the angry look of someone trying very hard not to look angry. She forced a little smile and held it for her husband to see and took his arm. O'Brien moved swiftly around the dance floor to head off Dev Barker, the company treasurer.

"Dev," O'Brien said, "let me give you a lift home."

Dev Barker's face was as smooth and red as a brandied apple, and he was carrying two drinks. "Thanks, Jack, but Cindy and I brought our own car."

"Why don't you tell Cindy she can drive the car home, and you ride with us?"

Dev Barker had put a fleck of toilet tissue on a shaving cut on his neck and had forgotten to take it off. He swallowed and said he'd be right back and hurried away. O'Brien avoided Debbie's eyes. If they'd been alone she'd probably have accused him of treating people like toy soldiers, lining them up and knocking them down any way he pleased. Dev Barker came back without his drinks and without his smile. They collected Debbie's Persian-lamb coat and asked the doorman to send for the car. O'Brien glanced around the almost deserted lobby.

"Someone has offered Frances Meredith thirty-five dollars a share for her stock in the company," O'Brien said. "She claims the bid's anonymous. She has till next Tuesday to make up her mind."

Dev Barker made a nervous, phony chuckle, as though uncertain how O'Brien expected him to take the news. "The Hornet's looking good and it's no secret."

"It's not looking that good, Dev. It's going to come in 18 per cent or more over estimate. We're being hit by price increases right down to the grommets. And if we give in to the wage demands in Detroit, labor costs will go up right across the board and our second run of Hornets will be under a new pay scale. Iran can't come in till Congress gives the okay.

The government may not want to absorb the increase. If they don't, we won't be able to absorb the loss."

Dev Barker still looked baffled. "What's the problem? You're worried because the stock is an attractive buy?"

"The stock is at a two-year high. And this morning we went up another eighth of a point."

"So?"

"It's the wrong time for the stock to be high. Any idiot who can read the *Wall Street Journal* knows the Detroit agreement is going to set labor costs for the next three years."

"You expect the New York Stock Exchange to wait and see?"

"It would make sense to wait four days and see."

"Apparently a lot of people are betting on Pacific Aero's past record."

"That past record is developing a few blotches."

"Come on, Jack. We've got the lowest overruns of any company in the top ten."

O'Brien watched his car pull up to the curb. He let Debbie and Dev Barker go through the revolving door first. The three of them settled into the back seat. It was a new-model custom-built Lincoln Continental, O'Brien's first. He had till now contented himself with a yearly change of Cadillac, but the extras on this year's Continental had enticed the small boy in him, even though it was the driver, not the passenger, who got to play with most of them.

O'Brien gave the chauffeur directions and pressed a button raising a glass partition between the front and rear seats. The car eased smoothly into traffic. "Last night, at Ellsworth Air Force Base," O'Brien said, "a Minuteman IV broke down during a routine ready-to-launch test."

Debbie flattened herself into the leather seat, allowing the men to talk around her.

"The Air Force thinks there's a bug in the new terminal guidance," O'Brien said.

"The Air Force has got to be crazy," Dev Barker said.

"Dev, just look at facts. We have contracts with twelve locals coming up for renewal in the next fourteen months. We have a strike brewing in Detroit. We're gambling double or nothing on that Hornet contract, and the contract is stalled in a demagogue's pocket."

"There's no way Senator Lasting can stop Hornet; no way. He owes the Navy this one."

"The Air Force is suspending all TG orders effective immediately," O'Brien said.

Dev Barker huddled back into the corner. His gray flannel vest corseted him but had the effect of making him look overweight. O'Brien reflected that he ought to have the vest let out an inch or else get a new suit.

"Dev, the Air Force ordered twenty-five hundred terminal guidance kits. We've sold them two hundred fifty. We've passed the break-even point and we've made about a million in profit so far. We're turning out two a day, and we're hoping to get up to ten a day. We're getting five hundred thousand a copy, and the Navy's talking about coming in. Until this morning, the TG was pure gravy: the kind of gravy this company needs to keep from starving. Now we have to halt production and idle upwards of a hundred men. It won't take *Aerospace Weekly* two minutes to piece together what's happened. The only question is, is word going to get out before Lasting's committee makes its recommendation on Hornet? If it does, we're sunk."

Dev Barker braced his shoulders.

"Dev, I want you to take care of something for me. Personally."

Dev Barker had been with Pacific Aero almost fifteen years. He earned forty-eight thousand and pulled down another fifteen in benefits. It was a damned cushy salary for the work involved, and O'Brien felt no hesitation asking him to lend a hand with odd and sometimes unorthodox chores. They both knew he'd have to hustle a hell of a lot harder as treasurer with any other company.

Dev Barker glanced at Debbie. She had a long-distance look in her eyes, as though she were not there at all. "Sure, Jack," he said. "Shoot."

"I want a breakdown of our last two stockholder lists by size of holding; a breakdown by geographic area; a breakdown by type of ownership—personal, corporate, brokerage house, foundation, fund."

"No problem," Dev Barker said.

"And I want to know how much the brokerage houses are holding in street names." All the brokerage houses had street-name accounts, stock bought and traded for clients in the broker's name. The device was basically a clerical convenience, but like the number on a Swiss bank account, it could be used as a mask.

"I want you to compare those two lists and see if you can

spot any unusual accumulation of stock in the last six months."

"So you really think there's a take-over in the works?" Dev Barker sounded almost hurt.

"We're easily in the last stage of one. Frances Meredith's stock will put the raider over the 10 per cent mark and he'll have to declare himself." Federal regulations require holders of 10 per cent or more of any corporation's stock to register with the Securities and Exchange Commission. While raiders could accumulate stock with complete secrecy below that amount, the 10 per cent rule had the effect of exposing their identity and intentions simultaneously; as speculators saw a chance to cash in on increased demand for stock, the exposure in turn drove prices up. Many raiders made killings not by taking a company over but simply by accumulating 10 per cent and unloading at the height of the demand that they themselves had sparked. "If Frances sells," O'Brien said, "the fight will be in the open next week. And if the committee stalls on Hornet, or word about the terminal guidance leaks, the stock will dive and the raider can pick us up for peanuts. We'll see some new faces at the stockholders' meeting next week. And a new board of directors."

Dev Barker adjusted the knee of his trouser leg so that the crease hung straight.

"What a lovely sky," Debbie remarked. O'Brien suspected she couldn't see the sky at all from the middle of the seat. Dev Barker leaned toward the window and said yes, it was a lovely sky.

"Dev," O'Brien said, "I'll need those lists first thing in the morning."

Wednesday

If the Pentagon's River Entrance with its steps and steps and steps was the Greek Temple, the Mall Entrance with its pillars was unquestionably the Southern Plantation House. Tate Erlandsen preferred the Mall, because if you had a sticker—and he had been able to wangle one—you could park without having to hike half a mile uphill, and if you were early you could stand in the pillar shade and watch the parade of government employees scurrying endlessly and importantly through the right-hand door and feel lucky not to be one of them.

For security reasons, the middle and left-hand doors were kept locked.

At 8:44 Tate went in. A guard sat behind the polished wood counter monitoring the flow, smiling at familiar faces, nodding at ID's flipped open, and very politely asking if he could help those he suspected of having no business at the seat of American military power.

Tate thumbed through the 461 pages of the DOD telephone directory. He found Lee Armstrong's number, picked up one of the black counter phones, and—omitting the exchange—dialed. He told Lee's secretary he was waiting. Then he stared at the wall, at color photographs of beaming heads of services, at cabinets of old flags, old awards, old weapons. An Army lieutenant hurried past with so many laminated ID's strung around his neck they looked like African tribal jewelry.

"On the dot, old son of a gun." In his uniform and decorations Lee Armstrong seemed taller and a little grimmer than he had the night before. He guided Tate around mail carts and corners and messengers on scooters. With one fluorescent light in three extinguished as part of the energy-saving drive, the corridors were pale-green tunnels, linked to one another like strands of concrete spider web.

"How's the peace?" Tate asked.

"We're keeping it; just. How's the war on Dumbarton Street?"

34

Tate grunted. "When I left the house, there were already two mothers picketing."

"Hell hath no fury like a woman."

They passed a great many clenched jaws, a great many open doors and television sets tuned to news bulletins. Tate glimpsed correspondents milling in tight knots in the press room. It was early for a briefing, but cameramen were testing focus and the green carpet and yellow backdrop curtain were bleached in klieg light.

Lee stopped at an open door and motioned Tate to go first. A chubby girl with hair the color of tinfoil sat at a desk emptying an envelope of powder into a styrofoam cup. "Coffee, Miss MacGruder," Lee said. "And no phone calls." They went into the inner office. Lee closed the door.

Tate's eye scanned the wall of framed photographs: Lee with his grinning kids, Lee with a grinning General Eisenhower, Lee with a big marlin that seemed to be grinning, Lee with a wife who was not grinning. Topping the collection was a garish orange-on-black abstract that looked as though it had been painted by a chimp or an eggbeater; it bore the clumsily printed signature *Jimmy Armstrong, First Grade*. Lee bypassed the desk and gestured toward four regulation Pentagon chairs grouped around a table.

"As of twenty minutes ago," Lee said, "we still don't know what the hell hit Silo 29. Senator Lasting's suspicion is going to be as good as yours or mine."

"Senator Lasting's suspicion will be that Pacific Aero hit that missile with all the incompetence it could muster." Tate wondered by what process of military procurement it had been decided that the cracks in Lee's ceiling should not be plastered, that the brass studs missing from the leather chairs should not be replaced. The view through the one window was a concrete wall. It was not an office a man was apt to advance out of.

"This is your counterattack." Lee slid a stack of documents across the table, its veneer pockmarked with cigarette burns. "And if you'll forgive a little authorial pride, it's pretty damned brilliant."

The upper sheets were not DOD or service letterhead, but plain typing paper. "Brilliant I don't doubt, but what is it?"

"Aircraft and weapons where Pacific Aero was the chief contractor."

Tate recognized the first item. "Right you are. I see my old pal, the two-and-three-quarter-inch dual-mode Sliding Airframe Missile." The SAM, a defense against Soviet anti-ship missiles, was actually an Army Sting missile. PA had put an RF antenna on another company's weapon and turned it into a Navy missile, at a healthy mark-up. Tate flipped through the stapled sheets. The secretary tiptoed in and placed a cup of coffee in a plastic holder at his elbow. She set a mug on the table for Lee.

"Okay," Tate said. "What do I do with it?"

Lee waited till the girl had closed the door again. "I told you we found Senator Lasting's leak. We've fed the Senator misinformation on each of these systems. Look at ROGUE, the all-weather defense against anti-ship missiles. The decimal point's wrong in the modification-to-radar cost. Real cost is three point two million. The Senator has a figure of thirty-two million: it's the kind of overrun he eats up. If he springs that one on you, just very respectfully beg to differ and hit him with Exhibit 2."

Tate lifted papers and came to a sheaf of Xeroxes fastened with a heavy-duty rubber band. Exhibit 2 was a copy of a DOD procurement order for 3.2 million, certified by the General Accounting Office.

"Or take Close-Air-Suport Weapon System," Lee said, "the laser-guided Runaway missile. The Senator has information that Runaway failed thirty-six out of a series of thirty-eight night-time tests last October at White Sands Missile Range. Supposedly we falsified the figures in testimony to the Appropriations Committee but not in our own records."

"Think he'll fall for this?"

Lee's fingers groped along the table, grazed a note pad, grasped it. "The old bastard wouldn't be stealing classified information if he didn't intend to use it. Now if he hits you with Runaway, you hit back with Exhibit 3."

"I think I grasp the principle."

"You might want to review all eleven of those weapons systems before you testify."

"Doesn't it seem a little crude that I just happen to have refuting documents for every weapon he happens to bring up?"

"Hopefully it'll seem crude and goddamned scary. I'd suggest you stuff your briefcase with typing paper and put it on top of the table, where he can see it. Let's go to contractors."

The contractors ran sheet after sheet dense with single-spaced names and addresses, every one of them from the state of Georgia.

"There were over twelve hundred subcontractors on Minuteman IV," Lee said. "Over seventy are located in or have subsidiaries in the Senator's home state."

"But if he's on to the launch shutdown, he knows the prob is in the terminal guidance."

Lee's pale-blue stare did not waver. "Page eleven. There were over two hundred eighteen subcontractors on the terminal guidance. Three of those subcontractors have subsidiaries in Georgia, and six are Georgia companies whose out-of-state subsidiaries contributed components."

"Sort of tenuous connection, isn't it?"

"I doubt the Senator will think it's all that tenuous. Georgia-McCann, Inc., is one of his heaviest campaign contributors." Lee tore a sheet of paper off the pad, wrote something, and slid it toward Tate. The block letters spelled: *Meet me in 3 minutes in the meditation room.* The meditation room was a nondenominational quasi-chapel on the third floor. Speaking was forbidden, and it was probably the one place in the Pentagon that wasn't bugged.

Frowning, Tate pocketed the note. "What did McCann do in the terminal guidance?"

"Eight miles of zinc wire."

"There's not that much wire in a TG kit."

"There is in two hundred fifty of them." Lee's chair squeaked as he rose. "Boy, I must have a defective kidney. That coffee's running right through me." He told his secretary he would be right back, and walked Tate into the corridor. The girl was watching them.

"Good luck this afternoon," Lee said. "Any problems, let me know."

They shook hands and went in opposite directions. Tate turned a corner, unfolded the note, and read it twice again.

"Well I'll be a—if it isn't Tate Erlandsen!"

Tate looked up into a smile spanning a well-built jaw, a head of curly hair cropped to show as few curls and as much steel gray as possible. A tanned hand grabbed his and pumped, and a swarm of briefcase-toting assistants came to a halt.

"Good morning, Admiral," Tate said. He couldn't imagine why Ilya Wanamaker had bothered to speak to him. They had been friends of a sort in the old days, but since Wanamaker had made Chief of Naval Operations they'd been best of strangers.

"Why don't you fellows go on ahead?" Ilya Wanamaker

suggested to the briefcase swarm. Half of them were in naval uniform, one- and two-stripers, and the other half were in that Brooks Brothers civilian uniform that Pentagon civilians adopt when they break the twenty-thousand-a-year barrier. They went on ahead.

"Well, how are you, fellow?" The Chief of Naval Operations turned full-face, full-smile to Tate. "What the hell brings you here to Valhalla?"

"I just came by to clear up a few points on Hornet," Tate said.

"Right, right. Say, I hope that works out."

"We're guardedly optimistic."

"I'd say you have grounds for guarded optimism." Ilya Wanamaker clapped a hand on Tate's shoulder and the hand stayed there just long enough to tell the forty or so Pentagonians who scurried past that Hornet was a damned fine fighter plane and Tate Erlandsen was the CNO's man.

"It's been nice talking to you, Admiral," Tate said.

"Come on, Tate, it was Ilya six years ago, it's still Ilya."

They hadn't seen one another since Canal Zone days, and probably they wouldn't meet more than twice between now and death, but if the CNO was buying your hardware and wanted to believe you were chums, you let him. "Nice talking to you, Ilya."

A sound like a contralto cuckoo filled the corridor. Pedestrians moved to the walls. A candy-striped go-cart zipped around the bend, speeding two medical officers and a heart-resuscitation unit to Ring E.

Ilya Wanamaker raised and angled his arm in a neat, economical gesture that pulled the shirt cuff back from the wristwatch. "We're pacifying some very angry newsmen in seven minutes. The President leaked the new nuclear sub to the White House press corps last night—the bastard."

"Maybe you can give the Pentagon correspondents a White House scoop," Tate said. "How about the cost overruns on the President's swimming pool?"

The CNO broke into a big grin that was utterly charming in its lopsidedness. "You should be in public relations, Tate."

"I am."

"Right, right. Hey, I hope it won't be another six years till I see you again."

"Maybe in six years we'll both be a little less busy."

A razor glint in the CNO's eye faded quickly into a smile.

"Right, right," Wanamaker said. "Maybe we can squeeze in eighteen holes of golf."

"Might as well think big," Tate said.

"Hi to Barbara for me. Say, she's okay, isn't she?"

Tate hesitated. "Doing just fine."

"That's great, really great." With a wave and a smile, the CNO turned smartly and strode off to his press briefing.

The door to the meditation room had been left unpainted, as though to put you in mind of old wood, of solid and good things. Tate opened it softly and stepped through. A sign in the small entrance space reminded the visitor that speaking was not allowed.

To the left, a doorway opened on the group meditation room. Folding metal chairs lined three dark walls. Hidden electric bulbs lit a wall of stained glass whose drifting abstractions suggested church windows with the saints removed. As Tate understood the room's function, it was here that committees reached particularly difficult to-bomb-or-not-to-bomb decisions.

The room was deserted.

To the right lay the solitary meditation room. Ten wing-backed chairs were arranged to give a view of the stained glass without giving a view of one another.

Tate saw Lee Armstrong in one chair and a young uniformed marine clenching a rosary in another.

He took a seat and felt embarrassed.

When the marine got up and left, he moved to the chair next to Lee.

"I dropped off Asher's plans last night with my physicist friend." Lee's voice was low. "Young fellow by the name of Bailey. He gave me some poop on what the Air Force was up to at Silo 29. They developed an experimental ceramic nose cone for Minuteman IV. It worked out in the tests, withstood heat and friction up to twelve hundred centigrade."

Tate stifled a whistle.

"Two years and twenty-five million dollars later they put it on a rocket and fired it. Damned thing shattered on re-entry. They thought it might have been a fluke, defective cone; they fired six more, all six shattered. Then Bailey and an Air Force physicist came up with the idea, instead of writing off the whole program as a dead loss, why not trick the Russians into wasting two years and twenty-five million of their own?"

Lee leaned sideways a moment to scan the dark behind his chair.

"The idea was to put the nose cone on a Minuteman IV and go through a routine readiness test launch while a Soviet spy satellite was passing close enough to get a look. Hopefully the Russians would swallow the bum steer and go off on a wrong tangent, wind up in the same dead end the Air Force did. It's kind of farfetched, but I can see Bailey coming up with it. He's a plotter, counter-counterespionage type. And I can see the Air Force might want to write off some of its loss as counterintelligence."

Tate grunted. "Even if Bailey's telling the truth, I don't see how it helps Pacific Aero. It doesn't explain the launch shutdown."

"I'm not sure he is telling the truth." Lee squeezed his knuckles till they were the color of bled veal. "Bailey phoned me this morning. He said Asher's plans were stupid, unworkable, illiterate. He said they and Asher should be buried. I've never heard him so worked up. He told me he'd shredded the plans."

"Shredded them!"

Lee flinched, as though Tate's had swung too hard. "Bailey's a young fellow, but he's not inexperienced. Either he way overreacted, in which case I'd like to know why, or he's lying, in which case I'd still like to know why." Lee lifted his pinkie and bit at a piece of skin near the nail. "What do you know about Firebird?"

"That was a Bolen-McKuen job. PA didn't have anything to do with it."

"Get hold of the DOD research and development reports to the House for the last five fiscal years. Look under R and D for tactical naval forces. Firebird's an alternate energy source in case of fuel blockade. A satellite gathers solar power and beams it by maser to your ships. It's in the development stage, low priority. They say they've spent a little under five million. At least that's the published information." Lee's whisper tightened to a pinpoint. "Tate, I only skimmed Asher's plans and my German stinks. But I can grasp the basics. Firebird relays energy to power stations, and Theta knocks out computer-missile communications. They're both the same kind of satellite, they use the same kind of cells to store solar energy, and they have the same kind of maser. They're built the same and they work the same. What it comes down to is, Firebird looks one hell of a lot like Theta with a new name and a new mission."

"That's quite a hypothesis," Tate said.

"I want you to go to Asher," Lee whispered. "Show him the published data on Firebird. Ask him how he thinks Firebird compares to Theta."

Tate fought a flare-up of impatience. "How's Asher going to know that? He's been out of the business ten years."

"Someone in the Navy's been playing with the procurement funds for fleet air defense. They're inflating items. Skimming the money off and putting it somewhere else. I'm sure they're putting it into Firebird. And I can't see any reason to fund Firebird on the hush-hush unless there's been some kind of rip-off."

"Come on, Lee. This doesn't have anything to do with me or PA or Silo 29."

"When Asher was trying to sell those plans and no one was buying, maybe a Navy engineer got a look at them. Times changed, we had an energy crisis, we had a maser breakthrough, and maybe that engineer thought: What's the harm if I borrow crazy old Asher's crazy old idea? After all, no one remembers the guy." There was a bitterness in the whisper more personal than principled, as if Lee were crusading not so much for dotty old professors as for all the forgotten drudges who'd ever been robbed of their nickel's worth of recognition. His hands were trembling and his face was horribly lined and it was a good thing, Tate supposed, that he was getting away to the Blue Ridge on Thursday.

"Come on," Tate placated. "Every department skims a little off of every other department. That's standard operating procedure."

"And that attitude is what's wrong with DOD finances." The accusation in Lee's eyes was unmistakable: that Tate had won his stars swimming from one end of a private pool to another; that Lee had had to hack through a jungle for his silver eagle; that Tate had sold his stars to the highest bidder and Lee was one of the last dwindling remnants of true soldiers. He had never put it in so many words but over the years he had implied it again and again and Tate was sick of the simpleminded injustice of it. "I stayed up till 5 A.M.," Lee said quietly, "working out a defense for your company. But if you don't want to take fifteen minutes to stop off at the hospital, I understand."

"Damn it, Lee, I haven't got fifteen minutes. Not today."

"Okay. We'll handle it through channels. Wait for Asher to find out and sue the DOD."

They had escalated to shouted whispers, like skeletons screaming at one another across a graveyard. It dawned on Tate that there was something wildly out of tilt about the argument, that Lee was near some kind of breakdown and if Tate could put up with boring senators at endless lunches there was no reason he couldn't cope with the slipped judgment of an overworked friend.

"Okay, okay," Tate conceded. "I'll dig up the reports. I'll see Asher."

Lee's face brightened and he was about to blurt something when a Wac came into the room. The stench of conversation hung over the chairs, blatant as cigar smoke. She gave both men a shocked look and vanished into the furthest chair. Lee made an apologetic gesture, pointed to his wristwatch, and rose.

They walked to the parking lot together. Lee said he would be having lunch in town; he would telephone Tate at the office to see how it went with Asher. He talked animatedly of baseball and waved good-by from the Mall Entrance steps.

Tate was relieved to slide into the solitude of the Bentley. A black Ford began to pull out in front of him. With a politeness that was almost insistent, the civilian driver let him go first.

Tate stopped in the doorway, not certain it was the right room. His eye took in gray wall, a window with a view of other windows, a pitcher lying on its side in an enameled bowl.

"Will you be taking him?" The old woman rose from her steel chair by the bed. She looked pained but in some mysterious way relieved to see him. "I didn't want to leave him alone."

For an instant Tate did not understand, and then it hit him that the body in the bed had a sheet pulled over its face. "Mrs. Asher?" he stammered.

The eyes saw his surprise. "You're not from the hospital?"

"No, I'm not." He took an uninvited step into the room. "I'm sorry."

She dropped into the chair again, thin in her pale dress. Hair the color of shadow clasped her head. "He gave his body to the hospital, to their medical school. There's a shortage."

"I'm very sorry," Tate said.

"Did you know him well?"

"Since yesterday."

Her eyes narrowed on him.

"My name is Tate Erlandsen. I'm with Pacific Aero. We had a—professional connection."

There was an instant of hooded suspicion. "Why are you here?"

"I'd hoped to speak with him. If there's anything at all I can do . . ." The offer drifted off helplessly.

"Could I be alone a minute?"

Tate waited in the hall, shutting out the smell of rubbing alcohol and disinfectant. There was a pay phone behind the nurse's desk. He realized he could phone Lee Armstrong and say he'd tried. He was off the hook.

Two orderlies passed him, pushing a roller cot. He turned to see what made them stop at the door. Mrs. Asher had folded down the sheet. She kissed the dead man on the lips and forehead. She came out of the room and walked away without a glance at Tate. There was not the least hesitation in step.

He went after her. "Mrs. Asher, can't I be of some help?"

"If you have a car, you would be very kind to drive me home."

The drive was strained. It was Mrs. Asher who broke the silence: she said the doctors had found a tumor. It had turned out not to be malignant; but her husband had not regained consciousness. "It happens," she sighed.

"I'm sure it happens," Tate said as neutrally as possible, letting her talk, not wanting to involve himself beyond the one good deed. She turned chatty and mentioned names of men who had designed missiles at Pacific Aero during her husband's time. Tate had to excuse his ignorance of them. She directed him to a dingy house on Thirty-sixth Street, not far from the campus of Georgetown University. She saw his expression.

"Can you imagine, they're raising the rent."

"Inflation, I suppose," he said.

"Or greed. Can I offer you something? Coffee? A drink? There's a little whiskey."

He was about to refuse when it occurred to him that she did not want to go back into the apartment alone. He parked the car, and they went up four stories in a wobbly small elevator with World War II graffiti—*Kilroy was here*—scratched into the wood. Mrs. Asher sorted out keys and opened the door to 4D. A dim corridor led into deeper dimness. She went quickly down the hallway snapping on lights. Tate followed her into the kitchen. He smelled cooking gas.

"The pilot light leaks," she apologized. "I try to leave the window open a crack. Sometimes I forget." She wrestled with a screw device on the side of the window that permitted it to be locked at any height.

"Let me try." Tate gripped the screw and gave it a hard wrench that almost took his thumb off. He raised the window. A humid breeze drifted in from the fire escape.

Mrs. Asher peeled off her white gloves, now smudged, and laid them on the table. She opened cabinets and searched among a congestion of dark jars.

"Coffee would be fine," Tate said.

"I could make real coffee."

"Instant is fine."

"Do you mind the real? I haven't had it in so long."

He observed her subtly agitated ritual of setting a coffee tin beside the stove, rinsing and assembling the filter coffee maker, digging a ring of measuring spoons from the back of a drawer.

"Asher couldn't drink coffee. He could only eat bland foods. For five years, eggs and cottage cheese. His cholesterol level was dreadful, but he had a stomach ulcer. It's difficult to choose between evils."

"Yes, it always is."

"Why did Asher go to see you yesterday?"

"He wanted me to pass some plans on to the Pentagon."

Her hand slowed; water overflowed the kettle spout. "Theta?"

Tate nodded.

She set the water on the burner and arranged six chocolate-chip cookies on a plate and set them in front of him. "He loved Theta."

"How many duplicates of the plans did he make?"

"Perhaps a dozen. He scattered them all over the industry. He even tried to put a set in the Library of Congress. No one wanted them. It broke his heart."

"And were the copies returned?"

"No one bothered. No one cared."

"What about work notes—did he keep copies?"

Tate followed the old woman through the small, shadowy apartment. Asher's metal filing cabinets were in the bedroom.

She searched the drawers. She pulled out a manila folder that had become flexible with age. She glanced through it, inhaled sharply, and handed it to Tate.

The tab was labeled *Theta*. The pages inside were crisp blank typing paper.

Mrs. Asher hurried back to the kitchen. She ignored the whistling kettle and thrust a finger toward the window. "I knew something was wrong."

All but one of the panes bore a good two years' city dust. But the pane beside the screw lock sparkled, throwing the fire escape into almost scrubbed relief. Tate reached beneath the open window and touched the putty. His finger came away with a gray, claylike dampness on the tip. "Not more than a few hours old," he observed.

She shook her head and tipped a jet of steaming water at the coffee filter. "When he was alive, no one wanted Theta. Now he's dead and they can't wait to rob him." The water dripped noisily and she stood hands on hips, muttering in a language that did not sound German enough to be Yiddish; possibly Hungarian. Her hands were shaking when she thumped two cups down on the table.

The coffee's unexpected bitterness almost made Tate gag. He reached for the sugar bowl. There was barely a teaspoon in the bottom. "Mrs. Asher, do you remember what time you left the house this morning?"

"I left the minute the hospital phoned. Nine, nine-fifteen."

"So you were gone almost an hour and a half. And this fire escape is on an alley."

"I don't understand this world any more."

"Is there a back entrance to the building?"

"Through the basement."

He took a business card from his wallet and jotted his home number. "You can always reach me at one number or the other. I'll see that your husband's plans are safe."

"You're very kind."

Tate let himself out of the apartment. He took the elevator down to the basement. He circled from the rear of the building to the side street. A truck backfired. Pigeons pinwheeled in the hot air as though a pillow of gray feathers had detonated. He slipped into a phone booth at the corner and sighted his car halfway up the block. He scanned the parked cars on either side of the street.

A heavyset man in a seersucker jacket sat in a black Ford. He had braced a newspaper against the steering wheel and kept putting a pencil tip to his tongue. Crossword-puzzle enthusiast. From time to time he glanced toward the door of Asher's building.

Tate lifted the telephone receiver and dropped a coin into the slot. He dialed his office. His secretary answered.

"Miss Monroe, you'd better write this down. Go to my home, right away. Take a taxi. Ask my wife for the copy of Asher's diagrams. *Ash* as in ash, *e, r*. They're in the study in the middle desk drawer. Make four sets of Xeroxes. Put two in the office safe. The original and other two go into a safe-deposit box. You're to rent the box in my name."

"I doubt I can do that, General. You'd have to sign the forms." Miss Monroe was an old priss. She offended Tate's conviction that secretaries should be sexy, not smart, but she had a useful habit of not making mistakes.

"Then rent the box in your name. You can do that, Miss Monroe, can't you?"

"Very well."

"I'd like you also to rent a post-office box. Mail both safe-deposit keys, in separate envelopes, to that box. Leave them there."

The man in the Ford folded his newspaper shut, looked at his wristwatch, and made a face.

"Send a letter to my lawyer immediately. Give him the combination to the post-office box and your authorization to open the safe-deposit box. To be used in the event anything untoward happens to me."

"Untoward?"

"Choose the wording yourself. You get an extra day's paid vacation if you can wrap all that up by noon."

He went to his car. He could see in the rear-view mirror that the black Ford pulled away from the curb at almost the same time he did.

With a burning sensation in his stomach, O'Brien reached the editorial page of the New York *Times*. He skimmed an outburst against government "bailing out" of a nuclear-sub builder. The phrase "socialism for the rich" stung him. He hurled the newspaper to the floor of the car.

The stereo speakers of the cartridge tape system whispered the slow movement of Brahms's Third Symphony. O'Brien read the early editions of the *Times* and Washington *Post* each morning on the way to work. Both papers were openly hostile to aerospace defense, but they were the agreed forums for government and defense department leaks and they contained the most up-to-date information available on policy struggles and shifts.

Usually Brahms helped him get through the chore. But not this morning. The car was mired in rush-hour traffic, and the veins in his forehead were pounding. He stared at the brick wall that separated the Pacific Aero plant from the highway. It was dotted with flower beds and box bushes that a Rockefeller might have placed at the entrance to his estate. A little of his anger left him.

As the driver aimed the Continental toward the Interstate 5 exit and spiraled down to ground level, the brick shaded off into fourteen-foot wire fences broken at hundred-yard intervals by entrance gates. These were manned around the clock by security guards working six-hour shifts. O'Brien gazed at the plant. He reflected that other men had conquered empires, but he had built one.

Twenty-two cinder-block monoliths clustered in the west, each rising twelve stories, where 14,000 skilled and unskilled workers handled design, data systems, engineering, electronics, and mechanical subassemblies. To the east, across a broad gash of runway and parking lot, loomed ten quonset-roofed hangars where 6,000 skilled men and women assembled and repaired the jet planes and missile components that had been PA's biggest earners in the 1960s and early 1970s. Though the newest of the hangars had been there six years and the oldest twenty-four, they gave the impression of prefabricated shelters airlifted to an asphalt Arctic and temporarily plunked down.

But there was nothing temporary about them at all. Not if Jack O'Brien could help it.

The car cut speed at the approach to Gate Three, the executive entrance. A group of women had bunched together at the guard booth. They were waving placards. The word *racist*, boldly lettered in red, hit O'Brien's eye like a fist.

"Sam," he told the driver, "slow down." He had a foot on the pavement before the car had even stopped. "Good morning, ladies. What seems to be the trouble?"

A tall black woman with an extravagant Afro stepped forward. "Mr. O'Brien, I'm Davidine Strokes: shop stewardess of electronics subassembly C-8."

"How do you do," O'Brien said.

"A foreman beat one of our sisters yesterday. We are here to protest."

"Which sister?"

The stewardess threw a nod toward a cringing Mexican. The others pushed her toward the front rank. She wore a bandage across one eye. The tip of an iodine-colored stain showed.

"Pleased to meet you, ma'am." O'Brien held out a hand. "Would you mind telling me how you got that wound?"

She was tongue-tied; a helping babble rose.

O'Brien had learned a little Spanish three years ago when he had to go to Peru to look over a copper mine. He was not about to get the story through shouting intermediaries. "*Señora*," he said softly, "*quisiera usted decirme como recibió esa herida?*"

"*Me sentía enferma*," she said in a near-whisper, "*me caí* . . ." She had felt sick; she had fallen; the *patrón* had struck her in the eye and on the arm. She lifted an elbow and showed the purple bruise.

O'Brien listened, nodding, to the all too familiar story. He knew the foreman would have his side of the story, equally familiar, perhaps equally pathetic. To get defense contracts, Pacific Aero had to meet government racial quotas. The company had instituted crash training programs aimed at blacks and Chicanos. The result had been a growing de facto segregation: whites occupied management and skilled positions, while nonwhites occupied unskilled and all too rarely made the jump to semiskilled. There had been repeated incidents of friction between foremen, who were mostly white, and minority workers. In eight years the number of tranquilizers that company doctors prescribed to employees had quintupled. The harm that these frightened people did one another was bad enough; the harm they did Pacific Aero could be irreparable.

O'Brien learned the names of the Mexican woman and of the foreman; asked if she had been to a doctor. She said the doctor in Building C had bandaged her and sent her home. O'Brien told her to go to Dr. Sloane, in the executive building; to phone him after the doctor had examined her. He apologized for the incident, shook hands that thrust themselves out at him.

He got back into the car, and the limousine eased through the dispersing pickets. Davidine Stokes's face, a mask of mute hostility, swiveled like a radar tracking him. Too bad she wasn't on the company's side, O'Brien thought; she had organized those women well.

O'Brien asked the driver to stop a moment at Hangar 3, the B-92 assembly. The B-92 was an updated, medium-range Air Force bomber that incorporated recent advances in maneuverability, electronics, and laser guidance. It also incorporated power plants, radars, and landing struts that PA had been putting into other craft and still had assembly lines tooled up to handle. Switzerland was negotiating to buy in, and while the company's gamble was close to four hundred million, once the B-92 hit profit it would hit hard, and PA would clear an astronomical 22 per cent of the eleven-million-dollar unit price.

Yesterday a snag had been reported in one of the prototypes. O'Brien wanted to make personally sure that the problem had been straightened out.

The limousine pulled into Hangar 3 and the foreman—a barrel-chested grandfather who'd been with PA twenty-eight years—came hurrying over. O'Brien got out of the car and clapped him on the shoulder. "How are we coming, Lou?" He had to shout over the noise of riveting machines.

"This will really give you a kick, Mr. O'Brien." The foreman pulled a handkerchief from his overall pocket and carefully unfolded it. He held out a quartz chip scarcely larger than an eighth-inch industrial diamond drill bit. "Three hundred twenty-eight circuits are micro-integrated on this chip, and one of them's defective."

O'Brien's eye traveled the line of prototypes in a sweep. There were five B-92 frames in different stages of completion. He watched the workers feeling their way across them like mountain climbers. His eye stopped at the fourth frame. A workman was applying bulkhead grommets to a hoseline that would eventually conduct fire-extinguishing medium to the cockpit. At the third frame, entrails of a radar system spilled through an uncompleted gap in the titanium skin.

"Lou, I don't know how the hell you do it," O'Brien said.

"It took a little looking," the foreman admitted. "Why don't you keep it? It's no good."

O'Brien accepted the chip. "I'll give it to my grandson. He'll get a kick out of it."

O'Brien gave a wave and got back into the idling Continental. The car pulled out of the hangar and carried him smoothly to PA's oasis, the three green, landscaped acres surrounding the executive building. It eased to a stop in the dogwood-shaded parking lot. O'Brien, as president of the company, had the space nearest the west entrance. The remaining diagonal slots were assigned to VPs and assistant VPs in order of descending rank: the lower your status, the further you walked from your car to the door. Fifteen out of the thirty slots were already occupied, mostly by Cadillacs.

O'Brien thanked the chauffeur and strode into the building. It was the type of glass-and-steel structure considered wasteful in these days of energy crunch, a graceful memento of the optimism and expanding economy of the early 1960s.

The temperature was sixteen degrees cooler—almost too cool—within the entrance. "Far elevator, Mr. O'Brien," the guard called.

"Thanks, Harry." O'Brien waited at the elevator. He was joined by a stocky man in his late forties. He recognized Bob Schick, vice-president in charge of special design projects. "Morning, Bob."

"Hi, Jack."

They got into the elevator and it gently lifted them.

"We may have licked the salinity," Bob Schick remarked.

It took O'Brien an instant to understand. Bob Schick was heading up a task force to get the kinks out of a prototype submarine-detection sonar buoy system. It was a Navy project, part of the DOD's attempt to break the pattern of company favoritism among the services and assign contracts on an ability-to-perform basis.

"Got a minute?" Bob Schick said. "I can show you." Excitement and overwork gleamed in his pinprick eyes.

O'Brien wondered when Bob Schick had last had a good night's sleep. "Sure," he said, and hoped it wouldn't take long. "I'd like to see."

The elevator stopped on the fourteenth floor and O'Brien followed Bob Schick down the corridor to the Special Design Division. Bob Schick showed O'Brien two blueprints.

"Pretty, hey?"

The blueprints looked as though they had been executed by high-speed plotters, mechanical devices that drew designs under computer control. "Beautiful," O'Brien said.

"Take a look over here," Bob Schick said. He led O'Brien to an input/output computer. A diagram glowed white against dark on the cathode-ray tube. An engineer was touching a light pen to the surface of the tube, drawing in an adjustment. Bob Schick asked him to show O'Brien what they'd come up with.

"The salinity was the problem," Bob Schick said. "It kept throwing the heat sensors off."

The diagram began to turn on its axis, imitating exactly the rotation of a three-dimensional figure.

"The sensors could tag whales," Bob Schick said, "and icebergs and rocks—"

"And seaweed," the engineer said.

"And seaweed," Bob Schick said, "but the salinity kept screwing them up."

"How did you lick it?" O'Brien asked.

"Copper ions," Bob Schick said. "Don't know why we didn't think of it before."

O'Brien said that Bob Schick and his team were doing great work. He rode up along in the elevator to the fifteenth floor, thinking it remarkable that he was co-founder and president of a company whose products he could no longer comprehend.

He stepped out of the elevator and passed through a corridor of vice-presidential offices, each door neatly labeled and most of them ajar. A shut door meant conference or no one home. In front of each office a secretary sat arranging her desk for the day's work. O'Brien called out a string of *hello*'s and *hi there*'s.

"Phil Marquis would like you to call him in Detroit as soon as you can. He wants to bring you up to date on the labor negotiations." Miss Kelly had risen from her desk to hand him the typed list of phone calls, with caller, time of call, subject of call, and—where necessary—*reply requested* all indicated. It wasn't even nine o'clock, and there had already been over a dozen calls.

O'Brien glanced through the open door behind Miss Kelly's head. He had the impression from the way she lowered her eyes that the new girl had been watching him. She wore a blue blouse today with a high, lacy collar; her hair seemed to be brushed a little looser than yesterday.

"The Olympic is redecorating half its suites, won't have them done by Friday's board meeting." Miss Kelly moved and blocked his view of the girl. "Rather than put any out-of-town board members in single rooms, I've booked suites at the Hilton."

O'Brien said, "Good," and shifted position and watched the girl roll a carbon set into her IBM Selectric. "Anything from General Erlandsen?"

"Not yet."

The new girl's name was Dempsey, Miss Susan Dempsey. He had been aware of her for almost three months. She had the smile of a very young girl and her lace blouse suggested the breasts of a young mother. From time to time when he saw her initials on a letter, O'Brien made a point of mentioning to Miss Kelly how very satisfactory *sd*'s typing was. Miss Kelly ran through assistants fast, and O'Brien wanted to be sure *sd* lasted. He had never spoken to Miss Dempsey and probably never would, but the sight of her earnest concentration at the typewriter touched some spot in him that was still capable of a pleasant sort of adolescent pang.

"Anything from Ellsworth?" O'Brien asked.

Miss Kelly shook her head. "We're keeping line three, red phone, open. Just in case."

More than once O'Brien had asked himself which would be the greater disaster: to lose his wife, or to lose his secretary. Miss Kelly was his shield and third hand. In subtle ways she was adviser, nurse, confessor, friend. In certain respects she understood him better than Debbie.

It was as shield that he valued her most. She intercepted a huge portion of the calls, the flak, the inquiries, the visitors, even the emergencies that came his way, and rerouted them to the department heads who could best handle them. Without her, he would have drowned in trivia.

"Miss Kelly, an employee by the name of Gabriela Revueltas will be phoning. Put her right through to me, will you?"

Miss Kelly took it down on her note pad with a flick of her pencil point.

"And could you get hold of Tim Boswell for me, right away?"

Another flick of the tip. "Oh, Mr. O'Brien; you'll be seeing Dan Jones of Seattle Guaranty at eleven. You might want to glance at the material in the yellow folder. It's been updated to closing business yesterday. And Bart Masters is in the next room."

O'Brien lowered his voice. "Who the hell is Bart Masters?"

"Texas Star Trust. You met him in Dallas eight months ago."

"Any idea what the hell he wants?"

"Probably to tell Dallas he shook hands with the president of Pacific Aero."

O'Brien put on a smile and stepped into the leather-and-chrome waiting room with its splashy abstractions shouting off the wall.

The Texan rose from the couch, one hand clutching a copy of *Aerospace Weekly*. He wore a business suit and boots. His sun-tanned jaw broke into a grin that reminded O'Brien of some earlier phase in the evolution of man. O'Brien wondered what the hell kind of a banker he was to come busting in without an appointment.

"Hi, Bart," O'Brien said. "Nice to see you again."

The Texan held out a strong hand that seemed incongruously clean. "I knew I wouldn't get a chance to say hello if that secretary of yours had anything to do with it, so I just walked right in. You're looking terrific, Jack."

"So are you, Bart. Say would you mind if I made a couple of phone calls? Then you and I can have a cup of coffee."

"Go right ahead, Jack. I'm having a great time with this magazine. Just give a shout when the coast is clear."

O'Brien went into his office and shut the door behind him. The office was the plum location in the building. Its two glass walls looked north and west, and if the accordion-fold partition were rolled back, he had an eastern view as well. He liked space, indoors and out. The distance from door to desk was as broad as a city avenue. The furniture clustered where the two glass walls met: leather, chrome, and plastic were expensively joined into a desk, chairs, a sofa.

The green phone on his desk was buzzing softly. He pushed the flashing button and lifted the receiver. "Tim, what are you doing about those pickets at Gate Three?"

"I'm working on it, Jack. A foreman got rough with one of the women, but the big problem is the shop stewardess. One of those organizer types. I'm going to see if an apology and handshake will do the trick."

"Give me a report."

"Will do."

O'Brien sat a moment staring at the lit, glassed-in shelves where he kept his collection of duck decoys. The only wood in his office was the pencils Miss Kelly sharpened for him daily and those fourteen ducks and the frame on the Jackson Pollock. O'Brien hated the Pollock, but he hated it under his breath: it had been a gift from the board back in the '60s, and it had tripled in value since. He loved the ducks. They had been a hobby for over a quarter century. One bore a three-inch gold plaque with a greeting from President John F. Kennedy.

O'Brien realized he was wasting time. He lifted the green receiver and told Miss Kelly to put him through to Phil Marquis in Detroit. At the buzz he lifted the black receiver. "Phil, how's it coming?"

"The local won't budge from 29 per cent."

Twice daily for the last week, O'Brien had been on the WATS line to Phil Marquis, vice-president in charge of labor relations at the PA plant in Detroit. The local was asking for a 29 per cent increase over the life of the new contract, but for an immediate across-the-board hike of ninety cents in benefits as well. As if the package weren't irresponsible enough, they wanted dental insurance, free eyeglasses, and maternity benefits for all dependents, including unmarried daughters. They'd even thrown in irritants like a demand for Ground Hog Day and a holiday to commemorate Michigan's statehood.

"No way, Phil. Not on top of the cost-of-living adjustment." O'Brien lifted the plastic bottle of Valium out of the desk drawer, put a ten-milligram capsule on his tongue, and washed it down with spit.

"Jack, these men read the papers. PA stock is up. And the Sea Condor is ahead of projection." The Detroit plant was a small operation, turning out engine parts and spares for commercial and military jets. It was also handling the Sea Condor, a run of 340 helicopters for the Marines. PA had entered a low bid on the Sea Condor as a courtesy to the DOD and as a tacit thank-you for the far more lucrative Hornet fighter craft. So unpredictably did the wheels of procurement grind that PA had wound up saying thank you before it had anything on paper to be thankful for. Surprisingly—considering the unrealistically low bid—the Sea Condor had started breaking even at the eightieth copy and might get to profit around the ninetieth. There had been talk of the Navy's buying in. "The men know they're the only PA plant that's in the black this quarter."

"That's a matter of bookkeeping. In three hours I could have figures showing the worst loss in ten years at that plant."

"We're awfully close to that Friday-midnight deadline." Phil Marquis' voice had all the bounce of a used-up tennis ball.

"We'll hit them with a few concessions once the Hornet's out of committee. Keep them negotiating as long as you can. Stretch it, Phil. Thanks." O'Brien hung up. After his stomach had uncoiled he opened the door to the waiting room. The

Texan was tapping his knee with the rolled magazine. "Come on in, Bart. Sorry to keep you waiting."

Bart Masters came smiling into the office and made a suitably impressed face. "That's quite a view."

"How do you like your coffee, Bart?"

"If you have some milk substitute and some saccharine, that would be just fine."

O'Brien sat at the desk, not in one of the chairs grouped for conversation, and Bart Masters sat facing him. O'Brien pushed a button for Miss Kelly and asked her to take care of the coffee. "What brings you to Seattle, Bart?"

"Seattle happens to be where my baby sister lives. You might say I'm taking the long way around to New York. Sure is good to see you, Jack. Been reading about that Hornet in the New York *Times*. It's looking good."

"We hope the committee will vote for it."

"You got that committee sewed up. They're just making a fuss for the folks back home. Say, Jack, any chance of kidnapping you for lunch before I head East?"

"I'd like to, but today's out." Miss Kelly came in with the coffee tray, and O'Brien asked, "Miss Kelly, how am I set for lunch tomorrow?"

"You'll be lunching with two members of your board."

O'Brien smiled at Bart Masters. "Miss Kelly always keeps me booked solid a month in advance. But as long as you came all this way, how'd you like a little tour of the plant?"

Bart Masters suddenly looked very eager. "I'd like that, Jack."

"Miss Kelly, could you get hold of Will Stevenson and see if he's free to show Mr. Masters around?"

Quentin Quinn calculated that in his three years as Pacific Aero's controller he must have made somewhere in the neighborhood of twenty-two hundred round trips to the junior executive men's room. Yet he still experienced a discharge of raw, electrical resentment every time he looked down that corridor and saw where the company had put his secretary. She sat not in an anteroom of her own but out in the hall with the secretaries of three vice-presidents in charge of subdivisions of production and twenty-two assistant VP's in charge of carrying out orders.

If her status depressed her, the fact didn't show in Miss Langston's pink-gummed smile. "You have a visitor, Mr. Quinn. The treasurer."

Quentin Quinn tried not to make a face and thanked her. He walked into his office. Dev Barker was standing by the desk playing with the lid of the humidor. Quentin Quinn wished he wouldn't. Those cigars were two-dollar Havanas.

"Sorry to barge in, Quent." The office was on the wrong side of the building, with a view not of the reflecting pool but of Building C. Sun bouncing off cinder block caught moisture on Dev Barker's face. His vest looked tight and his voice came out pinched and high. "I was wondering if you could help me."

"Glad to try," Quentin Quinn said.

"We'd like to know the effectiveness of that ad campaign we ran last January."

"It was a damned good campaign."

"Hard to be sure without figures. What I'd like to do is compare the last two stockholder lists. See how our appeal has shifted in terms of ownership: brokerage houses, mutual funds, foundations, corporations, personal. I'd like to know how we're doing geographically. And we might as well get a breakdown by size of holdings."

Quentin Quinn couldn't believe his ears. O'Brien must have told his treasurer to check the stockholder list for signs of a takeover. He'd probably asked Barker to handle the inquiry himself. But Barker could no more operate a computer than he could a drill press. Since he'd done a few favors for Quinn, he figured Quinn would help him out without asking questions.

Quentin Quinn had built his career on not asking questions. "Any rush on this?" he said.

"As soon as you can get to it."

"Give me half an hour."

Dev Barker lifted a pudgy hand in an economizing thank-you/good-by gesture. He about-faced and hurried out of the office.

Quentin Quinn telephoned the computer room and spoke with one of the whiz kids he had brought with him from his old company. He explained what he wanted. He replaced the receiver and sat staring out at the cinder-block view.

He had come to Pacific Aero from Houghton, King—one of the "big eight" national accounting firms—where he had been dissatisfied as supervisor. He was thirty-nine years old and his hair was beginning to go. It nagged him that after three years he was still on the next-to-top floor; that at an annual salary of forty thousand with another twelve in untaxed benefits he was the lowest-paid vice-president on the company staff. But he calculated that he had time and changing times on his side. After all, the chairman of the board of Chrysler and the president of General Motors were both CPAs just like him, and neither was over fifty.

Twenty minutes later he had ten yards of accordion-folded computer printout on his desk. When he saw how much stock had shifted into street-name accounts between December and March, he picked up the telephone and dialed four digits.

"Mr. O'Brien's office."

"Hi, gorgeous."

"Quentin, I can't talk now."

"Me neither. Is your bag packed?"

"Why should my bag be packed?"

"Because your boss is going to take you on a trip."

"Mr. O'Brien's not going on any trip."

"He will after Dev Barker shows him the stock movement in the last quarter. Now when Miss Kelly asks if any of you girls can fly to New York with O'Brien, you say yes. Got that?"

"What's this all about, Quentin?"

"Meet me in the cafeteria at three o'clock. I'll treat you to a cup of coffee and tell you all about it."

"The pension fund is holding about 5 per cent." Dev Barker had placed the printout on O'Brien's desk. Slump-shouldered, he stood reading it off fold by fold. "The Stern Foundation is holding another 5."

"Frances Meredith is on the board of that foundation." O'Brien took the carpet in broad strides. "If she sells, they'll liquidate upwards of half."

"The Benjamin Hess Foundation is holding 3 per cent, down from 6."

"They'll sell the works if Meredith and Stern sell."

"Two of our mutual funds have dropped. Samson is down from 5 to 3, American United is down from 4 and a half to 3. They may have gone down further. Our figures are practically three months old. Frances Meredith is still holding 3 per cent."

O'Brien paused to stare at the gold plaque in the side of the wood marlin. He thought of John F. Kennedy and an age of optimism that seemed as overstuffed and irrelevant now as a Victorian doll's house.

"You're holding 8," Dev Barker said. "Southern Electronics is holding 4, up from 3. They seem to be branching into aerospace. Last year they took over Pan-Rad."

O'Brien had followed the take-over of the Utah-based manufacturer of aircraft radio gear. The government ought to have brought an antitrust action but had not, a clear signal that in matters touching the ailing aerospace-defense industry they were prepared to look the other way.

"Maybe they liked the taste of blood." Today Dev Barker was wearing a light vest that fitted him as poorly as the dark vest he had worn yesterday. He hooked a finger into a buttonhole and made breathing room. "We'd be a good candidate for them. We're solid as aerospace goes, we're not mammoth, they could get us relatively cheaply."

"I don't like that kid they put on our board."

"Allan Martino?" Dev Barker said.

"Never says anything." O'Brien frowned. "Just sits there and takes notes."

"He usually votes with management, doesn't he?"

"He never looks you in the eye. Some of those Italian kids are as ambitious as Jews."

"We're all as ambitious as Jews," Dev Barker said.

O'Brien glanced at his treasurer and wondered if he was one of those liberals who got offended the minute you said "Jew," as though the word were some kind of insult. O'Brien respected ambition and he respected Jews who had it. He just didn't like Allan Martino.

"Rebus is holding 4 and a half," Dev Barker said; which didn't surprise O'Brien at all. Rebus International had been holding 4 and a half for over six years, even since they'd taken over Melvin Culligan's company and his holdings in PA. "There's been a real leap in Techno-Mutual. They've gone from 2 and a half to just under 10. And Pacific Aero has repurchased 15 per cent for treasury stock." Dev Barker riffled through the last dozen folds of printout. "Eleven months ago about 40.5 per cent of the stock was held by individual small investors. Two months ago that was down to 36.5."

"What about street-name accounts?" O'Brien asked.

"They're up, from half a per cent to 6." Dev Barker closed the printout. It made a heavy sound, like the shutting of a family Bible. "The take-over has been in the works at least six months."

O'Brien kept pacing. "Techno-Mutual's not interested in taking over any companies. They're cashing in on the stock rise. They could even be working with the raider—holding stock for him so he won't have to register. Frances Meredith is the linchpin. If she sells to the raider, she could swing anywhere from 8 and a half to 11 per cent. If we can keep her from selling and keep the stock up, Techno-Mutual will hold on to their 10 per cent—and we'll stop the raid."

"It'll cost you three and a half million at least to buy her out."

"How's our line of credit?"

Sunlight filled half the office, but Dev Barker kept hovering in shadow. "We're exercising nine million right now."

"What does that leave us?"

"About a million with Seattle National."

"We're exercising that line Monday. Set it up." O'Brien snatched up the green receiver and dialed 1. "Miss Kelly, get hold of Bart Masters. He's out looking at the Hornet assembly. Ask if he'd like to fly to New York with me in about— oh, an hour and a half." He lowered the receiver and saw Dev Barker looking surprised. "Masters spent half an hour this morning trying to butter me up. He's dying to get his bank into the Social Register. If I can set up a loan from Manufacturers in New York, he'll fall right in."

"What makes you think Manufacturers will come in?"

"Chrissakes, Dev, we're a good customer. Harry Pratt owes me a few favors. How many shares have we got outstanding?"

"Three and a half million."

"Okay, we'll make the raider buy more. At the board meeting this Friday I'll move that we issue another half million shares."

"The stockholders will howl, Jack."

"We'll tell them we're using the receipts to buy back some of our thirty-year debentures. Interest rates were sky-high when we set up that loan; they're lower now. It'll look like we're saving money. You handle the presentation, Dev. You're good at that." O'Brien paced to the glass wall and stared at the reflecting pond. He'd never understood how Arabs and Israelis could squabble over land until he'd seen the reflection of his own buildings in his own pond.

"And we'll make the bastard pay more," O'Brien said. "We'll start rumors, talk the stock up. Dev, I'm going to exercise an option for fifty thousand shares. It would look good if you bought a few too."

Dev Barker made a sound that wasn't quite a word.

"Drop a hint to the other officers. Get them on the band-wagon. Let a few of your friends know the company's look-ing good." O'Brien made a catcher's mitt of one fist and a baseball of the other and began pounding them together: an isometric movement that kept the upper arms strong. "Word will get out that management is exercising its options. It'll hit the newsletters and snowball. And we'll get out a letter to the stockholders. We'll say projected profits for the upcoming quarter will be up 8 per cent—up 10 per cent above the same quarter last year."

"That's sixty, seventy cents a letter," Dev Barker said.

O'Brien whirled on his heel. "Screw the cents, Dev. Do it."

"We could wipe out contingencies for expected increases in labor and overtime costs. We could account them as profit this quarter." It was a gamble: if they distributed their emergency reserves as profit and costs went up, they'd be sunk. Dev Barker's voice was almost as pale as his face. "Short-term profits would go up, but in the long run—"

"Not *go* up, Dev: they've got to shoot up." It was a straightforward matter of increasing cash on hand by any means feasible. A lot of corporations did it between audits. The losses would show up in a quarter or so, but in the meantime the company would have gotten over the hump. "What about bills: can we postpone payment on anything?"

"Ad bills. We could wait the full sixty days. It would mean giving up the 3 per cent discount." Ad agencies tradi-tionally gave a discount to clients who paid their bills in full within ten days, and most companies paid within the discount period. But tradition was not law.

"How much could we save?"

"We owe twenty-five million, we could pay twenty, keep five. Increase our earnings per share $1.43 or so."

"Good."

"We really ought to take that discount, Jack. Passing it up is like paying 108 per cent a year."

"If we don't get some cash in hand we don't have a com-pany." O'Brien didn't bother reminding Dev Barker where they would both be if the company got taken over. More than once in the past they'd come close to bending regula-tions, and O'Brien resented Dev Barker's suddenly getting cold feet like a kid on his first visit to a whorehouse. "Have the letter to the stockholders ready for my signature tomor-row."

Miss Kelly must have knocked, because she was crossing

the carpet toward them, pad and pencil at the ready. "Excuse me, Mr. O'Brien. Mr. Masters says he'd enjoy very much flying East with you."

"Call Execujet: have a plane waiting in an hour. I'll be taking Bart Masters and a travel secretary. Pick a good girl for me, Miss Kelly. You stay here and hold the fort. I'll spend the night in New York, fly back tomorrow."

Miss Kelly's pencil skimmed the surface of the pad, leaving a track of fleet hieroglyphics.

"Set up appointments with Barry Manners at the Stern Foundation, Lew Walters at Benjamin Hess, Fred Morgenstern at American United, Ted Samson at Samson Fund, Reuben Arbenjian at Techno-Mutual."

Miss Kelly somehow flipped a page without the pencil's stopping.

"I'll want to see Jacob Rosen at Klein Finch; Jonathan Thomas at Mason Stanley." Both men were partners at key brokerage firms. O'Brien couldn't expect them to tell him outright who was behind the street accounts, but they might be willing to barter some background with him. "What's that black fellow's name at Freedom Trust—the executive VP?"

"Aaron Winston," Miss Kelly said.

"Get me an appointment with Aaron Winston." Freedom Trust was one of the new black banks. O'Brien was not a customer, but he'd be a catch for them, and in a pinch they might loan a half million of sub-usurious interest. "And I'll want to see either Stainslav Kubrick or Morton Kelly at Kubrick, Sloan, Cohen and Rothstein." KSC&R had established a reputation among law firms for fighting take-overs. Kubrick was managing partner, Kelly a partner and CPA, and it wouldn't hurt to establish communication. "I don't care if I have to see them at two in the morning, I want to see them. And get Quentin Quinn on the line right away."

Miss Kelly picked up the green receiver and punched four digits.

"Dev, see if you can goose the computer department and—"

Miss Kelly passed the receiver to O'Brien.

"Quentin, I need something fast."

"Shoot."

"Analysis of all current projects. Any overruns higher than 5 per cent per unit I want spelled out in detail. Have it ready for me tomorrow evening."

"Roger."

O'Brien hung up. "Dev, see if you can goose the computer department and get a rush on the next stockholder list. Run a comparison with the other two, detail the trends. I want to know all about the little old ladies in Wichita with ten shares." He lifted the black WATS-line receiver and dialed Detroit and asked for Phil Marquis. The green phone rang and Miss Kelly answered and began saying something to a Mr. Channing, who was probably Hal Channing, head of public relations.

"Phil," O'Brien shouted, "I need a projection of the kind of settlement we can expect out there and I need it right away. I want you to spell out the increased cost in labor and overhead on all goods, broken down by unit."

"All right, Jack." Phil Marquis sounded so tired it made O'Brien angry.

"Get those results to Dev Barker posthaste. Thanks, Phil." O'Brien turned again to his treasurer. "I want to know how the Detroit agreements are going to spill over into our other labor agreements. Do a unit projection on all goods, detailed."

"It's awfully conjectural, Jack."

"Do it, Dev. Miss Kelly, is that Hal Channing?" O'Brien took the green phone. Channing was saying something and O'Brien cut him short. "Hal, we need to spiff up the old image. Can you map out a few campaigns and have them ready for me tomorrow evening?"

Miss Kelly looked troubled. "Will it be all right if I send Miss Dempsey with you?"

"Miss Dempsey will do fine," O'Brien said. "I like her typing."

Mort Dubrovsky stepped onto the fifteenth floor of the executive building and was lost.

Either way he looked, up or down the corridor, desks were angled like cars in a parking lot. The tops were so neat he didn't see how anyone ever got any work done on them, and at every desk a pretty girl was typing or telephoning. Behind each girl was a numbered door. He looked for the number that Timothy Boswell's secretary had given him, and he saw Timothy Boswell, jacketless, standing in a doorway waiting to greet him.

"Hi there, Mart." Boswell steered him into a room that Mort had expected would be an office. But it was just a room with a sofa, two chairs, an ugly painting, and a shut door.

"Why don't you call me Tim, Mart?"

Mort tried to figure the *Mart* business, and then it hit him: a typo in his company report. Pacific Aero kept close track of all its employees' performances, reviewed the record when weighing decisions to promote or freeze. Timothy Boswell had been dipping into his folder. Mort wondered why, and he wondered what Boswell had fished out besides the *Mart*.

"We've got a hell of a sticky problem here; this Davidine Stokes is shaping up to be a real nuisance."

Boswell sat on the sofa. Mort took the cue and sat on a chair. Boswell leaned out of his seat and put a hand on Mort's knee.

"We're both married men, Mart. We both knew how women are."

"Yes, sir."

"And I hate to say it, but we both know how blacks are."

Mort suspected Boswell didn't know a damned thing about blacks; just took Mort for a Ku Kluxer and was playing to it. "Yes, sir."

"Mart, we have over twenty thousand workers in this plant, and more than 10 percent of those workers are black and Chicano."

A lot more than 10 per cent where I work, Mort thought; and a lot less where you work. He bet even the cleaning women up here were white, and he bet there was no writing in the johns either.

"As you know, close to 80 per cent of our work is done directly or indirectly for the government, and we're committed to the same goals as the government, at least on paper. Now I know this Revueltas woman deserved it, and you know she deserved it, and for Pete's sake the United States Government knows she deserved it." Boswell's teeth glowed against his tan. His eyes were green as "go" signals. "But we're a company that's one tenth black and Chicano, working for the government of a nation that's one tenth black and Chicano, and we have to keep up a semblance of harmony."

Mort almost lost the grip on his smile. In Boswell's math nine tenths had to cater to one tenth.

"Now the easiest way to handle Davidine Stokes is the same way you'd handle any woman. If you'll play along, Mart, I'm going to pretend to give you one hell of a dressing down, and chances are she'll buy it and we won't have any more flak and she'll put her women back on the assembly line. Okay?"

"Excuse me, sir. If she's taken women off the assembly lines, they're wildcatting."

"I've spoken to the union, Mart, and the union's view is, if we can straighten this out informally, between us, with a minimum of fuss and bother, it'll save everyone a lot of pain and woe. Now if you want to go along with us, Mart, you'd be doing Pacific Aero a hell of a favor."

Mort still had three grades to advance in pay scale. "Okay."

Boswell rose and opened the door and let Mort go first.

This was definitely the office: desk as big as a grand piano, telephone console with twenty buttons, view of the reflecting pond, and Davidine Stokes on a black leather chair not bothering to get up.

"How long have you worked for this company, Dubrovsky?" Boswell pitched his voice differently now, like a drill sergeant's.

"Twenty-seven years, sir."

"Twenty-sevn years and you still don't know how to handle your workers?"

Mort glanced at their audience. Davidine Stokes could have been peeling potatoes for all the interest she showed. She dangled a lit cigarette, powdering Boswell's carpet, and stared at an empty spot on the wall.

"Christ, Dubrovsky: don't we deserve a little something for our money? This company pays you 326 dollars and 99 cents a week. What for?"

Mort swallowed back a denial, but the slip jabbed him. Pacific Aero paid him 326 dollars and 98 cents a week, not 99. So long as the vice-president was going to hit him with dollars and cents, why didn't he at least get the cents right? It was the same sort of inattention to detail that riled Mort when he looked at trainees' work.

"Dubrovsky, we don't strike workers at Pacific Aero. And we don't strike women. And certainly not a pregnant woman!"

"Who's pregnant?"

"Gabriela Revueltas is four and one half months pregnant." Davidine Stokes took a long drag of cigarette.

"If Revueltas is pregnant," Mort said, "she lied on her job application."

"The point isn't pregnancy," Boswell broke in, "the point is, you struck an employee of this company."

"If I'd known she was pregnant, do you think I'd have let her work on an assembly?"

"The point is," Davidine Stokes said quietly, "you hit her because she's a woman and she's Mexican."

"The point is, I hit her because she was doing a piss-poor job!"

A bubble of silence enclosed them, and Mort realized his mistake.

Davidine Stokes sighed and readjusted herself on the black leather cushion. "Mr. Boswell, we consider the continued employment of foremen like this an affront to every woman, black, and Chicano in Pacific Aero."

"Who's we?" Mort demanded.

Her eyebrows formed a smile.

"Miss Stokes and her shop have asked for your resignation," Boswell said.

Mort shot a glance at Boswell's eyes, trying to read them. They were glassed over, dead. His stomach told him there was a ventriloquist in the room by the name of Davidine Stokes and a dummy by the name of Timothy Boswell, and this wasn't playacting at all.

"Miss Stokes and I have discussed the matter," Boswell said. "Miss Stokes is willing to call off her pickets, provided you apologize to Mrs. Revueltas."

Mort tried to take a breath. His neck and wrists were running caterpillars of sweat.

"Understand one thing, Dubrovsky." Boswell's jaw made a fist. "Any repetition of this, and you're out."

"Okay, you want me to go right now and apologize to Revueltas?"

"Hold it, Dubrovsky. I want you to apologize to Miss Stokes first."

Mort looked at the playacting bastard with his vacation tan and his eighteen-dollar shirt and he wanted to say: *Boswell, you're as wrong about Stokes as you are about the cents in my salary.* But he said nothing. He held out his hand and swallowed hard. "I'm sorry, Miss Stokes."

She gave him a long narrow look. Her fingers stayed coiled in her lap.

Okay, you black bitch, Mort promised himself: *I don't care if you've got the whole board of directors kissing your African ass, Mort Dubrovsky is not kissing. Someday you're going to pay me back for this and pay me back good.*

Davidine Stokes rose, said goody-by to Tim Boswell, and

went. Boswell put an arm around Mort's shoulder and said, "Guess we really gave Stokes a run for her money, eh, Mart?"

"I hope so," Mort said. And then he asked, "Say, mind if I ask where you got my salary figure, that 99 cents?"

Boswell smiled. "We do keep records, Mart."

The midday sun was hot on Tate's Dacron jacket as he hurried toward the Senate. A mob of reporters and cameramen packed the steps, and a woman thrust a microphone into his face.

"Isn't it a fact, General, that you're here to defend the high cost of weapons of war, and your own son was killed by a bomb?"

He ignored feet, shoulders, microphones pressing against him; kept climbing. "I'm not here to defend the high cost of anything."

The crowd poured upstream alongside of him. "Some clergymen," a woman shouted, "say there's a moral connection between the deaths of our children and the manufacture of sophisticated weapons systems. Have you any comment?"

"I see a moral connection between the deaths of our children and the failure to maintain a credible defense."

"Isn't that a pretty old line, General?"

He studied her: mid-forties, breathing hard. "It's at least as old as you or me, ma'am, and it's one of the reasons we've lived to such a ripe and wise antiquity. Now if you'll excuse me." He pushed through into the Senate lobby, where the climate was air-conditioned, and cameras and hand-held mikes were not allowed. A guard made room for him on an elevator reserved for senators, and he reached the committee room just as the chairman was convening the afternoon session. The committee was running late, as committees always did, and Tate had to listen to members take jabs at a witness who had carried over from that morning.

"Now, Doctor, isn't there some kind of a contradiction here?"

Tate saw that the congressman from Philadelphia was questioning a middle-echelon paper pusher, one of the thousands of civilian barnacles that had encrusted themselves to the Navy and once a year got a chance to strut their loyalty in public. "You want more subs and you want more MIRVs on the sub-launched missiles. You justify this on the grounds that submarines are undetectable, that land-based missiles are sitting ducks, and the faster we get this nation's deterrent underwater, the safer we'll be. On the other hand, you want nine and one half billion dollars to research and develop a laser-amplified thermo-emission seeker which will track submarines and make sitting ducks out of them too. Now make up your mind, Doctor: which do you want—invulnerable submarines or infalliable sub tracking?"

"The crucial consideration, Mr. Congressman, is that both these capabilities will be in our hands, not the Soviets'."

The committee table, covered in green napped cotton like a gambling board, had been extended with an extra leaf. Witnesses sat at a much smaller table facing the committee. Microphones dotted the two tables. Reporters, staff, and witnesses waiting to testify sat in folding chairs ranged two-deep against the walls. The hearing was technically open, but so far as Tate could judge there were no chairs for the public.

"Doctor, this country's broke and you want ten billion to counter a three-hundred-billion sub technology that *we* brought into existence. When the hell do we stop chasing our own tail?"

"I hardly think you could call the Soviets an appendage of the USA."

"For God's sake. I yield, Mr. Chairman."

Senator Sam Houston Lasting of Georgia, chairman of the Joint Economic Committee, lifted his chins from his starched shirt. He held stage center with a long, thoughtful frown, then asked if any of the other committee members had questions to put to the witness. Twelve of the ten congressmen and ten senators, including the chairman and vice-chairman, had switched to anti-defense positions since the last elections, and there were no further questions. Senator Lasting called General Tate Erlandsen.

Tate and the man from Navy passed in the makeshift aisle like two passengers changing places in a lifeboat. Tate sat at the witness table, identified himself, took the oath.

"Good afternoon, General." The Senator's drawl struck Tate as thicker than necessary or natural, on the order of distilled molasses. His white circumflex eyebrows were astonishingly limber and accented every syllable he or anyone else spoke. "As I understand it, the military requirements for the Hornet naval aircraft, and specifically for the full run of 802 aircraft, are based on the two-plus war contingency, plus a 1974 rapid-deployment strategy. Now I am far from certain,

General—ah—Erlandsen, that 802 such aircraft can be justified even if we accept the astonishing assumption that we must be prepared to engage in two and one half wars simultaneously." The Senator shifted documents, rattling them close to the microphone. "The most recent study of the Office of Systems Analysis concludes that the 674 follow-on craft cannot be justified on either military or economic grounds, even if the Department of Defense succeeds in its widely advertised attempt to impose this craft on our NATO allies. Now, General, setting aside this doctrine of two and a half wars, setting aside the findings of the Office of Systems Analysis, we still have what is in my opinion the most troublesome point of all, namely, the performance of your company's prototype craft."

The Senator took a long swallow of water and rattled more papers.

"As I understand the matter, General, on July twenty-third of last year, during a routine test of the Pacific Aero prototype Hornet at White Sands, Nevada, the jet system experienced an unstable oscillation. One of the jets, as I understand it, vertically separated from the plane itself. Now is that correct, General, and what explanation does your company have to offer for this astonishing malfunction?"

"I'm not aware," Tate said quietly, "that any such malfunction occurred."

"Not aware." Senator Lasting stuck his thumbs under his suspenders and leaned back in his chair. "Now are we to conclude that if manufacturers choose to be unaware of such damaging test results, the malfunction becomes—to use your military word—inoperative?"

"The explanation is simpler than that, Senator. The Pacific Aero prototype wasn't off the assembly line till September of last year. It wouldn't have been possible to test it on July twenty-third."

Murmurs swept the room like a rush of litter along a windy street. The furrows in Lasting's face snarled.

"General, is it not a fact that in a letter dated August nineteenth of last year, your company requested a contract relaxation to lower the top speed from fourteen hundred to thirteen hundred miles per hour?"

"Not that I'm aware of, sir. The top speed of the Hornet tests out at eighteen hundred miles per hour."

The Senator quickly dealt out fresh documents. "Now during a test flight last September—you were able to test this plane last Sepetmber?"

"No, sir."

The Senator's smile became poisonous. "Now surely you would know if one of your planes failed an airborne test and killed a pilot, surely you would know that."

"Not in September, Senator. The plane wasn't tested till October."

"Surely you would know," Senator Lasting shouted, "if at any time a Hornet broke up in midair and the test pilot was killed."

"To my knowledge that never happened, sir."

"Just how selective is your knowledge, General?" Senator Lasting reached beneath the table, produced an eight-inch stack of bloated manila folders, and dropped them within a deafening inch of the live mike. "I have here documented evidence that on September twelfth of last year—"

"Senator, the prototype wasn't delivered to the Navy till September twenty-ninth."

Silence hit the committee room. Tate hefted his briefcase, bloated with two reams of fresh typing paper, onto the witness table. It impacted with an amplified thump.

The Senator's face became red. "Now, General," he shouted, "let us not bog down in nit-picking. The issue is the competence of your company to handle sophisticated defense systems!"

Tate nodded in agreement. He reflected that there was something sad about men who stayed in the Senate after they were seventy, something sad about men over seventy who had double martinis for lunch, and something very sad about having to do what he was doing.

"If I may beg the committee's indulgence to go slightly afield," the Senator said, "Pacific Aero did contribute and is in the process of continuing to contribute a so-called terminal guidance system to the Air Force's Minuteman IV missile, is that not so?"

Tate stiffened. "Yes, sir."

"And at a simulated test of the missile's readiness to launch last Monday night, the terminal guidance manufactured by Pacific Aero broke down, and crippled the Minuteman missile, did it not?"

Another silence engulfed the room. Tate held to the arms of the chair and tried to keep his voice down to a natural pitch. "I'm afraid that kind of information is beyond my clearance."

"Was the shutdown not caused by a malfunction in the system which your company built at a cost of three billion dollars?"

"I have no idea," Tate gritted.

"Does Pacific Aero take responsibility or does it not take responsibility for the Minuteman IV terminal guidance system?"

"Yes, sir. We designed the terminal guidance, we subcontracted the components to over two hundred eighteen corporations in thirty one states, and we integrated the system."

"Now all this is most vague, General, and most disquieting. To whom does Pacific Aero suggest the people of the United States turn for redress if they have been defrauded of billions in the name of national defense? How can any corporation have the effrontery to foist such shoddy goods on any customer, rich or poor? How can you, General, presume to ask that this nation buy even a paper glider from your employers—let alone a seventeen-point-eight-million-dollar Hornet fighter craft?"

"To answer your questions in order, Senator." Tate snapped the briefcase open. Two clicks bounced off the ceiling. "If it were discovered that there had been fraud or negligence in the manufacture of the terminal guidance, if for instance one of the subcontractors had sold us a lower-grade zinc than we specified, and this zinc had caused aberrations in the mircromodular circuitry, we would then say that Georgia-McCann, for example, was at fault along with Pacific Aero." Tate had named, of all the Senator's backers, the single greatest corporate violator of the 1974 campaign-financing law. For an instant the Senator's expression blanked out. Tate continued smoothly, "This wouldn't diminish our responsibility for failing to detect the fault, but it would be grounds for a collateral action in a civil suit."

"Damn it, sir," the Senator exploded. "You prattle of civil suits as though this were a game of writs and torts. We're talking of the security of the nation, sir! I am weary! This committee is weary! The people of this nation have poured their lifeblood and treasure into the all-devouring mouth of that chimera you call national defense, and they too are weary!"

Tate glanced at a guard, stocky in his short-sleeved blue

shirt, leaning in undisguised boredom against the double oak doors.

"Weary of rifles for infantrymen and cannon for tanks which do not work!" the Senator shouted. "Weary of lavishing funds from our exchequer on planes which do not fly and helicopters which do not function and battleships which sink in harbor! The United States of America is weary unto death of being left naked to her enemies with nothing for defense but broken promises!"

Tate noticed a thickset man in a seersucker jacket sitting with the reporters. As Tate's eyes met his, the man looked quickly down at his note pad and scribbled something. He had a pencil-line mustache and the beginnings of a double chin.

"You may tell your Pentagon masters, General—" The Senator waved a thumb in the air. "You may tell them the United States Congress writes blank checks for no man, for no corporation, no vested interest!" He scowled the length of the committee table. "Furthermore, General, this committee would be most interested to know if you've heard of any efforts by any parties to fund the Hornet without congressional approval."

"I don't follow you, Senator."

"Do you know of any negotiations, past or present or contemplated, to sell any portion of the first run to any foreign government?"

Tate knew the Senator was dying to mention Iran by name. The press had been screaming for months about the U.S.-financed arms buildup in the Persian Gulf area. Any allegation involving Iran meant headlines. The Senator wanted headlines. But he was afraid Tate would give him tit for tat, and he didn't want the name Georgia-McCann brought up again.

"I've seen nothing that would document such negotiations," Tate said. Company lawyers had seen to it that he had seen nothing, just as State Department lawyers saw to it that the Secretary of State received controversial briefings orally rather than on paper.

Senator Lasting glared at Tate. A shadow of cunning flitted across his frown. "We have a great deal of testimony to get through. I see no purpose served in questioning this witness any further at this point. With the committee's permission, I suggest that we excuse General Erlandsen for now and ask him to continue his testimony . . ." The Senator leaned to exchange whispers with an aide. "Next Monday at 2 P.M. At that time we can pursue more closely several of the topics he has raised. Will that be agreeable to you, General?"

"As you wish, Senator," Tate sighed.

"If there are no objections or further questions, this witness is excused."

Tate locked his briefcase and surrendered the chair to the next witness. He left the committee room and went to the water fountain and bent down to take a long swallow.

A treble chatter of secretaries approached and a group of young girls flowed past, leaving airborne hints of laughter and perfume.

Tate went down the stairs slowly. He negotiated the congestion at the main-floor elevators and stepped gratefully into the open. The sun blinded him. He paused a moment on the Senate steps, giving his eyes time to adjust. Giving the man in the seersucker time to catch up.

Tate decided they both could use some exercise. He strolled down from Capitol Hill to the Mall. It was the sort of sunny hot day that inspires Americans to jettison principle: there were no pickets, and a lot of tourists were letting a lot of skin show. Only the ducks in the reflecting pool, quacking an argument, seemed up to taking any kind of stand.

From time to time Tate glimpsed flashes of seersucker pacing him in the shadows of the trees.

Three dozen screaming schoolchildren were playing tag in the Doric colonnade of the Lincoln Memorial. Tate pried his way through them and took up position behind the statue of the gigantic Emancipator. He wound his watch and let his eye drift to where they had chipped Lincoln's Second Inaugural Address into the wall. Halfway down the first column of text the stone carver had made a typo, *EUTURE* for *FUTURE*. They had plugged the lower bar of the *E* to make it an *F*, but the plug didn't match the white Colorado marble and it looked like a typical governmental fumble.

It was ten minutes before the man in the seersucker jacket stepped into Tate's sight line. He had joined a group of tourists and he was pretending to study the mural depicting Charity, Fraternity, and the Unity of the northern and southern states. Tate walked up to him and tapped his shoulder.

The man turned. His pencil-line mustache was beaded with sweat and his hazel eyes were void of reaction.

"You can tell them it's no use," Tate said.

"I beg your pardon?" The man was built like a football tackle, but his voice was high and apologetic.

A low-flying jet roared an astonishing crescendo overhead, and for a moment Tate was shouting. "I've put copies in a safe-deposit box. If anything happens to me, this town will be drenched in Xeroxes."

The man looked genuinely baffled and a woman in a bright print dress glanced at them curiously. "You're making some kind of mistake," the man said.

"Just be sure you don't." Tate smiled. "Nice talking with you." He turned and went back down the steps.

"The Senator managed to speak to the secretary in charge of R and D," the voice on the phone said. "The source selection board will try to see to it that things are worked out fairly."

"That's very kind of the Senator." Tate swiveled as far as the cord allowed and stared out the window. Pacific Aero maintained its Washington staff of twenty-two in headquarters across the street from the FBI, a twelve-minute stroll from the Senate, and a ten-minute drive from the Pentagon. It was a good location: central, yet suitably modest for a company that was courting government favors.

"We're still getting a lot of Mickey Mousing from the General Accounting Office. They seem to be waging a campaign to persuade the Senator we won't need a ninety-eight-million-dollar strategic bomber in eight years or eighty years."

Tate picked up a carved walrus tusk from the shelf and weighed it in his hand. Barbara had begun the job of decorating his office. She had gotten as far as cocoa walls and Eskimo figurines. "You might remind the Senator," he suggested, "that missiles aren't credible against China. If you shot your SALT limit at the People's Republic, you wouldn't have anything left to use against the U.S.S.R."

"He's giving that argument some thought. A little fresh documentation from your end might speed things up."

"Okay, we'll have it to you by the end of the week."

Tate reflected that the Senator was getting greedy: two demands for bribes in less than three months. He broke the connection and dialed Miss Monroe. Before the phone could react, Miss Monroe's skeletal face materialized in the doorway.

"There's something wrong with the phone, General. There are clicks and I've been cut off twice. Half the time I can't get dial tones. I really feel a complaint has to be made." What could you say about a secretary who gave you five Xeroxes when you asked for four, two safe-deposit boxes when all you really needed was one? She was a thorough woman, Miss Monroe, thorough to excess, with an astonishing capacity for storing telephone numbers, correspondence, grudges, and confidential memoranda under her great-grandmother hairdo. The hair was parted, like pews in a Presbyterian church, down the middle, and capped like a pressure cooker by a small, tightly screwed-on bun. She was partial to skinny belted dresses that matched her hair, a sort of sky gray that you find only when you've traveled three thousand miles for a vacation.

"Any luck getting hold of General Armstrong?" Tate asked.

"His office says he's not expected this afternoon. I've tried his home and no one answers. About the phone, General: would you object if I drafted a very strongly worded letter—"

"Karl Marx was right. You capitalist moneygrubbers would sell anything." The top half of a man leaned into the office. Even on a hot Washington day, he had the lunacy to wear a three-piece tweed suit.

"Hi, Sam." Tate gestured Sam Liggon to come all the way in. "What's Marx right about this time?"

"You better watch out, Miss Monroe," Sam Liggon chided. "If you consort with this crypto-liberal you risk compromising the security of this nation." Miss Monroe gave a sniff and vanished.

Tate grinned. "Me, a crypto-lib? Would I work with money-mad warmongers like you, fattening myself on the profits of doom?"

"A hungry liberal would do anything." Sam Liggon headed up Pacific Aero's District of Columbia public relations team. A former newsman, he had happened to witness the fatal heart attack of an ex-movie queen in a Chicago hotel lobby and had won a Pulitzer Prize for on-the-spot reporting, at age twenty-four. That had been over thirty years ago.

"Shame on you fellows." Sam Liggon wagged a finger. "Trading the security of the American people for a few lousy billion. I have always said, aerospace contractors cannot be trusted to make anything that works, especially not doors. They should stick to rockets."

"What doors?" Tate asked.

"The door I refer to is the lid on a certain underground

silo at Ellsworth Air Force Base, South Dakota. According to an item which will appear tomorrow in Dudley Mayhew's nationally syndicated kvetch, the door doesn't open. As a result, the rocket she no getta out. As a result, the Russians have us by the balls, oi."

Dudley Mayhew was no joke: he had swung decisive blows in bringing down a vice-president, a vice-presidential nominee, the president of a midwestern telephone company, and a President of the United States. "Sam," Tate asked "where did you hear about this?"

"I happened to be having a late lunch at the Statler. Whom should I bump into on the way out but Fred Dunaway, Securities and Exchange Commission, on the way in. Plastered. They just unloaded three tons of thirty-day notes at 8 per cent to a Chicago bank. Dunaway invites me to join the celebration. I accept a ginger ale. Dunaway pats me on the shoulder like the good dog I am. 'If you thieves can't even build a door that opens,' he advises, 'why don't you get out of aerospace and go into deep-sea diving?' I enlighten the dear man that Pacific Aero is already up to its neck in deep-sea diving, and he says, 'Stay there.' He tells me a very hot news flash from the Dow news tape. It transpires that Dudley Mayhew is going to say in his column tomorrow that Senator Sam Houston Lasting said in his committee hearing today that the night before last the U. S. Air Force—Am I losing you?"

"The night before last what?"

"The Air Force tested the launch-readiness of a Minuteman IV in South Dakota. The silo door stuck and killed the launch. And that is the state of our deterrent. Dudley Mayhew says, who is Pacific Aero working for, the Pentagon or the Kremlin, or is it all the same nowadays?"

"When did it hit the tapes?"

"I heard it around—oh, two-thirty."

"Senator Lasting broke that story at the JEC hearing at three o'clock this afternoon."

"And you're wondering how Dudley Mayhew reported the hearing before the hearing happened?"

"That vicious bastard."

"Is it true?"

"He's giving it one hell of a twist."

"Adios, Hornet." Sam Liggon sauntered back toward the door. "I guess we'll all be looking for work next week, huh?"

Tate's phone buzzed. Miss Monroe's exasperated shout was

audible over a beeping busy signal. "General, you have a visitor."

"Ask him to wait."

"It's your maid."

"My maid?" Tate wondered what the hell his maid could want. "Send her in."

Martta Savolainen came into the office looking harried and uncomfortable. She had put on a raincoat and she must have been hot. "I'm very, very sorry to disturb you, General." She sounded unhappy but she also sounded comic with her *v*'s pronounced as *w*'s.

"Perfectly okay," Tate said. "What's up? House burned down?"

"I have to talk to you privately."

"I can take a hint," Sam Liggon said cheerfully. He waved and closed the door behind him.

Martta sighed and dropped into a chair. She was wearing her uniform beneath the raincoat, and Tate was relieved she was still dressed for work: it didn't seem likely she'd come downtown to give notice.

"Colonel Armstrong gave me ten dollars and told me to take a taxi." She opened her right fist. She had three crumpled dollar bills and forty cents in change and her fingernails had made dry crescents in the flesh. "He would like you to come right away and please bring the diagram, he says you know which one."

"Hold on. Colonel Armstrong is at *our* house and he sent you to get me?"

She nodded. "He says he can't use phones. He's been drinking, sir, I can smell it on his breath. He looks crazy and those crazy mothers are still picketing and I left a roast beef in the oven, and if anything has happened to it, I'll be crazy myself."

Jack O'Brien swallowed a ten-milligram capsule of Valium and chased it with a Dixie cup of water from the faucet marked *drinkable*. He crumpled the paper cup and dropped it into the toilet. He waited till the blue chemical carried it down the drain before sliding the bolt on the washroom door.

Miss Dempsey stood two feet away, in the galley, ladling cylindrical cubes from the ice machine into a styrofoam bucket. As she bent, the window of the emergency exit momentarily framed her head. A shoreline of cumulus haloed her. She had set up Cokes for the pilot and copilot. O'Brien reached out and tapped her shoulder. "Could you check and see if the pilot or copilot has got the electric razor?"

"It isn't in the cabinet?"

"There's not even a razor blade in the cabinet."

She hurried with the Cokes to the front of the cabin. O'Brien watched her lean into the cockpit, one hand braced on the doorframe. Her left foot lifted from the beige carpet, and the skirt rode up the back of her thigh.

The flight had been smooth. O'Brien supposed they were somewhere over Minnesota now.

Miss Dempsey turned and came back. She paused at the halfway point of the cabin, where Bart Masters' long, expensively booted legs sprawled into visibility. Masters drawled something and when Miss Dempsey reached the washroom she was holding the empty martini pitcher. O'Brien wondered at Masters' ability to absorb rounds.

"They haven't got the razor," she said.

O'Brien felt the stubble under his chin and along the jawline: invisible to the eye, but not to the finger. For some reason his beard grew faster when he worried. By the time he reached New York he'd look like a gorilla.

He knew the tranquilizer had gotten a grip because he wasn't angry about the razor, just hurt, as though Execujet had personally betrayed him. Stepping back into the cabin, with its seven beige-upholstered chairs laid out like a very intimate boardroom, he tried to remember exactly how many Valiums he had taken: one in the office, one a moment ago. Had he taken a second in the office, without thinking?

The plane's droning vibration gave him the feeling his head was wrapped in cotton. He forced his mouth into an approximation of a smile. "Say, Bart, where does a man spend the night in Kermit?" He sat down, and Masters looked quietly amazed.

"Kermit? Kermit, *Texas?*"

O'Brien had to be careful: the SEC would have his ass if he got caught lying. He had to do it all by implication; let Masters' eagerness do the lying for him. "You fellows have a branch office there, don't you?"

"Sure, we have a little branch in Kermit."

Miss Dempsey set two glasses on the table between them. The placement left no ambiguity as to which glass was whose. They were plastic, but she had put them in the freezer, and moisture had condensed in an inviting simulation of a chilled martini. Masters' drink was the real thing.

O'Brien's was water with a twist. He couldn't risk getting high, not with all the Valium he was taking.

Masters lifted his drink in a semi-toasting gesture and O'Brien reciprocated and sipped.

"Real estate's a hell of a lot lower in Kermit than in Fort Worth," O'Brien said. "So are the taxes. You'd pay five million two just setting up a three-thousand-man assembly in Fort Worth. And Kermit's nearer your New Mexico missile range. I can't imagine why no one's ever built there."

Four martinis and sunlight streaming in at twenty-five thousand feet lit Bart Masters' smile like a billboard. "When are you going down, Jack?"

"I have to wind up something in New York first." O'Brien leaned slightly nearer the Texan. "Bart, my board would murder me if word got out, but I'm seeing Harry Pratt of Mannie Hannie tonight." Eastern financial columnists promulgated a lot of supposedly inside slang, like *Mannie Hannie* for *Manufacturers Hanover Trust*. O'Brien had never heard a real insider say anything but MHT, but he resorted to the slang when he needed to make an outsider feel he was on the receiving end of a confidence. "We're setting up something short-term—thirty days."

Bart Masters nodded.

"I wouldn't mind swinging a little of it southwest," O'Brien said, lower. "If the rate was right."

"Excuse me, Mr. O'Brien."

The plane banked, and Miss Dempsey tipped into a blast of sunlight. O'Brien stretched a buttressing hand and caught her just above the waist. She felt slender to the touch, and her dress was a very pretty violet.

"A message came over the radio for you."

O'Brien wished she would smile, wished she would just hand the piece of paper to him like any piece of good news instead of standing there radiating uncertainty. He reached a hand and took the message. Angling it from Bart Masters' view, he scanned the copilot's neat block printing. ACCORDING TO PM DOW NEWS TAPE, DUDLEY MAYHEW'S COLUMN TOMORROW ALLEGES FAILURE AT ELLSWORTH AIR FORCE BASE DUE TO PA NEGLIGENCE. NO FINAL YET ON NY TRADING BUT PA STOCK VERY ACTIVE TOWARD CLOSING. O'Brien crumpled the message casually into a trouser pocket. "Good old Dev," he said, and smiled as though at some private joke shared with his treasurer. His elbow knocked over his glass.

Bert Masters began daubing at the spill with his napkin.

Miss Dempsey reached for the glass, but Masters stayed her hand. "I get the feeling your Miss Dempsey's been rationing us. How about bringing the whole pitcher, Miss D.?"

Miss Dempsey glanced at O'Brien, and O'Brien couldn't be sure whether or not Masters caught the glance. His eye signaled *yes* because there was no way of saying no to Masters at this point.

"I'll have to check with Dallas," Masters said, "but we could probably come in for—oh—half a million. Whatever rate Mannie Hannie offers, we'll go for—oh—a quarter less."

"A quarter?" O'Brien said as neutrally as possible.

"Hell, we're Texans. We'll undersell them three eighths."

Miss Dempsey brought the pitcher, and Masters drained his glass to make room for the fresh stuff. Miss Dempsey poured O'Brien's martini halfway to the top, and he wished she had poured it full because it was less conspicuous to nurse a full than to start with a half-empty. He was glad that she poured Masters' half-full too, so at least it didn't look like a conspiracy.

"I wish we would come in for more, but . . ." Masters raised his glass in another toast, and there was no way for O'Brien not to follow. He tried to dilute the swallow with saliva, but when the alcohol hit his stomach it lifted his heart like a cam raising a power hammer and dropped it hard.

"I'll have to give that some thought, Bart." It was only a fraction of what he needed and it was only a maybe, but O'Brien felt a slack-kneed relief that he fought to keep from showing. "I'll give that some serious thought."

Lee Armstrong's eyes were restless, sad. "What about your sister-in-law's husband? Have he and his submarine turned up yet?"

"Haven't heard a thing," Tate said.

Lee got up from the chair, paced the length of the study, stared at the shut door that separated them from the rest of the world. "Can I borrow the Theta plans? I'd like to take them down to the Blue Ridge; go over them."

"What's there to go over?"

"I'd rather not say just now."

Tate let a fist fall on the desk top. "Lee, would you spare me the mystery? Okay, so you think someone may have swiped Asher's idea and sold it to the Navy. You don't want lawsuits and you don't want congressional inquiries. I'm with you. But Asher's work notes aren't going to tell you if Firebird hatched out of Theta, because you need Asher to explain that scrawl, and Asher died this morning."

Lee's gaze, tracking motes somewhere in the middle of the room, shifted depth of focus and swung into Tate's.

"The original of Asher's work notes has been shredded." Tate held up fingers, itemizing. "His apartment was broken into within an hour of his death. All Theta notes were removed from his files. Possibly I'm the only person alive with a surviving copy. I'm being tailed. Now you can damned well tell me why."

Lee shook his head in instant denial. "I don't have anything in the way of hard fact."

"Yet you know my phone's tapped. You know I'm being followed."

"I'm not sure of that."

"Then why did you send my maid instead of phoning? Why are you afraid of the tail? Why do you give a damn if he catches you and me together?"

"Ease up, will you? I'm in this way over my head, buddy."

"Look here, Lee: you've dragged me into something and I have a right to know what the hell it is. And if you're not telling, you're not getting those work notes."

Lee's voice was small and tight. "All I have is a hunch."

"A hunch will do fine for starters."

"Someone in Navy R and D took Asher's idea and passed it off as his own. Then you came up with the original plans and it caused embarrassment."

"A Navy engineer is breaking into apartments and tailing me just to avoid embarrassment? Where does he get the time off from work? How does he manage to be at Asher's apartment and at the Pentagon parking lot at the same time?"

"At this point, it's not just one engineer and it goes beyond embarrassment." Lee dropped onto the sofa. He sat forward with his palms pressed together. "Millions of dollars have been diverted to a top-secret project. That happens all the time. Only this project may turn out to be a plagiarism and suddenly it's no secret."

"What do you mean, Lee? There's no top-secret project. They've been publishing Firebird in the R and D reports to the House for the last five years."

"Firebird isn't the secret." Lee crossed his arms over his chest, stared at Tate over a barricade of muscle and decorations. "The secret is Theta." His gaze was level, without humor or doubt.

"I'm listening," Tate said.

"Okay." Lee bounded to his feet. "Scenario. We make two assumptions." He placed himself in front of Tate, explanatory and almost eager. "One: Theta exists. Two: *we* have it—not the Russians. Now hold your horses: let's just kick the idea around, like RAND men."

"All right. Theta exists. We have it."

"What if someone pretty high up thinks he can cripple the Soviet deterrent with it?"

"No way. Theta couldn't do it. No weapon could do it."

"Why not?" Lee smiled as though Tate had unsuspectingly moved his king into check. "We've pinpointed all their land-based launchers. We know approximately where they've got their mobile launchers. They've only got sixty-one missile-launching subs, and they're noisy sons of bitches and we keep tabs on them twenty-four hours a day. Theta could hit any one of their launchers on land or sea and paralyze it."

"Maybe Theta could hit any one of their launchers. But how the hell can it hit all sixty-one subs and all one thousand silos—not to mention the launchers they've got on railway cars? You'd need more Theta satellites than in Asher's wildest dreams."

"No need for all that. You bluff them with an orchestrated demonstration. Let's call it the Warning Theta."

"You're slipping, Lee. Assuming the Russians would swallow a bluff, which is assuming a hell of a lot—"

"We bluffed them in Cuba in '62."

"Cuba wasn't their own soil. Assuming we stage a demonstration and convince them their deterrent is useless, what have they got to lose? They'll figure what the hell and launch everything at us from SS-11's to balalaikas. We haven't got a damned thing to hold them off with. We haven't got any option but to hit them back, and that's World War III. And that's why, strategically speaking, Theta is a dud."

Less raised a hand. "We don't panic the Russians. It's a civilized, understated showcasing. We throw a missile at a Russian ABM site, turn on Theta, and keep their ABM's grounded. We say, see what we've done to your ABM, we'll do the same to your whole deterrent. So put your hands in the air and come quietly to the SALT table and give us some real concessions."

"Which ABM site?" Tate asked. Russia, like the U.S., was allowed two. Unlike the U.S., it had not yet phased them out.

"If you're thinking along Hiroshima lines," Lee Armstrong said, "Moscow. Scare people, not machines."

Tate shook his head. He couldn't buy the notion. "People just don't think that way, Lee."

"You know damned well there are people who think that way," Lee Armstrong said, "and they're not all in nut houses. One or two of them are sitting over there in Arlington. Remember the warning-missile doctrine? The Secretary of Defense told Congress we needed super-accurate missiles. Why? So we could pick out military targets, show we meant business, not graze civilians. Sixty senators and four hundred congressmen asked what difference it made if that much holocaust landed two city blocks to the right or left, but the SecDef said he wanted it and he got it and the missiles got accuracy."

"Okay. He persuaded Congress. But he didn't persuade me. I don't swallow the warning-missile doctrine and I doubt the Secretary of Defense does and I doubt the Russians do. With Theta you're telling the enemy to lay down their deterrent. And that's crazy. No one wants a weak Russia. The Soviet threat is the one thing that keeps America from voting us all out of business."

"Then why did we built Theta?"

"Have we built it?"

"That is the question." Lee Armstrong thumped one hand into the other. "I've been speaking to one of the designers at Bolen-McKuen. He headed the team that designed Firebird. He'll be in Washington tomorrow. He's looking for a new position, been putting out feelers for a year or so. I told him you might be able to land him a spot at Pacific Aero."

Silence wooshed into the room.

"Why the hell did you tell him that?"

"Because if there's enough in it for him, he'll tell you what went into Firebird."

"That's a violation of security."

"Stop being a virgin. People in this town bat secrets around like ping-pong balls." The sunlit window threw a chessboard of light and dark across the carpet. Lee's feet marked out precise, nervous moves. "Firebird beams energy to a single station at a time. It has a narrow-focus antenna. Theta would cover a whole missile field at a swallow; it would use a broad focus. It might even have some kind of scanning mechanism or electron lens to diffuse the beam. We need to know two things: how efficient is the maser in Firebird—could it do a Theta job; and is there a broad-focus or scanning option?"

Tate shook his head and spread his hands out flat on the blotter. "Ask him yourself."

Lee wheeled, finger punctuating the air with jabs. "If I footsy with engineers, it gets noticed. For you people it's routine. Corky Corcoran's a top designer, and if anyone's watching it looks like Pacific Aero is greedy for Bolen-McKuen's talent. He'll be at the Hotel Washington, waiting for your call. Meet him tomorrow afternoon. Get him down on tape. I'll be at the 48 Club at five o'clock. It'll be crowded. When I see you come in, I'll go to the men's room. No one's going to tail us to the john. You can give me the tape there."

The madness of it did not anger Tate: all military men waded in murky waters, and anyone could stumble off the deep end. But the tone of voice, with its blithe presumption that he could be tossed orders like a buck private, was too much. He was on his feet pounding the desk top and shouting. "Now look here, Lee. I don't know what the hell's going on. But you don't know what the hell's going on either, and I'll tell you something. You need more than a weekend in the Blue Ridge, you need a month. You're talking a load of shit. You're looking like shit. If you advertise these theories of yours to Corky what's-his-face, to anyone, if word gets out what you're doing—and it will—you'll be invited to resign tomorrow."

There was a hurt, puzzled furrow between Lee's eyebrows. "You think that's the worst thing that could happen to me?"

"With military pensions what they are, yes I do."

"I'm a soldier, Tate. And once upon a time you were too."

Tate was not about to take that put-down twice in the same day. "Well, I'm in business now. And this Theta fantasy of yours hasn't got a damned thing to do with my job."

"What the hell do you think happened at Silo 29? And if that isn't part of your job, what is?"

"No one knows what happened there."

"It was a dry run. They were testing Theta."

"That is so stupid, Lee. Testing it on themselves? Stampeding Congress into an inquisition?"

"Okay." Lee shrugged his heavy shoulders. "I'm going crazy. No one broke into Asher's apartment or shredded his diagrams. No one's following you. And Leon Asher is still alive, gaily scattering his plans to the four winds."

Tate's mind raced in worst-possible-case projections. The age was paranoid, the nation gullible. If Lee were driven to blab publicly, to drag the press in, he would wreck what little career he had left, he'd have to yank his kids out of college, he might not even have the money to keep Thelma in booze. No matter how many doctors certified him bats, he would leave a legacy of uncertainty and distrust that would fuel the doubt-mongers and might cut into procurements for the next decade. The pragmatic course would be to humor him for twenty-four hours, get him packed off to the mountains, and pray that rest and solitude and open air restored his judgment.

If not . . .

"Okay," Tate said. "I'll talk to him. One condition. If it's a dead end, you drop it."

Lee thrust out a hand. "You've got yourself a deal, buddy."

O'Brien stared out the window. Black clouds sliced the sky like Frisbees in mourning. The plane was flying so low over Queens he could count socks on laundry lines. Then, abruptly, it was almost skimming the East River and he could see raindrops impacting on the water's shark-gray surface.

He looked for the finger of landfill that was the La Guardia runway. A stomach-twisting instant later than he expected, the white X's that marked the beginning of the landing strip shot past in a blur. The Lear jet touched down roughly. The asphalt tossed them back into the air. His stomach knotted again.

Wheels brushed runway a second time. Rubber squealed. The jets reversed and the safety belt dug into his stomach. The plane taxied toward the hangar.

Miss Dempsey disembarked first, buckling her portfolio. Bart Masters followed, adjusting his eighty dollar ten-gallon hat against the drizzle. O'Brien brought up the rear.

"Can we give you a lift to midtown, Bart?"

"No, thanks." Masters held out a tanned hand. "I'm heading the other way, out to Lloyd Harbor. Thanks for the ride. Very nice meeting you, Miss Dempsey." He touched a finger to his hat brim.

A young man from the New York office was waiting for O'Brien and Miss Dempsey. Holding a large umbrella with an annoying protectiveness over their heads, he steered them to a limousine. O'Brien had to stoop getting in.

"Did you have a good flight, sir?"

"Just fine," O'Brien grumbled.

As the limousine edged into the stop-and-start traffic on Grand Central Parkway, the young man opened a large loose-leaf binder on his lap. Glancing sideways, O'Brien could see it contained all of three sheets. The first was an almost blank page with the title *Agenda for Mr. O'Brien*.

"We've booked you into a suite in the Tuscany, sir. And we've put you in a room on the same floor, Miss—"

"Dempsey," the secretary said. She had taken the jump seat nearer O'Brien. He glanced at her, and for the hundredth time since leaving Seattle he saw smooth skin and soft brown hair and the uncaring clarity of young eyes. Her smile was cool and tolerant, and her light skirt reached barely halfway down her slender thighs. Miss Kelly had praised the girl's shorthand and said she possessed that mix of resourcefulness and ability to carry out orders that marks the good travel secretary.

"You'll be having drinks with Harry Pratt of Manufacturers Hanover Trust at seven o'clock in the Knickerbocker Club."

O'Brien grimaced. Harry Pratt was always saying the service was better at the Knickerbocker Club than at the Union Club, and the people were a little less stuffy, but the last time he'd had O'Brien to the Knickerbocker they'd had to compete with a Harvard *Lampoon* banquet in the next room. O'Brien wondered why the hell Harry Pratt couldn't just once invite him to the Union Club, where the people were snobs and the service stank and you didn't have to shout. "No time to go to the hotel, then," he observed.

The young man drew back a French cuff to look at a watch that told hour, minute, day of the week, and date of the month. "No, sir, not with this traffic." The nasality of the voice irritated O'Brien. "You'll be dining at 9 P.M. with Art Graves, the specialist in—"

"I know who Art Graves is, that's why I asked to see him."

The young man swallowed. "At 9 P.M. in the Oak Room, at the Plaza Hotel."

O'Brien shifted in his seat to look out at traffic-clogged ganglia of overpasses and underpasses, at billboards eroding in smog. His palms were damp and his heart was thumping in his ears, and he sensed that the pain in his stomach had settled in for a long stay.

He turned to see why the young man had stopped reading. "And tomorrow?" he asked.

"We're working on that, sir. We'll be in touch tomorrow morning at your hotel, first thing."

"Christ," O'Brien said, "I'm only going to be here a day, you know."

"We're aware of that, sir."

O'Brien shook his head and turned to gaze out the window at a tow truck that had smashed into the rear of a taxi. A row of flares marked off the accident zone, like candles at the foot of a statue.

The rain had stopped. O'Brien stood on the steaming pavement. A carillon in the zoo was chiming and little currents of air conditioning from the car stretched feelers toward him. "I don't know what time I'll get back to the hotel. Not till after dinner."

"I'll be there," Miss Dempsey said, and it made him feel better to think someone would be waiting for him. As she leaned forward to reach for the handle, her nylon-stockinged knee flashed in the limousine door. There was a cushioned slam, and her smile lingered in the shut window. She raised a hand and O'Brien waved back to her.

He felt alone, curiously adrift. He glanced at his watch and saw that he was twelve minutes late for his appointment. He hurried across the avenue, ignoring the red light like an accomplished New Yorker.

Harry Pratt's club was one of the row of millionaires' town houses along Fifth Avenue dating from the time when Sixtieth Street had been considered practically suburban. O'Brien told the porter that Mr. Pratt was expecting him, and the porter said he could go directly up to the reading room. Remembering that there was a washroom down a half flight, O'Brien said he would go up in a moment.

A hint of camphor persisted beneath the smell of lemon soap. An old Negro turned the hot and cold water faucets and achieved a comfortable mix and stood holding a cloth towel at the ready. O'Brien studied himself in the mirror. The beard growth was noticeable and it exaggerated the fatigue lines. He looked like an overworked executive. He asked the attendant if by any chance there was a razor and some shaving cream.

A toilet in one of the stalls flushed. O'Brien did not look at the man who took the washbasin next to his. When a voice said, "Hello, Jack," he glanced and recognized the young man as a member of Pacific Aero's board of directors. "Didn't know you were in town."

The attendant brought a razor and a canister of shaving foam, but he had the quickness to sense O'Brien's hesitation, and he placed them at the empty basin.

"Just in town overnight, catching a show." O'Brien smiled. It was curious that the first thing he remembered about the young man was his company, Southern Electronics: they had 4 per cent of the voting stock in PA and had insisted on having their own man on the board. He was always too tanned and he had a mustache like a silent-movie villain. O'Brien was surprised he could be a member of the same club as Harry Pratt. The last thing to come to him was the name, Allan Martino; he had trouble with that name, and he wished Allan Martino would go away and let him shave.

"Going upstairs?" Martino asked.

O'Brien said, "I have a date with Harry Pratt," just to make it clear he had no time to socialize.

"Harry's got a new sailboat," Martino said. "I went sailing with him last week out in the Sound."

"Harry's a good sailor, I hear."

"He won the Sewanhaka cup last year." Martino made no move to go, and O'Brien realized he was stuck with an escort. He reached into his trouser pocket, found he had no coins, and gave the attendant a dollar. He sensed Martino watching to see how much change he would take back.

"That's all right," O'Brien said, and the attendant pursued him into the hallway, beating his jacket with a little whisk broom.

They had a choice between the semicircular stairway and the small self-service elevator. It was a good twenty-foot climb from one floor to the next, and O'Brien would have preferred the elevator. But the young man had already taken the first three white marble steps. "Have you ever sailed with Harry?" Martino asked.

"No, I haven't," O'Brien admitted.

"You ought to sometime."

O'Brien felt woozy as they stepped into the reading room. A vein in his forehead was pounding from the climb and the heavy leather sofas seemed to float like buffalo fording a stream. Harry Pratt was sitting in a chair by a window, looking at his watch. It annoyed O'Brien that Martino crossed the room with him.

"He's all yours, Harry," Martino said, "safe and sound." There was a suggestion in the remark that Martino and O'Brien had been somewhere together, but O'Brien didn't know how to quash it without being rude.

"Thanks for the delivery." Harry Pratt's smile seemed perfectly cordial as he rose from the chair, but O'Brien sensed a quickness to the handshake.

"Enjoy your show, Jack," Martino said. "See you Friday."

Several old men were sitting with newspapers in chairs facing odd angles as though to ensure solitude. Younger men bent in huddles on sofas flanking the carved fireplace. The crystal chandelier, unlit, caught hints of coppery twilight through the windows. A few of the members nodded to Martino as he left.

"Allan's a nice guy," Harry Pratt said, and O'Brien couldn't tell if he meant it. "Good to see you, Jack. What brings you to Fun City?"

O'Brien could see by Harry Pratt's face that he'd been kept waiting a quarter hour and that was long enough. "I need two million for thirty days." The room murmured like a napping forest that would wake at the snap of a twig. "Putting up my three houses and my personal holdings, I figure I can secure 80 per cent of the loan. The rest will have to be on my good name."

"Why do you want the money?"

"Someone has bid for Frances Meredith's stock in the company. It looks like a take-over attempt." O'Brien paused to leave a gap for Harry Pratt to say something, but Harry Pratt had nothing to say. "I want to make a counterbid."

"How much does she control?" Harry Pratt asked.

"A hundred thousand shares of voting common. Her bonds and preferred and nonvoting are in trust for her kids."

"How much has she been offered?" Harry Pratt asked.

"Thirty-five a share. She has till next Tuesday."

"Do you know who's making the offer?"

"No idea. I thought you might have heard something."

An old man in a black waiter's jacket came with an empty pewter tray and asked if the gentlemen would care for a drink. Harry Pratt glanced at his highball, depleted to the ice, and said he might as well have another. "What about you, Jack?"

O'Brien did not need a drink on top of the martinis and Valiums and the climb up the stairs, but he knew he had a better chance of getting a loan if Harry Pratt got another highball.

"I'll have the same."

Harry Pratt gave him a look as though it were very strange to ask for the same when you didn't know what the same was, unless you were the kind of fool who didn't care what sort of whiskey got poured into your highball. "So you think with two million for thirty days you can head off an avalanche," Harry Pratt remarked.

"I can make a pretty good try."

"What's your plan?"

The evening sun, coming low through the western skyline and the trees of Central Park, shone directly in O'Brien's eyes. He could see very little of Harry Pratt except a silhouetted hand gesturing emptily and the bulk of a chair blotting out part of Fifth Avenue. "If you come in, I can put together enough to buy Frances Meredith's voting stock."

"And what do you do with the stock?"

"I'll farm it out to regional brokers." O'Brien had the impression that Harry Pratt was staring at the stubble on his chin.

"How do you know your raider won't just buy from the regional brokers?"

"I'll hold the shares six months. Then I'll sell slowly."

"And what if you can't afford to wait six months? What if your raider can?"

"He'd have to be pretty big."

Harry Pratt grunted. "What if the market drops? What if the stocks you put up as collateral go down?"

"I'll mortgage everything I've got." He wondered why the hell Harry Pratt was digging like that: Harry Pratt had never dug before.

"If I were you, Jack, I'd forget mortgaging and think about selling that house in Barbados and the place in Seal Harbor."

"I'll probably wind up doing just that."

Harry Pratt twisted in his seat and reached into his pocket to pull out a leather-bound agenda pad with perforated sheets. He shifted out of the glare and O'Brien could see his face better. Harry Pratt looked uneasy. He monkeyed with a gold automatic pencil and had a hard time getting the lead to work. "Give me a quick rundown. How's Hornet standing?"

"We'll have the contract within the month. First run, a hundred twenty-eight planes; seventeen point eight million per copy. Deliverable two years from contract."

Harry Pratt jotted. "You tooled up your lines a year and a half ago?"

"We had to. Only way we could get the job was to promise early delivery."

"You had a little trouble with the radar-guided fire control?"

In winged-back chairs so deep, there was no comfortable way to cross your legs. "We made a small investment on the basis of the original proposal. Then the Navy decided it would save money by going with another system."

"Lost your investment?"

"Not really. There are escalators and adjustments on the second run. We can negotiate the price up to make back the original loss."

Harry Pratt gave him a worried look. "Jack, are you gambling everything on this Hornet?"

"We play to win, Harry, but hell no, we're not gambling everything on it. We have the Army JH-IH helicopter—we've got the prototype and the first run, we're about to make money on that. Within a year and a half we should make thirty million profit on a seventy-five million investment."

"Heard you had some trouble with the propeller."

"The driveshaft of the rear prop had a bad connection; we're readjusting."

"How come you didn't adjust it in prototype?"

"It didn't show up till halfway through the first run."

"And I hear you've hit a snag in your corporate jets."

"The private market's down. A buyer's asked to delay payment on two jets."

"How much does that tie up?"

"Three million."

The waiter set down fresh highballs and Harry Pratt was occupied signing the chit.

"On the other hand," O'Brien said, "the Sea Condor helicopter is turning out to be a beaut."

"That's that little job for the Marines?" Harry Pratt asked.

"The run's three hundred forty. We'll be into profit with the thirtieth copy." Harry Pratt did not react, and O'Brien went on. "Fiber-glass bodies for sports cars are zipping along. We sold a thousand last year, probably sell twice that this year."

"What's your profit?"

"About 25 per cent."

Harry Pratt glanced at him impatiently. "In dollars, Jack."

"Oh, hundred—hundred ten."

"A hundred *dollars*." Harry Pratt wrote something on his pad.

"Right. And the B-92 is practically into profit. And we just sent out an order of about twenty modular kitchens."

"What's your profit on those?"

"We sell them for around a million each. We sold fifty last year, made five hundred thousand profit."

"Why's buying?"

"Piper, Cessna, Beech, Lear. The middling-to-big corporate jets."

"You said the corporate-jet market's down. Does that mean you've saturated?" Harry Pratt kept glancing around the club, like a man who thought he was being tailed. O'Brien wondered what was wrong with him.

"No sign of it yet."

"Jack, what about the rumor in Dudley Mayhew's column: you fellows did some kind of shoddy work on Minuteman?"

O'Brien speculated that he must be worth at least ten times whatever Harry Pratt was worth. A man who sat behind a desk adding up other people's assets couldn't be worth more than a quarter million. He wondered if Harry Pratt thought this inquisition was really necessary.

"I was in the air when that story hit the Dow tape. I came straight here from the airport. Haven't had a chance to read it."

"Apparently you built a door for the silo that sticks."

"Absolute nonsense." O'Brien sipped his highball and wondered if the bartender had forgotten to add water. He jiggled the glass to get the ice moving. The vein in his forehead gave a painful throb.

"Have you looked at the closing market figures?" Harry Pratt asked.

"Haven't had a chance."

"After that story came out, you dropped three and a half points." Harry Pratt reached into the other pocket for his wallet. He opened to a rear chamber and extracted eight inches of ticker tape and handed it to O'Brien. The tape was neatly scissored and folded. A generous black felt-tip circle enclosed the 15:49 PA quote.

"That was thoughtful of you, Harry."

"You're down to thirty."

O'Brien wondered if Harry Pratt was rounding him off low on purpose. "Thirty and an eighth."

"Maybe with a strong denial you'd be able to recover some of that."

"It'll be a very strong denial, I can promise you that, Harry." O'Brien took out his wallet and folded the tape as neatly as Harry Pratt had folded it and tucked it into a safe place. As he put his wallet back his elbow knocked his highball. He caught the glass before it spilled.

"In the last half hour of trading," Harry Pratt said, "your employees' pension fund sold two thirds of its PA stock. Not exactly a vote of confidence."

O'Brien tried not to show he was jolted. "Confidence doesn't have anything to do with it. They're just going for higher-risk, higher-return investment somewhere else."

"It still looks a little funny." Harry Pratt gave him an indecipherable look. Fear? "Our loan board usually meets on Monday. I suppose I can persuade them to convene tomorrow morning." Harry Pratt drained his second highball to the ice cubes. He dried his lips on a cocktail napkin embossed with the club's seal. He folded the napkin so that the daub did not show and tucked it under an ashtray. "I'll let you know as soon as I can."

"Thanks, Harry."

"If you had that Navy contract in hand, we could give you the money in six hours." The folds of Harry Pratt's face seemed to rest bodily on his button-down shirt collar. "But you don't have it, and you went ahead and gambled anyway. And you'll be bankrupt if it doesn't go through."

"You take risks in my business. That's how I built the company."

"We all take risks. But time after time you've done the same damned thing and rushed into production before you had a firm, legally binding go-ahead. Jack, there are times when you just can't take that kind of chance. Times when none of us can." Harry Pratt looked sad. "How's your drink?"

With its remote-control locks, its steel fence between passenger and driver, the taxi was a jail cell on wheels. O'Brien told the driver to let him off on the corner of Park and Thirty-ninth. He passed three dollars through the hole beneath the security mesh. Too tired to wait, he let the man keep an eighty-cent tip.

Dinner had been a waste. The Oak Room had been mobbed and noisy. Kittredge-Lowe's specialist in aerospace stocks had been polite, but when O'Brien had asked point-blank he'd said he knew nothing about any take-over. O'Brien was convinced the man had been holding back.

He was grateful that the half block to the hotel was downhill. His stomach felt hollow, his bladder oppressively full. Rain was falling again, draining the colors from the traffic signals. It was too short a distance to bother opening his umbrella.

The desk clerk said his bags were in his room. He followed a bellboy into the elevator and during the slow ride up resisted a yearning to lean his head against the wood.

The suite was at the end of a cool corridor that smelled faintly of lavender. The bellboy began demonstrating lights, television, air conditioning, but O'Brien cut the young man short with a dollar tip. He went into the bedroom and kicked off his shoes. There were four vases of fresh-cut yellow roses and two fifths of Jack Daniel's on the dresser and there was another fifth of Jack Daniel's with a pitcher of ice on the bedside table. He did not see his bags.

"I unpacked you." Miss Dempsey stood in the half-light of the doorway, her legs slightly apart, her skirt an inverted V of translucence.

"Who sent all the roses?" he asked.

"One dozen from the hotel. Three dozen from the Iranian consul."

O'Brien wondered if Iran was keeping twenty-four-hour track of him till the Shah got his Hornets. "I suppose I can thank Iran for some of the Jack Daniel's?"

"All of it. The hotel sent Cutty Sark. It's in the other room."

O'Brien took off his jacket. The shoulders were damp.

"I'll hang this in the bathroom." Miss Dempsey took the jacket and vanished.

He massaged his toes a moment and walked in stocking feet into the sitting room. A room-service table stood beside the color television, laden with cold lobster salad, fresh fruit, a bottle of chablis atilt in an ice bucket. Suddenly he was hungry. He dolloped huge spoonfuls of salad onto a plate and went to the sofa and began forking lobster into his mouth.

Miss Dempsey set a glass of wine on the coffee table in front of him. The skin of her breasts was slightly flushed just above the line of her blouse.

"Mr. Barker's been phoning," she said. "He called four times."

"Dev Barker? Did he say what about?"

"He only said it was urgent, and would you try to get back to him tonight. If not, you're to wake him up tomorrow morning."

It sounded like bad news if Dev wouldn't leave a message. "Could you get him on the phone, please?"

O'Brien could no longer ignore the need to urinate. He wiped his mouth on the cloth napkin, crossed to the bathroom, and closed the door behind him. Standing at the toilet he could see himself in the full-length mirror. He disliked the little bulge of colorless flesh when he loosened his belt; disliked the look on his face when he disliked the bulge. If he had seen the face on a poster, with its scalpel-etched worry lines, he would have thought it that of a hunted criminal.

He emptied his bladder, flushed. He shook his penis, resented its perseverance at holding on to the last drops of urine. An old man's penis, he reflected bitterly. A young man might envy its size, for with age it had become enlarged and dangling, but there was nothing else to envy about it, nothing at all.

He washed his hands at the black marble sink with gilt faucets; dried them on a thick cloth towel bearing the hotel's initials. He glanced in the medicine cabinet; used the mouthwash; sniffed the cologne, liked the smell of sandalwood, decided he was too old for it.

Miss Dempsey was sitting with the telephone cradled in her lap. "No one's answering."

He tried to remember whether Dev Barker had a sleep-in servant or not. "It'll just have to keep."

She smiled strangely. He could smell her: she had showered and sprinkled herself with baby powder.

"You might want to call your wife," she said. "She was planning a surprise party for your birthday tonight."

"Jesus, I completely forgot."

She handed him the phone. He lifted the receiver and hesitated.

"Area code 206," she said.

"Stupid of me. I never call home. Miss Kelly always dials for me."

She dialed for him. He was surprised that she knew the number. After a moment she handed him the phone. Inger, the Swedish maid, was saying hello, and he asked for his wife. There was a long silence, and he watched Miss

Dempsey walk slowly into the bathroom. He heard Debbie's voice.

"Happy birthday, Jack. We miss you."

"I feel like a dope. I completely forgot."

"You've got enough on your mind, you probably wouldn't have enjoyed a surprise party anyway. How is it going there?"

He heard rain pelting the windows. "Oh, so-so. How's it going there?"

"In about fifteen minutes we'll be sitting down to dinner. But confidentially, it's not much fun being a hostess without you."

"Say, you didn't by any chance invite Dev Barker?"

"No, just the Watsons and the Westervelts. Do you want to say hi?"

"I'm kind of tired."

Miss Dempsey came out of the bathroom. She was naked. "Give them my love," he said in a voice that was suddenly strangled.

"Are you all right, Jack?"

"Sure."

The breasts were small and firm. The brown nipples seemed to become larger as Miss Dempsey approached him.

"Miss Kelly promised you'd be back tomorrow, and I'm going to hold her to that."

His eyes dropped to the flat stomach, the full thighs, the strangely tiny feet.

"I'll save you a bottle of champagne and a piece of birthday cake."

Miss Dempsey slid gracefully to a sidesaddle position on the carpet before him, her legs pointing out to one side.

"It's homemade orange. Your favorite. And guess who baked it."

Unhurriedly, Miss Dempsey's hand explored the inside of his leg, brushed against his fly.

"Good night, darling," he said.

"I love you, Jack."

Surprised to feel his penis stir in response to the gentle pressure, he lowered the receiver back into its cradle. Miss Dempsey's hand nursed the swelling. She eased down the zipper of his trousers. Her fingernails tickled along the exposed surface of his underpants, which had suddenly become as alert as his own skin.

Her tongue nibbled along the shorts. Damp capillaries of

cotton pressed warmly against the part of him that he had long thought dead and useless. Drawing back the white flap, her fingers entered and stroked. With her free hand she unbuckled his trousers, tugged them down to his knees, drew down the shorts. Her hand enclosed his testicles, and he felt his penis struggle to awaken.

He could not believe the moist touch of her lips and the moister contact of her tongue circling the head of his penis and moistest and least believable of all, her mouth enclosing him. Debbie had never, but never . . . He stopped trying to believe and simply abandoned himself to hope and infinite sadness and, silently as a brave child, began to cry.

He closed his thighs around her head, cautiously, as though some crystal thing might shatter, and pressed himself timidly against her face. He heard a sound try to escape her and drew back, wondering if he had hurt her. But she gripped his buttocks and pulled him more tightly toward her.

He felt a glow in his stomach. He closed his eyes and tried to will it to spread.

This is not happening, he told himself. *There is no reason for this to happen. Debbie, forgive me.*

His hand reached for her and found hair soft and scented and light as spun candy. He tried to concentrate on here, now, this, tried to keep the glow from going out. He gritted and prayed and felt tears on his cheeks.

Her hands reached and grappled blindly with his necktie, his shirt buttons. He threw off his clothes. She brought him down and arched him back against the carpet. Trailing kisses along his navel, his stomach, his nipples, she crawled up beside him and touched her tongue to the tears and he thought of a mother cat grooming its young.

And then she smiled without mockery. And as he smiled she drew him on top of her, and they rolled slowly across the floor, struck chairs and table legs and sent oranges cascading over the rug.

And something changed.

He felt no shame or apology. Her hand guided him, strong and thick, into her yielding softness. Then he moved, more easily than he had ever moved, and he felt her arching in answer and saw her eyes shut and heard her shallow, quick gasps and he could not believe any of it.

He held back, knowing there was no danger, he would not lose the moment, he could hold back forever and still be young and hard. He heard her begging him and he knew the moment was there. He moved inside her with a certainty and a joy he could not remember even having felt before. He heard her crying his name, and he knew he was giving more and better than he had ever given any woman.

At the next-to-last instant he stopped moving, and her fingernails dug into his shoulders. He felt the semen rush from his testicles, felt her vagina constrict and swallow it and shudder, keep shuddering till finally she shuddered to a stillness and lay relaxed and limp in his arms, as he lay in hers, at peace, nothing mattering but this moment that he had never thought to find.

He kissed her and thought of calling her "Susan," and she half smiled at him. And, gradually, he began to believe it had really happened.

Thursday

"The bad news is official. Kittredge-Lowe is backing out." It was ten o'clock New York time, 7 A.M. in Seattle, and Dev Barker spoke with the shivery voice of a man yanked out of a hot shower.

"What do you mean, backing out? You're not making sense, Dev." O'Brien gripped the receiver so tight that his nails cut into his palms. He frowned through the sealed hotel window down at East Thirty-eighth Street. "We have a commitment from them, goddamnit."

While the government delayed the initial Hornet payment, Pacific Aero had found itself pressed for cash. The company had arranged for Kittredge-Lowe to spearhead a ten-million-dollar commercial-paper offering. The rate was to have been a point over prime, the loan repayable in three years. The deal had been in the works two months and Kittredge-Lowe had assured O'Brien, orally at least, that everything was set. The paper had been due to be offered next week on Monday, opening business.

"I spoke to Harry Walters personally, Jack, and he's very sorry but market conditions—"

"I take it by market conditions he means the Mayhew rumor and those so-called labor troubles in this morning's New York *Times?*" O'Brien had picked up a copy of the *Times* in the hotel lobby. The photograph on page 3—*pickets at prime U.S. defense contractor's plant*—had been cropped in a way that suggested a far larger and angrier group than O'Brien remembered.

"He phoned yesterday afternoon, so how much it had to do with this morning's New York *Times* I couldn't say."

Hard nuggets of panic began studding O'Brien's gall bladder. PA had been counting on that money to help meet its payroll till the Hornet funds came through. He tried not to let Dev Barker hear how badly the news upset him. "Okay, I get the picture. Hang tight, Dev. I'll get back to you."

He hung up. When he turned and saw Miss Dempsey standing in the doorway he had the impression she had been observing him for some time. She was wearing a high-necked, long-sleeved dress that made him very aware of the skin it hid.

"You've got a lunch date at twelve-thirty with Reuben Arbenjian," she told him. "He's asked you to meet him at the 21 Club on West Fifty-second Street."

O'Brien supposed Arbenjian thought the 21 Club was impressive, and he supposed that was a good sign. "What else?"

She told him what else the New York office had been able to set up for him. "Barry Manners of the Stern Foundation is unavailable: he left this morning for Aspen, Colorado. He's speaking at a seminar on the interface of art and technology."

Barry Manners' bothering with art struck O'Brien as awfully strange.

"Kubrick and Kelly are willing to talk to you, but they have to clear it with their partners, who are unavailable till next week."

It smelled to O'Brien like a conflict of interest: in all likelihood, with their skill at fighting take-overs, they had jumped the fence and were helping the raider.

"Klein Finch and Mason Stanley have to check with partners, partners unreachable till next week. Aaron Winston of Freedom Trust can meet you next Monday at three-thirty."

O'Brien had the sense of seeing and hearing and feeling through a porcelain glaze. There had been no taste to his low-cholesterol breakfast of soft-boiled egg white and toast and he had a headache from drinking eight cups of black coffee. "Get hold of Melvin Culligan at Rebus International, will you?"

Miss Dempsey consulted the Manhattan directory and placed the call. O'Brien stared at the walls and noticed for the first time they were pink, not a very pleasant or soft pink. The receiver made a dead sound in his ear and at first he thought Miss Dempsey had made a mistake. "Mel?" he said.

The hesitation was almost audible. "Jack? Are you in New York?"

"You know how it is. The phone system's in such lousy shape it's easier to come East."

"What's up?"

O'Brien tried to remember if Mel Culligan had sounded so jittery on the phone in the days before Rebus International had taken him over. "I want to see you, Mel. Soon as possible."

"Gee, Jack. I'm not really free at all. Not today. It's a shame you didn't call yesterday. Where are you?"

"The Tuscany."

"Uptown. That's a shame. I have a lunch date at twelve, then I have an appointment at two-thirty. I could have squeezed in something around two, but if you're all the way uptown . . ."

"Two's fine," O'Brien said. "Where do we meet?"

"What's the rush, Jack? We'll both be in Seattle tomorrow. You don't want to knock yourself out getting downtown for a fifteen-minute cup of coffee."

"Sure I do. Name the place."

Melvin Culligan explained that he was having lunch at his club, the Downtown Association, and he couldn't invite Jack, but they could meet after lunch for coffee; it would have to be brief. He sounded very worried and very embarrassed.

"See you at two then, Mel. Looking forward to it." O'Brien hung up and caught Miss Dempsey staring at him with that thoughtful look on her face again. "Miss Dempsey—Susan," he said. "Would you have a minute to go over to Fifth Avenue and stop at Cartier's?"

"Sure," she said.

"I want you to get yourself something in the—oh, five-hundred-to-thousand-dollar range. I'd do it myself, but—"

"Mr. O'Brien, that's not necessary." She didn't sound offended but she sounded quite definite.

"Charge it to me."

"I'm really not all that keen on jewelry."

"I like you very much, Susan. Very much. I won't be able to see you again except at work and that will have to be strictly work. I'd feel an awful lot better if you'd let me give you something."

She didn't say anything for a moment and then she shrugged and said, "Okay. You don't need to, but thanks."

She looked at him as though she were wondering whether or not to kiss him, and he was disappointed but in a way relieved when she did not.

When she got out of the car Barbara Erlandsen noticed that a woman in a canary-yellow dress was standing across the street staring at her. She had seen another woman in canary yellow somewhere that morning and as she hurried into the building she wondered if the color was becoming a fad.

The doctor's receptionist wore hospital white, but of course doctors' receptionists had to.

The receptionist smiled and said, "Good afternoon, Mrs. Erlandsen," which was accurate and perhaps pointed, since Barbara had had trouble finding a spot large enough to park the Mercedes and was two minutes late for her noon appointment. "The doctor will see you right away, won't you have a seat?" Barbara obediently took a seat.

Dr. Rigby shared a suite with several other internists whose names took up half a door. There were always patients waiting, and today they were all women, silent and nervous, with perfectly even hems on their unwrinkled skirts, like mannequins in shopwindows. Barbara was glad she had decided to wear her salmon Chanel.

The twice-monthly visits to the doctor were boring, uncomplicated things. You sat in the waiting room and when called you sat in the examining room and sometimes you sat afterwards in the doctor's office and were given a prescription or a progress report. It was strange that even the question of whether or not you were going to live could become boring: you got used to it and besides it was hard to believe you could actually die. You needed patience for all the boredom and sitting. And of course you needed money too. Dr. Rigby was said to be one of the best. Barbara suspected all sorts of rich men and beautiful women paid his bills without even checking the addition.

Dr. Rigby's nurse came into the room and asked for Mrs. Williams. Barbara opened a magazine, shoring up her endurance. She needed endurance because she was approaching a dangerous moment and approaching it defenseless. A defeat at this point, she knew, would be a defeat forever. Today a word would be spoken or not spoken, a blow would fall or not fall, and she would stride from the doctor's office not caring if she had to wear rags, or limp from it, mown down in her salmon Chanel.

It was practically twelve-thirty when the nurse returned for Barbara and led her into the examining room and left her to undress. When the doctor came in he did not close the door all the way. Male doctors couldn't close the door all the way, not with female patients.

"You're looking good, Barbara." The doctor was looking not at her but at a clipboard jammed full of the last visit's blood-cell and albumin counts. "Sputum's good. Blood's good. Urine's good. Any trouble urinating?"

The examining table had a green foam-rubber mattress. A carpet of white paper, changed for each patient like a disposable napkin, unspooled from a roll at the foot and stretched up to the angled headrest. Barbara sat legs dangling, and felt like a sandwich waiting to be wrapped.

"No trouble." She managed to smile even though she was terribly nervous.

"Any change in frequency of urination?"

"No."

"Good girl." He was younger than she, but he called her *good girl* a great deal. He lifted her left hand out of her lap and wound a rubber tube around her arm and placed the cold medallion of a stethoscope beneath it. He inflated the tube with squeezes of a little rubber bulb and listened. She could feel her heart surging in the arteries of her arm, and was afraid he would find her heartbeat much too fast. "Any headaches?" he asked. "Nausea or vomiting?"

"No vomiting," she said.

"Your blood pressure is dandy." He dismantled the apparatus and set it with practiced care in a box that looked like the carrying case for a clarinet. "Wish I knew how you did it. Getting enough sleep?"

"More than enough."

He put a finger under her chin and nudged her head up and back till the examining light was blinding in her eyes. "Close your eyes a moment." His hand grazed her cheek. When she opened her eyes again she caught a naked instant of something that could have been concern. He tucked it under a smile and went on tapping and prodding as though everything were beautifully normal. When he had finished he said, "You can get dressed."

His hand was resting on the inside of her thigh. She glanced at his trousers just below the white jacket and saw that he had a slight erection. It made her angry that he probably didn't even know it. He could call her by her first name and touch her wherever he wanted and tell her she was to live or die, but she had no rights at all, not to name or body or life. She wanted to hurl something at him.

But she got up quietly from the examining table and walked to the steel coat rack where she had carefully hung her clothes on hangers. She began covering her nakedness, aware of the carpet beneath her bare feet, aware of the doctor still observing her. She had been so hopeful and certain that there would be one more test result on that clipboard of his, yet if there had been anything, wouldn't he have said so? She felt empty and barren and utterly without use.

"Oh, by the way," he said. "I want you to go to Walter Reed Medical; would next Friday suit you?"

"What for?"

He looked embarrassed. "I'm afraid we've killed a rabbit."

She sank onto the steel chair. For a moment she did not feel any way at all, not happy or sad, not relieved or frightened. "It's definite?"

"How many rabbits does it take to convince you? Lady, you've gotten yourself knocked up but good. Dr. Neil Fitzpatrick is a friend of mine and he'll be glad to take care of you next Friday."

"I'll have to think about it," she said.

The doctor frowned at her. He had chestnut hair and a mustache and eyes that were usually humorous. She had decided it was the time in her life for a younger doctor, one who would live on into her old age, if she ever had an old age, and see her comfortably into death. "What's there to think about?" he said.

"I'm not an old woman and I'm not dead yet, and I want to think about it."

"You don't want a baby, Barbara."

She rolled one of her stockings back up her leg.

"Your husband doesn't want you to take the risk. He couldn't."

She didn't answer, and the doctor's frown hardened.

"Barbara, haven't you told him *anything*?"

"He has enough to worry about."

"Are you afraid he'll find you less attractive? Is that it? My god, you wouldn't have the problem you've got now if you weren't a very attractive woman."

She was tempted to tell him he was a handsome man and obviously needed to sleep with his wife more. Instead she said, "Thanks for the reassurance, but I don't brood about my appearance."

"Then why haven't you told him?"

"Because he's a soldier and he comes from three generations of soldiers. Soldiers collect trophies and they don't collect invalids. Masters and Johnson might not call it the perfect marriage, but I happen to love him and I want to keep him. I've seen too many people who don't have anything or anyone and I'm not going to be one of them and he's not going to be one of them either. I want this child."

He stood listening as though she were a recording he had played and replayed, nodding as though he knew her by heart. "At your age, Barbara, the pelvis is rigid—"

"I've had one baby already."

"There's a one-out-of-fifty chance the child will have Dawson's syndrome. Mongolism. After the mother's thirty-five the odds are catastrophic. Late children have terrific emotional problems. And your husband may not even want a child."

"I've paid my money, Doctor, and I'll take those odds. Tell Dr. Neil Fitzpatrick he can play golf next Friday."

"This could kill you. I'm not exaggerating. Pregnancy is absolutely contraindicated."

"Doctor, how many times have you told me I'm no more under death sentence than anyone else who might get run over by a truck? Well, maybe a truck will get me before the pregnancy does."

He stood speechless, jaw dangling.

She buttoned her salmon-pink jacket and kissed him on the cheek. "A for effort, Doctor. And thank you." She felt elated leaving the office.

And then, getting back into the Mercedes, she saw that woman in canary yellow again, sitting in a green Ford across the street.

"Since you're a major stockholder now," O'Brien told Reuben Arbenjian, "you have a right to know that we understated corporate profits in the last report."

"Did you have any reason for doing that?" Seated, Arbenjian was the sort of man who should have had a phone book to bring him up to table level. His deep tan seemed subcutaneous in origin.

"We had to establish contingencies on several projects," O'Brien said. He had ordered the hamburger—*boeuf haché,* as the menu put it—because there were no lurking bones or gristle and he knew exactly how much time and work each forkful would require. He chewed and let Arbenjian wait just long enough to get interested in what he was leading up to. "It turned out we were a little too conservative. We haven't even had to touch the contingencies."

"Which projects were those?" Arbenjian asked.

"The Sea Condor is coming in way under projection. The fiberglass sports-car bodies are showing profits we never dreamt of—20 per cent above projection."

Arbenjian's eyes made no secret of trailing a young woman in a low-cut dress picking her way through the press of tables. The maître d'hôtel, who had called Arbenjian by name, had seated them in the downstairs part of the restaurant, apparently the prize location. It seemed to O'Brien that half the women he saw were call girls on some kind of happy drug and the others retired madames on their third face lift. "21" did not seem to be a society place any more. The men were almost as flashily dressed as the women and everyone was shouting. Waiters did not apologize when they bumped into you and it was a strange place for a business lunch. Arbenjian seemed proud of the restaurant, as though it were a club he had been elected to.

"The modular kitchens have been going like hotcakes. And Hornet doesn't show any sign of overrun. Knock wood." O'Brien rapped the tablecloth with his knuckles.

"How do you know you won't need contingencies on Hornet?" Arbenjian lifted his wineglass and took an audible sip. He had made a great fuss with the steward, discussing various wines in a loud voice, finally opting for a 1967 Montrachet wildly overpriced at twenty-eight dollars a bottle. To O'Brien's palate the wine tasted poor. "I hear you risked quite an investment without even having a contract. Some people are saying you might even be wiped out."

"I know what some people are saying. The fact is, the contract is virtually in hand."

Arbenjian gave him a look admiring the audacity if not the honesty of the claim. "Do your stockholders know that?"

"Technically, till we've got the actual scrap of paper, the only thing we can say is that we're hopeful. As a matter of fact, I'm sending the stockholders a letter telling them in the strongest terms the law permits just how hopeful I am."

"And what makes you so hopeful?"

"It's a good deal more than hope."

"Then why are you shifting your debt into preferred stock?"

"That's the first I've heard about any preferred-stock issue," O'Brien evaded, smiling.

"Come on, you're strapped for cash."

"Rumors."

"I hear your bookkeeping's a mess. I hear you're overstating inventories."

"Everyone overstates inventories."

"I hear, if Congress ever gets a look at some of the items you're charging to research and development . . ."

"What items?" O'Brien challenged pleasantly.

"Fifty thousand dollars to Steuben Glass for Sea Condor. What have you got, engraved crystal in that copter?"

"Probably some Christmas presents to a few generals."

"Okay, but research and development? You better clean up your accounting, Jack."

It was the first time Arbenjian had ever called him by his first name, and it stung. O'Brien realized he'd better get used to that kind of sting. "The SEC hasn't closed us down yet," he smiled.

Arbenjian's eyebrows came together. "Yeah, but I hear that missile-silo screw-up is hurting you with Congress."

"If there were any truth to that silo rumor, I doubt you'd see company executives exercising quite so many stock options. The insiders would be the first ones to abandon the ship."

"I hear a few insiders are taking the jump."

O'Brien held the smile steady. "Naturally the major stockholders have had offers. Every speculator in the country wants to cash in on a good thing. Frances Meredith says some fool offered her thirty-five and an eighth a share." O'Brien added the *eighth* as a goad.

Arbenjian's knife, which had been bulldozing rice onto his fork, slowed.

"Can you imagine, thirty-five and an eighth, when our profits are up 10 per cent next quarter and we'll be declaring the biggest dividend in twelve years?"

Arbenjian laid his fork down on his plate, a clump of filet mignon still wedged between the gravy-soaked tines.

"I suppose Frances does present an inviting target," O'Brien said. "Old woman, big family, no real business background; and she's used to having trust companies do all her thinking for her. She probably strikes a lot of people as gullible."

Arbenjian took a swallow of wine. O'Brien had the impression he swizzled the twenty-eight-dollar Montrachet like gargle.

"Her grandson plays the guitar, doesn't he?"

O'Brien could not for the life of him imagine why Arbenjian brought up that guitar-playing vagabond, but he sensed that the man was reaching for some kind of leverage. "I believe one of them does."

"A friend of mine heard him at a benefit for Argo House—the drug rehabilitation center." Arbenjian stared at O'Brien, not quite smiling. "Apparently Harvey Meredith is really into that scene—music, I mean."

O'Brien understood exactly what Arbenjian was telling him: Frances Meredith's grandson was on drugs. The information could easily be checked out, so chances were he wasn't lying. But why did he want O'Brien to know?

O'Brien took a long swallow of Montrachet, buying time to work through a rapid calculation.

Arbenjian was gambling on a take-over. He needed Frances Meredith to sell as badly as O'Brien needed her to hold. He wanted O'Brien to dig out the dirt and threaten to publicize it, anger Frances Meredith into selling and wind up in a jail cell. That had to be it.

Well, it was just possible that O'Brien would surprise him.

"I hear Harvey Meredith's very accomplished," O'Brien said. "Very accomplished."

"Baby, we are in trouble, and that's spelled H-o-r-n-e-t. Thanks to Silo 29, we're down to ten votes on that committee, and a tie defeats us." Tommy Talmadge, Pacific Aero's lobbyist, had parked one buttock on the edge of Tate's desk. He wore a maroon shirt that emphasized his year-round tan.

"Any way around it?" Tate asked.

"How would PA like to open a four-thousand-man plant in Utah?"

"Is that the only way we can scare up another vote?"

"Votes are not cheap this year. Now if the head office could offer some earnest of their intention to move some part of the operation to Utah—buy some land, say—"

"Why not direct subsidy to the senator from Utah?"

"Sarcasm," Tommy Talmadge said, "will get you nowhere."

The phone buzzed, and Miss Monroe said there was a Mr. Corcoran waiting. Tate asked her to send him in. "Tommy," Tate suggested, "could we talk about this in a half hour or so?"

"Delighted. Just give a knock. I'll be right down the hall, slashing my wrists."

As soon as Tommy Talmadge was out of sight, Tate opened the bottom left-hand drawer of the desk and pressed the start button on the portable tape recorder.

"General Erlandsen?" The little man in the doorway wore

glasses and a hundred-dollar suit that could have used a hundred fifty dollars' worth of alterations. He looked as nervous as a bank teller cheating on his wife.

"Won't you come in, Mr. Corcoran? Good to meet you." Tate rose and shook his hand. "Could I offer you some coffee? Or a drink?"

Corcoran hesitated. "If you're having something, I'd join you in a drink."

"Sure. What'll it be?"

"Scotch on the rocks would be just fine."

Tate opened the bar and banged ice loose from the little freezer. He made two scotches. Corcoran sipped and smiled and waited for Tate to lead the way to the chairs. They sat facing one another across a low coffee table strewn with company reports and *Aerospace Weeklys*.

"Good of you to come all the way down." Tate lifted his glass in an unspoken toast. "I know how busy you must be up in New Jersey."

"As Colonel Armstrong may have told you, I'm not all that busy."

"I don't know whether I should be sorry, or glad to hear it." Tate set down his glass. "Mr. Corcoran—"

"Call me Corky. Please."

"Corky. Pacific Aero has a problem. Colonel Armstrong thought you might be able to help us out."

Corky Corcoran's gaze crept to the window, to the facade of the FBI building, as though someone up there were compiling evidence of his treachery. "Absolutely, I mean, if I can."

"You designed Firebird, didn't you?" Design and engineering decisions, in satellites as in missilery, were made by computer, and Tate was aware of the flattering implication of the question.

"I was one of the team."

"We think Firebird infringes on one of our patents."

Corcoran's forehead squeezed, tugging at a cap of dark blond hair. "I'll tell you whatever you need to know."

The club's initials fluttered in Gothic monogram from a flagpole above the door. O'Brien stepped into the big, brightly lit lobby and his sense of Wall Street's mobs and even of the present dimmed. The door swung behind him and a porter asked if he could be helped.

O'Brien explained that Melvin Culligan was expecting him.

He watched the porter go with an age-lamed gait to the barroom and stop at one of the tables.

O'Brien stared at the fireplace, unused in summer, and at the cloakroom with its counter as long as a bar in the Ritz, where two uniformed attendants sat reading newspapers. The coat racks were seasonally empty, the hat racks laden with packages and briefcases.

"Hello, Jack, good to see you." Melvin Culligan, tall and gray and tanned, lobbed a greeting from ten feet, hand already outstretched. "Why don't we talk upstairs?" He gave O'Brien a gentle steer toward a stairway decorated with prints of old ships. Clusters of young men politely bypassed clusters of old men. In their black suits they gave an impression of murmuring monks.

Melvin Culligan was wearing a brown suit and it seemed rather daring in the context, like a sports car among Rolls-Royces. He asked about the weather in Seattle and O'Brien said it was just fine. They stopped at the second landing at a room of dark wood panels.

"Two nice chairs over there," Melvin Culligan observed. The chairs looked no nicer and certainly no more private than any of the other chairs and black leather sofas scattered in conversational groupings. They sat beside a carved stone fireplace and Melvin Culligan said, "You must have something pretty urgent on your mind if it couldn't wait twenty-four hours."

"It can't wait," O'Brien said.

"Okay. Shoot."

Leaded windows let in a translucent notion of weather and sun. One very old man with a *Wall Street Journal* huddled in a wing-backed chair as though it were an overcoat in a wind blast. The room did not strike O'Brien as a place for a private talk. There was no covering babble. "Pacific Aero's in trouble," he said quietly.

"What kind of trouble?"

"Take-over attempt."

A sweetness of pipe tobacco thickened the air, spiced with the less cloying pungency of cigar smoke. Melvin Culligan nodded. He seemed uneasy.

"The raider has picked up close to 10 per cent of the company in his own name and in street-name accounts," O'Brien said. "He's made a bid for Frances Meredith's 3 per cent. He's persuaded a go-go fund to pick up another 10 and hold it for him."

A servant in waiter's black went from chair to chair offering coffee from a pewter pitcher. Melvin Culligan asked for coffee for both of them. He sat with a sad expression waiting for O'Brien to go on.

"If Meredith sells to the raider," O'Brien said, "it will trigger a small landslide. If I can get Meredith's shares, we'll stave off the landslide. We can keep the stock high enough so that the go-go fund will hold on to what it's got. And we'll beat the raider."

"Is Meredith going to sell?" Melvin Culligan asked.

"She'll sell to me if I can raise three and a half million by next Tuesday."

"Can you?"

"We've got a line of credit for a million through the end of the year. I've asked MHT for two. If they come through, and I should know today, I can get the rest."

"Where do I come in, Jack?"

"If MHT falls through, I'll need two and a half million. I can secure 64 per cent."

Melvin Culligan made a thoughtful face. In the old days, when he'd run his own company, he'd run it well and he'd made his own decisions and he hadn't been afraid of risk. Six years ago he'd been absorbed by Rebus International, a multinational with heavy Middle Eastern backing, and O'Brien wasn't sure how many of his own decisions they let him make nowadays. Rebus was known to have holdings in American forestry, Japanese steel, Iranian shipping, Arabian oil, South African diamonds, Bolivian bauxite, and Australian beef. They even had a small Swiss-based airline that flew insane routes like Los Angeles–Taipei. In the available reports most of Rebus' funds were mysteriously though quite legally reported as "consolidated from operations." Though it was foolish to extrapolate from the tip of the iceberg, O'Brien supposed they were worth a hundred billion at least and he couldn't imagine Melvin Culligan had sold out to them cheap.

"Jack, as a friend, I wish I could say yes. But at the moment I haven't got that much personally, and the company . . ." Melvin Culligan looked apologetic and miserable. "Rebus got burned in '71. They lost over thirty million in the Penn Central commercial-paper deal. They're very, very shy of paper. Look, I'll be glad to ask. But you know what their answer will be. They want to give you ninety million now for the Hornet buy-in, and you're strapped for money. Why the hell don't you swallow a few scruples and shake hands on the deal?"

O'Brien wondered if Melvin Culligan had any idea how many times in the last twenty-four hours he had wished he could swallow a few scruples and shake hands on that ninety million. *If only I could,* he thought. But he heard himself say, "It's the wrong time to take that money, Mel."

"We can arrange it as a loan from three dozen banks." There was something hungry in Melvin Culligan's eyes, as though he and not O'Brien was the beggar. "We can funnel it through three hundred banks. Rebus' name won't show up on a single scrap of paper."

"Congress would shut us down overnight."

"How the hell will Congress know? You have to take chances in this life, Jack."

"Maybe I've taken a few too many."

"I'm surprised at you."

"I'm surprised at myself."

Melvin Culligan stirred a lump of sugar into his coffee, taking great pains to dissolve it. "When do you hear about MHT?"

"I expected to hear this morning."

Melvin Culligan seemed to be debating whether or not to say something that was very much on his mind. "Jack," he said finally, "they're not running a philanthropy out there." He nodded toward the window, in the direction of Wall Street. "If you're worth more to a raider than you are to your own stockholders, the raider's going to get you."

O'Brien realized that Melvin Culligan would be no help at all. He nodded.

"I've been through it myself," Melvin Culligan said without bitterness. "They stripped me of my own company. It's like having an arm cut off. But you survive."

O'Brien looked at his friend. "That's true," he said. "You see a lot of one-armed men."

"A hell of a lot more than you used to, that's true," Melvin Culligan slapped O'Brien's thigh. "Now let's talk about serious things. How's your golf game holding up—still shooting in the eighties?"

Despite the heat, Jack O'Brien closed the door of the phone booth before dialing the hotel. He asked to be connected to Miss Dempsey's room. "Hi, it's Jack O'Brien. Has Harry Pratt returned my call yet?"

"Not yet, sir."

"All right. I should be back in about an hour or so."

Through the wall of cracked, dirt-stained glass he watched a wave of pedestrians flush across Wall Street and Broad, sweeping traffic to a standstill. He searched the phone book and found that the page he wanted was one of the few that had not been ripped out. He deposited another dime and dialed. A woman with an overstuffed shopping bag stationed herself outside the booth door and crossed her arms.

"Argo House."

"May I speak with Harvey Meredith, please?"

"Who? Oh, you mean Harv. Sure."

Someone covered the mouthpiece on the other end, and O'Brien had the sensation of pressing his ear to a seashell. He heard a relay of muffled shouts and finally a soft-spoken "Hello?"

The voice astonished him with its gentleness.

"Hello?" it repeated.

"Do you know the West Side Argo House?" O'Brien asked.

The private investigator, a thick man in his late forties, made a grunt. A little below average height, he wore a wrinkled white shirt unbuttoned at the collar and rolled up to the elbows and a striped necktie yanked half loose. From time to time his hands made isometric gropings along the edge of the desk and cords in his forearms stood out.

"There's a young man connected with Argo by the name of Harvey Meredith. I want to know if his grandmother is Frances Meredith of Seattle. If so, I want everything you can find out about his involvement with drugs, any criminal record he may have, what his activities are at present, what sort of associates he's going with."

"Sex life?"

O'Brien swallowed. "Yes." He had found the agency in the classified directory. *Domenick Mandel, confidential investigations by professionals. Fast, precise, discreet.* He had chosen them for the *fast* and because they were two minutes' walk from the phone booth. "I've got to have this information by nine-thirty Monday morning, Seattle time."

"Let me get a few details on Harvey Meredith." Mandel prepared to make ball-point scribbles in a notebook.

"I've told you all I know."

The ball-point tapped the blotter.

"I knew him ten or eleven years ago, when he was a child."

"Do you have a photograph?"

"No. He used to have blond hair, that sort of childish blond that always turns brown when they get older. He came to New York three or four years ago to study music—against the wishes of most of his family." O'Brien shifted uneasily in the chair. The office furniture seemed a dispiriting parody of his own, with Naugahyde making do for leather, aluminum for chrome, and Formica for everything else. The bookbindings on the shelves were bluntly phony and he doubted that Mandel had chosen or ever looked at the two Picasso harlequins framed in plastic above the water cooler. "His grandmother had—still has—faith in him. I suppose she's been giving him money. She thinks he's involved in studies. I heard a rumor he's involved in drugs. Was involved. I'd like to find out more. His grandmother is a close friend of mine."

"What's Harvey Meredith's connection with Argo House?" Mandel's hair was a horseshoe of close-cropped gray, and his nose looked as though it had taken a dive in a heavyweight bout. His voice betrayed no expression and his eyes did not waste movement.

"He played guitar at a fund-raising gala there last week."

"Doesn't necessarily mean he was on drugs."

"I phoned Argo House a few minutes ago and asked for him. He's there."

"Speak to him?"

"No."

Air conditioning filled the room with whispers. Mandel lowered his eyelids, like shades half drawn. "The way we'll get information fastest out of Argo House is to pay for it. Drug court records are open. Police records are not open."

"I understand."

"It'll cost you three hundred a day. Plus bribes and expenses. You get two investigators. We get three days' advance."

"I can give you an out-of-town check."

"Charge card would be easier for us."

"American Express?"

"Fine."

O'Brien slid the card out of its compartment in his wallet. Mandel buzzed the intercom, and a woman with hair reverting to dark at the roots fluffed into the office to take care of the charge forms. O'Brien asked if he could use the phone.

Mandel stared out the window and made a polite show of not listening while he rang Susan Dempsey at the hotel.

"Mr. Pratt called two seconds after you hung up. If you call him right away, he should still be in his office." She gave him the number. He repeated it mentally, making sure he had it, and thanked her.

"May I make one more call?"

Mandel said, "Sure."

O'Brien asked the switchboard for Harry Pratt's extension and identified himself to the secretary. He heard Harry Pratt sigh.

"Jack, I tried my damnedest. The committee feel we're overextended in short-term and they're awfully leery of the commercial-paper market. The vote was eight to seven against. Look, if it's any help, I could personally lend you a quarter million."

It was a perfectly safe offer to make; as a creditor of the company Harry Pratt would get his money back no matter what. It sounded like a way of saying he felt sorry for O'Brien.

"That's good of you, Harry. Thanks anyway."

"Give a little more warning when you're in town next time, maybe we can swing dinner."

The woman returned O'Brien's credit card and a duplicate of the executed charge form. Her fingernails were bright orange, and an automated smile puffed her face.

Mandel was watching him. "There's a bottle of good bourbon in the safe."

The kindness hit like a slap of cold water in the face. O'Brien stared at the investigator and something in him groaned, *What in God's name do I think I'm doing here?* "Mr. Mandel," he said, "I'm afraid I've made a mistake. I don't want any investigation. Please keep the advance. I'm sorry to have wasted your time."

From five hundred yards it seemed strange to Elmer that anyone would erect cyclone fence around two acres of nothing. At three hundred yards he saw the little shed, and at two hundred he saw that the man sitting in the shade was armed. Coming closer he saw the air shafts poking up from the ground, barely taller than the sun-stunted scrub.

It wasn't till the guard let him and his lieutenant guide through and they were on top of it that Elmer saw that twelve-foot steel square almost flush with the dirt, the hairline barely visible where the seventy-six-ton door split in two. The steel was painted dingy to blend in with the dirt and grass and even through shoe leather it was hot to the foot.

The second door was man-sized, not missile-sized, and it weighed a modest half ton. It opened in response to a signal from the lieutenant's hip radio.

They reached the on-site control center of Silo 29 by taking an elevator 120 feet down into the South Dakota earth. They stepped out into a fifty-foot corridor linking the six-man living space with the six-man working space. Iron blast doors, eight feet by ten by three, sealed each iron-and-steel chamber. In the work center a third, heavier door sealed the thirty-foot tunnel that led to Minuteman IV.

Elmer did not ask questions until the lieutenant had completed what was obviously a prepared speech.

"Let me make sure I've got this straight." Elmer flipped a page of his notebook. "You say that the launch mechanism activates only if two keys are turned at the same time in the locks on the two control panels?"

The lieutenant was a big man, suntanned as though to compensate for the days lived underground. He gave Elmer an impatient look. "That's correct. At launch signal, Lieutenant Hamilton and I turned our keys simultaneously to test mode, counterclockwise from the vertical."

Elmer observed that the missile control panels were spaced just far enough apart that one man wouldn't be able to work both controls at once.

"And who," Elmer asked, "gave this signal?"

"The computer at Control Center 3. Signals to test-launch are always generated by the computer. An actual signal to launch would have to come from NORAD headquarters at Cheyenne Mountain."

"How does the computer generate these signals?"

"It generates them randomly to catch us off guard."

"But last Monday you weren't off guard."

"That was an exception. Dr. Provenson told us there'd be a test at 22:46."

"But you say Provenson didn't give the signal himself."

"No. His team reprogrammed the computer."

The reprogramming surprised Elmer. The revised program, being top secret, was not subject to verification by Pacific Aero's team, and it certainly was not subject to inspection by Elmer. His clearance went only to secret, and he knew nothing about computers. So Pacific Aero had only the Air

Force's word that the Air Force's own program was not at fault.

"Is your key the same as your buddy's," Elmer asked, "or different?"

"Different."

"And you both carry your keys on you at all times?"

"While we're on duty. When we go off duty, we give the keys to our replacements."

"At the signal, you say you both turned your keys counter-clockwise, test mode. Now what should have happened?"

"The computer should have verified that the missile was in ready-to-fire state."

So as to give the least fragmented picture possible of the missile, eighteen color television screens were arranged on the wall of the work center in a six-by-three pattern corresponding to the placement of cameras within the silo. A gleaming steel puzzle that disintegrated and reassembled itself as the cameras scanned, Minuteman IV could be seen resting in its ten-story, twelve-foot-diameter cocoon. Along with monitoring and communications systems, it was supported by six mammoth coil springs that could absorb the shock of an eight-megaton warhead impacting three quarters of a mile away. Though it weighed 70,000 pounds at launch and stretched almost sixty feet from fins to tapering nose, on TV it seemed barely a six-foot model, an unborn dolphin harassed by crews of midgets in overalls.

To the right of the screens, electronic panels reported on the status of 256 subsystems. The missile's guidance system, like the never-sleeping brain of a living thing, evaluated internal conditions and reported around the clock both to the on-site computer and to the remote-control center four miles away. It displayed its findings in fan-shaped dials, in half-inch squares of red, yellow, and green that blinked to indicate one state and shone to indicate another, tiny tiles in a mosaic that never tired of redesigning itself.

Elmer supposed that when the PA crew went home, the mosaic would be unblinking green. "How long does the verification take?" he asked.

"With the Pacific Aero terminal guidance kit, it ought to take thirty-one seconds."

Elmer watched a nervous lieutenant colonel trying to monitor all eighteen TV screens at once. "If the missile passes verification, then what?"

"On a launch, the missile takes an additional seventeen seconds to ignite, and then she goes. On a test, the computer tells you you're ready and closes the door again."

"Now exactly what did happen when you turned the keys?"

"We went into countdown. At nineteen seconds the computer signaled an unspecified malfunction in the terminal guidance and shut down pending rectification."

"And approximately four seconds later Dr. Provenson was dead?"

"That's what they tell me."

"So Provenson died up in Control Center 3 more or less the same time that something killed the launch down here."

"More or less."

"And where did the body go?"

"The body was flown out by helicopter and that's all I'm allowed to say."

She had chestnut hair and a violet dress, and she held herself in a manner that suggested, at thirty yards, a certain availability. If she wasn't following Tate, she still had been going his way—and that had included one loop around the block—a persistently long time.

Tate turned off C Street Northeast onto the concrete drive that separated the back of the New Senate Office Building from the Senate Annex. It was a high-crime area, heavily patrolled, and a member of the Capitol police force nodded as though in recognition of a fellow law-abider.

Summer weeds were beginning to encroach on the stone steps that led up to Schott's Court. Tate opened the iron gate and, turning to close it, could see the girl in violet just coming around the Annex. She had not lagged or gained a yard.

The day was muggy and Tate climbed slowly.

The little street at the top of the stairs looked like an alley that had barely been snatched from the jaws of slumhood. Recent renovation was evident in the brightly painted, slightly cutesy façades of the row houses. Tate stopped at the door of a brick building with fresh white trim. He looked over his shoulder. The girl in violet had reached street level. He went into the club.

The three ground-floor dining rooms smelled of corned beef and crab cakes. Late lunchers were overlapping with early drinkers, and conversations had reached the not-quite-shouting pitch of a good cocktail party. A hostess asked if Tate would like a table and he said no, thanks. He walked to the bar and stood in the doorway, eyes adjusting. At a table near him two men and a woman were drunkenly discussing a soy-bean acreage bill.

Tate did not see Lee Armstrong at the bar.

His first reaction was surprise. He checked his wristwatch to make sure he had got the time right. The time was right, and he was relieved, hopeful in fact that Lee had changed his mind. He decided he had earned a drink. The stools at the bar were taken, but there was room to stand. He ordered a Chivas Regal. The press of the crowd straitjacketed his elbows to his side and he stood awkwardly sipping. He raised his eyes to the smoked mirror behind the ranked battalions of bottles to survey the fellow drinkers. They were a loud, overweight fraternity, defying the heat of the day and the distress of the nation with their collegiately bright ties and shirts and jackets.

Two thirds of the membership were lobbyists representing the ten dozen richest corporations and interest groups in the nation. The other third were staff aides to federal regulatory agencies and congressional committees. The club admitted its descent from the old Quorum Club, which had been organized in 1961 by a Senate Democratic Majority secretary who had later wound up in jail. You came here to do in a relaxed, open way what you'd have had to do in paranoid secrecy anywhere else in post-Watergate Washington: to deal, to influence—in some cases, to write—the major legislation that passed through the houses of Congress each term.

At the far end of the bar, Tate saw Lee Armstrong half in shadow, huddled over a drink. He sat tensely, as though his slacks and sports jacket and open-necked tennis shirt made him itch. His eyes were waiting in the mirror for Tate's. They were pregnant with the sort of uneasiness that does not invite strangers. There was a suitcase wedged under his stool; he rose, adjusted it so it would not trip the unwary, and eased his way through the crowd.

Tate finished his scotch and ordered a refill before following. He had to stand sideways on the staircase to let a fat senator pass. The self-closing device on the men's room door was adjusted too heavily, and he had to shove.

A merciless camphor permeated the air. The john had been redecorated in cut-rate opulence, with formica wood and wallpaper patterned in imitation red velvet. The toilet stall was wide open and unoccupied. Lee Armstrong stood at one of the urinals, picking at his nails with clippers on a key chain. Tate went to the other and unzipped. "I'm afraid you're going to be disappointed."

Lee's face went dark like a sky with the sun yanked out. "Didn't you get the tape?"

"Forth-five minutes' worth. Poor Corcoran spilled his guts. He really wants that new job."

"What did he tell you?"

"Everything he knew. Firebird's an updated Agena rocket, highly maneuverable. Uses commercial GE photoelectric and energy cells."

"Exactly the same as Theta!" Lee blurted. "What about the maser?"

"Corcoran never saw the maser, but the refrigeration's taking away about 97 per cent of the energy input."

"Which means the maser's ten times as efficient as the old synthetic ruby. Efficient enough for Theta. So if the beam is broad-focus, and there's a scanning mechanism—it *is* Theta!"

Tate was silent a moment. "Corcoran doesn't know about the beam or the scanning mechanism."

"Doesn't *know*?" Lee challenged.

"It came in a sealed unit."

Lee nodded, grinning like a crazy prospector who'd stumbled on gold. "So it *could* be Theta!"

"And it could be King Kong." Tate reached into his pocket and produced the cassette. "Judge for yourself."

Lee accepted the tape in unsteady hands and deposited it in an inner breast pocket. His eyes paced to the door and back. "Could you give me a five-minute lead?"

"Glad to," Tate said. "I have a drink waiting."

The phone on Tim Boswell's desk purred, and the secretary said, "Mort Dubrovsky to see you."

"Who?" Tim Boswell asked.

"Mort Dubrovsky from Building C. He says he spoke with you yesterday and it's important."

Tim Boswell went into the anteroom. Mort Dubrovsky was wearing a jacket that didn't even attempt to go with his grease-stained trousers. "Hi, Mort—Mort, is it?"

They shook hands. "Mort's the name, Mr. Boswell."

"Something important's come up?"

"It's important to me, sir. Yesterday you said the company didn't pay me 326.99 a week to go around hitting pregnant women."

"That was for Miss Stokes's benefit. I thought we understood that."

"I understand that part. What I don't understand is the 326.99. I brought my paycheck so maybe you could explain it to me." Mort Dubrovsky took a long envelope from his jacket pocket. He raised the flap and lifted out the stub of a company paycheck as carefully as if it were a saint's relic. "Period ending 6/2. June second. Regular hours, thirty-seven and a half. Regular earnings, 326.98. Gross earnings, 326.98."

"What's the problem?"

"You said 99 cents. The check says 98 cents."

Tim Boswell fought down a surge of impatience. "I apologize, Mort. I must have made a one-cent slip."

"But look down here, year-to-date accumulations." Mort reached again into his jacket and pulled out an electronic pocket calculator. He punched buttons clumsily and had to clear the table twice before he got the division key to work. Dividing the gross pay accumulated to date by the number of weeks paid, he arrived at 326.99—Tim Boswell's figure. He repeated the operation with the Social Security tax; federal withholding; state tax; and union dues. In each case, the deduction for that week was a penny higher than indicated by the accumulated-to-date figure. While a total of $129.78 had come off Mort's salary, only $129.74 showed in the company's accumulations.

"Now, Mort," Tim Boswell said gently, "the payroll calculations run into tenths and hundredths of cents. There's a certain amount of rounding off week by week. It all comes out even on a yearly basis."

"I went back to the first paycheck stub I got this year. Every payday I'm getting three to four cents less than my cumulative says I got. I can show you the stubs."

If Dubrovsky was telling the truth, and Tim Boswell could see no reason for him to lie, then something was wrong. Tim Boswell decided he'd better check into it. "Mort, could I borrow that?"

Dubrovsky returned the stub to its envelope and handed it to him.

"And thanks again," Tim Boswell said, "for helping with Miss Stokes."

"My pleasure, I'm sure."

"Happen to remember where you were at the time of the test?" Elmer asked.

"Sitting on my bunk, writing a letter to my mom in San Diego." The specialist first class, a rangy boy in Air Force fatigues, kept running his fingers through his crew cut, as though the hair had just been amputated and he hadn't quite gotten over the shock.

"Notice anything out of the ordinary?"

The SFC glanced around the cube with its three double-decker beds, shower and chemical toilet stalls, steel chairs and table. The usual pinups and travel posters tried to give the walls a lift. You knew it wasn't a prison cell because there were too many electrical appliances and a phone and there were no windows to put bars on.

"There's eighty tons of stone between this bunk and that rocket. All you hear is the buzz. Seemed like an ordinary test to me."

On the table a portable color television set was picking up a commercial channel in surprisingly sharp focus. "How do you get that clear a picture?" Elmer asked.

"Remote-control center picks up the picture from Rapid City. It comes down here by cable. Only way anything can get down here is by elevator or cable."

"You fellas sure have all the conveniences."

"Yeah, everything but sunshine." The SFC opened the new-model two-door refrigerator and took out a plastic package half covered in snow. "Care for a hot dog?"

"No, thanks."

The specialist snapped three hot dogs from the bundle and laid them parallel on the grill of a small radar oven. Elmer watched him unwind black adhesive from around the coiled electric cord.

"That a new radar oven?"

"Been here longer than I have."

"Thought it might be new with that cord all taped up."

"We taped it up Sunday."

"How come?"

"Orders from the CO. No weenie roasting while Dr. Provenson was on the premises."

"Guess those radar ranges are against regulations. You have to bootleg them in?"

"Hell no. All the silos have got them, right out in the open."

"Provenson have a thing against hot dogs?"

"Search me." The SFC peered through the oven door. His hot dogs were already coming up blisters.

Barbara stood in the doorway a moment to admire the burgundy walls and dove-gray trim, the milky glow of the ribbed skylight. The gallery was as still as a photograph. A student in blue jeans and sunburst T-shirt had set up an easel to copy a painting. She stood out of his sight line and peered at the original, George Inness' "The Lackawanna Valley," and wondered what made it worth his attention.

She stole a look at the student. The bearded half of his face was nothing but black fuzz and the clay-red half was mostly eyes, and both halves were grimly serious. She moved on.

A man in gray worsted and a woman in canary yellow had taken seats on one of the sofas. They sat so still they could have been posing. There was a space between them. They were each alone and yet in some indefinable way they were linked in their silence. The man was bald and he was looking at his hands. The woman's hair was cut a little too short, as though she worked in one of the men's professions where you had to wear a cap. She was looking straight ahead. Her expression was a blank.

Barbara could not be certain if it was the same woman in canary yellow whom she had seen when she had dropped off the Mercedes at the garage for its tune-up; or the same woman who had stood with her in a bus queue on Pennsylvania Avenue and taken a place three seats behind her. It seemed to her it was the same, and she debated turning back. She slowed, snared in uncertainty. Her legs did not want to take her past the sofa.

She felt the woman's gaze grow rigid and slide through her. The woman put a cigarette between her lips. Smoking was not permitted in the National Gallery; surely the woman knew that. Barbara hurried past the sofa and into the next room and did not look back.

She found herself in an indoors sunken garden, with pillars rising from a manicured jungle of potted plants. There was a trickling stone fountain with lyre-playing cupids. A uniformed guard stood against the wall and a girl on a bench was turning the pages of a musical score, nodding time to some symphony inside her head. The stairwell with its black marble Mercury fountain was visible halfway down the almost deserted corridor.

Barbara slowed as she came into an octagonal room. It was little more than a passage between galleries, but four paintings had been hung on the walls. She studied the little brass plaques. The artist's name was Thomas Cole, and the paintings formed a series, "The Voyage of Life." "Infancy" showed an angel in the sky watching over a babe adrift in a rowboat; "Youth," a young man eagerly rowing toward castles in the clouds; "Manhood," an older man in a boat caught in a storm and abandoning his oars to pray; and in "Old Age," the same angel in the sky beckoned to an exhausted old man in an exhausted old rowboat.

"If you'll pardon my frankness—" The man in gray worsted who had been sitting on the sofa stood beside her. He looked like a minister and he wore a hearing aid. "I think they're the sort of corn that belongs in a granary, not in the National Gallery."

"I'm not certain," Barbara said, wondering why he had spoken to her.

"The analogy of life and the river is pretty trivial," the man said.

"But it sums up a nineteenth-century way of expressing things."

"What way is that?"

"Oh, a sort of sweet pessimism. Stephen Foster and Edgar Allan Poe."

The man was thoughtful a moment. He looked at her. The irises of his eyes were a fragmented green, like broken glass. "They're shit!" he screamed.

Barbara did not speak. For a moment she did not move. She could hear the man breathing very fast. She said to herself: *I will turn away slowly; I will walk; I will not run.* She turned and something struck her hard in the left shoulder and spun her back around. The man lunged for her hands. She thrust her purse behind her. Her wrists made a cracking sound and she heard the purse slap the floor. The man seized her right hand and, almost lifting her off the floor, slammed it against the frame of "Infancy." An alarm shrieked and the painting tipped crazily to the end of its wire.

She jerked a knee up into the man's groin. Something hissed from his mouth and he let go of her and hunched forward, hugging himself. Barbara backed off. *Don't watch*, she told herself: *get out.*

The woman in canary yellow blocked the doorway. She had locked both hands into a double fist and she swung them

at Barbara's stomach. The surprise stung. Before Barbara realized what had happened her knees buckled and she felt the
wood floor slam into her. She tasted blood on her lips. Suddenly the pain exploded, filling her stomach and pressing up
against her lungs. The man staggered toward her. His shoe
took aim. She could see black leather and a flapping loop of
shoelace. She jerked away.

The shoe smashed squeaking into the waxed wood par-
quetry, barely an inch from her ear. It drew back and she
tried to yank herself clear, but the woman in yellow was
holding her legs. Barbara could only get half clear, and this
time the shoe slapped her head against baseboard. She
clenched her teeth and a gasping sound ripped itself from her
knotted throat.

Her body began to shake, first her hands and feet and then
her limbs and then her abdomen. She lifted her head and saw
the woman in canary yellow jabbing at her Chanel skirt with
a metal nail file. The strokes were raw and deliberate as
though the woman had a precise timetable. Barbara opened
her mouth and sank her teeth into the woman's leg.

The woman screamed and released her. Barbara scrambled
choking to her feet and fumbled with one hand at a loose
stocking. A guard came rushing into the room. The man in
gray worsted grabbed for her and the woman in yellow came
hopping toward her, face wrinkled like a mad dog's, and
yelled, "Stop her!" Barbara dodged their oustretched hands.
The guard tried to block her and without thinking she
knocked him aside. Her heart was pounding and her eyes
were streaming. The galleries blurred into the corridor and
shouts whipped the air.

She swerved toward the stairway and threw a look back at
the wavering shapes of her pursuers. In that instant she lost
track of the steps: there were too many and they came too
fast. Her right foot hit wrong and skidded. Her hand shot out
for the banister and she stumbled forward and down. A roar
filled her ears. She heard children shrieking. By the time her
feet found solid floor a chorus of voices had arisen to assault
her. She opened her eyes numbly.

"She was vandalizing the painting," a woman shouted, the
woman in yellow. "I saw the whole thing."

Someone, something had straitjacketed her arms. She
stared at the encircling anger of unknown faces. Someone
said, "Crazy. We get two of them a week." She abandoned

herself to a paroxysm of sobs. She felt as humiliated and helpless as if she had urinated in public.

Anonymous hands dragged her to a room below street level. It was a cellar room: beige paint and lampshades could not disguise that. She was able to catch her breath. Through a crack of open door she could see the tile wall of a bathroom adjoining. Voices bubbled out but she only half listened. Hours seemed to go by and she began to be quite certain she would be late for dinner.

"I'm seven weeks pregnant." She tried to sit straight in the chair of molded, orange-flecked plastic. Her purse was gone and she didn't want to cry without Kleenex. If her face ran, she was sure to lose credibility with the people who were staring at her. Her watch was smashed and that made her ache. "I practically fell down a flight of stairs and I want to see a doctor."

"I *am* a doctor." A man in a tapered tan suit looked her over like a young mayor making a three-second stop in a ghetto. "Are you in pain?"

"Not yet."

"Do you have any idea why you tried to smash the painting?"

"I didn't touch the painting."

"A guard and two witnesses say you did," a man who had said he was head of museum security stated. He wore a necktie embossed like a paper napkin, and his fingers kept touching the thick knot.

"The guard wasn't even there," Barbara said. "If he'd been there it wouldn't have happened."

"*I* was there," the woman in yellow said. "I saw the whole thing."

The head of museum security watched the woman in yellow. He did not tell her to go on, but he did not tell her to shut up either.

"She was trying to rip that painting out of its frame. I have never seen such savagery inflicted on a work of art. When this gentleman tried to stop her, she kicked him. Kicked him I won't tell you where, but it was the dirtiest kick I've ever seen. Why, even in the Marines I'll bet you don't see kicks like that."

"I kicked him in the groin," Barbara said. "It was self-defense."

"And I suppose," the woman in yellow cried, "you bit me and attacked the painting in self-defense?"

"I did not attack anything. I was looking at the painting. This man struck up a conversation with me." Barbara glanced at the man in gray worsted. He was adjusting the control of his hearing aid. He did not seem to be in the same room with her. "Before I knew what had happened he grabbed one of my hands and slapped it against the frame."

"Which hand?" the head of museum security asked.

She studied the head of museum security, trying to gauge his friendliness or lack of it. He wore a signet ring that made a brass knuckle of one finger and his stomach bulged on either side of his belt. His eyes repudiated her smile. "Does it make any difference which hand?" she asked, for she couldn't remember.

"The exact facts make a difference."

"I did not strike up a conversation with this lady," the man in gray worsted said. "I did not grab her hand or attack her in any way."

No one spoke, and Barbara said, "They're both lying. It's quite obvious they're in collusion."

"Why should I bother to lie?" The woman in canary yellow thumped both hands to her hips. "I don't know you from Eve."

"Then why have you been following me since ten o'clock this morning?"

"You're bananas," the woman in canary yellow snorted.

"You were waiting in a green Ford when I left the house. You followed me to the doctor's. You were at the garage when I took my car in for a tune-up. You were on the same bus with me. You followed me to the hairdresser's and you followed me here."

"I don't even own a Ford, green, purple, or otherwise. Why, I don't even own a car."

"She's lying," Barbara told the doctor. "They're both lying. And if you don't believe me I wish you'd phone my husband."

Resting a lean buttock on the edge of the desk, the doctor crossed one cordovan shoe behind the other and lit a filter cigarette.

"I've been attacked," Barbara burst out. "I've been forcibly detained. I want to phone my husband. I have a right to phone my husband, haven't I?"

"Her husband might be able to help," the District of Columbia patrolman suggested. He was young enough to be a rookie. He wore a hip radio and his holster had an extra slot

for a ball-point pen. There were half circles of sweat beneath
the armpits of his shirt and his voice was high and his face
was a beardless, unlined blank. "It could be she's a repeater."

"Phone him." The doctor slid the telephone across the desk
toward Barbara.

"Dial 9 first," the head of museum security said.

Barbara dialed 9 and then Tate's office number. A recorded voice told her the line was temporarily out of order.
"Out of order," Barbara said. "May I call home?"

"Be my guest," the head of museum security said.

Barbara dialed home. She was baffled when she got the
recorded voice again. "They say that number's out of order
too."

The doctor's eyes flicked over her appraisingly.

"There's something wrong," she said. "Someone's playing
tricks with the phone. Look, my husband works three blocks
from here. General Tate Erlandsen—Pacific Aero Corporation. Couldn't someone go get him? He could be here in five
minutes. He'd clear everything up."

"You're Mrs. Erlandsen?" the doctor asked.

"Of course I'm Mrs. Erlandsen."

"Do you have any proof?"

"Proof?"

"Do you have a driver's license or charge card?" the doctor
said gently. "Anything with your name on it?"

"I haven't got identification." She glanced at the man in
gray worsted. "That man took my purse."

The man in gray worsted held up two empty hands. "I
don't have anyone's purse."

The museum guard stepped forward to place an alligator
handbag on the desk. He was a skinny man and he had a
habit of jerking his head like a caged bird. "We found this
upstairs," he said. "On the floor."

"Is this your purse?" the doctor said.

"Dear God, yes." Barbara snatched the handbag and
snapped open the bronze clasp. She found her wallet and
fumblingly thrust it on the doctor. "Everything's in there—
charge cards, driver's license."

"And your New York City Public Library card," the doctor
observed.

"I don't have a New York City Public Library card. I live
here, in Washington, D.C."

"Betty Engels," the doctor read from a card in the wallet,

"12 Barrow Street, New York City. Social Security card, Betty Engels. BankAmericard, Betty Engels."

"That's not possible." Stagnant puddles of cigarette smoke clogged the room. Barbara's lungs had difficulty drawing breath. "I've never heard of Betty Engels."

"You're carrying her New York State driver's license," the doctor said. "Height five foot four. Blue eyes. Blond hair. Two violations." He pulled another card partway out of the wallet. "In case of accident or death please notify next of kin, Mrs. Florence Engels, 259 Ware Street, Dorchester, Massachusetts."

"That's not true. There must be something here with my name." Barbara dumped the purse empty over the desk. She did not bother with the quarter that rolled to the floor and no one else bothered either.

"While you're looking," the doctor said, "maybe we might give Mrs. Florence Engels a call and tell her there's been an accident."

Barbara examined the purse's contents quickly, feeling she had thirty seconds to assemble a jigsaw puzzle.

The doctor lifted the telephone receiver and dialed a number written on one of the cards from the wallet.

She sifted through cosmetics and pennies and Kleenex. She found a cellophane-wrapped mint and an unfamiliar key ring. Her own keys were gone, but she doubted they'd had time to do a complete switch. There had to be something of hers they'd overlooked.

The doctor said the line was busy and hung up.

"Here." Barbara showed the doctor a linen handkerchief. She was sorry it was not quite fresh. "It has my monogram. *B.E.* Barbara Erlandsen. That wallet is initialed. This pen is initialed." She plunked a fourteen-carat gold pen down onto the blotter. "See? *B.E.* My compact: *B.E.*"

The doctor's eyes were very blue and seemed to regret they could not be more convinced. "*B.E.* could also stand for Betty Engels."

"No. I'm Barbara Erlandsen." She saw that the doctor and the guard and the head of museum security did not believe her at all, and for the first time she realized they might not let her go. The patrolman looked troubled, as though he wanted to believe her. "Phone my husband," she begged them. "Ask him who I am."

"Let's start by phoning your mom." The doctor lifted the receiver and dialed again.

"They changed my papers," Barbara told the patrolman. "They picked a name with the same initials as mine. Please phone my husband. Phone my maid. Phone my sister. My sister lives in Washington. Her husband's with the Navy. Janey Breckenridge. Mrs. Thomas Breckenridge."

"Mrs. Florence Engels?" This time the doctor had got an answer.

The room and people suddenly seemed very unreal, and Barbara knew she must struggle to keep reality in her mind's focus. The pale rug worn down where the door had scraped quarter circles over it, that was here. The doctor's nose sending out smoke jets of parallel randomness, the ticking of the patrolman's wristwatch, the shades of relief showing on the other's faces, those were here and now. She must sit straight and stay calm and control herself.

"This is Dr. Mark Stimson. I'm phoning from the National Gallery in Washington? We've got your daughter here."

The doctor talked and listened and kept glancing at Barbara. She could imagine how she looked to him: the strap of one shoe split, the heel of the other wrenched off, her skirt ripped, makeup running, her hands hugging the arms of the chair as though for anchor.

"Miss Engels," the doctor said, holding out the receiver, "you mother would like to talk to you."

"I am not Miss Engels. I don't know any Miss Engels. My mother is dead."

"She won't talk to you, Mrs. Engels." The doctor listened a moment. He picked up the gold pen and tapped it against the blotter. The pen had been a birthday present from one of Barbara's aunts in Minnesota and she had had it almost twenty years and she wished inanimate objects could speak. "We can keep her under observation till you arrive, yes. All right, Mrs. Engels, we'll let you know."

The doctor hung up and seemed to reflect a moment, and then he beckoned the patrolman and the head of museum security into a huddle on the other side of the room. Barbara heard them whispering from a great distance away. Finally the patrolman came and took her elbow and helped her to her feet.

"Let's go, ma'am." His eyes had the flickering softness of a deer's, and she realized he was almost as young as her son had been. "How about a little ride?"

"But my husband's expecting me," she said. "I'm seven

weeks pregnant and I almost fell down those stairs. Couldn't you please just phone him?"

Tate swung the Bentley broad onto Dumbarton Street and slowed at the third house from the corner. His eye took in the brick and pillars, cushioned in dogwood and laurel and azalea, and he saw with relief that the pickets had gone home. Braking at the two-car garage, he pressed the electronic signal button beneath the dashboard. The door grumbled upward. He was surprised to see that Barbara's blue Mercedes was not there.

Foreign cars were Tate and Barbara's little rebellion. Friends tsk-tsked about public relations, but Tate had found that American cars simply didn't hold up as well as some of the European models. And the annual pressure to junk last year's Cadillac and get this year's was too close to procurement logic: he needed a rest from all that.

He gave a last tap to the gas pedal, and the Bentley slid forward into the naked dimness of the overhead 100-watt bulb. He left the keys in the ignition and entered the house through the kitchen. Martta Savolainen was sitting at the spotless formica-topped table, her face pale and angled toward a newspaper that looked like Hawaiian with umlauts. The lights on the electric stove were all out and he could see through the glass door that the oven was sparklingly empty. He remembered Barbara's mentioning that they were not dining in.

"Do you know where Mrs. Erlandsen is?" Tate asked.

"No idea," Martta said.

"I'll be upstairs," Tate said.

He had been soaking a blessed half hour in the tub with the hot water trickling when the phone rang and Martta yelled up from downstairs. He wrapped himself in a towel and, dripping water across Barbara's broadloom rug, crossed to the bedside telephone.

"Tate," the voice on the phone said, "Janey. Where the dickens are you?"

The question was absurd even for his sister-in-law and Tate said, "Where do you think I am? At home."

"The reception's at seven-thirty," Janey said, "and it's after eight now."

Barbara had mentioned a reception at the Chilean Embassy, but Tate had not realized she had promised Janey a lift. "That's too bad, Janey, but Barbara's not home yet."

"Where is she?"

"I don't know."

"What do you mean, you don't know?"

"I mean I don't know where she is and I intend to wait till I hear from her. So if you're in some kind of rush you'd better drive yourself to that reception."

Something clanked, and he supposed Janey had shifted the receiver from one hand to the other and had banged a bracelet. "That's very unlike Barbara," Janey said.

"It's not at all like her," Tate agreed.

"You don't suppose something could have happened?"

"Her car's gone," Tate said, "and I'd like to keep the phone open in case she's trying to call."

"She thought they might be following her," Janey said.

"Who might be following her?" Janey's fondness for making things mysterious could be infuriating.

"Those pickets, those mothers-for-life. She phoned me from the hairdresser's and she said someone seemed to be following her, a woman in a horrendous yellow dress."

"I don't see why a mother-for-life would follow Barbara to the hairdresser's. Those mothers looked pretty unkempt to me. Anyway, they all wore blue jeans."

"They're fanatics and it wouldn't surprise me if something has happened to my sister."

"That's why I'd like to keep the phone open."

"I'll check back in half an hour," Janey said.

Tate finished drying himself and took his time dressing. The hallway was dark and there were no lights on in the living room or dining room. He could hear Martta working a blender in the kitchen. He made himself a scotch and took it into the study and sat with the door open. The blender went off and the house seemed to be holding its breath.

He sipped slowly and it struck him that something was out of place. His eye scanned the shelves. The books and shadows were all in their familiar places. It was the desk that troubled him. The lower left-hand drawer was not quite flush with the others.

Drawers often popped open in the house, moved by some crazy volition of their own, but he remembered locking the lower left-hand drawer, and keys did not turn a hundred eighty degrees by themselves. He slid the drawer open.

The Sony tape recorder was lying on its side, and all that was left of his conversation with Leon Asher was three ripped inches of magnetic tape and the smashed segment of a four-inch plastic reel.

The phone rang on the desk. Tate lifted the receiver and heard someone say his name. "Barbara?"

"Thelma Armstrong," the voice corrected. "Have you got a moment, Tate?"

He wondered why Thelma Armstrong would be phoning in the middle of the evening asking if he had a moment. "Sure," he said cautiously, lifting the segment of reel from its spindle. "I've got a moment."

"It's a terrible favor to ask, but I haven't got the car." Thelma's voice was flat, the words bunched in knots. "The police drove me down, but I can't face riding back with them. I know it's silly, but I'd like to talk to you, and if it's not too much trouble . . ."

The voice trailed off. Tate fingered the fragment of plastic reel. "What's the matter, Thelma?" he asked. "Where are you?"

"I'm in a phone booth just inside the emergency entrance of Bethesda Naval Hospital. The police have offered to drive me home, but I don't honestly trust them."

"What are you doing at the hospital?"

"Lee's car went off the turnpike and he died ten minutes ago."

"Jesus," Tate whispered. He knew there was no point asking questions. "All right, Thelma. You wait by the phone booth inside the emergency entrance. I'm on my way."

Barbara felt the squad car brake and realized they had come to a stop. The policewoman passed her out to the patrolman. Her feet grazed steps numbly. Glass doors swung shut behind them. She saw the lobby with disquieting clarity: The ocher walls glistened like fevered skin. Fluorescent lights cast a pulsing glow and shadows lurked in ambush. Twin doors led to a corridor fringed with human shapes on stretchers and crutches.

Two orderlies brought a wheelchair and told her to sit. When she said she wanted to call her husband they pushed her down into it and fastened her with strips of white canvas. Half the instincts in her body screamed to her to claw, kick, run. The other half warned her to sit still, go along calmly, risk nothing more that might dislodge the speck of life she prayed was still clinging to her womb.

The patrolman held a door. The orderlies sped her through a long corridor. The air changed. She smelled disinfectant.

They were in an elevator and the light bulb was broken. Darkness overtook them as they rose.

They stopped on the fifth floor. The orderlies said hi to an armed guard in a folding chair. They wheeled her into a small cell-like room and untied her. There was a white cotton smock on the bed with a pair of paper slippers tucked into a fold. They told her she could undress herself. She said she wanted to phone her husband. They said a doctor would see her as soon as one was free but not to count on Friday. Things were busy Fridays. Someone might be able to see her Monday.

She said she was sick, she was pregnant, she had almost fallen down a flight of stairs, and she had been kidnapped. They told her she was lucky to get a room at all and she would just have to wait her turn the same as anyone else. They advised her to behave herself and they took her clothes with them.

After the orderlies had gone, she went to the door and tried the handle. They had locked it. She sat on the steel hospital bed. Her leg had scratches halfway up the thigh. Her left foot dangled like a broken sandal, bruised where she had aimed a kick at a policewoman. She passed her tongue along her lips and felt dried blood. One of her eyeteeth seemed loose in the socket but she didn't want to know. Her stomach gnawed. She combed her scalp with both hands but found no blood.

Her ears were alert. Voices whispered in the hallway. She watched the door. The whispering passed by and she sank back against the pillow. The linen smelled boiled. She was afraid she would be very late for dinner.

Voices nagged at her memory. She tried to ignore them, to concentrate on here and now and not slide somewhere else. She lay down but could not find a position that did not ache. A swift and total sense of isolation engulfed her. Her ears clawed for some sound she could cling to. The smell of rubbing alcohol rushed in from nowhere.

A nurse was rubbing a damp cotton ball on her arm. Barbara had not heard the woman come in. "What's that?" Barbara reached up a hand to fend off the hypodermic.

"This will make you calm," the nurse stated. She was a heavily built woman and the needle jabbed quickly.

"No drugs," Barbara begged.

"There now, that wasn't so bad, was it?"

At first from a distance and then gradually closer Barbara

heard it: the putter of the power mower cutting long unhurried swaths. It slowed at the far end of the lawn and grew louder as it approached her window. It brought a smell of fresh-cut grass and for some reason it calmed her.

She realized they had brought her back to the clinic in Kansas.

The red brick observatory sat tiny and copper-domed in the flatness of a sugar-beet field three miles east of Box Elder, Pennington County, South Dakota. The people at the college had told Elmer that if he took the dirt road, and hurried, he might catch Wiley Herndon before Mr. Herndon locked up for supper.

Elmer's rented Nova screeched into the three-car parking lot just as a twenty-year-old and beautifully preserved Pontiac was revving up for departure. He shouted to the driver, "Mr. Herndon, have you got a second?"

The driver glared from his Pontiac with a look that said no, he did not have a second, but Elmer was on the asphalt waving a wallet flung open to nothing in particular.

"The name's Connally, I'm from *American Astrology Magazine?*" Elmer leaned down to the driver's window. "Thanks for not laughing. We're running down a story on some UFOs, and the long and short of it is, you were on the telescope Monday night, weren't you?"

Mr. Herndon wore wire-rimmed spectacles that seemed to sweat in sunlight. "I'm on from 11 P.M. to 7 A.M. every day this week, and I'm very tired."

"I appreciate that, Mr. Herndon. You wouldn't happen to remember any unusual sightings around 11:46 Monday night, would you?"

"I wouldn't remember a thing. That's why astronomers keep logs."

"If you could take a look in that log, our readers would be mighty grateful. And of course *American Astrology Magazine* would pay you for your trouble."

Mr. Herndon got out of the car. He unlocked the observatory door, and Elmer followed him into a widowless, one-room darkness. Mr. Herndon pressed a button and fluorescence struck a twenty-foot telescope, steely and gleaming as a missile, its nose pressed to the sealed rift in the dome.

Bent over the desk, Mr. Herndon turned pages in a two-by-three-foot ledger. Elmer edged near and peeked. The sheets, stamped with dates and hours and minutes, were intermittently speckled with writing as precise as a certified public accountant's.

"I'm afraid your readers are going to be disappointed. We have no sightings from 11:43 to 11:47. The telescope blanked out."

Elmer put on his best incredulous face. "Now how can two lenses and a mirror blank out?"

"It's not a question of two lenses and a mirror, Mr. Connally. The telescope amplifies radio signals electronically. Otherwise it would never see past Pluto on a clear night. Our amplification got wiped out for three minutes."

Elmer's pocket notebook was jammed with jottings. He scribbled on a clear space inside the cover.

"I'm afraid it was a power surge," Mr. Herndon apologized with a hint of satisfaction, "not a UFO."

Traffic on the beltway was light. For almost twenty minutes Thelma sat silently beside Tate, eyes cast down with a sullen lack of curiosity at the lights and dials of the polished mahogany dashboard. Her body swayed on the leather seat with the motion of the car, and Tate drove very carefully.

"The police say the Buick's a total loss," Thelma remarked suddenly. "I don't suppose it matters. I've still got the VW. It gets better gas mileage."

She was silent a while, and Tate said, "You don't have to talk about it."

"I want to talk, I've got to talk. You see, it isn't just Lee—it's much more than that." Thelma's hair was a harried fluff and she had lost one of her trapezoidal tin earrings, and her eyes were red. "It happened on Chain Bridge Road, west of Tyson's Corner. Lee crashed the Buick into a concrete culvert. The highway police found him just after six. They said the crash was alcohol-related. Well, they're full of crap."

Tate had heard that people confronted with death sometimes became angry instead of sad, and he supposed that was what was happening to Thelma. She didn't seem sad at all. "I'm awfully sorry," Tate said. "I really am awfully sorry, Thelma."

"Sure you are," Thelma said in an odd voice.

It was the second time that week that Tate had driven a widow home from the hospital, and he went into the house with Thelma and let her keep on talking.

"Two years ago," she said, "they told Lee he wasn't going to go any further in the Army." Tate and Thelma were sitting at far ends of the sofa. She had been twisting the painted beans on her necklace and now there were gaps where two chick-peas had worked loose. "Lee would come home evenings, wouldn't hardly talk to me—he'd open up a bottle of Jim Beam and go out on the terrace and watch the sunset. Some nights he wouldn't even come inside for dinner."

Thelma rose and went to a carved oak cabinet and got out a half-full bottle of Jim Beam sour mash and two tumblers with eagles etched into the glass. She left the room and came back with a silver bucket of half-formed ice cubes and apologized that the fridge was on the blink.

"Lee knew he was drinking too much," Thelma said, "and he started seeing an Army psychiatrist." She poured herself a stiff drink and let Tate fix his own. "I don't know to this day whether it was Lee or that Army psychiatrist, but one of them came up with this idea that we should have a little place in the country. Nothing fancy. Just a place to get away from pressure and work; where you could sit and look at trees. We thought about the Blue Ridge and how much we'd loved it on our honeymoon, and we drove down to see if we could find a few acres of woodland. Nothing too expensive."

"I suppose the mountains must have changed," Tate said.

Thelma nodded. "If you go up high enough, there are still trees. We bought ten acres, five hundred dollars an acre. Sank almost all our savings into it—had to postpone the new car and washing machine. That shack cost close to six thousand dollars, but it made us real happy for almost a whole summer. Well, come fall, Lee said the Army psychiatrist thought he should get away from everything and everyone and go down to the shack by himself. 'Lee,' I said, 'at least put a phone in that shack, let the phone company run a party line in so I can phone you,' and Lee said, 'Nope, no phone, doctor's orders.' "

Tate shifted weight and took a swallow of his bourbon and realized there wasn't a damned thing he could do or say to make anything easier for her.

"Well, the last straw was the weekend of September twelfth. Our twentieth wedding anniversary. Lee told me he had to go down to the mountains alone. You could have knocked me over with a feather. I didn't say a word, but I was stunned that Lee would actually forget our twentieth wedding anniversary. To make a long story short, after Lee went driving off, I took the bottle of Jim Beam out on the terrace and I don't mind telling you, Tate, I had a few. I was angry. Angry isn't the word. I was livid. And I went through the Pentagon phone book and I found the number of that Army psychiatrist and I called the Pentagon and said who I was and I said it was an emergency and I got that Army psychiatrist's phone number.

"Well, I got that psychiatrist on the phone and said I would appreciate knowing just what the hell he thought he was doing sending my husband out to some shack in the woods and leaving me high and dry on my twentieth anniversary. That psychiatrist sounded like you could have knocked him over with a feather. 'Thelma *who?*' he said, and I said, 'Lee Armstrong's wife, in case you didn't know Lee Armstrong still had one, and he might not at the rate this so-called treatment is progressing.' "

Thelma leaned forward to freshen her drink. "That Army psychiatrist said, 'Mrs. Armstrong, I did treat Colonel Lee Armstrong several months back, but he is under no treatment by me at this point in time.' Well, you could have knocked me over with a feather. I thanked him for his trouble and I drank three percolator pots of black coffee and I got into the VW and I covered a hundred miles in an hour and twenty minutes, and if there was any rubber left on those tires it was a miracle. I got to Boonesville around two in the morning. I snuck up to that shack and I put the key in the lock and I opened the door real quiet."

Thelma took a gulp of bourbon, and Tate said, "Thelma, are you sure you want to tell me this?"

She sat down her glass with a thump. "The dust in the shack was two inches thick: why, you could have written your initials on the floorboards. Lee wasn't there and no woman was there and if I'd had any sense I would have seen that there wasn't any car there either. Well, I turned the VW right around and drove straight home and I spent our twentieth wedding anniversary crying. I didn't know if Lee was dead or alive or if he'd left me, and by the time he showed up Sunday night at 9 P.M. I frankly was past caring. And when that man started telling me what a good rest he'd had himself in the mountains I said, 'Lee Armstrong, you shut the hell *up* because I burnt the tires off the VW and practically killed myself getting down there and back and I've seen for myself that no one's been in that shack all summer and

I'd appreciate knowing where the hell you've been all these weekends that I couldn't go along.' "

Well, she had never seen a face fall so flat. Lee had said, "Honey, would you mind if I fixed myself a drink?" Thelma had said he could have as many Jim Beams as he wanted, but he had better tell her the truth here and now, or this wedding anniversary was going to be their last. Well, he had a drink and he had another drink and finally he told her the craziest story.

Thelma kicked her shoes off and drew her feet up under her skirt. "He told me for over a year he'd been a sort of traveling salesman for the Pentagon, selling old Army and Air Force and Navy stuff to get a little money to help buy the new stuff. I said, 'Then why the hell did you lie to me?' Turned out he was selling this stuff to foreign governments and it had to be secret because if the newspapers got hold of it they'd blow it up out of all proportion. I said, 'Why the hell would newspapers care who you're selling scrap metal to?' He said a lot of liberals would say ten-year-old fighter planes are not scrap metal and we haven't got any business selling them to Arabs and Chileans and God knows who-all. I said, 'Lee Armstrong, frankly it sounds like a load of hooey.' "

Tate said that actually the Department of Defense did sell several thousand tons of outmoded armaments every year to foreign governments. Some of the sales were sensitive and had to be kept secret, and of course, a military man couldn't discuss classified material with anyone, not even his wife. "It wouldn't surprise me in the least," Tate said, "if Lee had been involved in that sort of thing."

"Well, classified or not," Thelma said, "Lee reached into his pocket and he pulled out a matchbook. It was brand-new and it was written in Saudi Arabian. That was good enough for me. I said, 'Lee Armstrong, in the future when you've got something secret to do, just come right out and tell me and let's not have any more of these lies.' "

Tate would have liked to ask for coffee, but he knew from other evenings in the Armstrong living room that Thelma's percolator was not kind to coffee. He didn't suppose he ought to ask her for anything, not at the moment, not even permission to use the phone and see if Barbara had gotten home yet.

"Tate," Thelma asked, "do you remember that business in Chile when Allende fell? Because I was following it in the newspapers, and the Chileans weren't flying any ten-year-old planes, they were flying American F-12 fighter planes, brand-new. And I don't mind telling you, Tate, Lee looked pretty grim when that fact hit the headlines. And then the mess in Cambodia. The United States was sending aircraft and ammunition to the Cambodians and the Communists were hitting right back and it came out that the Communists were using American ammunition. That didn't make any sense to me at all and I could see it bothered Lee too."

Thelma eased one stockinged foot out from under her skirt and jiggled it off the sofa as though to get circulation going again. "Well, as if Lee and I didn't have enough on our minds, along came the Benzikoffs. Yuri Benzikoff—maybe you've seen photographs of him? He's as fat as a teddy bear and he laughs and laughs and he's the last person in the world you'd think was a Russian nuclear physicist. Well, he came to the U.S.A. to look at some of our nuclear power plants. We had a team looking at theirs, and supposedly it was one of these détente things. Well, the assistant to the assistant director of the Atomic Energy Commission gave a reception for the Russians. Lee was what you'd call the token soldier, and I was the token wife. And we got to talking with Mr. and Mrs. Benzikoff."

Thelma freshened her drink to the brim. "I don't know how sincere they were—not very, I don't suppose—but I don't mind telling you, the Benzikoffs were charmers. He was a fat man, laughing all the time, and Mrs. Benzikoff—why, when I saw her, I thought she was his daughter or his secretary maybe, but his wife . . . You could have knocked me over with a feather. She's what you'd call a raven-haired beauty. Thirty, maybe thirty-five years younger than Mr. B. She had a nice figure, wore nice clothes—she didn't *look* Russian. You'd have thought she was a ballerina. Something in the way she did her eyes; *Swan Lake,* do you know what I mean? We got to talking, the four of us, and we really hit it off. The B.'s said they were sick and tired of nuclear physicists and what a relief it was to meet real people for a change and couldn't we all have dinner."

Thelma hesitated. She seemed to want someone to say she had done the right thing. "You had to be polite to them," Tate said. "They were guests of the nation."

Thelma nodded. "So Lee asked at the Pentagon if that would be all right, and it was all right and we all had dinner. They took us out once, and we had them over for a barbe-

cue. Well, Saturday morning I always send Lee's uniform to
the cleaner. That Saturday I found a piece of paper in the
pocket with a phone number. I was curious, and maybe I
shouldn't have, but I phoned the number."

"Perfectly natural thing to do," Tate said.

"I wasn't going to say anything, just see what kind of voice
answered. Well, a voice answered and said 'Hotel Washington, may I help you?' and without even thinking I said,
'Are Mr. and Mrs. Benzikoff staying at the hotel?' "

"Perfectly natural thing to wonder," Tate said.

"They were at the hotel. Well, I don't mind telling you I
saw red, and when Lee got home that night I said, 'Lee, I
saw you and Mrs. B. talking and giggling the night we had
that barbecue.'" She sulked a moment, remembering. "I
said, 'Lee, what's her phone number doing in your pocket?'
'Okay,' Lee says, 'I'll tell you what we were talking about.
Mrs. B. and I were talking about arms reduction.'

"Well, apparently Mrs. B. had kept saying how stupid it
was that America was arming both sides in Indochina, how
stupid it was that Russia was arming both sides in Guinea,
how stupid it was that the U.S. and the U.S.S.R. were both
arming both sides in Ethiopia. Apparently Mrs. B. said the
U.S. and the U.S.S.R. ought to get together and stop peddling
arms right and left. And she said Lee ought to come to their
hotel room because Mr. B. had something to show him.

"Well, Lee didn't know what the dickens was happening
but it could have been important and so he took a chance
and said okay. When he got to the hotel room the next evening, Mr. B. had a loose-leaf folder on his lap. In that folder
he had thirty-two photographs of—I don't know what you
call them, radar profiles of MIRVed Minuteman IV decoys.
Does that make sense?"

Tate nodded. "Radar profiles of MIRVed Minuteman decoys make a great deal of sense."

"Mr. B. told Lee the Russians had had the profiles for over
five months and they came from a highly placed source in the
Pentagon. Of course, Lee didn't believe a word of it, but he
played along and nodded and smiled. In that same loose-leaf
folder were twenty-nine other photographs. Mr. B. said they
were radar profiles of the Russian MIRVed decoys."

Thelma hesitated and Tate said that made sense too.

"Well, at that point in time no one knew for sure whether
or not the Russians even had MIRVs and this was news to
Lee. Mr. B. said there were eight MIRVs on the land missiles

and six on the sub-launched, and he handed Lee these photocopies and he said they were the radar profiles and the timing and the trajectories of all the decoys.

"Mr. B. said the whole arms race was out of control and all SALT did was raise the ceilings instead of lowering them, and everyone was cheating anyway. The only way to bring arms under control was to exchange information at the top. Mr. B. thought he and Lee could have a good ongoing relationship trading secrets. Well, Lee took the loose-leaf folder and went straight to the Department of Defense intelligence. Turned out the U.S. profiles were correct, every damned one of them. Maybe the Russians got them by monitoring American tests. Maybe they really did have a source at the Pentagon. There was no way of knowing for sure. The Russian profiles looked authentic, but the U.S. hadn't monitored any Soviet MIRVs and no one wanted to take the Russians' word for anything. The DOD told Lee the only thing to do was play Mr. B. along. They gave Lee some photocopies to give Mr. B., and Mr. B. gave Lee more photocopies, and Lee never knew for sure what the dickens the information was or what it was worth or who was fooling who. He was just following orders, and his orders were to keep channels with Mr. B. open. Well, three weeks later Mr. B. went back to the U.S.S.R. and that looked like the end of it. Three months later the Russians tested their first MIRVs and a U.S. weather satellite monitored the test, and Mr. B.'s profiles all fitted.

"In the meantime," Thelma said, "Lee kept making these business trips, selling weapons to the allies and raising money for new weapons, and we kept telling friends he was going down to the shack in the Blue Ridge. Seemed to me he was beginning to accept the situation and he was beginning to drink a little bit less. Well, along came Hornet. The Department of Defense wanted to lay off eighty of the first run, to offset costs, and it was Lee's job to peddle forty-two of them to Denmark."

Thelma sighed. "Orders are orders, and Lee went to Copenhagen and set up the deal with the Danish Ministry of Defense. Well, on his second trip to Copenhagen, who pops up like a bad penny but dear old Yuri Benzikoff, fatter and louder than ever. He's visiting professor at the Niels Bohr Institute of Physics and he's so glad to bump into Lee, what a small world and how about a beer? So they go sit in a café in Tivoli Gardens and after yakking through four beers Mr. B. finally gets to the point. He'll give Lee the plans of the Rus-

sian MIG 125 fire control and smart missiles if Lee will give
him the Hornet fire control and missiles. Mr. B. gives Lee
one photo—a sample, he calls it—some kind of mercury
switching mechanism. Lee shows it to the DOD, they like it,
they want the rest. They say they'll fake the plans Mr. B.
wants, and the U.S. will pay for real information with phony
information. So a man by the name of—I forget; Bailey, I
think—some kind of genius in advanced strategy—he fakes
some Hornet plans."

The Jim Beam in Thelma's glass had sunk to the halfway
point, and she spoke with the earnestness of a woman longing
to be absolved but damned if she'd admit she had sinned.

"A couple of weeks later, Lee took the fake plans to Copenhagen. He met a Danish friend of Mr. B.'s in the beer
garden, they drank five beers apiece. When Lee told me they
switched microfilm right there at the table I said Lee you are
crazy, but Lee said so long as you do it in the open nobody
notices or cares. Well, the Danes didn't notice or care—they
signed up for forty-two Hornets. Only the day after Lee arrived back in Washington with the signatures on the contract,
all hell broke loose. He hadn't been back more than twelve
hours when a CIA agent in some defense bureau in Moscow
uncovered Russian plans for a radar-guided fire control."

Tate remembered that day. October seventh. The Russians
had developed a system identical to Hornet's. The Navy had
made Pacific Aero scrap the fire control and start again from
scratch. The company had lost close to a quarter billion.

"I've never seen Lee go through a fifth of Jim Beam so
fast. 'Thelma,' he says, 'those are the same plans I gave
Benzikoff.' 'Lee,' I say, 'why the dickens would anyone
ask you to pass real plans to Mr. B.? That doesn't accomplish
a damned thing except waste five hundred million dollars.' "

Lee was sick with worry, Thelma said, and as if they
hadn't enough on their minds, along came Silo 29.

"You handed those Theta plans to Lee, and Lee gave them
to Bailey. He didn't trust Bailey, not after the Hornet mess.
He knew Bailey was involved in some kind of double-cross
and he wanted to give him enough rope."

Thelma's face had become very gray: there was no way of
knowing whether from grief or bourbon, fatigue or remembered anger.

"You know what happened. Bailey shredded the plans.
Asher died and someone broke into his apartment. They followed you from the Pentagon."

"Who's *they?*" Tate asked.

Thelma dipped a hand into the bucket and dredged a sliver of ice out of the puddle and dropped it into her Jim Beam. The ice bucket had begun to tarnish around the engraved lettering, but Tate could decipher a portion of a farewell and the names of some of Lee's Army platoon buddies.

"They?" Thelma repeated. She thought a moment and then she said, "Bailey, the Chief of Naval Operations, those people. They're all involved in Theta."

Tate could not tell whether this statement was Thelma's paranoia or her husband's, or whether it was just Jim Beam talking.

"At first," Thelma said, "Lee thought the whole Theta thing might be some kind of a scheme to kill land-based missiles: you know, show them up and move all the money into sub-launched missiles. I said, 'Lee, I've heard of rivalry between the services, but even at the Army-Navy football game Navy never played *that* rough.' But Lee kept worrying about our sister-in-law."

"Why the hell would he worry about my sister-in-law?" Tate said.

"Her husband's sub, the one that didn't show up in Rota, Spain. Lee asked me a half dozen times: why is a nuclear sub with armed warheads given new orders the day before a missile in Silo 29 breaks down? I said, 'Lee, unless you know what those orders are, I don't see how you can say there's any connection.' But you know Lee—never content to see both sides of the picture. He had to see the worst side too. This morning he got up at five-thirty, wouldn't tell me where he was going. Came home at lunchtime with two Xeroxes. Copies of submarine orders."

"Lee *copied* submarine orders?" Tate said.

Thelma's shoulders made an impatient gesture, as though Tate were being a pointless stickler for rules. "For three months there's been a standby authorization for the *Intrepid* to run sonar tests in the Barents Sea. The authorization was activated last Sunday. Lee made Xeroxes of the backup carbons. You see what it means, don't you?"

"No," Tate admitted, "I don't see what it means."

She stared at him in silence. "The orders prove Wanamaker is doing it."

"Doing what?"

Thelma drained the glass and passed a tongue tip over her lips. "He's bypassing the State Department and the CIA and the President. He's going straight to the Russians—bluffing them into laying down their defenses. This week, the *Intrepid* will fire a warhead at the Moscow ABM. You'll see."

"Jesus Christ!" Tate had to get his breath. "Even if Wanamaker were a complete madman, there's no way an order like that could get through the Joint Chiefs."

Thelma's body retained its erect, despairing confidence. "Look at the *Pueblo* mission. There's no way an unprotected intelligence ship could have been sent into North Korean waters, yet the order got through the Joint Chiefs."

"The *Pueblo* was a fluke," Tate said.

"Then this is another fluke." Thelma braced a hand on the arm of the sofa and stood up. She went to the liquor cabinet and rummaged in a drawer beneath the bottles. She handed Tate a plain white envelope. "See for yourself."

He opened it. Lee had Xeroxed the plaintext and code.

Thelma sank back into the hollow she had worn in the sofa. She gave Tate a hard stab of a look. "When Lee left the house this morning, he had a copy of Asher's plans and he had two tapes and he had a copy of those orders. The highway police gave me back an empty briefcase."

The night was still, but the suburban house creaked like an old barn standing up to a gale.

"Someone took those orders. Someone killed my husband and someone took his papers and someone had a reason." Suddenly Thelma's face looked a good deal older, but it also looked alarmingly redder, and Tate did not think it was a good sign that she was refilling her glass.

"And what reason would anyone have had to kill him?" Tate asked quietly.

"They knew that Lee knew, and they had to stop him from getting on that plane."

"What plane?"

She looked at him with a sort of amusement. "Lee wasn't going down to the shack. He was going to Copenhagen. He was going to give the plans and the tape and the *Intrepid* orders to Benzikoff. He was going to get Benzikoff to take them to Moscow and leak them back through the CIA."

"I don't see the point of that," Tate confessed.

"If Soviet Theta plans turned up now, they'd wipe out any notion Wanamaker had of a Theta lead. He'd have to call of his bluff."

It was the kind of reasoning that made sense after three

Jim Beams, and Thelma paused as though it might make sense to Tate if he gave it a second or two.

"Lee was overworked," Tate said, "and it seemed to me he was close to some kind of breakdown. And you've had a shock."

Thelma drew her shoulders back. "You think Lee was imagining it all?"

"If he was betraying secret orders and handing plans to the Soviets, I think he was showing very poor judgment."

Thelma's eyes snapped open. "There was a 51 per cent chance and he had to take the risk."

"And he's dead."

"Maybe there are worse things than being dead," Thelma cried. "Maybe it's worse to be drunk every night. Maybe it's worse to spend your life dying behind a Pentagon desk. This was the first decision Lee made for himself in fifteen years. It was a brave decision and it was the right decision and they've killed him for it. I'd like to know what you intend to do about it, General. Keep on peddling overpriced bazookas?"

Thelma set her glass on the table and hid her face behind her hands and broke into tears that sounded horribly like a crow's cackling.

"I don't think you should spend the night alone," Tate said.

"I asked you a question." With an abruptness that was crazier than anything she had yet said, Thelma's voice was sober and measured. "They've killed my husband and I want to know what you're going to do about it."

"The first thing I'm going to do is telephone the doctor that lives next door."

"I don't need Dr. Burns. I need an answer."

"He'll give you a sedative and see that you sleep. He may not want you to stay here alone. You can come to our place if you like. I wouldn't drink too much more, Thelma."

She gave him a look of unsheathed contempt. "You can be the goddamnedest bastard."

"I'm trying to help."

"You don't know the meaning of the word *help*. You've never had to worry two minutes in your life. You've had your pick of the richest women and the top commissions and the highest-paying jobs. Lee had to work his way through school and the Army. Lee had to sweat blood for every single thing he ever got. But everything came to you free, General. Even credit for jobs that Lee did."

"I never tried to take credit for anything Lee did. I never wanted credit."

Her eyes climbed him like claws. "Lee was a fool. He saw you operate for ten years and he still liked you. Well, I don't like you one bit, General. I don't think you're sexy, I don't think you're honest, in fact I don't think you're a very nice person at all."

Thelma's mouth was bent into a tight, satisfied bow, as though with that arrow she had shot down her husband's murderers.

"Thelma, do you want me to call the kids?"

"You don't need to call anyone: I can take care of myself, thanks."

But Tate needed to get up from that sofa, and he got up and phoned the doctor next door, and Dr. Burns hurried over in his bathrobe with his black leather satchel. Thelma insisted she was just fine, thank you all very much, and Tate left them arguing and phoned home. The woman's voice that answered on the fourth ring was not Barbara's and it had none of Martta Savolainen's hesitance. "For God's sake, Tate, where have you been?" It was his sister-in-law Janey.

"That's a long story. I don't suppose Barbara has showed up?"

"No, she hasn't, and the police inspector's been waiting over an hour and he can't start without you."

"What police inspector?"

"His name is Mac-something and he doesn't have a warrant and he refused to touch a thing unless you authorize him."

Tate heard muffled exchanges and realized his sister-in-law had placed her jeweled fist around the mouthpiece. He stared at a blue and red finger painting that the Armstrongs had framed and hung in the hallway and wondered if it dated from their children's kindergarten years.

"You can't authorize him over the phone," Janey announced, unmuffled. "I just asked and he says no."

"What the hell are you and a policeman doing in my home?"

"Two policemen. We're sitting in the living room. I told them Barbara is missing and I told them about those mothers-for-life and the sooner you get back here, the better. So will you please hurry?"

Tate left Thelma on the sofa pressing a cotton wad to the crook of her arm. He hit seventy on the Little River Parkway. It was not till he stood on the doorstep of his home looking through his pockets for the keys that he realized he had gone off with Thelma's Xerox of the submarine orders.

Silhouetted in the flickering candlelight, Debbie poured them both more wine. The clock chimed and it made O'Brien weary to realize it was only seven o'clock: his body was still on New York time.

"Poor Jack." Debbie lifted a hand and touched his cheek. "You've been working much too hard."

He smiled and gave a half nod and watched her slide the bottle back into its silver bucket.

He liked to watch Debbie preside at the dinner table. She reminded him of a good secretary, able to monitor several variables at once: the food, the level of wine in the glasses— and able at the same time to listen intelligently and ask the correct questions. At such times he saw that in her way she was a pro, too. Even this meal, for the two of them, with the food already set out and three candles, was a professional job, and he knew she had planned this moment very carefully.

"It's nice not having Inger," she remarked.

He wondered if she had fired the Swedish girl. "Where is she?"

"I gave her the night off. I thought you and I would like a vacation from servants. You know, rough it."

It was a light, tasty meal: chilled vichyssoise, fish soufflé—she had three books on soufflés and regarded them as her specialty—and an endive salad with low-cholesterol corn-oil dressing to compensate for the excess of the soufflé. She had brought up a bottle of the good chablis from the wine cellar. He knew she had a reason and he wondered what it was.

"Jack," she said very gently.

He looked at her. She was watching a candle flicker and it seemed to make her thoughtful.

"Couldn't you just ask Frances straight out not to sell? Wouldn't a direct appeal be better than catting-and-mousing till Monday?"

The question made him angry. Perhaps the trip from New York and the accordion stretching of his day across time zones had made him angry and he was only looking for some pretext to detonate. Debbie was always criticizing him for bringing the office home, and though he had to admit he was

often at fault in that regard, he'd never brought the office
into the dining room and he felt like telling her so.

But it was her dining room and her home too; had been
for over fifteen years.

When they'd moved into the house Wayne had been eight
and Suzie had been six. Now Wayne was at Harvard Med
writing home letters about radioactive tracers. Suzie was married to the owner of a Holiday Inn in Georgia and had an
eight-month-old baby of her own and did not write very often. The dining room had changed less in all those years than
the family. The house had grown bigger and the emptiness,
but the dining room had persisted as it was.

From the start Debbie had wanted French Provincial. He
had acquiesced because for the first time in their lives they'd
been able to afford antiques, and he discovered a bit of the
collector's bloodlust in him. Since they entertained business
contacts at home, his tax accountant had advised him he
could write off a third of the nineteenth-century table and
eighteenth-century chairs as business expenses. He used to
joke with Debbie when they dined alone at one end of the
table that they were eating off Pacific Aero's third.

After Debbie bought books on the subject and seriously took
up the study of old furniture, the Wedgwood plates in the
breakfront had changed to Sèvres, and instead of saying
French Provincial she had started saying Louis Quinze. Now
that the children were gone there were no marks or smears
on the wallpaper, except for a ghost by the baseboard where
seven-year-old Suzie had drawn Winnie the Pooh in raspberry
jam. The paper was not actually paper, but hand-blocked
French watered silk, and its continued cleanliness surprised
O'Brien in the light of Debbie's decision, after the children
left, to get along with only one cook and one full time maid.

"Frances has a right not to be pressured," he said.

"Isn't she being disloyal, selling out like that? I mean,
couldn't you make a straightforward appeal to loyalty?"

"We don't know she's going to sell out."

"Oh, Jack," Debbie said in a way that was as cuttingly soft
as a mother's pity, "she wouldn't have bought it up otherwise.
Frances Meredith is not a woman who asks anyone's permission, and she doesn't do her thinking out loud. She's a tough
old pragmatist, and I'd be dead certain she's made up her
mind and her conscience is bothering her. She wants you to
let her off the hook."

"Possibly." He looked at her obliquely. Her hair was curly

and soft in the candlelight and he suspected she had washed it quite recently. They were usually at ease with one another at times like this. He realized how very friendly he would have felt toward her at this instant if she had not asked about Frances Meredith.

"If she does sell," Debbie said, "does it make a terrible difference?"

"How do you measure terrible differences?" he said.

"Am I butting in?"

"Of course you're not."

"Because this time I want to butt in, even if the last thing you need is a backseat driver."

"A man can always use a second opinion."

"Oh, Jack, I've let you down."

He thought of the girl he had made love to in the New York hotel room. "How?" he asked.

"I've never been brave enough."

"You're plenty brave."

"I mean brave enough to give you that second opinion."

The turn of conversation made him uneasy, because she was leading up to something they both knew he didn't want to hear and in a way she had tricked him into giving her permission to say it, and there was a chill in his stomach.

"It's nice to have you home again," she said. "It's like before the children."

He managed to laugh. "We didn't live like this before the children."

"Didn't we?" she said. "I used to cook for you all the time."

"You used to scramble eggs. Now it's soufflés."

"I can still scramble," she said, looking straight at him.

"I don't want you ever to have to scramble again."

"All I meant was, think of the awful things that can happen, that do happen—think of wars and concentration camps and cancers and children who die. Somehow you've got to try to survive them, haven't you? Maybe it's the horrible things that bring out the survival in us, maybe that's why it's easier to survive the horrible things than the things that aren't quite so horrible."

"What are the things that aren't quite so horrible?"

"Not having three cars. Not having servants. Not belonging to country clubs and having all the things you think you want."

"I see you've already voted me a salary cut."

"I wasn't talking about salaries. I was talking about you and me."

"If all we've got is the fact that we're not in a concentration camp, I'd say it's not a hell of a lot to show for thirty years."

She touched his hand. "Jack, there are women who lose a breast and spend their lives feeling deformed. But they've still got *life*."

"That's a fine noble view, Debbie, but I'd just as soon not have to hear it, not at this juncture."

"I'm only trying to tell you how much I love you."

"I know you love me, and if you're saying the company is just a company and it doesn't matter who built it or who runs it, you're probably right—in the long run. But in the long run we're all dead and so by that kind of logic living doesn't matter much either."

"But living does matter." Her expression was sad, as if she saw she had driven him away. "Living is what matters most."

He didn't answer. The phone was ringing. She looked at him as though asking him to make some sort of choice.

"Do you want me to get it?" she said.

"Probably for me," he said.

It was Phil Marquis calling from Detroit and sounding tired. "We just finished counting ballots. The men rejected the offer by eighteen votes."

"Jesus Christ," O'Brien said, "I told you not to let this happen."

"Take it easy. There's no walkout. We're going to keep negotiating till we come up with something. The men will clock in tomorrow and there'll be a slowdown."

"What the hell kind of slowdown?"

"They'll work to rule till we hammer out a new proposal. If you let me give them Ground Hog Day, we should be able to vote tomorrow afternoon."

"Ground Hog Day makes us look like idiots."

"They need a concession, Jack. It's either that or pregnancy benefits for all dependents, including unmarried daughters."

"Give 'em Ground Hog Day. Call me the minute you have an agreement."

"It'll probably be the middle of the night."

"Call me."

When O'Brien came back to the dining room, Debbie was still at the table, staring into the candle flame. "Detroit," he said. "They're still negotiating."

She looked at him and got up and began clearing dishes. "There's cheese and fruit," she sighed.

"Can you think of any reason your wife would want to leave home?" the policeman asked. "Did you argue?"

"My wife and I are best of friends," Tate said. "We haven't argued for six years."

"Six years is a long time not to argue." His head half averted just beyond the perimeter of lamplight, the officer observed Tate obliquely. He was an elderly man, all sags and furrows, gawky and stooped in a coffee-colored summer-weight suit. He kep pushing his steel-rimmed spectacles back up his nose. "How did she act in the last few weeks; did you get the feeling anything was bothering her?"

"Not at all."

For a moment the corners of Janey's mouth, drawn taut in the cooled air, were the only thing that threatened to move in the stillness of the bedroom. A young policeman, doleful in plainclothes, leaned like a resentful toll taker in the bathroom doorway. The air conditioning was humming. Martta Savolainen, who was treating the whole thing as an impromptu if grim party, had set Janey's highball and a tray of crackers and dip on a table. Janey was ignoring the highball and no one was dipping crackers.

"Did your wife have any special friends that you know about?" the old policeman asked.

"You mean affairs?" Tate asked.

Shock seeped like a stain across Janey's face.

"I mean, is there anyone she might have gone away with?"

"I don't know."

"My sister never mentioned anyone to me," Janey said in a voice that was as righteous and clipped and unbidden as the slam of a door.

"Any money problems?" The policeman eyed the dressing table with its triple panel of mirrors and the jewelry boxes stacked slightly out of alignment. The police had searched the boxes. Though doubtless there was a pattern to the way Barbara embedded her treasures in their velvet matrices, Tate did not know it, and with his poor memory for baubles he had been able to discern nothing missing. The police had not mentioned robbery, and Tate did not think it was what they had in mind.

"No money problems," Tate said. "Absolutely not."

"Any problems with children?"

"Our only son died seven years ago."

The old policeman eyed him strangely. "That was when you stopped arguing, right?"

"Approximately."

"What about health: did she have any problems in that line?"

"What do health problems and lovers have to do with this?" Janey broke in. "Those lunatic mothers-for-life were picketing this house for three days, and my sister told me she was being followed."

The inspector gave her a look instead of an answer. "What about you, General: any feeling you're being followed?"

"No."

"Mack," the young policeman called from the bathroom. The old policeman excused himself and Janey shot Tate an exasperated grimace. A moment later the old policeman called Tate into the bathroom and asked if any of the four toothbrushes in the rack were his wife's.

"The yellow ones," Tate said. "One for morning, one for evening."

The old policeman swung open the door of the medicine cabinet. "What do you know about these?" He handed Tate a small brown plastic bottle that contained a dozen small white pills.

Janey had crowded into the doorway and Tate could see she didn't want to miss a thing.

"Tranquilizers," Tate said. "She takes them now and then to help her sleep."

"That's not what it says on the label," the inspector said. "Prednisone, thirty milligrams, one capsule twice daily."

"It's a controlled substance, I suppose. The doctor has to put something on the label."

"You ever heard of this stuff Prednisone?"

Tate watched the younger officer, curiously uninvolved in rituals of questioning, brush an inventory taker's glance along the cabinet shelves.

"All those tranquilizers have gimmicky names," Tate said.

"What about this Dr. Robertson Rigby—know him?"

"I've never met him. He's her internist."

"You're sure it's a tranquilizer?"

"My wife told me it's a mild tranquilizer. She wouldn't have any reason to lie."

The old policeman gave Tate a look that was more pitying than inquiring. "Are you still with the military, General?"

"Retired. I work for an aerospace outfit in Seattle."

"How's business?"

There was a slyness in the man, and Tate sensed he was being questioned not for answers but for involuntary slips. "Fair to middling."

The old policeman put the brown bottle back in its place next to the unwaxed dental floss. "You don't happen to know the license number of your wife's car?"

"I'm sure I could find it."

"That might help."

Tate asked the policeman to come with him to the morning room. Barbara stored her documents in a safe-deposit box but she was fond of saying you couldn't run to American Security and Trust every time you forgot your IBM stockholder ID number, and she kept Xerox copies in a brown folder in her desk. Janey trailed close behind and stood like a bank security guard watching Tate search the drawers.

He found a copy of the Mercedes registration tucked behind the Social Security card Barbara had had to get when she had done five weeks' paid work with Project Outreach. He handed the automobile registration to the old policeman, who copied the number into a little pocket notebook and said Tate had been very helpful. The policeman promised to be in touch just as soon as anything turned up and he said that in many of these cases there was no actual kidnapping involved.

After the policemen had gone Janey said, "I suppose there's some kind of difference between a kidnapping and an 'actual' kidnapping?"

"I don't suppose there's any difference at all," Tate said. "That's just the way policemen talk. It's meant to be reassuring."

They were in the living room and Janey had dropped into a chair. It matched the sofas and the other chairs with their bright print cloth that never wrinkled and never looked sat on. Tate was uncomfortable in the room and it was not simply because his sister-in-law was there. He had never been fond of the colonial red walls and the almost theatrical contrast of the tall, white-shuttered windows. He had never played chess at the Regency game table with its pierced panels and lacquered chairs. Barbara and her decorators had put the room together, impeccably and expensively, out of antiques gathered from all over the eastern seaboard, which was a little like putting your life together from the hopes and memories of other people. Tate did not feel it was his room.

Janey had an elbow on her knee and her chin was cupped in the palm of her hand and the position would have better suited a woman in slacks or riding breeches. She studied Tate with a grim, thoughtful look. "I don't think it's reassuring at all, and I think you're being awfully calm about all this."

"She's only been missing a few hours," Tate said, "and I'm not being calm about a damned thing."

"My nerves are shot. I'd like another drink."

"Help yourself. That's what it's there for."

Janey went to the bar and made herself a scotch with a token splash of water. She was obviously worrying very hard, and her high heels began methodically trampling the flower design in the carpet. "What do you intend to do?" she snapped.

"I'll do what the police suggested. Stay by the phone and keep out of their way. And you might consider doing the same."

She gave him a glance of irritated sobriety. "You don't really think those policemen are going to do a damned thing, do you?"

"I think they'll probably do something, yes. Why else would you have phoned them, Janey?"

"They seemed awfully calm to me." She lapped at her drink with tiny, dissatisfied sips. "I can't imagine anyone that calm accomplishing anything."

Tate saw they were on the brink of a discussion, and the last thing he could have borne at that moment was a discussion with his sister-in-law. He stood in the crook of the Steinway and saw that the music to Debussy's *Children's Corner Suite* lay on the music rack, open to "Golliwog's Cakewalk," and he wondered when in the world Barbara had had time to play Debussy.

"I don't suppose there's any point in our waiting by the phone together." Janey drained her scotch to the ice cubes.

"I don't suppose there's really much point," Tate agreed.

Janey's eyelids made a quick flicker and she said in that case she would go home and wait by her own phone. Tate walked her to the front door and promised to call the minute he heard anything. Janey had parked her purple Porsche not quite parallel to the curb. Instead of using the flatstone path she took a shortcut across the lawn, her heels raising welts in the grass. She did not bother to wave good night and Tate did not bother either.

As he went upstairs, Martta passed him coming down with

the tray of crackers and dip. The servant gave him a reproachful look and he said he was sure Mrs. Erlandsen would phone soon. He closed the bedroom door.

He stared at the Victorian sofa that Barbara had placed facing the fireplace. He had always intended to light a fire on one of their anniversaries and get them both a little high on champagne and make love to Barbara on that sofa.

Death, at least in Tate's mind, had some kind of unconscious link to sex. He had never known a friend or relative or even a President of the United States to die but that he had felt disloyally horny immediately afterwards, and he knew he wasn't really thinking about the sofa: he was trying not to think about Lee Armstrong.

He had never especially liked Lee Armstrong.

The man had been stiff and he had never laughed and toward the end he had definitely been a little crazy. But the fact was, Tate would never see that stiff, crazy soldier again, and all sorts of recollections flooded his mind unbidden and it seemed to him Lee Armstrong hadn't been half bad, all things considered: a little unimaginative perhaps and obviously not promotion material, but a hard-working little Pentagon colonel who had borne despair a lot more gracefully than many.

Tate's eyes burned and the stacked jewelry boxes on the dresser top disturbed him. On his way to the bathroom he made a mental note to put the boxes back in their drawers. He found the little brown plastic bottle in the medicine cabinet and took it back to Barbara's desk in the morning room. He got her bank statements out of the middle drawer and snapped the rubber band off the most recent. There were two canceled checks written that month to the order of Dr. Robertson Rigby. He looked through the preceding month's statement and the ones before that. His wife did not keep bank statements beyond the three years required by the Internal Revenue Service, but in that time she had paid Dr. Rigby just under eight thousand dollars.

Tate lifted the telephone receiver and asked information for the doctor's number.

After eight rings a woman answered. Tate said he wished to speak to Dr. Rigby and the woman explained that she was only the after-hours answering service. Tate gave her his name and number and said it was an emergency, would she please have the doctor call him back immediately.

A big man with a badge pinned to his shirt sat high in his chair and tried to wrestle three sheets of paper into a typewriter. His efforts did not appear to be helped by a transistor radio at his elbow blaring the latest bulletins.

Elmer Connally leaned across the hip-level partition and made his bid for the man's attention. "Excuse me, is the sheriff in?"

Eyes the color of concrete swung toward a half-open door and then back to Elmer. "What about?"

Elmer explained what about. The man dropped a piece of carbon paper. He rose clumsily, knocked on the door, and nodded Elmer through.

The sheriff stood at a window licking mayo from a ham and Swiss on rye off his fingers. "Yes, sir," he invited through a mouthful, and set the sandwich on the ledge. He had a full, sunburnt face, and a generous, well-fluoridated smile. "What's on your mind?"

"Sheriff, around 11:45 P.M. last Monday, would you happen to know if there were any deaths due to pacemaker failure in the northern half of the county?"

The smile went into instant eclipse. The sheriff crossed the room and shut the door. "Yes, I would happen to know. Now suppose you just tell me who you are, and why you're asking."

"He's not touching the accumulated figures. He's skimming off from the week-to-week figures." The boy lay stomach down on the rubber raft. A current kept him bobbing against the concrete shore. His arms were folded beneath his chin and he stared across them at the printout piled at poolside like a child peering at a fabulous toy castle. "If you took the trouble to compare, you'd see the weekly doesn't quite tally with the accumulated-to-date. But you'd probably think it was just the rounding off."

"And is it the rounding off?" Tim Boswell asked, nakedly and unashamedly ignorant in the face of younger knowledge.

"To an extent. He rounds the weekly salaries down. He rounds taxes and union dues up. He pockets the difference." With his undergraduate swimmer's body and his face haloed in beard, the boy looked as though the Vatican had lowered the age requirements for sainthood. "That way the full tax gets paid, and he's not stealing from the government."

"Nice of him."

"Nice for you too, Dad. Otherwise Pacific Aero could be stealing from Uncle Sam."

"How's he doing it?"

"He's adding instructions to the program. Probably he has some extra cards punched. He throws them in at the beginning of the run and takes them back at the end so no one finds out." The boy wedged a finger into a fold of the print-out and flipped it back. "Look here. Your original program has a rounding-off option. ROUND. Couldn't be simpler. Since you're dealing with dollars and cents, only the first two digits to the right of the decimal are significant. The rounding-off option says if the third digit to the right is less than five, forget it; if it's more than five, forget it and add one to the preceding digit." The boy craned up and forward on one elbow and moored himself to the aluminum ladder. He turned through folds till he found what he wanted. "Now look here. Your man rewrites the rounding-off option. He says if there are any fractional cents in the weekly gross salary, knock them off and credit them to United Fan Jet. With taxes and union dues, round the figure up and credit the difference to United Fan Jet. Now that could come to practically a nickel per paycheck."

"And the final instruction is to total United Fan Jet credits and print a check?"

"That's the next-to-last instruction. The final instruction is to forget all instructions from 120 on. Instant amnesia."

"So if we have twenty thousand take-home salaries then he's skimming off . . ."

"It could come to over a thousand a week."

"More than I take home." The sound of the television set flared up from the study as someone changed channels. Tim Boswell turned his glass in his hand and extracted a musical note with the tip of his finger.

"Dad, have you ever heard of this United Fan Jet?"

"Of course not."

It was a mild evening, alive with crickets. The floodlights in the rhododendrons, beginning to bloom in the gathering dark, threw a mantilla of shadow across the lawn. The pool water mimicked the half moon in fragments.

"Your auditors don't audit the weekly payroll, do they?"

"I'd assume they just audit the gross," Tim Boswell said.

"He doesn't monkey with the grosses, so they balance." The boy smiled. "All he has to do is get the cleared Fan Jet checks back from the bank or the accounting department and destroy them."

"And I send you to college to learn that."

"They have a seminar in it. Computer crime. Very popular. There's another in computer poetry. Not quite so popular."

Tate started out worried and by the time he located the Rigby home he was worried and exhausted. Worry and exhaustion took the edge off one another and he parked the car and walked to the Rigbys' door feeling numb. The Rigbys' was the only ranch-style house on the suburban street, brashly out of place among its half-timbered neighbors. He gave the bell two jabs. A minute passed before the door swung open. A woman stood staring at him, head tilted so that honey-blond hair drenched one shoulder.

"Yes?" she said.

Tate supposed that only the lady of the house would answer the door in a dress that made so little effort to hide her nipples. He smelled something, and it was more than Mrs. Rigby's perfume. Marijuana. The sixties had finally caught up with suburban Washington.

"I'd like to speak to Dr. Rigby," he said.

"Are you a patient?" She had the pronounced squint of someone who thought she was prettier without her glasses. "He never sees patients at home."

"I'm not a patient. Could you just tell him General Erlandsen is here?"

Her eyes gave him a quick scan, but her cool held up. She turned and vanished and reappeared almost instantly with a tall, suntanned man. He wore slacks and an open-necked raspberry-colored shirt and she was saying something bad-tempered to him. He made a gesture, half placating and half silencing, and came down the hallway toward Tate. "Hi," he said. His mustache followed the neat line of his smile. "Bob Rigby."

They shook hands.

"I didn't mean to bust in on your party," Tate said.

"No sweat." The doctor glanced toward the lit doorway and then across the hallway, where a door stood ajar on a darkened room. "Why don't we talk in the library?" He touched Tate's arm and led the way. Flicking on a brass table lamp, he swung the door shut. He gestured, allowing Tate the maroon leather easy chair.

"Would you mind telling me what these pills are?" Tate handed the doctor the little brown bottle.

Dr. Rigby dropped limberly onto the sofa and sat rubbing the back of his head. The muscle under his silk shirt sleeve was well developed. "Your wife is getting sixty milligrams of Prednisone a day—and she'll keep getting it for the rest of her life."

"She told me they were tranquilizers."

The doctor smiled. "Well, they're a corticosteroid. And they're working. Let's get one thing very straight, General. At this moment, she's a cheerful, functioning human being. She's no more under sentence of death than you or I."

Tate fought to keep his breathing even. "And just what kind of death sentence is that, Doctor?"

"Okay. It's called systemic lupus erythematosus. Informally known as lupus. It's an inflammation of the connective tissue. The fibrin—the protein that forms the fibrous network in the coagulation of blood—dies. The tissues or any organ in the body can alter. Which confuses diagnosis, to say the least. Thanks to antibodies in the blood serum, we can recognize the disease. Probably it's an auto-immune disorder—but we don't know for sure. The cause is unknown. It occurs chiefly in young women. But children get it and adults can get it." The doctor thrust a brown-eyed glance across the softly lit space that separated him from Tate. "It's a chronic, relapsing disease. It can flare up without warning and kill the patient in a matter of weeks. Or there can be periods of remission."

"Is she dying?"

"Not at the moment." The doctor bent sideways to open a cabinet beneath the bookshelves. He took out a tumbler and a half-empty bottle of Johnnie Walker Black. He poured a generous double shot. As he handed the glass to Tate a gold necklace barely thicker than a thread glinted in the open V of his chest hair. "I gather this is all news to you. Well, relatively speaking, she's lucky. The disease could have attacked the lungs, the spleen, the joints. It didn't. It did hit the kidneys, but that's par for the course. In practically every case of lupus you find kidney inflammation or lesions of the kidney tubes. In your wife's case, we're doing periodic needle biopsies, keeping track."

"I'd like the unvarnished truth, Doctor. What are her chances?"

The doctor studied him, as though evaluating his tolerance for unvarnished truths. "The bad news is, there's no cure. The good news is, we're in remission and have been for al-

most three years. There are cases on record of remission lasting as long as thirty years." The doctor sat back: not smiling,
not grim. Stoned, Tate suspected: almost certainly stoned.
"It's a crazy disease. No rules. Almost as hard to tag as syph.
It can look like a kidney problem or arthritis or rheumatic fever or any of the collagen disorders. It can hit the central
nervous system, and you get a psychotic or epileptic episode
at the outset."

"She was very depressed when our son died," Tate said.

"I know."

"She was hospitalized for depression."

The doctor gave a flick of a nod. "Diagnosis can be
damned tricky. You treat certain types of depression with
tranquilizers, and certain tranquilizers aren't good for the kidneys. But she's off tranquilizers now and her kidneys are doing pretty well."

"They said she was mentally ill."

"In your wife's case there was apparently a psychotic episode marking the onset."

"They said it was guilt. Four different psychiatrists said she
was angry at me and couldn't face it. Another said she was
angry at her father and couldn't face that."

The doctor opened his hands in a gesture that neither gave
nor took, confirmed nor denied. "I only know what she had
when I examined her, General."

"Are you telling me she wasted three years of her life in
that clinic?"

"General, some free advice. Don't flirt with guilt. You had
no way of knowing the truth, and no one can give her back
the years she spent behind barred windows. What we can give
her is the hope of a relatively normal life span. There are
four essentials. One: keep track. We're doing that. Two: keep
the kidneys going. We can do that too. Three: keep sensitiz-
ing agents to an absolute minimum. That's a big order. She's
got a gamut of verbotens from aspirin to sunshine."

Tate thought back. He had never been aware of Barbara's
avoiding aspirins. How stupidly unobservant he had been.

"Four, the point where you can be of real use: physical fatigue and emotional stress have absolutely got to be avoided.
That goes for everything from arguments to too many dinner
parties, and above all it goes for pregnancy." The doctor let
the silence italicize the prescription: and then he rose.

"I don't suppose there's much worry about pregnancy,"
Tate said.

"Considering her condition and age, I'd say there's a hell of a lot. I've told her she's a fool not to abort the fetus."

"Fetus?"

The doctor's hand, blunt and oddly clean, paused three inches from the doorknob with its recessed lock button. "She didn't tell you she's seven weeks gone?"

"She didn't tell me a damned thing."

The doctor shook his head. "If I were you, General, I'd use all my powers of persuasion to get her to change her mind."

Jack O'Brien heard the ring in his sleep and was able to revise his dreams to accommodate it, but there was no revision that could accommodate Debbie's saying, "Phil Marquis from Detroit," or the cold solidity of the receiver in his palm, or the voice crackling in his ear, "Jack, have you seen the early edition of the Detroit *News*?"

O'Brien felt he'd bumbled into the second half of someone else's dream. The fluorescent hands of the alarm clock clasped a pie-shaped segment of time between two and four. "No, I haven't seen it. What's happened?"

"A company spokesman is quoted as saying the stockholders and board of directors are quote absolutely outraged over the proposed pregnancy coverage. It's a quote license for immorality and quote cannot be tolerated."

O'Brien sat up straighter. "Who the hell could have said those things to a reporter?"

"Sounds like a member of the board. He says labor has quote dragged the nation down to the status of a third-rate power and now it's trying to quote scuttle our defenses. We're in a mess, Jack. The local took one look at that and they're calling a walkout. We were practically home free, that's the shame of it."

"Goddamn." O'Brien was silent a moment. "You'd better get some sleep, Phil." He leaned across his wife, groping in the dark for a cradle to lay the receiver down in. Her night cream smelled faintly of roses, and the press of her hip against his was as comfortingly familiar as the curve of the banister on the stairs.

"What did he want?" she asked.

"He says there's a blind item in the Detroit *News*. It upset the local and they're calling a walkout after all."

Debbie took his hand and gripped it, and they lay still and side by side, like figures on a stone casket in a cathedral.

Friday

Tate did not sleep. Since the police had not said he had to stay home, he went to work at his normal hour. If there did turn out to be kidnappers he thought it best that they find him calm and resolute and functioning. He gave Miss Monroe an envelope containing Lee Armstrong's purloined submarine orders and he asked her to put it in the safe. He did not feel calm or resolute but he managed to dictate several letters, and he supposed that was a form of functioning.

His sister-in-law kept phoning and he had to keep telling her there'd been no word from Barbara. He felt dizzy, like a man treading the edge of a precipice who had made the mistake of looking down, and it came almost as a relief when Miss Monroe told him he had a visitor, an Inspector Maclean from the District of Columbia police.

Tate did not recognize the name but he recognized the old policeman from the night before. He had come alone this time, and he carried a caved-in Stetson in one hand and a very inexactly folded Washington *Post* in the other. He passed a cheerful glance along the shelf of Eskimo sculpture and at the view of the FBI building and helped himself to a seat. "We've checked the jails, the police blotters, the hospitals, and the morgues. Negative. So we know she hasn't been arrested and chances are she's not sick or dead. Not yet. Unless she's using an assumed name. Or no name."

"I don't see what you mean by no name," Tate said politely.

"She and her purse might have got separated. She could be an unidentified corpse."

The idea made Tate sick to his stomach.

"If she doesn't show up in forty-eight hours, we'll look into that possibility. In the meantime we've checked hotels and airlines. Also negative." The inspector reached deep into the pocket of his rumpled jacket. He produced a small spiral-bound notebook, wilted from body heat, and turned to a page near the end. "We know a little about her movements yesterday. She left the house around ten in the morning, had a doc-

162

tor's appointment at noon. It was a half-hour appointment. She stopped at the Aquitaine pharmacy around one-thirty. At two-thirty she left her Mercedes at Henry's Repair Shop on Massachusetts Avenue for its tune-up. Nice car, Mercedes. I gather she gets it tuned up pretty regularly?"

"Twice a year," Tate said.

"She had a hairdresser's appointment at four-thirty. Monsieur Alvin." The rambling recitation and the sleepy, disheveled appearance could not disguise the face that the old man was observing Tate closely. "She was ten minutes late. Monsieur Alvin scolded her personally and trimmed and rinsed her hair. Trim and rinse cost thirty, she gave him a fifteen-dollar tip. She told him she was going to a reception at seven-thirty and she intended to wear an old dress as a form of protest."

"That was the Chilean Embassy," Tate said. Barbara had often said that she did not like the Chilean junta.

"She made one telephone call on Monsieur Alvin's personal phone. That was probably the call to your sister-in-law saying she thought she was being followed by a woman." The inspector looked up. "Now about this woman following her. Your sister-in-law thinks it might tie in with the women that were picketing your house. Mothers for Life."

"I frankly don't see why they'd follow my wife," Tate said. "Don't you think they'd more likely follow me?"

The inspector propped his notebook on his knee and began writing with an old-fashioned lead pencil. "Now your wife left Monsieur Alvin's around five-thirty. Where did she go?"

"No idea at all. She might have decided to stroll for ten minutes. It was a pleasant evening. She likes strolling. Before sunset."

"It's a great city for strolling," the inspector said, "before sunset. We've checked with the doctor and we've checked with the pharmacy. Those pills your wife takes are a controlled substance. She gets them in batches of sixty. She left a prescription with the druggist yesterday, but he was out of them. She hasn't had a refill in twenty-four days, and there are twelve pills in that bottle in your medicine chest. So she's traveling without spares."

Though the old man was presenting the visit as a sort of progress report, Tate sensed he was more interested in goading for reaction, feeling out Tate's role in all this.

"How many people know your wife's sick?"

"I didn't know myself till yesterday. Obviously she'd hoped to keep it secret."

"She was hospitalized for a nervous breakdown six years ago."

"Depression," Tate corrected. "And she did not have a relapse and go strolling off to commit suicide. That's an idiotic idea."

The inspector looked at him thoughtfully. "Then the question is why would anyone snatch your wife and not contact you for ransom?"

"You must know a good deal more about kidnappers than I do."

The old man glanced at him almost mischievously. "Ninety-nine point four per cent of the time they're after money. But in your wife's case, General, I wouldn't be surprised if they were after something else. I wouldn't be surprised if your phone rings and someone asks you a favor. Let's just hope it rings before your wife starts needing those pills."

At the instant the avocado-green telephone on Tate's desk gave a short, sharp ring.

Jack O'Brien arrived at his office forty-five minutes before the nine-thirty board meeting. Miss Kelly said that Elmer Connally had been waiting almost fifteen minutes to speak with him.

O'Brien hurried to his office and found Elmer Connally stooping to stare at a duck decoy on the lowest shelf.

"Beautiful work," Elmer said. "I don't suppose you could make a thing like that by machine." There was a bad knick on Elmer's chin, as though he had tried to shave in the washroom of a speeding bus, and his Dacron polyester suit looked as though he had spent two nights in it. O'Brien offered coffee and Elmer said no, thanks, Miss Kelly had already filled him up.

"Your wife's worried about you," O'Brien said. "Have you been home?"

Elmer said he would go home as soon as he briefed O'Brien. He said that the missile-base computers generated test-launch signals on a random basis. "The idea is to catch the crew unawares. Now in Silo 29, Dr. Provenson's team reprogrammed the computer so that the test launch would be triggered by a signal from the perimeter-acquisition radar. Dr. Provenson was with Air Force intelligence, and what the hell he was doing in that control center no one's been willing to tell me. He dropped dead just about the time the computer shut the launch down. Now a specialist first class told me while Provenson was in the silo they weren't allowed to use the radar cooking range. Those radar ovens are dangerous for anyone who's got a pacemaker in his heart. They interfere with the pacemaker's microwave signal. Which leads me to theorize that maybe Dr. Provenson had a pacemaker. Ergo no microwave cooking while he was on the premises."

An air-conditioned chill flowed through the room, insistent as a current in the ocean.

"The microwaves tie in with another little oddity. Not many people make long-distance calls at 11:46 at night, but the ones who do can be pretty desperate. The local phone company got eight complaints between 11:44 and 11:50 about interrupted calls. All eight were long-distance microwave relays."

Elmer paused, like a professor waiting for questions. There were none.

"This got me to thinking about general microwave disturbances in that area. Which got me to thinking about observatory radio telescopes, because they use microwave amplification. I checked with two observatories in an eighteen-mile radius. Both their telescopes were wiped out at the same time as the launch failure."

O'Brien still said nothing, but his head came around, like that of a cat tracking an infinitesimal, possibly hostile sound.

"So I checked with four police departments in the area; asked about deaths around 11:45 Monday night that might have been due to pacemaker breakdowns. Turns out they know of one farmer who died of heart failure just about then. His pacemaker stopped. There was a young housewife, an epileptic. They'd implanted a brain-wave setter to head off seizures. Her husband says she had a seizure at 11:45 or so. My guess is, some kind of microwave disturbance flooded the area and knocked out the microwave link between the Minuteman IV and the computer in Silo 29."

Elmer had come into the office carrying what seemed to be a sawed-off broomstick wrapped in brown paper. As he began removing the paper, it began looking like a furled four-by-three-foot map.

"This brings us to point two. If you look at the path of those disturbances, they lie in a straight corridor, about a half mile wide and thirty-six miles long."

Elmer rolled the map open on the desk top. O'Brien shoved aside letters and gift crystal and engraved silver, made generous room for it.

Elmer went on. "The computer was waiting for the radar to spot something in the sky. We can rule out a missile, obviously. But if you start looking at satellites, some interesting things turn up."

The office was very quiet. There was no movement. O'Brien's eyes scanned the map of South Dakota, enclosed in segments of six neighboring states.

"For instance, there are over 17,800 known—that means unclassified—man-made satellites orbiting the earth at this moment. Over half of those are American. The United States Bureau of Astrophysical Data keeps track of their orbits and movements, and the information is available to the public. Not freely available; you have to pay retrieval-time computer cost. For which I am billing Pacific Aero seventy-eight dollars."

"How the hell did you get into their computer?" O'Brien asked.

"The University of Washington, Seattle campus, has a shared-time program. They plugged me right in. What came out is downright fascinating. At 11:46 last Monday night there were two unclassified satellites in the air space of the missile field at Ellsworth. One was eighteen miles higher than the other. Give or take forty seconds of arc, they both passed almost directly over Siló 29. The lower satellite was Akula-3, excuse my Russian. A weather satellite. Which is to say, a spy satellite photographing optical spectrum and infrared radiation and radioing information back to terminals in the U.S.S.R. Obviously it uses some kind of microwave transmitter. But it wouldn't be transmitting over the United States, and even if by accident it did, the transmission would be damned feeble by the time the signal reached the ground. Certainly not enough to blow out pacemakers or computers.

"The higher satellite is a U.S. Navy job—Firebird 111. According to *Aerospace Weekly*, it's an experimental energy-relay satellite. It picks up solar energy and transmits it by microwave to a station in Arizona. So far it's done things like beam enough kilowatts to run a television set for an hour and a half; at least, that's all they're publishing about it."

Elmer laid a piece of tracing paper over part of the map. He aligned a mark on the paper with a town in Pennington County and another with a town in Meade. He had drawn a thick line between the marks. Names of towns showed through.

"This line is the projection of Akula-3's orbit at 11:46 P.M. last Monday. Aside from passing through Ellsworth Air Force Base itself, it doesn't touch a single area in the corridor of microwave disturbances. Not only that, it's at an angle of about seven degrees to the corridor."

Elmer moved the first piece of paper aside and laid a second in its place. On this one he had drawn a different line.

"Here's the projection of Firebird 111's orbit, 11:46 P.M. last Monday. Now do you notice anything?"

O'Brien frowned. "This one doesn't go through your microwave corridor either."

"Notice anything else?"

"It's to the left of the corridor."

"What else?"

"The orbit's almost parallel to the corridor."

"It's *exactly* parallel to the corridor."

O'Brien hesitated. "Do you suppose the Navy satellite was somehow leaking radiation?"

"How many leaks have you heard of that are focused and aimed? Firebird was locked in."

O'Brien's eyes squinted. "Locked in on what?"

"Look again at your microwave corridor. Notice anything about Silo 29?"

O'Brien looked again. "It's—exactly in the center."

"Right. The microwaves began ninety seconds before Silo 29, and they stopped ninety seconds after Silo 29. Make anything of that?"

O'Brien was thinking sadly of America, where nothing is impossible if there is someone who wants it badly enough. "It looks as though—as though they weren't taking chances."

Tate lifted the avocado-green receiver. "It's Mr. O'Brien," Miss Monroe said. "Urgent." Tate covered the mouthpiece and asked the inspector to excuse him a moment. The old man told him to take his time and O'Brien came on the line sounding jittery and far away.

"I've got a board meeting in five minutes, Tate, so I'll give this to you shorthand. The company's in trouble. Someone's picked up over 12 per cent of the stock. We're being flim-flammed."

Tate watched the inspector take off his wire-rimmed glasses and blow on the lenses.

"We've had a phony strike threat out here, labor troubles in Detroit, Silo 29 leaked to Dudley Mayhew—it's too much to be coincidence. We don't know exactly what's going on, but it could be someone in the Navy wants to discredit the land-based deterrent once and for all. They're going all out to sink the Air Force and they don't care who else gets drowned."

"That's quite a theory," Tate said neutrally.

"Elmer Connally's been down to Silo 29, nosing around. There was some kind of microwave disturbance in a thirty-six-mile corridor. Radio-relay phone calls were interrupted, telescopes wiped out, people with pacemakers dropped dead. Including that Air Force intelligence fellow in the control center—Provenson. Elmer has twenty pages of details. We think it was caused by a naval satellite, a thing called Firebird. Elmer got the orbit and the time and it checks out. What worries me is that it doesn't look at all like an accident. They were aiming at Silo 29 and they wanted to kill that launch."

An expectant silence came across the line. Ghost fragments of chatter on neighboring circuits crowded in, like air feeling out a vacuum.

"I want you to be prepared for the worst, Tate."

"Okay," Tate said, feeling he'd been sandbagged. "I'll be prepared." The connection went dead and he hung up.

The inspector's dark eyes met his calmly. "You had a son, General."

"Yes, I had a son."

"He was kidnapped seven years ago." It was difficult to tell whether this was a statement or question. Tate sensed that the old man was prospecting, using every scrap of dynamite he could to blast out the veins of secrecy and falsehood in him.

"That's right. My son was kidnapped by Communist guerrillas in Panama and it has nothing at all to do with my wife."

"You never can tell, General. The past is never a hundred per cent dead."

"My son *is* a hundred per cent dead, Inspector, and frankly, unless you have some reason for bringing it up, it's a painful subject."

"He died in an explosion in Dorchester. They were building bombs, weren't they?"

Tate did not deny it.

"Kids," the old man said in the tone of one parent pooling disgusts with another. "He *was* just a kid, wasn't he?"

"My son was an extraordinary young man."

"That's a shame, General. I sincerely mean that, and I respect you. For the way you handled it then and the way you're handling it now." The old man gathered up his newspaper and notebook and hat and gave Tate's hand a shake and said he would be in touch.

The call came an hour after the old man had gone.

Miss Monroe buzzed and said the Pentagon was on line seven. She wouldn't have said "Pentagon" if she had known who it was, and Tate didn't waste time asking. He picked up the receiver and gave his name.

"General Erlandsen, you're a very hard man to get hold of. Could you hang on just one moment, please?"

The connection went staticky and then with an ear-popping burst of clarity an Admiral Anne Gurney announced herself. "And how is the Congress treating you, General?"

"Leaving me alone for the moment, thanks."

"I'm sure you're managing to fill your time. General, could we see you today?"

Tate hesitated. "Sure."

"Could you come to the Pentagon, be at the Mall entrance, at five?"

"Could you give me some idea what this is all about?"

"It will be a fairly high-level discussion." Admiral Gurney had a voice of peach-blossom honey hand-filtered through a silken sieve. "The Chief of Naval Operations would like to speak to you personally."

"Concerning what?"

"You might say it's a family matter."

Tate felt an adrenal spurt and his heartbeat accelerated. "Admiral Gurney," he said, "have you got a pencil there?"

She said, "Just a minute," and then, "Go ahead."

"You may tell Admiral Wanamaker that he is to have my wife here at my office by two o'clock this afternoon. I don't mean two-thirty and I don't mean five after two. I mean two o'clock, fourteen hundred hours; I'd translate that into bells, Admiral, but I don't have my conversion table handy."

There was an instant of baffled hesitation. "Naturally I'll be glad to tell him," Admiral Gurney said, "but I really don't see the point."

"If she is not here, unharmed, I'll tell the police everything I know which as you realize is a great deal or you wouldn't be phoning. The District of Columbia police force may not have a third of the defense budget to work with but they have been known to catch a few cheap criminals in their time. Not that anything you do is cheap, Admiral."

"General, are you feeling all right?"

"You know goddamned well how I'm feeling, Admiral. Get her here by two."

Tate slammed the receiver back into its cradle. When the phone buzzed again, a half hour later, his heart was still thumping like a fist in his chest. It was not Admiral Gurney or anyone from the Pentagon calling, but his sister-in-law Janey, wondering if he had heard from Barbara yet.

By the time O'Brien got to the boardroom, all the other members had arrived and all but two croissants had vanished from the elegant little breakfast buffet. The chairman said, "Ah, there you are, Jack," and suggested the meeting be called to order. He received sixty thousand dollars a year for calling the meeting to order, and he did it very smoothly.

The corporate secretary read the minutes of the previous meeting. "Any additions or subtractions," the chairman asked, "before the minutes go into the corporate records?"

Cornelia Barnes Lonsdale, who had once been assistant secretary of the United States Treasury and ambassadress to Kenya but whose party was currently out of the White House, lit a very long cigarette.

"Tell us, Jack," the chairman said when the silence had gone far enough, "what about this labor situation? Have the men in Detroit really walked off the job or is that just a rumor?"

Beyond the walls of plate glass, shifting clouds toyed with the sun.

"It's a token walkout," O'Brien said. "The men are angry that negotiations are running into the weekend. We expect to have the whole matter wrapped up in a day or so."

"Can you give us an idea how the walkout and the settlement are apt to affect profits and costs?"

O'Brien took his glasses from his jacket pocket and sat cleaning them with a handkerchief, postponing the moment of answering. He was not about to volunteer that the walkout was costing upwards of eighty thousand a day, with spillovers that could go as high as another twenty. He took a swallow from his water glass and could not get rid of the feeling that a tranquilizer had lodged itself in his throat. "My controller has prepared a detailed projection on a per-unit basis. Why don't I just read you his conclusions, and if there are any questions we can dip back into specifics."

There were no objections at all till the last ten minutes of the board meeting, when Cornelia Barnes Lonsdale lit what was by O'Brien's count her fourteenth cigarette and loudly coughed.

"Mr. President," she said, "in view of all the company's troubles and the fact that it's your management that's led us into them—I fail to see any reason why the hell we should keep you on." She recited O'Brien's failures: racial flare-ups at the home plant; strikes in Detroit; pay settlements inflating labor costs 18 per cent above government guidelines; the Minuteman IV failure at Ellsworth; the almost certain loss of the Hornet contract after the company had gambled five hundred million on it; the calamitous drop of PA's stock on the New York Exchange.

"I explained that," O'Brien said. "We're facing a take-over bid."

"Well, if anyone's fool enough to want to take over Pacific Aero, I say God bless him, because he'll do a damned sight better job than you!" Mrs. Lonsdale lit her fifteenth cigarette and had two going at once. "I propose a motion terminating Mr. O'Brien's presidency at the earliest possible date."

Lieutenant General Robertson Chambers thrust a hand into the air. "I propose a motion tabling Mrs. Lonsdale's motion." Since his retirement from the service, General Chambers had carved out a second career as figurehead American eagle on the boards of various companies doing business with the government. He had never really left West Point, and when he had had a little to drink he was fond of saying he would vote against Navy on anything.

"You can't do that, General," Mrs. Lonsdale shot back.

"I hope this board realizes," the General said, "that if there were more men like Jack O'Brien, labor would never have been able to drag this nation down to the third-rate status we now occupy."

"We're still ahead of Russia and China," Mrs. Lonsdale said.

"And the only reason for that is men like Jack O'Brien. I am absolutely outraged and this board should be outraged at the demands of the Detroit local." It came to O'Brien that Lieutenant General Chambers might have gotten drunk at a party and allowed some Detroit *News* reporter to goad him into that unattributed salvo. "I say there's hope for America so long as we have men like Jack O'Brien who aren't afraid to take a stand against licensed immorality."

"The only thing I've seen Jack O'Brien take a stand against," Mrs. Lonsdale said, "is the well-being of this company."

The chairman rapped his gavel. "Will the meeting please return to order."

A black hand touched the air, and Harold Santa asked to be recognized. "Mr. Chairman, we already had a motion pending before Mrs. Lonsdale's. Mr. O'Brien has asked whether the board will entertain the issuance of five hundred thousand shares of common stock."

"Absolutely criminal," Mrs. Lonsdale twisted out her cigarette in her neighbor's ashtray.

"The board will note on the president's proposal." The chairman turned to the man on his left. "Mr. Donahue?"

Donahue, a pipe-smoking two-time Nobel runner-up in economics, shook his head. "We haven't seen the breakdown for this quarter and I think this proposal is sheer fiscal irresponsibility. I vote no."

"Mr. Santa?" the chairman asked.

Harold Santa, the only black in his law firm or on the board of PA and a very well-paid man, said he had all possible faith in management. "I vote yes."

"Mr. Wilkinson?"

James Wilkinson's forebears had come to America on the *Mayflower*. Their beachheads in banking, slave trading, and insurance had been wiped out decades ago, and this fourteenth generation of the Pilgrim fathers earned his livelihood renting his name to corporations new enough to feel they needed his sort of roots and big enough to meet his sort of price. "I vote nay."

"Mrs. Lonsdale?"

"Absolutely opposed. Nay, nay, nay!"

"Mr. Biddle?"

Angus Biddle was a president of a Wyoming university. He got five thousand dollars four times a year for lending humane window dressing to the board's decisions, but he had never impressed O'Brien as understanding a damned thing about Pacific Aero. "I see no way to sanction such a move. I vote nay."

"Mr. Butterfield?"

So far as O'Brien had been able to piece together, Raymond Butterfield's background was in engineering. He served on the board of a multinational construction company that had been putting up refineries in the Soviet Union. He was very much the same sort as Allan Martino: young, manicured and tanned, with an innate sort of sleaziness that no amount of good tailoring could cover. His company owned 2 and a half per cent of PA and it had been impossible to keep him off the board.

"Opposed," Butterfield said quietly.

"Jack, you're in favor of course."

O'Brien nodded.

"General?"

Lieutenant General Robertson Chambers gave a snap of a nod.

"Mr. Martino?"

Allan Martino glanced at O'Brien. It was reasonable to suppose his company would be opposed to any dilution of the ownership they had picked up. "Opposed."

"Mrs. Meredith?"

"Jack's pulled us out of some tight squeezes before. I'll go along with him. In favor."

"Mr. Culligan?"

Melvin Culligan gave O'Brien a long and disappointed look. "Floating further shares can only weaken what little control management possesses. I think many of our stockholders who held on to their stock because of their faith in the company will feel betrayed in having their equity undercut in this manner. I realize the bylaws provide for it, but I'm not sure it's at all right. With grave reservations, I'll vote with Jack."

"I vote in favor," the chairman stated.

The corporate secretary counted the X's and checks on her pad. "We have a tie, Mr. Chairman. Six in favor, six opposed."

"In that case the chair casts its second vote in favor of the motion."

"Seven in favor," the secretary tallied, "six opposed."

"The motion is carried." The chairman touched his gavel to the tabletop.

"I see Mr. O'Brien has a hard-core cabal of loyalists supporting him." Mrs. Lonsdale stabbed out yet another cigarette in another ashtray. "It would be futile to vote on my proposal. I withdraw it."

The chairman turned to the General. "Do you care to withdraw your motion, General?"

"Absolutely not."

"I believe the issue is moot," Mr. Biddle said.

The chairman consulted his wristwatch. "Which brings us to exactly one o'clock. Do I hear a motion to adjourn?"

"Tate," the man from State Department Munitions Control said, "this had better be off the record." He nodded toward the steward, who was preparing to serve them coffee.

"Why don't you just leave the coffee, Charlie?" Tate said.

"Certainly, General Erlandsen." The steward brought cups and a pewter pot of rich-smelling coffee. He shut the door quietly, and Tate and the man from State were alone in the private dining room of Tate's club. Lunch had gone on a long time and it had started late, at two-thirty—the only hour the man from State had said he could arrange. It wouldn't have surprised Tate if in fact the man from State had had two lunches today. He had scarcely touched his brook trout. Neither had Tate.

"The Secretary wants to declassify the B-92 sale to Switzerland," the man from State said.

Tate poured coffee for them both. He had waited at the office till two-fifteen. Barbara had never showed up. "What's the Secretary trying to do?" Tate said. "Kill the deal?" He had not made good on his threat to call the police. He had no proof, only an instinct.

"He wants a little open debate in Congress." Foreign sales amounted to a sixth of American aerospace-defense gross and up to half its profits. Congress had appointed itself watchdog of the peace and had wrenched from the Pentagon the right to examine and veto all deals over twenty-five million.

"He's never done anything openly before," Tate said. "Why start now?"

The man from State said that if the U.S. knocked Britain and Belgium out of the Swiss market, their balance of payments would hurt. And that would hurt NATO. "Britain and Belgium have said that would hurt NATO very much."

"You know damned well if he declassifies, Congress will scream 'merchants of death' and kill the deal. Those planes carry smart bombs and they can take nuclear cruise missiles."

"Well," the man from State conceded, "PA may have to postpone the sale."

"Postpone it, hell. France will step in and we'll lose it."

"Those are the risks." The man from State bit down on a huge forkful of lime chiffon pie. "Now for the good news. The Secretary's not going to let Congress block the Hornet sale to Iran. He wants the Shah to have those planes, and he's got the SecDef to agree to stretch the Navy's delivery schedule. The Shah will be getting equal priority with the Navy during the production run."

"So far," Tate said, "Navy hasn't got a delivery schedule to stretch."

"Navy will have a delivery schedule, don't you worry."

"The Secretary of State may have a lot of things in his pocket, but Congress isn't one of them. We can classify all the deals we want, and Congress still holds the twenty-five-million-dollar trump."

"We're breaking the sale down into lots."

The man from State began describing the breakdown and Tate was thinking that his wife had vanished and an assistant to the CNO had said *family matter.* Didn't that mean something? He wondered why he clung so to the idea that his wife had not vanished voluntarily.

"Iran will get twenty-five million worth," the man from State was saying, "Chile will get twenty-five, Panama will get twenty-five, so will Lebanon, Argentina, Venezuela. They'll resell to Iran. Liberia will resell to Jordan. That way we get around the Israel lobby, and everybody's happy."

"That kind of Mickey Mousing is fine with tanks and bazookas," Tate said, "but twenty-five million will buy you just about one-point-five Hornets."

"So? You'll jiggle the prices. Hell, it's only paper. The hardware goes straight to the Persian Gulf."

"In other words you don't care if the Shah has his fighter planes before the Navy? You don't care if Jordan has them before Israel?"

"We only have one small concern, and that's the commissions."

The Department of Defense collected a 2 per cent commission for putting together foreign arm deals. Since the DOD was the sole agent in the field, the commission amounted to a healthy flow of cash independent of congressional purse strings. "We can pay the 2 per cent," Tate said. "No problem."

"The kickbacks, Tate. Lebanon takes 10 per cent. God only knows what Panama's going to want."

The setup sounded messy to Tate and it sounded typical of

the Secretary of State's increasingly Byzantine secret agreements. It was also the type of governmental end run around the law that was apt to prod an election-year Congress into a witch-hunt. Tate's instinct told him that if State needed the deal badly enough, they'd put it together without PA's help.

"I'll talk it over with management," Tate said.

The man from State was silent, and his silence scalded.

Tate realized he had broken a rule. He had been brooding about Barbara and for a moment she had seemed far more real than missiles and aircraft and he had forgotten that you never say *no* to State, you say *I'll try*.

"Times are changing," the man from State said. "The market's changing. I should think PA would want to keep abreast."

Tate realized he had missed the whole cue. The man from State was dangling a deal. If PA helped State cement their secret diplomacy with the Arabs, State would help PA secure an inside track in the defense market of the coming decade. An inside track at this point could mean the difference between drowning slow and drowning fast. The man from State had even gilded the offer with that remark about *changing markets*. It was an open secret that the Administration wanted to shift atomic energy to the private sector. One consequence of the move would be to free a select handful of American corporations to leak nuclear technology to highest bidders the world over—at no small benefit to the balance of payments. State was hinting that PA could be among the chosen few.

But State was notoriously generous with hints. The bait smelled fraudulent and Tate was thinking about the inspector, wondering if the old man had tapped Tate's phones and started a mail surveillance and sent out plainclothesmen to inquire as discreetly as police could into infidelity, drink, money, all the easy and obvious reasons for a woman's suddenly vanishing.

"Sounds interesting," Tate told the man from State. "I'll have to talk to the home office and get back to you."

The eyes of the man from State were suddenly hurt, rebuffed. He asked about PA's labor problems in Detroit and he nodded through the answers. He made a remark about the weather and finished his coffee in a gulp and looked at his watch and said he had to run. He left half his lime chiffon pie on the plate.

Tate walked him down to the street. The good-by was

cordial, but they didn't fix a next meeting. Tate wondered if he had miscalculated and handed Lockheed a three-billion-dollar contract.

He walked to the garage where he had parked the Bentley and he gave his ticket to the manager. The manager said just a minute, have to phone upstairs. Tate waited at the foot of the concrete ramp. Someone was using some kind of machine in back and the noise blotted out any attempt at thinking.

Tate used the garage whenever he used the club. He was a good tipper and he knew most of the day shift by face. But he did not know the face of the attendant who brought the Bentley down the ramp.

The attendant got out of the car smiling, holding the ignition key, blond and gawky and not much older than a boy. He stretched out his hand. Tate moved to meet him, and as he reached to accept the key it occurred to him: *Why didn't the kid just leave the key in the ignition?*

The space between him and the boy was suddenly hard and rigid and he realized the car was three yards up the ramp, halfway around a curve, invisible from the street. The air smelled of hot motor oil and the machine in back kept throbbing.

Tate reached for the key. The boy's hand clamped shut on his. Tate tried to yank loose, but the kid was strong.

A man stepped out from behind the Bentley. He was nattily dressed in Treasury agent black, and he came at Tate hunched and grinning.

"General Erlandsen? We wanted to make sure you didn't forget your appointment." The man glanced at the kid. "That's okay, Jim."

The boy released Tate's hand.

"If you mean Ilya Wanamaker," Tate said, "the answer's no."

The man's arm shot out and slammed Tate into the Bentley. There was a solid thump of good British construction and nerve endings screamed along Tate's spine.

The boy opened the door of the back seat and the man shoved Tate in. The boy slid into the seat beside him and took out a penknife. The knife looked like regulation Cub Scout issue, but then again so did the boy. He flicked open a three-inch blade and reached a hand over to unzip Tate's fly.

The man in black got into the front seat and the Bentley began moving down the ramp.

"My brother was a marine," the boy said. "He was killed in Cambodia. What did you do in Cambodia, General?"

The car eased into traffic. The boy pressed the tip of the knife to Tate's stomach, just above the penis. Tate did not make a movement or sound. There was no real pain, only a sting like an insect's bite, and a pinprick of red on the tailored undershorts.

The boy kept his knife out for the entire drive to the Mall Entrance parking lot, but he did not cut Tate again. The man in black opened the back door and helped Tate walk. He dropped the car keys into Tate's pocket.

None of the people scurrying down the Pentagon steps even threw a curious glance. The man in black steered Tate into the building and the security guard nodded and let them pass. A woman was waiting for them.

"General Erlandsen? Anne Gurney." Her smile was all cheekbone and the nameplate on her navy-blue bosom reminded you she was an admiral. "We'll be meeting with Admiral Wanamaker in the National Command Authority." She offered a gleamingly clean hand; her voice had a crisp finishing-school bounce.

"Have you seen the NCA lately?" In the nicest possible way Admiral Gurney pulled Tate along with her. "They've put in new chairs."

The evening exodus was on: all escalators were running downhill, and the stream of employees had accelerated to a churning rapids. The man in black had fallen several yards behind them, and after three turns of corridor Tate could not see him at all. Which didn't mean that a dozen men in black weren't back there somewhere.

Tate followed Admiral Gurney through twisting air locks of corridors and through two sets of heavily guarded doors, oaken and thick-paneled, plastered with warnings to unauthorized persons to keep out. An Army lieutenant was waiting for them at the National Command Authority. He gave Tate a coolly frisking glance and the Admiral handled introductions.

The windowless chamber was blanketed in a white noise of televisions, teletypes, and typewriters. Voices spoke in a library hush. Phones outnumbered humans two to one and kept ringing with burglar-alarm unpredictability, each color phone with its own distinct jangle. There were no women on duty, and almost half the men wore Army uniforms.

The lieutenant escorted Tate and Admiral Gurney past four teletypes clattering wire-service printouts. Through an open door Tate could see a fifth teletype clattering nothing. A young man with horn-rimmed glasses, obviously one of the presidential translators who were on duty around the clock, sat by the machine reading a paperback thriller.

"That's the hot line," Admiral Gurney whispered. "Most people think it's a telephone to the White House, but it's a teletype right here in the Pentagon."

Tate had never stepped into the NCA without having the hot line explained to him. Once he had been permitted to watch it bang out a Cyrillic essay on the dietary habits of the Russian sable. He knew that *line* was a partial misnomer, that in addition to the two commercially leased trans-Atlantic, trans-Scandinavian cables, there were two high-frequency radio satellite links.

The lieutenant led them to a doorway and stood aside. Tate had last been in the soundproof room three years ago. The drapes were closed, covering the front wall with its three projection screens. That meant no films, maps, or photos.

They called it the Joint Chiefs of Staff Emergency Conference Room, though its uses were far more routine than its name. Public tours through the Pentagon had been discontinued since a bomb had gone off in a powder room in 1973, but special visitors and journalists were still given a demonstration of the room's flashing real-time gadgetry, and at eight-thirty every morning it was the scene of operations and intelligence briefings for the Joint Chiefs. Two movable lecterns, apparently leftovers from the morning's session, stood idle and empty by the gold drapes.

Sixteen blue chairs were spaced around the oval conference table. The blue looked regal and brand-new. Two of the chairs were occupied.

"Hello, Tate. Thanks for coming." Ilya Wanamaker rose from his seat, hand outstretched. He nodded toward the other man at the table. "Dr. Bailey, General Erlandsen."

Tate said nothing.

The lights had been turned low, suggesting a theater just before curtain rise. Grunting something that sounded like *hello*, Dr. Bailey rose partway from his seat. Behind the black gash of ear-to-ear glasses, Tate glimpsed a face that seemed a single iodine-stained scar.

"Sorry to drag you all the way out here," Wanamaker said. "We thought a little privacy might be in order."

On the wall, a security warning panel flashed eight green rectangles around a central core of red. Among the greens were rectangles marked *record*, which meant no one was recording; *micro* and *TV*—the four microphones on the maplewood table and the five cameras slung from ceiling beams were dead; *curtains*—Tate could see for himself that the curtains were shut. As the lieutenant closed the door, the single red rectangle, *door*, turned green. All rectangles green meant no one was in the projection room, no one was in the glassed-in communications booth, there were no taps on phones, no phones off hooks. In theory, they were as alone and cut off in that room as technology could contrive for four people to be.

Admiral Gurney dropped into a chair. Tate took the seat between her and the Chief of Naval Operations.

"You saw a great deal of Colonel Armstrong this week," Wanamaker said.

Tate realized he could be brave and keep his mouth shut or he could be sly and tell them what they already knew. "My wife and I had the Armstrongs to dinner Tuesday," he said.

"Why did you do that?" Wanamaker asked.

"We were friends, Admiral. We've been friends since our days in the Canal Zone."

"And you saw him Wednesday morning."

"We had to map out a strategy for the Joint Economic Committee hearing."

"Were you mapping out strategy in the meditation room?"

To the right of the security warning panel, four display panels reminded Tate of scoreboards in football stadiums, ready to click out a message or a figure at the tick of an electronic impulse. They displayed row upon row of nothing. Time-lapse clocks clustered further to the right, all hands pointing to twelve hundred hours. Another display board, with initials of the National Emergency Command posts running down the left of the gaps, was blank. It was a room waiting for something to happen, a room where time could not start without an emergency to kick it off.

"He went to your home Wednesday," Wanamaker said. "You met him at the 48 Club yesterday."

"That's true," Tate said.

"When Colonel Armstrong was found dead, he was carrying tapes of conversations between you and Dr. Leon Asher, and you and Andrew Corcoran. How do you explain that?"

"He stole one from me and I gave him the other."

"Why?"

"Colonel Armstrong was worried about Firebird."

Wanamaker's eyes—staring without apology from beneath thick black eyebrows—seemed to be taking Tate's measure, and they gave the impression of being accurate to the millimeter. "How much do you know, Tate?"

"I know Firebird can function as a jammer. It can hit the radio link between missile and computer and abort the launch."

Wanamaker and Gurney exchanged glances.

"You tested it last Monday night at Ellsworth Air Force Base," Tate said. "You timed the test to coincide with a little demonstration that Dr. Bailey here worked out for the Air Force. Dr. Bailey must be a pretty busy moonlighter, helping the Air Force trip up the Russians and helping the Navy trip up the Air Force." Tate stared straight at Bailey and saw not even the shadow of a blink behind the onyx opacity of the dark glasses. "The test succeeded, give or take a couple of snags. The microwaves can't discriminate. They knock out missiles and pacemakers and telephones and brain-wave setters and telescopes and anything else that happens to be operating in the wave-length. But I suppose you'll iron out the kinks."

Soundlessly, Admiral Gurney opened a manila folder and one at a time handed Tate five sheets of fresh Xerox. He recognized what must have been a third-generation copy of Asher's diagrams. "These were also found on Colonel Armstrong," she said. "What do you know about them?"

"They're Leon Asher's plans for a satellite-based missile killer. He offered them to the Pentagon twelve years ago and got turned down. About three years ago one of your whiz kids decided to plagiarize the idea."

"What about these?" Admiral Gurney showed Tate two more Xeroxes. Smudges suggested they had been taken from flimsies, carbon backups of orders coded and radioed to the U.S.S. *Intrepid*. Glancing at the precoded plaintext, Tate saw that one was the standby order to proceed to the Barents Sea to test the new sonar; the other was the order dated last Sunday, activating the first. "Why did Colonel Armstrong have copies of these orders on him?" she asked.

"He had a crazy idea that someone had a crazy idea of provoking the Russians into a test situation. He thought these

might be a signal to proceed to the Barents Sea and fire a nuclear warhead at Moscow."

Wanmaker's eyebrows bunched together in a dark, pained
knot. "But no one in his right mind could believe the
President would give an order like that."

"Come on, Admiral," Tate said. "That line about only the
President pushing the button is pure publicity and you know
it. Hell, the first time BMEWS was broken in, the moon activated the radar warning system, and we were within eight
minutes of throwing an all-out pre-emptive attack on Russia—without the President's even being *consulted*. Now if the
moon can order a nuclear attack, and come that close to suc-
ceeding, I submit it wouldn't be too hard for the right man in
the right place to pull the same thing off."

The Chief of Naval Operations stretched out his legs and
crossed one gleaming black shoe over the other; as he listened, his high, sunburnt forehead made intelligent, troubled
wrinkles.

"Anyone," Tate said, *"anyone* with the right codes and
with radio access to that sub can give the order to hit Moscow. The man who turns the key to launch the warhead is
completely in the dark. He only knows one thing: the code's
right. But does he know whether or not it's a valid command?
Does he know if there's been foreign penetration of the command system? Or domestic penetration? He doesn't know and
he's not expected to. Under the systems we've got now, there's
no time for certainty. There's not even time for a declaration
of war. He turns that key and he doesn't ask questions. He's
a soldier, Admiral, just like you or me."

Wanamaker shut his eyes and shook his head as though the
whole discussion had taken a predictable but terribly painful
turn. "You've got it all wrong, Tate. It won't be a nuclear attack. We don't want to kill people. That's the whole point.
We want to *save* lives."

"Murder is a funny way to save lives."

"What do you mean," Wanamaker asked, "murder?"

"What the hell do you think I mean?"

Admiral Gurney looked concerned and a little sad. "If we
were killing people because they knew of these documents,
that would include Mrs. Asher and everyone Leon Asher ever
showed his plans to, and obviously it would include you."

"I don't see why. Asher's plans went into the unsolicited
super-weapon slush pile over ten years ago. No one in the
business has that long a memory, not for rejects. Your biggest

worry is renegade Pentagon insiders and physicists you don't own."

"We're not criminals." Tate detected a hurt in Wanamaker's voice. "We've bent one or two domestic laws, granted. But no more so than in any run-of-the-mill military intelligence operation."

The silence stretched so long as to be an admission.

"Tate, we're not killing people. We can't kill people. We don't *want* to kill people. No one knew about Provenson's pacemaker till he died. He'd kept it a complete secret. Asher so far as I know died of natural causes. Isn't that so, Dr. Bailey?"

Bailey nodded.

"As for Colonel Armstrong, the police say he was drunk and ran his car off the road."

"And you just happened to be passing by and picked up all the papers in his briefcase?"

Wanamaker tapped fresh tobacco into his pipe. "A state policeman opened the briefcase and saw the submarine orders. He contacted Naval Intelligence." Something in the CNO's eyes pleaded for understanding, as though Tate had him at moral gunpoint. "Look, Tate. Even if we had our hand in aspects of this—and we don't—extraordinary situations call for extraordinary measures. You of all people know that."

"I used to think I knew it."

"This country's at war. Call it what you will: cold war, détente, international economic collapse—call it peace, if you want. It's still war, and you can't fight a war democratically. You can't go to the Congress or the President or the press or the people and put your strategy to the vote. Democracy is a noble goal, but it's a poor weapon."

Why, Tate wondered, did the world have to be full of crusaders? Why not gardeners or carpenters? His eyes drifted wearily to the three missile warning panels at the rear of the room: the 440-L across-the-horizon system, looking at the Asian land mass of the U.S.S.R. and the People's Republic of China; BMEWS, the ballistic missile early warning system, looking north from Alaska, England, and Greenland toward the U.S.S.R.; and the submarine-launched missile warning system, with four radars scanning the Atlantic, one the Gulf of Mexico, and three the Pacific. Colored lights reported the readiness/functioning of each radar. Four were red, which meant "off line"—under repair; one was yellow, partly operational; and the rest were green, functioning.

"Colonel Armstrong had no grasp of what we were planning." Wanamaker's shoulders came forward and braid glinted like gilded rattlers. "He was way off, Tate: way off. We have a team, a strategy, and a technology. And they're all rock solid. In the coming week, you'll see how solid."

"When you blow up Moscow and launch World War III?"

"No one's blowing up anything. The missile won't be armed. It hasn't got a warhead." Wanamaker sat back to let the point sink in. He looked very satisfied, like a commander who had made up his mind, who was going to get this thing done and get it done right.

Ilya Wanamaker was famous for getting things done and done right. Tate knew his track record and it was littered with achievement. Wanamaker was a McNamara without an F-111, a Kennedy without a Bay of Pigs. It took a Vietnam or a Dallas to stop a man like that, and Ilya Wanamaker had a knack for steering clear of lost causes and ambushes. Within six years of taking his commission, he had risen to command his own attack cruiser. In a peacetime era when naval skirmishes were scarcer than czars' teeth, Tate had marveled at Wanamaker's ability to bring home the victories: the man had broken blockades, imposed blockades, rescued Americans, shelled rebels, faced down Russians, gotten himself hated in Lebanon, Greece, Guatemala, and Indonesia, and made himself adored at home. At forty-eight he had been one of the youngest admirals ever appointed CNO. His critics said he ran the Navy like a goddamned football team. He had forced racial integration on the service from top to bottom, backed pay hikes, scrapped half the fleet, advocated nuclear fuel 100 per cent, and swung every dollar he could into the submarine-launched deterrent. He had lambasted what he called the Navy's pay-and-sink procurement policy and had instituted the float-first, pay-later policy that had forced three shipbuilders into receivership and made billionaires out of two others. He was anathema to the oil companies, three shipbuilders, and a lot of old-school officers, and he was the second coming to the rest of the Navy, the Atomic Energy Commission, and the public. He was a tough man to stop once he'd decided to get a thing done.

"ABMs are clustered in a single field," Wanamaker explained. "They're short-range. They're small and they can be fired individually. With one Theta, we can cope with ABMs.

We can provoke the Russians into attempting an ABM response and show them they can't do it."

"And what the hell good is that going to do?"

"It's the old Hiroshima trick. Show them one and they'll believe you've got a thousand. Except at this Hiroshima no one gets killed."

"But a lot of people are going to get killed, Admiral. There's no way the Russians are going to know that missile isn't armed. As far as they're concerned, it's nuclear attack. They're going to react: and you haven't got the Thetas to stop them."

Wanamaker shook his head angrily. "We're at war, Tate. War's a gamble, the same as life. A nation that hasn't got the guts to gamble is a nation on the way down. We've got a lead, we're using it."

"Jesus Christ," Tate said, "am I understanding you? You've built Asher's Theta device. You've launched it. You've tested it. Sometime next week its orbit takes it within range of the Moscow ABM. You're going to launch an unarmed missile at Moscow from a sub in the Barents Sea. The Russians won't be able to shoot it down because Theta will have knocked out their ABM. The missile will impact harmlessly and the Russians will realize we've got a missile killer that checkmates the whole Soviet deterrent. And then they'll *surrender?*"

"You don't understand the Russians, Tate." Ilya Wanamaker smiled. "I do. My mother was a White Russian—still is. And I know that what worked at Hiroshima will work twice as well in Moscow."

"If you're so damned confident, why not let the President call the shots?"

"Because he's a coward. He'd scrap Theta if he knew it existed; or share it with the Russians. He's convinced himself and half the Congress that the Russians are our friends. He thinks he's forged an invincible détente."

"For God's sake, Ilya. You're a chief of staff. You're a military man. You took an oath to obey your commander in chief."

"I'm serving my commander in chief," Wanamaker said.

"You can't believe that. This weapon is illegal. It's forbidden by treaty. You had no right even to build the damned thing."

"The President never wanted those SALT treaties," Wanamaker said. "The liberal press forced him into them. Détente has been a one-way street: we're giving up everything to the Russians. The tide has been shifting in favor of them for over two decades. Well, for the first time since the A-bomb, we've got the weapon to impose a Pax Americana. In one move, we undercut every advance in thermonuclear technology and delivery of the last thirty-five years. And when the world sees that Theta works, no one's going to quarrel with success. Not the President, not the liberal media, and certainly not the Soviet Union."

"Ilya, it's mutiny."

"I'm putting the United States back in the driver's seat," Wanamaker said. "And once we're there I'll hand the reins to the President. You call that mutiny?"

"And what if the President doesn't want the reins?"

"He'll take them. After Yalta and Suez and Cuba and Vietnam and Angola and all the other humiliations we've suffered at the hands of the Communists, there's no way the people of this nation will give up a victory that falls into their laps without a single shot being fired."

"There'll be shots fired," Tate said. "I can promise you that, Ilya." His eye traveled along the control booth. From that little glass chamber ran the communications links to the alternate, survivable command center buried beneath a mountain on the Maryland-Pennsylvania border, ninety miles north of Washington. The glass was dark, the booth empty. There was no emergency, not yet.

"There'll be no trouble," Wanamaker said, "so long as outside of this room you keep Theta and these documents and Colonel Armstrong's theories to yourself."

Outside of this room? Tate wondered. Ilya Wanamaker was not the sort of commander who would ask when he could coerce. He could keep Tate prisoner or kill him, yet it sounded as though he was going to throw away his one trump, physical possession of the enemy.

It took Tate a moment's bafflement to realize that he held a higher trump, a date with the Lasting Committee next Monday at 2 P.M. Faced with the choice of Theta or Hornet, Wanamaker was choosing both. *Greedy Ilya*, Tate thought, *and God bless you, Senator Lasting.*

"Why should I keep anything to myself?" Tate said. "Why should I help you?"

Admiral Gurney dealt eight plastic charge cards onto the table; a driver's license; a Georgetown library card; a Smithsonian Institution membership pass. They were all Barbara's.

Wanamaker's eyes held Tate's. "She might never walk again. Or talk or taste food. Or breathe. It's up to you."

Tate thought he had prepared himself, but he felt a twist in his stomach. "And how do I know you haven't already killed her?"

A cloud of thoughtfulness darkened Wanamaker's face. "How would you like to field that question, Dr. Bailey?"

At each place at the table there was a command conference telephone, with the blue DOD insignia set into the dial. Bailey leaned forward to lift his receiver. "Put the call through," he instructed. His voice was surprisingly young.

In a time-sensitive situation, when security was of purely academic concern, conference calls to the other command posts could be placed in as little time as seventeen seconds. This call was taking well over thirty seconds to place, which made Tate certain it was going by secure channels.

"We don't want to hurt her," Wanamaker said, exhaling pipe smoke. "We'd be very sorry to have to do that."

Barbara did not move at the sound of the door slamming open.

"Have you eaten at all?" The nurse shook her by the shoulder.

"I don't remember."

A look of concern that was not at all gentle crossed the nurse's face. "There's a phone call for you. Come on."

Barbara rose. Her paper slippers whispered on the linoleum. Slumped, dead-eyed women filled the chairs lining the corridor. The nurse nudged her through a door marked *Private—Hospital Personnel Only*. She pointed to a telephone receiver lying off its hook on the steel desk top. Barbara snatched it up.

"Hello?"

The nurse took a sentry's position at the door of the cramped office.

A voice on the phone said, "Hello, do you hear me?"

Barbara had expected to hear her husband, but the voice was not Tate's. "Who is this?" she pleaded.

"Who *is* this?" The question blurted from the two-foot wall speaker. The narrow-band carrier wave made the voice sound as though it came from the bottom of an aquarium.

"Let me speak to her!" Tate stabbed at the glowing button on his telephone and grabbed for the receiver.

Admiral Gurney deflected his hand with a neat sideswipe of outstretched fingers. "We can't permit that, General."

Dr. Bailey clapped his receiver back into the cradle, and the wall speaker went instantly dead.

"Where have you got her?" Tate cried.

"There's absolutely nothing to worry about." Wanamaker's were the eyes of a commander who knew he was right and didn't care how many people had to die to prove it. "You have my word of honor, Tate. Just hang in till Monday. At 19:06 Greenwich Mean Time all of this will be history and you'll have your wife back again."

"Look, she's a sick woman!"

"We know." Wanamaker struck a match to relight his pipe.

"You don't know a damned thing. She could die without proper medicine. Prednisone, thirty milligrams twice daily. For God's sake, write it down."

"Bailey," Wanamaker said, "write it down."

"And no other drugs. She's got bad kidneys and she's pregnant."

Wanamaker's eyes flicked up. "Congratulations."

"If you've done anything to harm her—" Tate could find no words to complete the threat. Wanamaker met his gaze as serene as one who knew power by lifelong cohabitation with it; who knew by instinct and experience in whom and in what power was vested, and in whom and in what it was not; who knew how to cajole with power and how to kill with power and who waited for no man's permission to do either. *There are such men,* Tate realized: *there are such men, and this one is my enemy.*

"We don't want to kill her," Wanamaker said. "We sincerely don't want to have to do that."

Dr. Bailey made a stumbling attempt to join Wanamaker and Gurney in rising. Wanamaker held out a hand in crisp farewell. "Talk to you next week, Tate. It'll be a whole new ball game. You and Barbara will come to dinner and we'll have a laugh about it."

At that moment Tate hated Ilya Wanamaker more than he had ever hated any man in his life.

Admiral Gurney consulted her watch. "It's late, General. You'll need a pass to get out. I'd better walk you."

On the way to the Mall Entrance, she told him about the exhibit of Rumanian art she had seen at the National Gallery. She talked with an animation that was absolutely crazy in the context of what had just been said in the conference room. Tate wondered if there was an upper-echelon brain fever that sooner or later decimated all high commands.

A guard nodded them through the outer door. Sunset was beginning to drench the Arlington hills and forests fire-storm red. Admiral Gurney said she had found the Brancusi sculpture especially interesting and speculated that his were among the few works of Art Deco that would prove to have long-term survivability.

There comes a point where the people who aren't crazy have got to stop caving in like dominoes to the people who are: Tate realized, as Admiral Anne Gurney prattled a good-by on the Mall Entrance steps, that she had just led him to it.

Driving back to the city, Tate didn't see any black Fords in the rear-view mirror, but he didn't know if he could rely on his eyes. A headache made the highway wobble unpredictably through his field of vision and it was a miracle he didn't wreck the car.

He slowed to an illegal stop behind a road-repair sawhorse near a pay phone. Downtown Washington was afraid and it emptied of people after sunset. The street was practically deserted. The sun caught only upper stories now, and darkness was seeping rapidly upward from the sidewalks.

He did not know how much longer Ilya Wanamaker intended to leave him alive, but 19:06 GMT Monday gave him sixty-seven hours, which was very little time.

Not enough time to go to the press. Besides, why would the press believe Tate Erlandsen, lackey of the military-industrial complex, and even if they did, who would believe the press?

Not enough time to go to a senator or congressman: most senators and congressmen would have left town for the weekend by now, and even if he could find one who believed him, a congressional inquiry would take months.

And even if he could wangle a presidential appointment and bypass the President's assistants and get to the President in time and make the President halfway believe him—Theta still had a legitimate mission as Firebird; the *Intrepid* still had a legitimate mission testing sonar.

There was no way you could pluck a satellite out of the sky and open it up and expose it as a killer. Any attempt would drive Wanamaker underground, Theta and all, to bide his time a little longer.

Wanamaker had to be headed off some other way.

Tate eyed the distance to the telephone booth, considered shadowy doorways and open-mouthed alleys and wondered if by some stretch of luck or design he was about to die in one of them. Pocketing the car keys, he hurried to the booth. He searched the directory and deposited his dime and dialed.

SAS told him yes, they could reserve a space on that evening's eight-thirty flight from Kennedy Airport, New York, to Copenhagen. Yes, they would honor his credit cards. He gave them a false name, simply to hold the space. He calculated that if he could reach Washington National Airport within the hour, a shuttle plane would get him to New York in time.

He drove to the office and found a parking space near the building. The night guard knew him. He went up without signing the book and let himself into the Pacific Aero suite.

He took his raincoat and overnight kit from the closet. He opened the safe and gathered up his passport and two of the Xerox copies of Asher's work notes and the submarine orders. He took eight hundred dollars in petty cash and a thousand in traveler's checks. The papers went into the inner pocket of the raincoat and the overnight kit went into a TWA flight bag and the passport and money went into his wallet.

He looked out the window into the street. He saw one woman waiting uneasily at a bus stop. He saw no men in black or seersucker, no garage attendants with Cub Scout knives. Which didn't mean they weren't there.

By the light of his Tensor lamp he wrote Miss Monroe a note apologizing for the theft. He left the light burning. It had been a gift from Barbara.

He knew he was crossing a boundary and he knew what it would cost him. He knew he could never come back except as a dead man or a criminal; he knew he might never again see the last person on earth he loved. He knew he had no choice.

He folded the raincoat over his arm and hurried down the thirteen flights of fire stairs. The light in the window and the Bentley parked in front might fool whoever was tailing him, but not for very long. Tate estimated at most a fifteen-minute lead, and he'd used seven of those minutes washing and packing.

He stepped out of the building onto an unlit alley that let out on Ninth Street between a stationery store and a cafeteria. A cruising yellow cab was coming his way.

No one killed him between Washington and New York and no one killed him as he waited in the SAS terminal at Kennedy Airport. Tate stared through the glass wall at the jumbo jet that he would have to board if his luck held out.

A man in an SAS uniform was checking passports at the boarding gate. Tate was using his own passport. It was a calculated risk. He doubted Wanamaker had put out an alert for him, but with bureaucracies anything was possible, even efficiency, and if the word was to get Erlandsen, airport security might just be quick enough to do it.

The raincoat was folded loosely over his left arm, swinging in relaxed arcs. He could feel the weight of the papers in the pocket. There were six people in line ahead of him, if you called it a line, dozens more behind him. He was dimly aware of a woman pressing the sharp edge of a parcel into his back. He took a deep breath and moved forward, passport extended and conspicuous, nothing to hide.

His head ached and his heart was thudding in his ears.

The man ripped off part of his boarding pass and did not bother to look at the passport. "Have a good trip, Mr. Erlandsen."

The *mister* was reassuring.

Tate followed the passengers streaming through the accordion-fold ramp that linked terminal and airplane. A stewardess glanced at what was left of the boarding pass. She directed him to a seat by a window and gave him what he supposed was a first-class smile.

He rolled up his raincoat and slipped it beneath the seat. He fastened his safety belt and watched passengers boarding. Mostly they looked innocent and unremarkable, just as the garage attendant had looked that afternoon, and none of them looked at him. Tate shut his eyes and thought of the wall speaker in the Joint Chiefs of Staff Emergency Conference Room, the imploring sound of Barbara's voice. His hand made a fist.

The seat next to his remained empty right up to takeoff. Warning lights blinked and reading lights dimmed and jets howled and the craft gave a behemoth shudder and began lumbering forward along the runway.

The plane did not explode.

Twilit terminals streaked past Tate's window. The craft began to lift and he felt the growing emptiness beneath. The air passed in a screaming rush that was only partly muffled by the walls of the cabin. Shapes of harbor and cities shrank, excruciatingly small. The country below staggered and slipped and gradually lost definition.

For a long while Tate felt nothing but the vibrations of the jets. Slight shifts in acceleration rocked him in his seat. The craft flew easily, lightly through gathering night. He had the illusion he was beyond the reach of anything on earth.

But gradually he became aware of a desire to rip off his safety belt and claw his way jibbering through an exit. He knew it was only panic and he knew it would subside if he would just sit very still.

It didn't subside.

He found himself turning in his seat, eyeing the matron in blue behind him, the young man in jeans riding first-class across the aisle, wondering which of them was in the employ of Ilya Wanamaker. When the stewardess asked if he would like a drink he said yes, thank you, and he found that the drink helped.

Harsh keys rattled the corridors of sleeplessness. A bar of light jumped across the wall of Barbara's cubicle. Two nurses stood in the open doorway side by side, speaking in low voices.

Suddenly the cubicle bristled with movement. A nurse approached swiftly. Barbara's throat flexed to scream. The nurse leaned down beside her and spoke in an iron caress of a whisper: "Don't make things hard for us, Betty, you'll only make them worse for yourself."

A cold hand thrust itself inside the hospital smock. Barbara struggled. A needle touched her naked hip. There was a single blotting moment of pain and then she felt a false and terrifying serenity. Her fists unclenched and her knees relaxed.

She would have liked to stay awake. She would have liked to have her anger and her fear back.

But the nurses just kept standing there and gradually Barbara was aware of a cool feeling like death pushing out the living rage.

"Atta girl, Betty." They smiled. "Atta baby."

Tate could not doze off. He stared out the window. The jumbo jet was two hours into the abbreviated night of the Atlantic crossing. Noiseless as nurses in a hospital ward, Nordic blond stewardesses went up and down aisles, checking sleeping passengers.

Tate was calmer now. He was thinking of Asher and Armstrong, who had died, and he was thinking of his wife, who might die as a result of what he was doing, but he was trying to concentrate on clouds. He watched a distant sierra of cumulus somewhere over Newfoundland catch glints of midnight sun. It struck him that clouds and mountains could look uncannily alike. He had once spent two weeks in the cordillera in southern Panama, and the differences between Panama's cordillera and Newfoundland's cumulus were not great, not after dark, certainly not after two drinks.

It was a question, he supposed, of smell. Cumulus would smell of ozone. The Cordillera San Blas had smelled of rot. He had been unofficial chief American adviser to a division of government troops, and the smell had been too strong simply to be napalm or dead rebels. He had been convinced it was the smell of Panamanian earth, and for some reason it was almost unbearably acrid at night.

There had been a rumor that rebels were hiding in Chiparillo, to the south, and he had been detached from the main army to flush them out. The Panamanian command gave him fourteen American M-60 machine guns, eleven American M-79 grenade launchers, seventy American M-14 rifles, a ton and a half of American ammo, three Panamanian lieutenant commanders who had between them four years of training, and all the farmers he could conscript en route. The further south he got, the more Panama smelled like fried garbage.

When it existed back in the 1960s, the hamlet of Chiparillo stood on a bluff fifty feet above the Paraní River. It consisted of a church and general store built of stucco and eighteen shacks built of wood. Three of the shacks belonged to wealthy farmers and had floors. The population of the ten-mile metropolitan area was forty-three. This figure excluded livestock but included the priest who came by Land Rover the last Sunday of every month to celebrate Mass and hear forty-two confessions.

A hill sloped six hundred yards from the hamlet down into the forest. To the west and south, below rock outcroppings, the hill had been plowed with American plows and fertilized with American fertilizer and Panamanian coffee bushes grew. To the east were no contours to hold the soil and deep ravines gouged the land and nothing took root.

On the night of Abraham Lincoln's birthday, three Panamanian lieutenant commanders with carefully trimmed mustaches stood at the edge of the forest and took turns squinting through a pair of infrared binoculars at the hamlet on the hill. The eastern slope was jagged, with the profile of broken glass, and Chiparillo presented the silhouette of a thirty-car freight-train wreck. Tate reached a hand to his shirt collar and crushed an insect beneath his thumb. He suggested the men could sneak uphill in the dark and begin their charge from the cover of the rock outcroppings.

The night had condensed into a secretion that dripped from leaf to leaf with the sound of water bugs hopping. The light of a crescent moon stretched high across the tangled trees like an impaled parachute. A hundred and twelve sweating farmers milled in the forest, slapping at mosquitoes. Those who could stomach it drank Coca-Cola from hot cans. It was forbidden to smoke. The enemy on the hill might see the light.

The lieutenant commanders spread the order and gave the word, and Tate watched the armed farmers fan out in three battalions. At a noiseless, creeping run they advanced on the rocks. They had scuttled almost halfway up the hill when a man in the right-hand battalion, who must have mistaken a bird's screech for a signal, released a flare.

Answering flares shot up from left and center, ripping the sky red and pinpointing the troops in garish spotlights. The town opened fire. A mortar began lobbing 155-millimeter rounds into the hillside. A machine gun sprayed 82-millimeter steel pellets in a clean, sweeping downpour. Earth and flesh spattered like hot grease. The farmers scattered in jibbering panic.

A few tried to make the hopeless uphill dash to the cover of the rocks. Some dove to the ground. Most turned and ran for the trees. One sergeant, trying to goad his men into advancing, stepped into an explosion of soil and orange smoke and fell back as his legs turned to powder beneath him. In less than a minute, dozens of bodies in all degrees of dying littered the slope, and the survivors were in full downhill rout.

A farm boy at the bottom of the hill, trying to fire an M-60 over their heads, cut down a retreating wave of his fellow troops.

Tate motioned seven American advisers to follow him.

He ran east through the forest, clambering over and under trunks that blocked the path. Huge, skin-smooth leaves of low-reaching lianas brushed him and he dodged man-tall root systems of toppled trees that reared up in shadow. When he reached the ravine he slung the M-16 automatic rifle around his neck and dropped on all fours and crawled. Halfway up the hill, the ravine became deep enough to risk an almost-upright stumbling run. Ten yards from the town the ground leveled and there was no cover.

His hands itched. They were bleeding.

The rebels were concentrating their fire to the west and south. Mortar flames licked the church wall red. There was only the tinny crack of three Soviet-made AK-47 rifles, firing in counterpoint, and the screech of mortar rounds impacting at ten-second intervals. The machine gun had stopped.

Tate took the ten yards in a running crouch and hunkered down behind a wood shack. When he got his breath halfway back he felt his way toward the open space between shacks. He took it in a jump, catching light for an instant, hit the darkness and tumbled against packed earth.

He lay for a moment listening. There was no break in the firing to indicate the rebels had seen him. He raised himself to his feet and pressed into the shadow. Five yards away a three-legged terrier lay dead in the moonlight.

He unslung the M-16 and with fumbling fingers set it to automatic. He moved toward the sound of weapon fire. When he glanced back he saw one of the Americans following right behind him. Weeds grazed his khaki trousers with a whisper.

A rifle shot zinged in his direction.

He flung himself down. The ground beneath him crackled. He was crawling through coffee beans that had been spread on planking to dry. Two shadows darted between shacks, and a hand grenade came dancing out across the planks, winking sparks.

"Incoming!" Tate yelled. He dove sideways. Hot metal and coffee geysered, and the night smelled like breakfast. An adviser got to his knees behind Tate and opened automatic fire. A shadow pitched forward from the doorway of the shack.

Tate slipped over the dead rebel and advanced in a stoop till he could see the church wall and the abandoned mortar and the machine gun with the dead man still embracing it. A girl was trying to kick the man loose and thread a belt of cartridges into the magazine.

"*Manos arriba!*" Tate shouted. He made a jabbing motion with the rifle. She let go of the belt and put her hands in the air.

By then the other Americans were washing the town down in M-16 rounds.

In all they found eleven rebels: three dead, five dying, and three hiding in the church with spent weapons. The priest was in the church too.

The rebels had lashed the priest's bare feet to the crossbar of the crucifix. They had cut the jugular vein at the base of his neck. They had ripped him from breastbone to testicles and he had spilled across the altar like slaughtered game.

Tate was not a Catholic and he was not even a religious man, but a year later, sitting at after-dinner coffee with his wife and son and the new admiral of the U. S. Eighth Fleet, he still couldn't get the priest out of his mind.

The Admiral was saying, "The only questionable decision you made, Tate, was not shooting the whole bunch on the spot. Tell me: how many of that scum did you bring back alive?" The admiral's name was Ilya Wanamaker, and at that point Tate had known very little about him. People said that his father had run the fifth-largest cattle ranch in Texas, that his mother had been and still was a White Russian. The Arctic blue of his eyes made Tate uneasy.

"We brought back three alive," Tate said, "eight dead." He found himself wondering what sort of a world it was where people could tie a man upside down and gut him and say that was war. He was a career officer and he'd gone to officer's school and he knew that sort of thing wasn't war.

"I hate to back up these banana dictatorships," Wanamaker said. "But if we tolerate rebels in Latin America, we're going to wind up with communism on our own doorstep." It had been before détente, and a lot of people spoke that way, just as nowadays they spoke of better understanding through trade.

"It's an invalid argument," Tate's son said. The boy held himself erect in his chair, tall and tanned and aloof, like someone who rode horseback a great deal and owned his own horses. The narrow set of his eyes telegraphed the unstained determination of the very young. Tate wondered what those professors had been teaching Randy at MIT.

"It's a damned valid argument from where I sit," Wanamaker said. "We stopped communism in Chile, in the Dominican Republic, in Guatemala, in Honduras. If we'd helped Batista wipe Castro out of the Sierra Maestra, Cuba would still be a free country."

"Randy's on vacation from college," Barbara said. That long-ago evening, she had worn a close-fitting lime-green gown and the candle had caught blond highlights in her hair and she had glowed. "He's majoring in math."

"And minoring in politics?" Wanamaker said.

"I have one or two opinions." Randy was a little drunk and rather touching in his vehemence. He was barely seventeen years old. "Bad logic makes a bad foundation for anything, including military policy."

One of the club stewards bent down to say there was a telephone call for Mr. Randy Erlandsen.

"Must be Lisa." Randy folded his napkin. "She promised to call Christmas Eve."

"And who is Lisa?" Wanamaker asked after Randy had gone.

"A girl in Boston," Barbara said.

The main terrace of the country club, glassed in for dining and dancing, overlooked the American golf course and the American governor's mansion. Far beyond a fringe of palm trees, two battleships of the Eighth Fleet, visible by colored lights strung to their smokestacks, rose solid and gleaming from reflections rippling the surface of the Gulf of Panama, proof tangible of the American presence.

The band, twelve native Panamanians in tight black trousers and parakeet ruffles, attacked a medley of current Broadway show tunes. Wanamaker and Tate took turns dancing with Barbara. When in half an hour Randy had not returned to the table, Tate sent the waiter to look for him.

"He was pretty drunk," Wanamaker said. "Maybe he went home."

Barbara sent little let's-get-going signals to Tate. They wished the Admiral a merry Christmas and they drove home with the top of the Buick down and they were worried. A wind from the harbor was swishing the palms that divided the Avenida del Country Club, and the night smelled thickly of mimosa. Barbara adjusted a black lace shawl around her bare shoulders and said, "How did Lisa know where Randy was? The servants have the night off. There's no one home to answer the phone."

"Lisa Fairchild is a very resourceful girl," Tate said.

A light was burning on the front terrace, but there was no one home. A piece of paper had been slipped into the space between the tiles and the door. Tate watched his wife bend and pick it up. Her expression froze, and she handed it to him. "It must be a joke," she said.

But he could tell from her voice that she thought nothing

of the sort. The note was typed in Spanish. They said they
would return Randolf Erlandsen when the three surviving
rebels were released. Failing compliance before the New
Year, they would execute him.

Tate found out then that few things in life turn out the
way you expect, not even the bad things.

The Panamanian government opened negotiations with the
rebel leaders. An American Assistant Secretary of State inter-
ceded behind the scenes. On New Year's Eve, twelve hours
before the deadline, Tate flew in a Cessna four-seater to a
little town in northern Colombia to sit in on the final stage of
negotiations.

The rebel leader, a young man who wore American blue
jeans and kept combing his hair at the negotiating table,
wanted a quarter million dollars' worth of medicine and another quarter million in cash. The Panamanian negotiators
were willing to comply, which struck Tate as suicide, since
the money would obviously buy ammunition. The American
Assistant Secretary of State, who had come only for the day
and had worn a suit and a Porcellian Club tie, said he had no
objections. Tate was silent till the rebel leader said he wanted
not just the original three, but an additional fourteen prisoners freed.

Tate thought of that priest, and he placed his fists on the
tabletop and accidentally jiggled the Assistant Secretary of
State's coffee. "I won't go along with this," Tate said. "I
won't barter one life for all the people they've murdered and
all the people they'll go on murdering."

The Assistant Secretary of State was staring at him as
though he had gone crazy. "Your own son, Tate?" he said.

But Tate was an Army man, and in the Army you sometimes had to make tough decisions.

Three hours later, in the limousine carrying him home
from the airport, he took his wife's hand and tried to explain.
The hope in her eyes strangled. Her fingers slid free and she
turned to stare out the window. The Panamanian mountain
peaks were bleeding in the sunset.

If he had not been an Army man and toughened in combat, Tate doubted he could have survived the days that followed. Other officers, tactfully, coped with decisions that
should have been his and devised a paper stream of make-
work to keep his self-respect flickering. There were items
about him in the American papers, and well-wishers kept

shoving clippings at him in the officer's mess. Everyone said he had been brave, even the New York *Times*. He kept expecting to find his son's body mutilated and tossed on the front doorstep as a rebuke to Yanqui imperialism.

It was the day after the President issued an executive order advancing him from brigadier to major general that Randy came home. The chief of security had just alerted the base command to a Czech-made petnam charge found under the officers' gymnasium. Tate's phone rang and Barbara sobbed, "Randy's home."

Tate reached the house three minutes later, still wearing his tennis shorts, and Barbara had a blinking, shocked look. "Have they hurt him?" was the first thing he asked.

"He's in his room packing."

Randy looked leaner and tanner. He was wearing clean dungarees and an MIT T-shirt edged in blue. His hair was combed. Tate tried to embrace him but the boy said, "Come on, Dad. They didn't cut off my ear or castrate me. I'm whole and I'm healthy."

"Then why can't you stay with us a little longer?"

Randy wound a pair of socks into a ball and placed them in a suitcase next to a stack of fresh-laundered button-down shirts. He said he had to start thinking about mid-year exams. He looked pretty damned determined for a kid.

"Randy, give me a chance," Tate pleaded.

"No hard feelings." His son held out a hand, and it was the last time they ever touched. "You had a tough decision to make. I understand."

That spring there were letters from the dean of undergraduates about Randy's marks. Finally, there was a letter about drugs and, swiftly, another about expulsion. Tate placed a long-distance call to Lisa Fairchild, his son's girl in Boston, and in a voice barely under control she said Randy had moved into a commune in Dorchester and she knew nothing else about it. The boy ignored all written and phoned appeals from his parents. They had lost him and there was nothing they could do.

Barbara went into depression, and Tate requested a transfer back to the States, where she could at least get medical attention. The President gave him another star, and just before Christmas, when they were guests of friends in Palm Springs, a man from the FBI asked to speak to them.

"Dorchester," he said. "Near Boston. A two-family house

in a mostly black neighborhood. The group called themselves the *patriatistas*. They were activists."

"We don't know them," Tate said: simple statement of fact, no value judgment.

Even though it was the mild sort of evening that had lured millionaires to Palm Springs from all over the nation, the FBI man was sweating. "The kids were making bombs," he said. The kids had failed to take precautions. An FBI team had been combing the rubble for four days and nights and had found a print on a fragment of the middle finger of a right hand. The print matched one taken three months ago, when Randolf Erlandsen had been arrested on suspicion of narcotics trafficking.

The FBI man said he was sorry. He left a phone number. Barbara stared at the unfinished Christmas tree.

She'd grown up on Park Avenue and Long Island. She'd been educated at good places: Miss Porter's and then Vassar. Her father had rented the Plaza ballroom for her debut and she'd been around the world three times before she was twenty. The family had approved of her marrying a third-generation Army man and they'd left her two million, and until Randy was born she had taken an interest in the piano and civil rights. But Tate could see that nothing in her life had prepared her for this.

"Tate," she said, "I'm going to die."

He had to put her into a clinic in Kansas. Even though the press made a fuss and the President gave him another star, he thought things over and realized he was no longer an Army man. He resigned his commission, and a representative of the Pacific Aero Corporation asked if he would care to work for a subsidiary of the company. The law forbade his working for a defense contractor until he'd been retired five years, so the parent company gave him a secretary and an office in a Detroit subsidiary that made helicopters for businessmen. They called him a technical consultant but no one ever consulted him. He had free time and eighty-five thousand a year, which he supposed was a fair price for an option on a four-star general. He flew to Kansas every week.

Barbara's room was a cell, softened with hypocrisies: a calendar, a photograph, a beer stein of daffodils on the sill of the barred window. On their anniversary he took her a book of cat photographs. The nurse's aide had suggested it as being more suitable than jewelry. Barbara glanced at the flyleaf, where he had written: *To Barbara my beloved wife on our twentieth wedding anniversary, with love always, Tate*. He wrote *love* on the things he gave her each week. He watched her turn the pages.

They had cut her hair short, leaving her face pale and unprotected. Her eyes were huge and he wondered what kind of drugs they were giving her. Silence ached in him. There was nothing to say that hadn't already been said. The minutes trickled by and when he could stand it no longer he said, "I'll be back next week."

When he looked back from the doorway, she had shut the cat book in her lap. He saw that the web of hope that had once stretched from her to every other thing in the universe had collapsed, neatly severed at every strand.

He talked with the doctor for the few seconds it took the elevator to reach the ground floor. "Mrs. Erlandsen is doing better," the young doctor said. He seemed tired and his white smock had stains.

Tate stepped from the smell of disinfectant into the smell of mown grass. The sky was the color of sea and the earth was the color of thirst and they met in a horizon that was uninterrupted for 360 degrees. A lonely stand of pines, very far away, reached like a baby claw scratching at the hem of heaven.

He stared a long while at the Victorian stone façade of the clinic and he wondered how people could believe in God. It was never a problem he had had, believing in God, but he wondered if the Panamanian priest at the end had believed in God.

Eventually the clinic released Barbara, and she seemed to get better.

His five years elapsed, and the law allowed him to sell defense equipment to the Air Force and the Navy. Pacific Aero told him he was now working for the parent, not the subsidiary.

At the time, he hadn't minded at all. He had realized that the major events in his life were past. He hadn't been sorry at all, facing an eventless future. On the contrary, he had been grateful.

Saturday

As the taxi crossed over the Sortesdam Canal, for one surrealist instant Tate's unslept eye thought the city planners must have ripped out the broadest, longest avenue in all Copenhagen and put sky in its place. Then a swan gliding through a cloud gave him back reality.

He wondered if they were following him.

Of course they weren't following him. They had his wife and they'd said they would kill her, and no man would leave his wife to be killed, so why should they bother to follow him?

Tate turned to look out the rear-view window. Of course they were following him. The only question was how many and how far behind.

The taxi let him out near the intersection of Blegdamsvej and Frederik den femtes vej, and he paid the fare with ten of the kroner he had bought at the airport bank. Two buildings of dark yellow stone, one gabled and the other mansarded, sat right-angled to one another at the corner of a park. Joined at the edge like unmatched Siamese twins, they were set back from the street by a hedge and bike stands. A temporary-looking wood building had been erected in the courtyard, one-storied and weathered; rose beds planted around it lent it a sort of fleeting permanence.

The nearer stone building bore the sign *Nordita, Nordisk Institut for Teoretisk Atomfysik;* the further, *Niels Bohr Institutet 1920.* Tate opened the little gate and crossed the courtyard to the door of the Niels Bohr Institute. He pressed the buzzer. No one came to answer.

With fleeting panic he wondered if the Institute was open Saturdays, especially sunny summer Saturdays. Traffic and cyclists passed on the avenue in orderly packets and no one answered the door. *It's not too late,* he thought: *I can still turn back.* If they saw him turn back now, surely they wouldn't hurt Barbara.

He walked back to the door of the Nordisk Institut. He pressed the buzzer, waited, turned to see if anyone was watching him from the street. The door opened. A man in a dark suit, with frown to match, said something to him in Danish.

"Do you speak English?" Tate asked.

"Yes?"

Tate wondered why it was that Danish doormen looked like American bank presidents. He was glad he had shaved and showered on arrival at Kastrup Airport. "I would like to contact Dr. Yuri Benzikoff. I was told he is a guest lecturer here."

The man's eye followed three girls in short skirts as they fluttered past on the sidewalk. "Yes, he lectures here Thursday afternoons."

"I've got to contact him immediately."

The man hesitated. "I shall see what can be done."

Tate followed the man into the building and up a stairway. His feet kept finding sponge where they expected solidity, and his eyes, not yet adjusted to the interior light, kept producing black spots that flew at him like bats. The man opened the door to an empty office and let Tate go in. Somewhere a lone typewriter shot out a burst of muffled clatter and fell silent again. The man asked his name.

"Will you wait here please, Mr. Erlandsen?"

Alone, Tate laid his raincoat on one of the chairs and prayed he could stay awake. He passed a lingering gaze across the two shut doors, the edge of the desk glinting in a torrent of improbably bright sun, the tall window that seemed to be the source of streaming, exploding photons. He could see a corner of the park in unreal, scalpel-sharp focus. He walked closer to the window to count blades of grass that had never known litter or drought.

Smooth lawn arched across hillocks and valleys and down to an unexpected lake. Toy sailboats nibbled their reflections. Trees that were four and five feet thick at the base ballooned up into twenty-foot bursts of silver-speckled green. Formal flower beds, flung down in a playfully informal manner, vibrated bright as Tarot trumps scattered across deep velvet. A building that was in fact the *rigs hospital*, the national hospital, in its context looked as magical as a castle.

An old man, in jacket and tie, sat on a bench with a book while a baby played near his feet. Several yards away, in another world, a young man and woman lay on the grass embracing. Three ducks strutted Indian-file across a path.

A woman entered the room. *"Ja—onskede De at tale med mig?"*

"I'm sorry, I don't speak Danish."

"Forgive me. Your name sounded Danish." She spoke insidiously correct English, and her green eyes blazed cool assurance.

"It probably was, once."

"May I help you?"

"I'd like to see Dr. Benzikoff."

"I am Dr. Benzikoff." She was a short, lightweight woman with raven-black hair. Her gaze raked him up and down.

"Excuse my surprise. I thought Yuri was a man's name."

"It is. Yuri Benzikoff is my husband. I am Ilona Benzikoff." She sat in a chair and crossed her slender legs.

"I have to speak with your husband."

"What is this in reference to?" Pulling a silver cigarette box from the pocket of her lab smock, she snapped it open with switchblade quickness and jabbed it toward him. The box had Cyrillic script engraving. He declined with a headshake.

"I can only discuss that with your husband."

"Who are you, Mr. Erlandsen?"

"I'm a retired general of the United States Army. At the moment I work for an American aerospace-defense company."

She lit her cigarette, took a deep drag, and exhaled. Her eyes lapped kittenishly at a skim-milk cloud. "My husband lectures Thursdays. He's very busy with his students and with his theoretical research. And he's been ill. Possibly he could arrange some free time, if you could give me an idea what it is you wish to discuss."

"A weapon."

Metal clanked in her pocket as she crossed her legs the other way. "Will you be in Copenhagen long?"

"I arrived two hours ago and I'm leaving on the noon flight."

"Well, what a pity." She got to her feet with startling rapidity. "My husband is busy and he is convalescing from a prolonged illness. In any case, weapons are not his interest. He is in theoretical physics, you know. Not applied."

"My information—" Tate tried to explain. He had crossed the boundary and he could not go back, but the flight had wrecked him and his hands were shaking like a liar's and the words wouldn't come. *What if they've killed Barbara,* he wondered: *what if they've killed her and this woman still won't believe me?* "My information has a bearing on relations between our countries."

The third law of thermodynamics states that science cannot build a machine which will reach a temperature of absolute zero. Science had not built Madame Benzikoff's eyes.

"My husband is not concerned in politics. You have come to the wrong person, Mr. Erlandsen. Yuri Benzikoff cannot help you." Behind the slanting green stare, a spiked portcullis dropped. "I am very sorry you have made this senseless trip. I have much to do. Excuse me."

Madame Benzikoff left the room. Fatigue hit Tate in a tidal wave.

"Ilonka, shto tî dyelayesh—?" A fat face was poking through the open door. The face looked at Tate and changed languages. *"Unskyld—har De set min kone?"*

"I'm sorry. I don't speak Russian or Danish."

"Are you English?"

"American."

The face put on a broad smile and bobbed into the room on a fat, bouncy, checker-swathed body. "How do you do, I am Russian. They told me my wife was here."

"Dr. Yuri Benzikoff?"

"Yes." He was a wild-haired, stumpy, but not quite ugly person. His hand and eye betrayed the mild, habitual haste of a fat man who had spent his life waddling one step ahead of disaster. "I call Ilonka my little neutrino. Because she vanishes through walls."

"Doctor, my name is Tate Erlandsen. I was formerly a general in the United States Army. At present I work for Pacific Aero, an aerospace-defense manufacturer."

Dr. Benzikoff de-escalated to a simple, interested smile. "Then you can tell me something. Dr. Bohr, who built this house, he was a great admirer of your American western movies. Do you like movies?" He nodded as though he had heard a *yes.* "Dr. Bohr had a theory why it is always the hero who shoots the villain in the western-movie gunfight. Do you know Dr. Bohr's theory?"

Tate felt he was asleep, making this up. "I don't know the theory."

"The bad guy has to make the first move. Bad guys always make the first move, yes? The bad guy has to decide when to make his move, and this question of decision, it slows him down." He whipped an imaginary gun from an imaginary holster and gave it an imaginary twirl. "But the good guy acts on conditioned reflex. He shoots as soon as he sees the bad guy move. Nothing to decide, nothing to slow him down. That is why the good guy always wins. Now, tell me, General: do you think Bohr's theory holds when the cowboys are the Soviet Union and the United States?"

"I would hesitate to test it."

"But if we apply Bohr's thinking—"

"Doctor, you might be interested in this application of Bohr's thinking." Tate hoisted his raincoat, delved into the left-hand pocket, and extracted the single-folded manila envelope. He dealt out five Xerox sheets on the desk.

Dr. Benzikoff approached the desk. His eyes ripped into the plans as matter-of-factly as the claws of a bored cat.

"It's an orbiting satellite that converts solar energy into electricity to power a maser that—"

"Yes, yes," Benzikoff said. "I see what it is meant to do."

"The purpose is to disrupt communication between computer and rocket and kill the missile launch."

Dr. Benzikoff almost lost control of his eyebrows. "This is marvelous fantasy. My compliments."

"The device has been built. And orbited. And disguised as an American Firebird satellite."

Dr. Benzikoff shook his head. "Firebird we know about. Not possible."

Tate dug into the envelope and dealt two more documents onto the table, the submarine orders. "An unarmed missile will be launched at Moscow from an American submarine in the Barents Sea. The Theta device will paralyze the Moscow ABM system. Moscow will be unable to defend itself. You have to give these plans and these orders to your government immediately."

"To my government? This is not my field."

"The only way we can stop this is to convince the CIA that Russia already possesses Asher's device. The attack is planned for 10 P.M. Moscow time the day after tomorrow."

Dr. Benzikoff took a shuffling step backward. "The government would not believe me. This is not my field."

"They have records of the test. The Akula-3 satellite photographed a trial run of the device last Monday morning at Ellsworth Air Force Base, South Dakota."

Benzikoff's glance interlocked with Tate's. "General, can you meet me this evening at seven o'clock in Tivoli Gardens?

There is a woman who does caricatures; she has a stand near the roller coaster. Meet me there."

"We haven't got time."

"It cannot be done any other way. I cannot take these documents here. There is a trolley stop in front of the Institute. The trolley will take you to downtown Copenhagen. Go have a good time, meet me at seven. I must find my wife before she gets angry at me." Benzikoff scurried guiltily from the room.

Absurdly, Tate was thinking of his noon flight home. *There are other planes*, he told himself: *just hang on and stay alive and stay awake.*

He stared with sleepy envy out the window at the old man on his bench. It suddenly occurred to him that the old man could be a plant, and he stepped back from the window.

There was no way of turning off the forty-watt bulb, so it was never night in the cubicle. Barbara lay on her right side. The pain came and went in unhurried waves. It felt like the first stirrings of menstrual cramps, but it was not her time of the month and besides you didn't menstruate when you were pregnant.

She refused to think of miscarriage. *Not fair, not possible.*

If she lay very still on her right side the pain hurt less and she was able to link short thoughts together. She thought of the telephone down the hall and she thought of the bathroom. So far they had taken her to bathrooms on other floors, but if she said she was weak they might relent and let her use the bathroom on this floor. She could sneak into the office and call for help.

They had kept giving her injections. She didn't feel awake. But the pain in her abdomen was real, it hurt, it anchored her to here and now.

The buzzer, she told herself. *Reach over your head and push the buzzer.*

She shifted position by inches. It took forever but it was better than making herself dizzy. When she could see the buzzer cord knotted to the metal headboard she lifted her hand toward the cracked plastic button. Her depth judgment was off. It was like skeet shooting with a rifle that had faulty sights. She had to calculate the error in judgment and calculate the compensation. It took so long to think it all through that she lost track and had to start over again.

Gradually the anger of helplessness built up and she swung

at the cord. Her fingers grazed plastic and she repeated the
swing. She managed to grab the button. She pushed and
didn't stop pushing. She couldn't hear any buzzing. For all
she knew the button was a placebo but it was her only
chance and she held on for dear life.

They could be anywhere, Tate reminded himself: *they
could be anyone. Stick with the crowds. You're safest with
crowds.*

He took aim at the most crowded street he saw, a
pedestrian mall gently swollen with shoppers and strollers
that wound through a manicured jumble of close-packed old-
fashioned houses. He walked slowly in the corridor of glittering storefronts. He clung to the thickest human clusters,
eased anonymously into the unhurrying polyglot indifference,
borrowing not just the coloring but the tempo and destination
of strangers.

Of course, they could be in the crowd too.

Leisurely reflections of pedestrians unspooled in shopwindows. He slowed to stare at an arrangement of cloisonné
music boxes, translucent ceramic plates and painted porcelain
figurines. The day-to-day survival of useless, pretty things
seemed a trick of unaccountable conjuring. He saw that the
shop was crowded. He went in.

He lifted a coffee mug decorated with large, whimsical
flowers. It was a modern piece, cheerful and loud. He sighted
the doorway through the handle. His heartbeat stumbled and
stopped.

A heavyset man in a plaid jacket was just stepping across
the shop's threshold. He wore a pencil-line mustache. Tate
had seen the same man outside Mrs. Asher's apartment, at
the Senate hearing, at the Lincoln Memorial: he had been
wearing seersucker.

The man petted a teak monkey. Very slowly, he surveyed
shelves of cups and figurines.

Tate's heart was beating too fast. *All right,* he told himself:
*you were expecting them to come after you. You knew it
wouldn't be easy, so stop feeling sorry for yourself and stop
feeling scared.*

The man in the plaid jacket lifted a teapot, made a disappointed face at the price, and put it back. He turned and
with a deliberate lack of haste left the shop. He paused in the
street to study something in the window, never once looked at
Tate, and passed out of sight.

Tate waited fifteen seconds by his wristwatch. He slipped out of the porcelain shop and walked the opposite way from the man in the plaid jacket. He took a quick survey of the first side street. The greatest crowd had gathered at the plate-glass window of a shop marked *Porno.* He joined them.

The window offered nothing but a view of the tidy bright shop interior with its bins and shelves and milling, well-dressed patrons. Neatly lettered overhead signs marked various categories as clearly as Dewey decimal classifications: *humiliation, bondage, children, homo.* Tate had the impression that in pornography as in aviation English had proven itself the language of concision.

He followed a group inside. He stopped at a poster of a young man and woman and felt a stab of envy complicated by nostalgia for a mystery that had once been happy.

A French sailor stumbled into him and almost knocked him into a shelf of plastic dildoes and feather vaginal ticklers bright as fishing lures. At a cash register several feet away a young man stood smoking a pipe and smiling with the engaging hospitality of an on-duty proprietor. Across the shop, at a row of bins in the *children* department, the man in the plaid jacket stood examining a packet of photographs.

After a long study the man dropped the photographs back into their bin. He looked up at Tate. His face showed neither surprise nor recognition. He came one bin closer and lingered at *bondage,* then turned toward the young man with the pipe and asked something. The young man pointed across the store toward *lesbian.*

The man in the plaid jacket excused his way through a cluster of lederhosened, laughing tourists, veered straight toward the *strong sapphic action* bin, and then in a shift of purpose as abrupt as it was smooth vanished through the door into the street.

Tate realized he must not let himself be trapped indoors or even stay in one place. By the time he reached the door the plaid jacket was gone and the sky had clouded over and the color had faded from the blur of tourists and shoppers. He picked his way across cobblestones. He had to stay alive six hours.

Her thumb ached from pressing the buzzer, but Barbara did not let go till she heard the clinking of keys. A voice grumbled, "All right, all right," and the cubicle door opened so hard it thumped against the wall.

"What's the matter with you?" The nurse was a short woman. She might have once been pretty in a Hispanic way, but she had a scar that wrenched the line of an eyebrow into a scowl. Barbara wondered if she had gotten it in a fight with a patient.

"I have to go to the bathroom." Barbara fought the dizziness and sat up.

"You piss too much."

"I'm sorry."

"You're not the only patient on this floor, you know. We got our hands full."

"I'm sorry. But it's painful and I've got to go."

The nurse sighed. "Put on your slippers."

Barbara slid into her tattered paper slippers. The nurse let her out and locked the door of the empty cubicle. Barbara looked down the corridor. She saw the door marked *toilet*, and beyond it the open door of the room that had the telephone.

"If it's too much trouble for you," Barbara said, "I can go by myself."

"I gotta go with you," the nurse said. "Rules." She motioned Barbara to the elevator.

"I'm very weak. Couldn't I use the bathroom on this floor?"

"This is the men's floor. We got so many women we had to move some of them down here. Women can't use the men's john."

The elevator was crowded with orderlies in dirty smocks and porters in undershirts and Barbara felt dizzy and faint. They rode up a floor, and the nurse went with her into the women's bathroom.

Three sinks, three toilet stalls; the smell of disinfected, overkill cleanliness. No windows. Barbara realized she would have to make a break past the nurse. The woman was smaller than she, but she didn't know how much strength she had left. And she didn't know if there was a phone on this floor.

She chose a stall and swung the door shut.

"Leave that door alone," the nurse snapped.

Barbara let the door swing open of its own weight.

The nurse shoved a stool into the sight line and sat. She pulled a magazine out of her uniform pocket. The page never turned.

Barbara was able to void slightly. There was a stinging sensation when she relaxed and it didn't go away when she stood up. Something pressed uncomfortably between her lowest rib and hipbone.

"So that was the emergency?" the nurse said.

They went back to the elevator. An orderly aimed a stretcher in and steered it between them. Barbara pressed against the wall. The old man in the stretcher never opened his eyes. The orderly jabbed a finger at the emergency button. He had a crescent of dirt beneath his nail.

The elevator skipped Barbara's floor.

When the stretcher got off, two men with pails and mops got on. The mops smelled mildewed and Barbara felt dizzy again. The elevator stopped and a fat nurse barked, "Getting off," and pushed Barbara into the corridor.

The door jerked shut and Barbara realized she was alone, unsupervised.

She studied the corridor quickly. Women in striped robes had set up chairs in a campfire circle around a TV set. The volume was turned loud and actors were machine-gunning one another. She considered doors. She saw a telephone booth, back against a wall in half shadow where an overhead light had burned out. A nurse came out of a door, looked at her, and kept on walking, like a waitress in a restaurant too busy to bother taking an order.

An old woman patient sat in a rocker, alone, her gaze clinging to smudge marks on the wall.

"Can you lend me a dime?" Barbara said.

"Sure, honey." The woman had very few teeth. She lifted herself out of the rocker and shuffled into a ward.

Something made a moist, kissing sound. Two men in T-shirts were mopping down the floor with ammonia.

The old woman came back, dime clenched between thumb and finger. "I won it in Bingo," she said. "Enjoy."

Barbara thanked her and hurried to the phone booth. There was no light inside, but she could hear a dim dial tone above the noise of the TV. For one panicky moment she could not remember her home number. Her fingers remembered. She dialed.

There were five rings. The intervals between them stretched into eternities. She saw a nurse cross the corridor carrying a tray of medicine and white Dixie cups.

Answer, she prayed: *someone please answer*.

On the seventh ring there was a click and the Finnish maid said, "Erlandsen residence."

She was so relieved her eyes watered. "Martta, it's Mrs. Er-landsen."

"Mrs. Erlandsen," Martta cried, "are you all right?"

"There's been a terrible mistake. I'm in the hospital."

"Hospital? What hospital?"

She realized she didn't know the name of the hospital and tried not to break down in tears.

"Mrs. Erlandsen," Martta kept saying, "I can't hear you, speak louder."

Barbara's nose had begun running. "I'm in a mental ward. I don't know the hospital. It's in Washington. They've got me under a wrong name."

"Mrs. Erlandsen, please speak louder. I don't understand."

The receiver was yanked from Barbara's hand and a nurse was shouting at her. "What the hell do you think you're do-ing? All over the floor!"

The receiver was shouting Barbara's name. The nurse slammed it down into the cradle. Barbara fought to stay in the booth but the nurse yanked her spinning into the cor-ridor. The linoleum was speckled bright red and Barbara re-alized her nose was pouring blood.

The nurse twisted her wrist to read the plastic ID bracelet. "You shouldn't be on this floor!" the nurse exploded. "You're violent! Violents don't belong on this floor!"

Barbara tried to claw loose. "Just one phone call—please!"

"You calm down, sister."

"Damn you, let me phone!" Barbara dug her fingernails into the nurse's forearm.

"Hey, Wendy," the nurse shouted, "straitjacket, on the double!"

Tate kept shifting his raincoat out of the way of passers-by. The plans hung heavy in the left-hand pocket.

Sunset reds gashed the sky. A rising tide of twilight en-closed the park. Inverted electric-bulb outlines of pagodas and pavilions grew brighter in the lakes. The illuminated fountain began spraying sparks in a sunken garden circumfer-enced with trees and hedges. At the end of the long central promenade, the polished glass wall of the concert hall glowed like an airline terminal.

He did not see Benzikoff.

Smells of sausage and beer and hot mustard and deep-fried potatoes poured from the food stands. From the outdoor café terraces and the pavilions of luxury restaurants came subtler smells of spice and coffee and pastry.

"Caricature?" the woman offered.

Tate had been standing beside her booth for seventeen minutes, and she must have assumed he was in line. He smiled and said, "No, thanks," but her charcoal was already making swoops at her easel. The walls of the booth were hung with samples of her art; all of them profiles with huge noses.

And he did not see Benzikoff anywhere in the crowd.

An amusement-park area sent out shouts and machine clatter. At the outdoor variety stage, a family of clowns cavorted and collided on bicycles, unicycles, tricycles, and, for a finale, motorcycles, and kept a watching crowd in continuous explosions of laughter. A dance hall radiated rock music, all thump and tinkle. From an opposite direction where an outdoor pantomime theater lifted its Chinese pagoda proscenium came wisps of waltz from another century. Along a lane of trees with tiny lights strung in the leaves, old people sat on benches nodding to sounds of Mozart from a band shell.

But he did not see Yuri Benzikoff.

Each direction he looked lights edged the view in filigree, like the lace borders of a Victorian Valentine's card. Tivoli was a fairy-tale garden, without litter or cruelty or bad temper. Crowds moved neat and smiling along its pathways. It was not at all like anything in America.

He waited and thought: *No one is going to come: I've thrown everything away and I've killed my wife and I'm going to get myself killed and it will all have been for nothing.*

"General Erlandsen?" A short woman with steel-blond hair was smiling at him. He recognized Ilona Benzikoff under a wig. "Yuri thought it would be easier if I came."

"Would you mind if we talked somewhere else?" Tate took Mrs. Benzikoff's arm and pulled her through the crowd into a line of teen-agers waiting to get onto the roller coaster. He heard the caricature artist shout something. He had forgotten to pay.

Tate bought two admissions. An attendant herded passengers up onto the boarding platform and into the cars. Each compartment sat two and had its own waist-high door. There were no locks on the doors and no restraining bars on the benches. The attendant motioned Tate and Mrs. Benzikoff into the last compartment of the next-to-last car. He swung the door shut on them. The train bumped forward several feet and stopped to let passengers into the last car.

"Why has he sent you?" Mrs. Benzikoff asked.

The train bumped into a tunnel and darkness enclosed them. The cars angled themselves for the upward climb. Tate had to raise his voice to make himself heard over the clatter.

"No one sent me," he said. "All I'm asking you to do is take these plans and pass them—"

"Make Armstrong understand," Mrs. Benzikoff cut in. "We don't want any more. No satellites, no bogus missiles, nothing."

The train burst from pitch black into a fanfare of light. A dizzying drop below, the fairway was immaculate and bright and distant as a child's Christmas.

"Listen to me," Tate said. "Theta is real."

"I shouldn't even be talking to you."

"Theta is real and it's set to go off in forty-eight hours."

"It's not our concern."

"It *is* your concern. There's no time to argue and bargain."

"I'm not arguing, General."

The descent came without warning. Tate thrust his feet against the partition. His stomach was suddenly in free fall.

"Now you listen to me," Mrs. Benzikoff hissed. "Colonel Armstrong passed my husband misleading and false information. It was expensive information."

The car dove, hit darkness, bottomed out.

"It was expensive to buy; it was expensive to repair the damage it caused. Moscow has advised my husband to sever with Colonel Armstrong."

"Theta is real!" Tate realized he was shouting. Cracks of illumination swept the train. His instincts flashed a warning. He turned and squinted. He could make out only a four-foot gap between cars, a lump of shadow hunched forward in the car behind them. Light struck a shoulder and Tate glimpsed plaid striping. "Theta is up there," he said softly, enunciating, "a hundred twenty miles over your head."

"Do you understand the meaning of advice from Moscow?" There was more than mere coldness in Mrs. Benzikoff's voice. Tate heard the slight vibrato of fear. "My husband earns sixty-three thousand rubles a year—one of the highest salaries of any physicist in the Soviet Union. Why should he risk his position—perhaps his life—playing games with Colonel Armstrong?"

"If Theta were just a game," Tate challenged, "why is there an American agent in the car behind us?"

Mrs. Benzikoff watched Tate a moment. Three cracks of light flashed by. She turned her head to throw a glance behind them. "Who is that man?" she said in a whisper edged in panic.

"He's all the proof you need. He followed me from Washington."

"Who are you working for?"

"I'm not working for anyone."

The car was moving slowly now. Mrs. Benzikoff thrust a fumbling hand outside the compartment. Metal groaned and the train struggled up toward the light, fighting gravity for each inch of gain. Tate turned again just as the fairway glare hit them and flooded the next car. Light shot through scaffolding and grooved the face of the man behind them. It was the face that had followed him three thousand miles, a heavy face with damp eyes and a pencil-line mustache mimicking the wry line of its smile.

"You're not even American!" Mrs. Benzikoff cried. "You couldn't trap Yuri, so you're trying to trap me!"

The train had spent its last dying erg of momentum and had come almost to a standstill. Down on the fairway child musicians in scarlet Queen's-guard jackets and beaver hats marched through the throngs, oom-pah'ing a hearty brass military medley.

Tate watched the man in the next car brace both hands on the railing. They held a gun. The man's eyes and the barrel of his silencer took aim. There was four feet, one twentieth of a second between him and Tate.

Tate heard the door catch snap loose. He wheeled around. "Mrs. Benzikoff, get down!" he shouted.

Mrs. Benzikoff slid quickly sideways, away from him. He grabbed for her. She lashed her hand out. Fingernails dragged across his face. There was a stinging in his cheek and he saw astonishment in the Russian woman's eyes as the car banked and lurched into its final downward swoop.

Tate dove for her too late. She was looping out the open door and through the scaffolding. The wig fluttered loose. Her head met a girder and came apart like a doll's. Something hissed past Tate's ear. The car shot round a turn and plunged back into darkness.

Tate huddled down in the seat. His mind raced. The man in the next car was going to try to kill him as soon as the

train stopped. A woman was dead, a woman who needn't
have died. Tate felt sick and wondered what he was doing,
saving the world by risking his life and everyone else's too?
He realized that was exactly what he was doing, and there
was no turning back, no hesitating now.

The train slowed at the approach to the boarding platform.
Tate vaulted over the door and shoved quickly through the
waiting passengers. A backward glance told him the man in
plaid was trapped in the crowd. That gave Tate a lead.
Maybe only three seconds, but a lead.

He pressed the raincoat tight against him. Someone yelled
and he saw the caricature artist waving a stick of charcoal at
him. A moment later he heard shouts and whistles at the
roller coaster. He kept pushing through the crowd, putting
people between him and the man in plaid. He slipped
through an exit turnstile just as a police car pulled up at the
curb and two policemen sprinted toward the gate. They were
the first grim Danes he had seen all day.

So now it was not just the Theta people who were after
him, it would be the police too. He had forty-eight hours and
he couldn't go to Benzikoff: he had to find another Russian,
the right Russian. *Keep calm*, he told himself: *there's still
time and the world is full of Russians.*

The light was red at Bernstorffs Gade. Police cars were
massing at both ends of the block. He looked behind him. He
did not see the man in plaid. That meant nothing: there
could be others, they could be wearing anything. He managed
to take several deep breaths before the light went green. He
fought the impulse to run—running would mark him—and
he crossed the street with the surge of pedestrians and walked
into the Central Railway Station.

Young people had camped out on the floor with sleeping
bags and knapsacks, card games and picnic suppers. They reminded him of the joyless, uncomfortable protesters who used
to settle in for night vigils in front of the United States Senate. He threaded a way through them and reclaimed his flight
bag from the checkroom. He emerged by the front entrance
beneath an arch of flags of all nations. A small car marked
Taxa was waiting at the taxi stand. He asked the driver to
take him to Kastrup Airport.

Settling himself and the raincoat in the cramped back seat,
he glanced through the rear-view mirror. No policeman or
man in plaid bounded out of the station.

The cab eased out into Vesterbrogade, the six-lane, central

downtown artery. Idling through a three-minute light show of automobile and bicycle and pedestrian stop-go-turn signals, the driver managed a right-hand turn onto H. C. Andersens Boulevard. Traffic was moving slowly past the Tivoli Gardens. Blue-and-white police cars bunched up at the gates, their sirens repeating the same two urgent notes like stuck records. Sidewalk strollers had slowed to a curious shuffle.

Tate scanned the bogged-down traffic for some other car that might be carrying a man in plaid. The taxi crossed a bridge. A canal on the left reflected streetlights. On the right rose nineteenth-century office buildings, whimsically turreted like the castles of a fairy-tale bureaucracy.

The cab took fourteen minutes to reach the airport. At night the glass terminal had the blinding dazzle of an electrified pavilion. People flowed along inner walkways like streams of excited particles beneath the surface of a brilliant-cut gem.

Tate went in, studied announcements of departing flights. Aeroflot, the Soviet airline, had a plane to Leningrad in two days. Finnair had a flight leaving at nine that evening for Helsinki and Leningrad. He saw that SAS acted as sales agent for all carriers, and he took his raincoat and flight bag to the ticket counter with fewest people in line.

"Is there any space left on Finnair's Leningrad flight?" he asked when his turn came.

The young woman behind the counter smiled. "There is always space on the Leningrad flight."

"I'd like a one-way ticket please."

"First-class or tourist?"

"Tourist."

"May I see your visa, sir?" She had violet eyes that harmonized with the gray airline jacket.

"I don't have a visa," Tate said.

"I'm afraid we can't sell you the ticket without a visa. You're an American citizen?"

"Yes."

"If you go to the Soviet Consulate Monday, it shouldn't take more than one or two days."

Tate saw three policemen enter the terminal and make their way toward the information booth. "Monday's too late."

"You could fly to Helsinki. There are boat tours from Helsinki to Leningrad. You sleep on the ship and you don't need a visa."

Tate's impatience flared. "It seems odd that a visa depends

on the traveler's last port. If the Russians will let me in from Helsinki, why won't they let me in from Copenhagen?"

The young woman's smile seemed strained at the edges. "The visa is waived for Finnish boat tours. I don't know the reason; perhaps it's Russia's gift to the Finns. If you're in such a hurry, it's the only solution I can suggest."

Tate realized he was angry at the young woman for something that wasn't her fault. He was more tired than he knew. "How long does that boat trip take?"

"I shouldn't think more than twelve hours."

"I'll fly to Helsinki."

The young woman took his name from the passport and issued him a ticket. He paid in fresh ten-kroner notes.

"Any luggage?" she said with weary politeness.

He held up the flight bag. "I'll carry it on."

The waiting area of Kastrup Airport was a bright indoor esplanade of restaurants, snack bars, and duty-free shops. Black-and-white closed-circuit televisions displayed arrivals and departures, and color television sets beamed a barely audible symphony concert and a subtitled Doris Day movie.

Dodging Danish boys who zipped through the crowd balancing luggage on two-wheeled scooters, Tate found a row of chairs half hidden behind a bank of potted palms. He chose a seat at the very end and arranged the raincoat on his knees. He had almost an hour and a quarter before departure. He watched a parade of Africans, the men in business suits and the women in florid tribal gowns. They intersected a parade of nuns, equally tribal in their white wimples and habits. His eye stopped at a television set perched above the snack bar.

Doris Day had vanished. The screen showed a line drawing. It suddenly came to him that it was a caricature of a man's head. He glanced toward a TV that had been showing the concert, and he saw the same image. With a queasy jab of recognition he realized that the nose could have been an exaggeration of his own. The artist in Tivoli must have given the police his description—and the unpaid-for caricature.

A wave of paranoia hit him full in the chest. He hunched down in his seat, darted glances about the terminal. He saw no Danish policemen, no one in plaid. When he glanced back at the television screen, Doris Day had returned.

His hands were shaking and his gums ached and his heart was skittering like a ballerina's slippers. He realized he had not slept in almost three days.

The phone was one of four arranged around a steel pillar like points of the compass, with plastic sound-insulating boxes that came down to one's waist and afforded a hemi-demi sort of privacy. The man in shirt sleeves did not hurry toward it. In his twelve hours in Copenhagen, he had learned to approach Danish telephones far more cautiously than it was necessary to approach Danes. He lifted the receiver, its weight and balance subtly but disturbingly different from the American variety. Into the slot he dropped two 25-øre pieces, small coins with a candy-shaped hole in the center. He dialed the exchange. When the operator asked, he recited the four digits in guidebook Danish.

As the call showed signs of going through, his knees relaxed. A voice in the receiver rasped the identification word *sidewalk*, and he said, "Green light here. I'm at Kastrup Airport. Erlandsen tried to make the transfer in Tivoli. He failed. The documents are still in his possession. He's booked passage on the twenty-one hundred flight to Helsinki."

He detected a slight syncopation before Sidewalk said, "Your Helsinki contact is 21-21-32."

He repeated the number, returned to the snack bar and asked the waiter for a pencil and wrote it down on an SAS napkin.

The snack bar was one of several glittering commercial islands running down the center of the vast steel-and-glass atrium that separated the airline ticket counters from the boarding gates. The man in shirt sleeves chose a seat that enabled him to watch Erlandsen without having to turn or stare. A simple glance over the rim of his beer glass was enough to tell him that the General was still slumped, only more so, in the green chair at the end of the row.

The man in shirt sleeves eyed travelers wandering the terminal with nomadic lack of purpose, waiting for the hour of their flights. He eyed his companions at the snack bar: they confirmed his impression of the Danes, hard-working weavers, carpenters, potters, and merchants who had shrewdly lifted their entire nation into the middle class. Part of Danish shrewdness, he suspected, was exploitation of the weakness of others. He held in his lap, cover down, a leaflet handed him on the city's pedestrian mall—a "sexionary guide" telling the tourist where to get what, and wishing him "funny sex experience."

"Tuborg," he said to the waiter, and seconds later a spar-

klingly expectant glass and a steaming, uncapped beer sat on
the counter before him. He pointed to a lobster smørrebrød
garnished with shrimp salad, and it quickly appeared beside
his beer.

The General's head had fallen forward onto his chest. He
had something of the no-strings look of a dropped mario-
nette. The man in shirt sleeves wondered if the General was
going to miss his plane.

He stared at shelves on the other side of the snack bar.
Pastries. Finely layered chocolate and mocha and orange and
rum cakes; fresh fruit tarts; custard-filled shells . . .

The speakers said something Danish about Helsingfors, and
then something in a strange language that must have been
Finnish. The same voice announced in English that passengers for Helsinki could now board at Gate 43.

The man in shirt sleeves glanced across the snack bar
through bobbing heads of travelers. His eye riveted on the
empty curve of a green chair. He slapped down five ten-
kroner notes and did not wait for change. In one spin he was
off the stool and barreling toward a sign, far across the terminal, that said *International Departures* in five different languages.

The sea of travelers parted in deference to his speed. He
did not see Erlandsen.

International Departures branched into two corridors. He
saw that one was marked 38—50 and half skidded around
the turn, dodging three young men carrying guitar cases. The
corridor branched again, 38—42 and 43—50. He prayed 43
would be the first gate.

It was not.

The corridor was filled with people, and not one of them
resembled Erlandsen. Lit from above by overlapping pools of
fluorescence, they made a strange democracy of old and
young, business suits and blue jeans. Some slowed at
rampways labeled *Amsterdam* and *Roma* and *New York*,
boarding passes extended to men in spotless midnight blue.
The others flowed on past doors marked *Paris, Berlin, Zurich,*
fewer and fewer of them, till at the final rampway marked
Helsinki there could not have been more than twenty.

The man in shirt sleeves counted: nineteen. And Erlandsen
was not one of them. *Could the ticket to Helsinki have been
a trick?* the man in shirt sleeves wondered. If the ticket had
been a trick, he was dead.

He saw a door marked *männer/men/hommes*. He walked

to it quickly and pushed through. It was very quiet in the men's room and at first glance it was very empty.

The two toilet stalls were open. Light skittered and thrashed in a fluorescent ceiling light like some trapped dying thing. The urinals flushed automatically, making him start and glance to the side. He caught his face, frightened, in a mirror.

The stall doors were at slightly different angles. The door open less far than its twin drew his eye. He saw the slightest hint of a shadow in the space at the bottom. Someone hiding?

Three tiptoe steps brought him to the toilet stall. He bent to peek and heard a movement behind him. He spun in time to see a man in stocking feet who had stepped from the other stall. In his upraised hand the man held a brown beer bottle.

The man was Tate Erlandsen, and the beer was Carlsberg, and the man in shirt sleeves felt the bottle smash into his right temple.

"We've come across an irregularity in one of the programs," Tim Boswell said.

Quentin Quinn glanced at him. "Didn't know you were so deep into programming. What kind of irregularity?"

Tim Boswell stared out across the lawn. The rubber float bobbed in the pool and fallen leaves queued up beside the filter. "Two plus two makes three."

Quentin Quinn looked oddly vulnerable in the lawn chair, like a dentist's patient awaiting the drill. "Can I ask which program?"

"Payroll." Tim Boswell scanned cinnamon flecks of dead grass prematurely dotting the lawn. "The fellow who programs it is skimming off fractional cents. His name is Hutton, Floyd Hutton. You don't happen to know him, do you, Quent?"

"Matter of fact I do. We worked together before Pacific Aero."

"That so? You're friends?"

"Wouldn't call it friends. But he's damned good at his job and I'd hate to see him screw up over some trivial sort of lapse in judgment."

"It may not be all that trivial."

"He's a kid, Tim. Not much older than your boy." Quentin Quinn shifted weight. His carefully exercised shoulders and thighs bulged trimly through his tennis shirt and slacks. "Have you reported him?"

"Not yet."

Quentin Quinn picked up his glass and drew lines in the moisture that had formed on the side. "Have you thought of giving him a good scare and letting him off with a warning?"

"I've thought of it."

Quentin Quinn's eyes tightened against the sun. He seemed to deliberate a long while before choosing the words. "There might be some sort of accommodation that would be worked out here."

"What kind of accommodation, Quent?"

"It's a little slick, but I think it could be done. The way I understand it, Tim, this kid's got a problem and Pacific Aero's got a problem. His problem is he did something foolish and Pacific Aero might fire him for it. PA's problem is a local in Detroit that's hollering for two pounds of flesh." The servants had the afternoon off and Martha was in town at the flower show and the kids had gone camping, but Quentin Quinn lowered his voice as though the shrubbery had ears. "That local is basing their demands on the Sea Condor figures. The Condor's coming in way under projection; it's showing a fantastically early break-even and nice profit, and they think they deserve a cut. Now what if—this is wild, but just hear me out—what if we got this programmer to play with those Sea Condor figures a little? What if we had him shift a few profits away from Sea Condor so it didn't look quite so good? Now that would help the company, and it would help you as labor chief, Tim. The local wouldn't have a basis for their demands."

"How are you going to shift profits?" Tim Boswell asked blandly.

Quentin Quinn gestured with a light clumsiness that threatened to knock his vodka tonic off its coaster. "Hell, the Hornet interceptor and the Condor use the same wire and the same titanium and the same bolts. We could say the Condor's grommets should have cost a penny more and the Hornet's should have cost a penny less and someone got them mixed up. We could make the Condor look like a pretty sick bird, just tinkering with unit costs. We could wrap this whole problem up, kill two birds with one stone, and it wouldn't have to go any further than you and me."

Boswell did not speak for a moment. And then he said, "How's your vodka, Quent?"

The controller of Pacific Aero smiled. "Oh, wouldn't mind a freshener."

The blond immigration officer looked again, this time directly into Tate's eyes. Tate fought to hold his legs and hands steady, above all to meet the inspector's eyes.

The moment was long and silent and when the inspector stamped the passport he did not smile. "Welcome to Finland, Mr. Erlandsen. Have a good stay."

"Thanks very much." Tate pocketed his passport and stepped through the gate. He warned himself not to let his guard slip. He had gotten through immigration, but immigration was not customs. Customs was always tougher. And even if he got through customs, the terminal was sure to be infested with police. And if he got past the police there were bound to be Theta people following, waiting.

The terminal was an immense nexus of intersecting glass and wood and steel surfaces. Through one raked wall of sheer transparency he could see night and runway and armies of distant pines, untouched by reflected hurry and glitter. His searching eyes found the Finnish/Swedish/English/German/French sign for baggage claim and exit, and he joined travelers swarming in that direction.

"Where's the red bag, Poppa?"

Tate's way was blocked by a woman reaching out to grab her husband's arm.

"You had the red bag, Momma." Poppa, who could have been in his seventies, had florid skin and lush white hair and a big relaxed smile that looked as though it had floated three thousand miles on scotch and water. He wore a natty blue polo shirt with an alligator trademark over the left pectoral sag and flopping off-white slacks that pushed his stomach upward and out like a bra.

"That girl took the red bag." The woman wore a straw hat and a cotton dress of peppermint stripes crisscrossed with deep travel creases. She had eked out her fifties with powder and rouge and a curly blond wig that was closer to infancy than youth. "*Do* something, Poppa."

It occurred to Tate that if the Scandinavian police were looking for an American who had posed for a caricature and murdered a Soviet physicist, they had their eye out for a man of his description traveling alone.

"Excuse me," he said. "Can I help?"

The woman looked stunned with relief. "Why, that's right sweet of you. That young Finnish lady has taken our red bag. I've got the baggage check right here."

Tate took the woman's baggage check and caught up with the Finnish girl. She had set the red suitcase down on the customs counter and was waiting for the inspector to get to her with his piece of chalk.

"Excuse me," Tate asked her, "do you speak English?"

She gave him a baffled look. Her dark hair made an extraordinary contrast to her Baltic blue eyes and Tate stared longer than he should have. He pantomimed with the check, matching it to the tag on the red bag. The numbers on the tag and the check were off by about thirty thousand. He apologized in English.

When he returned to the American couple, their confusion was worse. "We owe you an apology," the man said.

"The bag's right here at my feet," the woman said, "and I'm so blind I didn't even see it."

"Next time look a little harder before you leap, Momma."

"Here, let me help." Tate picked up the culprit red bag. He brushed aside the couple's grateful protests. The bag gave him a piece of luggage to show customs; and the owners were so indebted that they offered him a ride to the city.

Helsinki was one of those idyllic towns where the taxis queued up for the people. As they emerged from the terminal, the woman semaphored a cab, told the driver, "Helsinki, s'il vous plaît," and plunked herself in the back seat between the two men.

"You're American of course," she said.

"Yes, I am," Tate admitted.

"So are we. Vacation?"

"Yes."

A smile inched across her face. "Us too. Poppa hasn't had a vacation in twenty-eight years."

"Too busy working," the man said. "Own my own business in L.A. Grommet factory."

The cab slowed and turned right onto a highway. A sign gave the distance to Helsinki in kilometers and two languages. A red light made them wait while absolutely nothing went by.

"Now that Poppa's retired we decided to have us a real vacation. Poppa's mother's people were Finnish, which is why we're starting with Finland. Oh, by the way, I'm Edith Gormley." She held out a hand bristling with rings and long-reach bracelet charms.

"How do you do? I'm Tate Erlandsen."

"Hal Gormley." Mr. Gormley stretched across his wife and

gave Tate's hand a quick hard shake. "Nice to meet you, Mr. Erlandsen. You saved our lives back there."

Mrs. Gormley gazed at his flight bag. "You're certainly traveling light, Mr. Erlandsen."

"My luggage was delayed in Copenhagen."

"Is Copenhagen as wide open as they say?" Mr. Gormley winked.

"Poppa." Mrs. Gormley extracted a blue Naugahyde document case from her purse. She flipped through travel folders, airline tickets, and typed itineraries and yanked a sheet of letterhead halfway free. After an incredulous squint at it she leaned forward in the seat. "Driver, we'll be going to the *Vaakuna* Hotel." She sat back. "Well, I must have pronounced it right, he seems to understand." She hunched sideways, pressing against Tate, to catch herself in the driver's rear-view mirror. She adjusted the placement of a blond ringlet. "Our travel agent recommended the Vaakuna as one of Helsinki's better hotels. Will you be staying there too, Mr. Erlandsen?"

Through the car window Tate could see endless pines massed against a sky that had more stars than he would have thought possible. "Yes," he decided.

"They say it's very difficult to get hotel space this time of year. The Russian tours are so popular, you know."

"You don't need a visa if you leave from here," Mr. Gormley put in. "So everyone going to Russia figures they might as well come here first."

"Have you ever been to Russia, Mr. Erlandsen?" Mrs. Gormley's eyebrows held a high questioning arch.

"No, I haven't."

"Neither have we. We're very excited about our two days in Leningrad. They say it's just beautiful; the only city in Russia that the Communists didn't ruin."

The road was so empty it could have been a highway on the moon; except, Tate remembered, there are no pines on the moon. They passed a gas station. Scrubbed and glassy, it looked like something out of America before America had started falling apart. He sensed an uncanny lack of the exotic about this country.

Mr. Gormley said, "We're taking a Swedish boat from Helsinki to Leningrad tomorrow afternoon."

"It's a Finnish boat with a Swedish name, Poppa."

Tate thought how ridiculous old married people were, and

he wondered suddenly if he and Barbara would ever be ridiculous old married people.

Mr. Gormley shook his head. "This whole business is too international for me."

"When will you arrive in Leningrad?" Tate asked.

"Monday morning," Mrs. Gormley said. "They promised us we'd see the sunrise in Leningrad Harbor."

"They say," Mr. Gormley said, "sunrise in Leningrad Harbor is something."

How crazy, Tate thought, to be sitting with Theta plans in his raincoat pocket listening to silly old married people prattle about sunrises as though the sun could be counted on. "I've never heard anyone mention the Leningrad sunrise," he confessed.

"Our travel agent went last year," Mrs. Gormley said, "and she couldn't talk about *anything* else."

There was no suburb, no warning. Without transition they went from country road to city boulevard of trolleys and traffic and bright store windows, shot across a square of soaring glass, and plunged into twisting valleys of dark granite.

"Are you sure you pronounced that Vaakuna right?" Mr. Gormley asked when the taxi pulled to a stop. "This looks like a railway station."

"It is a railway station." Tate pointed out the other window. "That's the hotel."

"What a pretty hotel," Mrs. Gormley observed. "So many flags."

A doorman came to meet them. The lie worked; an embarrassed desk clerk apologized that Tate's reservation had been lost and promised to send his luggage up the minute it arrived from the airport. A bellboy who really was a boy took the Gormleys and Tate up to their rooms. They were all on the same floor, and as the bellboy unlocked Tate's door the Gormleys made him promise to join them in the bar just as soon as he settled.

Tate hung his raincoat in the closet. He surveyed his home for the night.

The bathroom had a sunken, needlepoint shower with a curtain that drew around into a 360-degree tent. The bedroom was furnished with a black-and-olive lack of clutter that eased his sense of overload. A glass door led to a balcony overlooking a large, deserted square. He recognized the railway station, a little less monumental when seen from above than from the street. A band of young men passed by singing and tossing their white caps into the air. A lone car honked at them.

The balcony ran the length of the building, partitioned by chest-high panels that seemed to be made of opaque plastic.

Tate listened a moment to the singing. He felt a stab of nostalgia, not so much for America as for song. He latched the balcony door open a crack to let the air circulate.

The hotel had provided letterhead stationery in the desk and a magazine called *Helsinki This Week* on the bedside table. He glanced through one of the articles, a blitz of did-you-know? data. He ripped the magazine into four long strips and stuffed them into an envelope. He licked the flap of the envelope, pressed it shut till it stuck, and wrote his name across the front.

He took the envelope downstairs to the clerk at the front desk. "Could I leave some papers in the hotel safe?"

"Certainly, Mr. Erlandsen." The clerk sealed Tate's papers into a large brown envelope and gave him a receipt. Tate put it in his wallet.

"Would you know anything about the boat tours to Leningrad?"

"There are several," the clerk said. "Which one are you interested in?"

Tate did not want to seem odd or anxious or even memorable. He took time to pass a glance around the split-level, curving lobby with its fountain and enormous clock whose free-floating numerals clung as if by magnetism to the wall. Five men had scattered themselves among the chairs and sofas, but none wore uniforms and none wore plaid and none were watching him or even pretending not to. *Does that mean they're not here?* he wondered; and he asked the clerk, "Is there any chance of getting on the boat that leaves tomorrow?"

The clerk, a young man with neatly cut dark hair, seemed to resist a temptation to smile. "The Leningrad cruises are very popular." He turned to twirl dials, opened the hotel safe, and added Tate's envelope to the pile of others, all bulging with mysterious deformations. "You might wish to inquire at the shipping office. You could try Aurinko Laivatoimisto—it is on Eteläinen Makasiininkatu, very near the harbor. They open for two hours at noon on Sunday."

Tate's hands were not steady and his leg muscles were shaking inside his trousers. "I'm sorry, that name and address went too fast for me."

The clerk smiled a neat smile. "I shall write them down for you."

Mr. Gormley called out, "We thought maybe you'd pushed the wrong button in the john!" The Gormleys had taken a table for four at the edge of the terrace, by a boxwood-hedged parapet overlooking the city.

"Poppa!" Mrs. Gormley scolded.

"I had to leave some things in the hotel safe." Tate sat in the chair that Mr. Gormley pulled out for him. He looked around the terrace and he wondered: *Have they followed me, are they here?*

"They say you can't be too careful, even with traveler's checks. Sure you're not too cool without your jacket?" Mrs. Gormley's eyes had crashed in blue craters of fatigue, and fresh powder did nothing to camouflage the debris. "We could take a table inside."

"Thanks, I need to be cool. It's been a very long day."

"Long for us, too." Mrs. Gormley gazed out at the city.

In the near night a tower rose with one of those glowing, glassed-in top-of-the-whatever nightclubs, not quite near enough for Tate to make out the dancing figures clearly. Below, the electric contacts of trolley cars sparked on Manner-heimintie. The broad avenue, named for the country's first president and national hero, ran through the center of Helsinki, a magnet drawing light and movement from the surrounding dark. A ripple of traffic flowed past the sweep of stone steps that marked the House of Parliament, where once upon a time a Finnish student had assassinated the Russian governor. At the other end of the avenue a flock of celebrators surged out of a glass-and-steel hotel.

"Pretty city, isn't it?" Mrs. Gormley said.

"How's your room, Mr. Erlandsen?" Tipping back his head, Mr. Gormley drained his glass down to the ice cubes. "Comfortable?"

Tate watched Mrs. Gormley. Her charm bracelet rattled as she talked and it rattled as she listened. He realized Barbara would be a Mrs. Gormley someday, if she lived, and he would be a Mr. Gormley, if he lived. "Very comfortable," he said. "I've got a view of the railway station."

"So do we," Mr. Gormley said.

Mrs. Gormley moved her glass an inch sideways. "I couldn't help noticing, Mr. Erlandsen, what artistic fingers you have. Are you a pianist?"

"I haven't played the piano for almost forty years. I could never read flats."

Mrs. Gormley leaned forward. "What an interesting ring. You're married?"

"Momma, you're not fooling anyone. Quit prying."

"I wasn't prying. And you'd better drink a little slower, Poppa."

"Why should I drink slow on vacation? Miss!" Mr. Gormley's hands made castanet cadenzas in the air. A waitress crossed to the table. "Could we have another round? *Otra vez mismo*. Make them doubles."

"Poppa, you're going to be sick as a *dog*."

"Will you stow it, Momma?"

Mrs. Gormley bit down hard on a frown. "Just don't blame me when you wake up wishing you were dead."

"And just don't you tell me you told me so. I get enough of that guff in L.A."

The waitress asked them to pay for the drinks they had had.

"Here, let me." Tate raked fingers through his pockets, but could dredge up nothing more negotiable than his room key. He signed the bill, copying his room number from the heavy metal tag.

"That is disgusting," Mrs. Gormley said when the waitress was out of earshot. "Poppa, you didn't even *try* to pay for those drinks!"

"So what? I'll pay for the next round. And the round after that."

"You drink too much."

"And you run off at the mouth too much." Mr. Gormley nudged Tate and spoke in a whisper that was shriller than a shout: "That isn't the only place she runs off at."

"Poppa, shut up."

"Travel loosens Momma up something awful." Mr. Gormley stuck out his tongue at his wife.

"I have got a splitting headache. Excuse me, Mr. Erlandsen." Mrs. Gormley rose from the chair. "Poppa, I said I have got a splitting headache."

"I know what you've got. And Mr. Erlandsen and I got a round of drinks on the way."

"Then good night." Mrs. Gormley's short stubby legs stomped a retreat from the roof terrace back into the restaurant.

"Don't mind us," Mr. Gormley said. "Plane trips always get us to arguing. But we're real happy."

The headwaiter had said the Dubrovskys could wait at the bar without losing their places in line. Mort ordered beer. Tina and her Aunt Mary were drinking whiskey sours—a buck seventy-five for a lot of fruit salad. Mort glanced toward the line of customers waiting to be seated.

"That line hasn't moved in fifteen minutes," he said.

"We've only been waiting ten minutes," Tina said.

Tina had had the idea of coming to the steak house. It was one of those places where the baked potato cost a dollar fifty extra. She'd said the least they could do when Aunt Mary came all the way from Rochester, New York, was to take the old lady out. Tina had put on her blue dress and white gloves. Mort had let her bully him into a jacket and tie.

Aunt Mary was nibbling the orange peel from her drink. Tina was sipping. Mort finished his beer and signaled the bartender for another.

"Honey, slow down," Tina whispered. "That's your third."

"It's not my fault they can't seat their customers." Mort glowered at the line. He saw eleven men like him, guys who had spent their lives turning bolts so they could buy their families a mortgage, a car, a color TV; so they could feel proud putting five dollars in the collection plate on Sunday and taking their wives out once in a while.

They looked very tired in their jackets and ties.

And then Mort saw a man and a woman walk right to the head of the line as though there weren't any line at all. The woman was laughing. Mort recognized the laugh and he recognized the Afro beehive and he recognized the face, all cinnamon and blue eyelids and crimson lips.

Davidine Stokes. She was with a white man and they were walking to the head of the line and no one had the guts to stop them. Mort thumped his bottle onto the bar and got up from the stool.

"Mort, where are you going?" Tina said.

"I'll be right back."

Mort brushed past the line and picked his way through the crowded tables. Davidine Stokes was sitting alone, leafing through the menu. Her white dress looked a hell of a lot more expensive than Tina's blue dress.

"Why, Mort Dubrovsky, what a surprise." She closed the menu.

"Stokes, get off my back."

"I wasn't aware I was *on* your back, Mr. Dubrovsky."

"Well, you are, and I'm not giving piggyback rides to anyone, white, black, or pink."

"Why so liberal, Mr. Dubrovsky?"

Mort sensed a cunning streak behind the smile that ran like a gash of snow across her face. "I'm no racist just because I tell one of you people to do something right for a change. I'm not going to apologize when I'm the one who should be *getting* the apology." He thumped a fist into his palm for emphasis and sent an unexpected shock wave up into his skull. "You may have every vice-president in the company scared shitless of you and your Zulus, but *I'm* not scared and I'm not running and I'm not apologizing."

Davidine Stokes gazed at him a moment and her voice was suddenly very different. "Don't you ever get tired of being drafted into other people's crusades?"

"Who's crusading?"

"You are. Race is a crusade, like communism or Standard Oil or the U.S.A."

"And what the hell have you got against the U.S.A.?"

"Me? Nothing. The U.S.A. is the best damned thing that ever hit this earth. John D. Rockefeller can break out of the poorhouse and turn a billion. Henry Kissinger can break out of the gas oven and wind up Secretary of State. Yeah—and you and I can starve. They conned you, Dubrovsky: they told you you're a boss just like them and you believed them. Look at your hands. You've been picking cotton your whole damned life just like me. We are the same, Dubrovsky, and if you could get your eyes off skin you'd see it."

"You are a load of Communist crap, Stokes."

"*Miss* Stokes," a male voice cut in.

Mort turned and saw a thickset white man in his late thirties with curly dark hair and a full mustache. He wore mocha-colored slacks and a satin-collared jacket and a half-open shirt.

"I said Stokes," Mort said, "and I meant Stokes."

The man came forward faster than Mort could react. He twisted Mort's shirt collar into a noose and shoved him backwards. Mort smelled sandalwood cologne and clove mouthwash and bath soap and thought he was being bulldozed by a goddamned pharmacy.

"Get your nigger-loving hands off!" Mort cried.

A fist caught Mort on the side of the chin. The momentum

sent him lurching into a pillar. He spun around to hit back and swung into a shoulder-wrenching half nelson.

Davidine Stokes burst out laughing. "Sorry, Mr. Dubrovsky. I think my honor is being defended."

The restaurant was hushed and Tina's face was a full moon of shock. "You shouldn't have done that, Mort." She daubed at his nose with a Kleenex.

"I know that guy," Mort said.

"Leave them alone." Tina tugged at his sleeve. "Come on. Let's get out before the manager throws us out."

"Where the hell have I seen that face?"

"Forget it, Mort. You think you know everyone when you're drunk."

Gormley had been explaining what it took to build a grommet factory from a two-man operation into the biggest in metropolitan L.A. Tables around them had emptied in broadening semicircles, and Tate did not think it was solely deference to early Finnish closing hours. The waitress seemed surly when she brought another round; possibly she was hinting that the man from L.A. had been loud enough long enough.

Gormley jabbed a hand into a pocket and slapped a wad of paper down onto the table.

"That is not money," the waitress said.

Finnish money came in pastel greens, blues, and purples. It did not come in bright orange folders marked *AB Aurinko Laivatoimisto OY* and bearing the elegant script notation *ticket for Mr. Gormley*.

Tate signed the bar check and placed his room key on the table. The waitress verified the room number with a single unsmiling glance. Mr. Gormley raised the dregs of a vodka tonic in a toasting gesture. Instead of reciprocating, Tate set down his glass and stood.

"Where you going?" Gormley slurred.

"Sorry, Mr. Gormley, I'm bushed."

Tate ignored Gormley's look of fleeting, skeptical sobriety and returned to his room. He went into the bathroom to splash cold water on his face. Slipping his watch off his wrist, he remembered Finnish time was an hour ahead of Danish, and he realized they were well into tomorrow.

A noise came from the bedroom. He turned off the faucet. Something scraped softly, was silent, and scraped again.

He peered into the dark room. Light filtering up from the

street outlined the window. The lamp on the desk made a T-square silhouette. Whatever it was, scraped again. He saw that a breeze was lifting the curtain window. The hem was dragging across the Danish coins that he had left on the desk top.

He moved across the bedroom and could see the bed, its striped spread tight and virginal in the half light. He reached for the wall switch and flicked.

A blinding emptiness filled the room. Traffic stirred down in the square and something scraped again. His eye went to the balcony door, still open a crack. He caught his reflection in the window, frozen in mid-turn like a figure photographed without warning. Something shadowy darted behind him, but when he whirled there was no shadow, only light streaming onto a shut and locked door, and he realized the movement had not been the reflection of anything in the room.

He flicked off the light. A humanoid shadow was trying to heft itself over the little partition separating his balcony from the neighbor's. He flung open the balcony door.

"Stop right there," he said.

The shadow was making pathetic movements like a de-clawed cat trying to tug itself up a high sofa. The head half turned in the dark. A hand went up defensively. A foot groped for purchase. The shadow cantilevered itself outward, arms flailing, and began a backwards somersault.

Tate lunged for the legs.

He wasn't even able to catch a shoe.

The raincoat opened like an umbrella, slowing the free fall by some incalculably small degree. There was no scream. Half a heartbeat later, the raincoat impacted with a smack on the balcony below. It fluttered, accommodating itself to a face-down outstretching of arms and legs. Gradually it settled.

Tate peered over the railing. He could see no movement beneath the raincoat. A woman in a bathrobe rushed onto the balcony screaming Finnish. She crouched by the body and then looked up. Tate yanked himself out of her sight line.

He slipped back into the room. He went quickly to the closet and patted the pocket of the raincoat. The envelope was still there. He inventoried Xeroxes. All accounted for.

He crossed to the straight-back chair where he had hung his jacket. He counted the money in his wallet. None missing. He looked through the several chambers of the wallet, was dissatisfied, and emptied it onto the desk.

The receipt for the envelope in the hotel safe was missing.

He sat on the bed, pushed fatigue and drink out of his head, took stock. Someone had broken into his room. They had taken the receipt, which meant they knew the envelope was in the safe and had assumed it was the plans.

He had baited the trap. The bait was gone. There could be no question. They had tailed him from Copenhagen. The woman on the balcony below was certain to phone for help. The receipt would wind up in the hands of the police; they would know the name Tate Erlandsen and they would know he was in the hotel.

He couldn't risk arrest. He couldn't even risk questioning.

He took the elevator downstairs and told the desk clerk he was going for a walk. The boy didn't so much as glance at the raincoat on his arm.

The night was cool as Tate strolled into the square. His watch told him he had less than forty-eight hours.

The psychiatrist looked at Barbara with cool fatigue. He was a plain man, short and dark-haired and young, but without the grace of youth. He said, "You must be tired, Betty."

Barbara sat very straight on the edge of the bed. She nodded. "Yes, I'm a little tired. I've had a nosebleed and I'm pregnant."

"This won't take long," the psychiatrist said. He wanted to know the date and who was President of the United States. He asked her about her parents. She spoke quietly and without cunning and she could smell peppermint from his smile. She said her parents had been ordinary people and they had lived in New York and she had loved them and they were dead now.

He kept asking his slow and meticulous questions and she sensed he found her insane in a very ordinary way. He asked what her name was.

"They say my name is Betty Engels."

"Do you agree with that?"

"Frankly, no."

He stared at her an instant, then got up from the stool and knocked on the door for the nurse to unlock it. "Betty," he said, "I have a feeling you're going to be all right very soon."

But he turned out to be as wrong as he could possibly have been.

Sunday

"Is there any chance," Tate asked, "that I could get to Leningrad on today's cruise?"

"I am very sorry, sir." The young woman in the shipping office offered a berry-lipped, very apologetic smile. "We are completely booked through the summer."

There was less than thirty-six hours left. He had spent the night sitting on a bench in the railway station, the one hotel in Helsinki that didn't demand a passport. He'd bought toiletries and he'd washed and shaved in the men's room, but he didn't feel clean and his body kept urging him to make a unilateral surrender to sleep. "I have to get into the Soviet Union today."

She gave him a look of pained sympathy, as though it were a terrible thing that anyone would have to go to the Soviet Union any day of the week. "The flights to Leningrad and Moscow are very rarely full."

"I haven't got a visa."

"I see. There are day trips to Tallinn by boat." She bent to pull a polyglot brochure from a pigeonhole beneath the white enamel counter top. Behind her, the plate-glass view of a cobbled street dipping to a blue blaze of harbor seemed a curiously well-chosen painting. "Tallinn is not so popular as Leningrad. I believe it is not so pretty either. But you would not need the visa."

"Could you book me to Tallinn today?"

She gave him the red-lipped apology again. "I am sorry, we do not have that franchise. Do you know the Vaakuna Hotel, near the railway station? There is a travel agency in the lobby that books trips to Tallinn."

It didn't seem likely that the boy who had been at the front desk last night would still be on duty: Tate took the risk of being recognized and returned to the hotel. The travel agency in the lobby was not open. He could not tell from the Finnish and Swedish signs on the door whether it was closed for the morning for the day or forever.

He would have to ask.

The day clerk, a well-fed man in his fifties, was trying to explain to an American woman that he did not know what the airline had done with her luggage. Two men were waiting in line behind her: a stocky, dark Finn with almost Mongolian eyes; and another man, Nordic, with tight colorless lips.

The American woman went sighing to the elevator, and the short man spoke to the clerk in rapid, syncopated Finnish.

The tall man stood tapping a billfold against the edge of the counter.

Tate could not tell which of them it was who said the name *Erlandsen*. The clerk scanned the honeycomb of message boxes. His hand stopped at Tate's keyless box. He turned, shaking his head, and the tall man opened his billfold and withdrew a piece of crumpled paper.

Tate could see the hotel crest on the safe receipt. The clerk nodded.

A group of tourists bustled into the lobby, chattering loud German.

The clerk made conciliatory, promissory sounds. The tall man gravely tucked the receipt back into his billfold. The two Finns moved away from the reception desk. The clerk smiled at Tate. "Yes, sir?"

"Rien, merci." Feeling conspicuous and foolish and vulnerable, Tate hurried across the lobby and out onto the sidewalk.

The two Finns followed him and stood several feet away in close, muted discussion.

Tate ignored the hounds of survival that bayed in his blood, telling him to make a break for it. He moved casually to the curb and waited for the light.

He realized that outside of telephoning the Soviet Consulate, he had very few options left: and he doubted a Soviet consul would be eager to help. Russia had been raping Finland for over a hundred years and was still trying to get her to say "I do." Harboring him from the Finnish police could hardly speed the courtship.

"Mr. Erlandsen!" someone called. "Hello!"

Tate whirled on his heel. A maroon jacket had skittered out of the hotel to wave one arm at him. The jacket enclosed a Hawaiian shirt, and the shirt more or less enclosed Hal Gormley.

"Is your head in one piece after last night?" Gormley wore dark glasses almost big enough to hide his unsteady grin.

"More or less." The light went green. "Mr. Gormley, if you'd excuse me, I'm trying to make this light."

Tate could as easily have been speaking Esperanto to a deaf baboon. Gormley took a piece of scratch paper from his trouser pocket. "The hotel doctor looked at Edith. He says she's got to have some . . . *ree-see-nee-erl-you.* That's Finnish. Castor oil. He says the only thing to do with these bugs is blast them out and sit tight for a day. Poor Edith's going to miss Leningrad. I suppose I should stay with her, but she said to me, don't be a fool, we've come six thousand miles, one of us might as well go the last hundred."

"I hope she'll be feeling better soon." The light changed again and a flood of trolleys, automobiles, and cyclists flashed past.

"She was in real pain all night," Gormley said, "sick as a dog."

And what about *my* wife? Tate wondered. The two Finns had turned to stare at the two Americans. They could have been simply curious or simply appalled at Gormley's wardrobe or they could have heard Gormley shout his name. Tate started walking along the sidewalk, away from them, and Gormley fell into step alongside.

Two men in blue-and-white uniforms came around the corner of the hotel. Helsinki police. They saw Tate and stopped.

Gormley made a face as though he had been stung. "My God, am I dumb. Mr. Erlandsen, what are you doing for the next three days? I've got an extra ticket to Leningrad. How would you like to come along with me?"

Tate moved back against the row of shopwindows, drawing Gormley with him. "That's very kind; I'd like to."

Tate was now sure the police weren't simply following him: they were enclosing him. He kept walking with the deliberate pace of a window shopper. He stared at a display of men's summer clothes, draped on mannequins improbably well heeled and groomed. He caught the reflections of the Finns in street clothes. They were standing three yards away, watching him.

Gormley pulled leaflets and folders from his various pockets. He handed Tate a red Aurinko Laivatoimisto folder with Edith Gormley's name neatly penned across the cover. "Better be on board by five."

"How much do I owe you?"

"Forget it—I'll take it out in bar bills!" Gormley laughed loudly. "Well, I'd better go see Momma." He waved a crazy *au revoir.* Stuffing papers back into his pockets, he bounced into the hotel.

The far lanes were choked with cars and trucks now. As the traffic light blinked from red to yellow to green, cars and motorcycles began to trickle up the nearer, east-bound lanes.

The two Finns were walking in Tate's direction.

He hesitated at the curb. East- and west-bound lanes had separate lights and both were against him. But the main burst of east-bound traffic was still lagging twenty yards away. He estimated anywhere from one to one and a half seconds to try to reach the island in the center of the street.

He stepped into the traffic. Horns honked and brakes slammed and cars swerved and gave him a second's clear corridor, enough to attempt the dash. He made it to the concrete divider. He rested a moment, catching his breath, looking for a gap in the west-bound traffic.

And then he saw a blue-and-white car passing west-bound, the driver turning to glance at him and the policeman seated next to the driver talking into a radio mike. The police car braked at the end of the island and signaled a U turn.

Traffic was rushing in a continuous blur. East-bound was lighter, but not yet light enough for the police car to nose into. There were no gaps at all in the west-bound. Tate saw he would have to make his own gap. He took a breath and plunged.

Blood screamed in his ears. He could dimly hear shouts and horns and screeches of brakes. A sports car cut sharply away from him and clipped a van and rebounded halfway up onto the island. He kept running. A fender grazed him. He saw the sidewalk three leaps away. He dove and heard metal slamming into metal. He kept going.

His foot hit curb. He knew his leg had been cut but there was no time to feel pain. People were staring. He slowed to a half-run, from half-run to a walk. His right knee wouldn't bend.

Fine Baltic sunshine poured down on him and he kept walking. The sidewalk ran along a glass-and-steel shopping center. The Sunday strollers, neat and well dressed, seemed in no great hurry. He came to a pedestrian walkway in the middle of the block. Here the food shops and cafés were open and students were playing guitars and people were pitching coins at them. He turned up the walkway, stopped to listen to three boys singing "Hang Down Your Head, Tom Dooley" in Finnish, risked a backward glance.

He heard a sound that might have been a police whistle.

Barbara had lost all notion of day or time. Forty watts could be a twilight or an overcast noon. She lay unmoving on the metal bed, her head back on the meager pillow. She kept a finger pressed to her upper lip, stanching the nosebleed. The nurses had refused her ice: "What do you think this is," they had laughed, "the Hilton?"

The nausea had become constant and with each hard-won breath she felt she was one jolt from throwing up. The cramps came in stabs now, sharp and deep and cutting. Something was very wrong inside her.

Her hand could not find the buzzer. She rolled onto her stomach, winced through the dizziness, searched the headboard. The cord had come untied. It was lying on the floor. She could not reach it from the bed.

Very slowly she sat up, lowered her feet, touched cold linoleum. She winced again and fought the sudden certainty that this time the nausea would go all the way. She took a deep breath, held it. The nausea receded.

When she could look down again without feeling dizzy she put her feet on the floor and stood. She kept a hand on the bed to brace herself. She stooped and gathered up the cord. The buzzer was a shattered ball of plastic and wire.

She gritted, trying to keep her head above the waves of nausea and disappointment. She pulled herself back onto the bed. Her fist clutched a handful of red-spattered sheet. She thought, *That's only the nosebleed.*

And then she realized it was in the wrong place to be nosebleed. The nausea hit in a rush and she doubled over and retched but nothing came up. Her eyes watered and she tried to call out but her throat could muster only a dry rattle.

She staggered to the door and fell against it and tried to pound. Her fists made scarcely a sound. She blinked her eyes clear and took quick inventory of the cubicle. The bed. The light bulb. The chair. It would have to be the chair.

The chair was wood. Almost too heavy to lift but not quite. She found strength to swing it back, then smash it forward into the door: once, twice, again, till it broke into sticks and her hands were bleeding and her throat, at last, found a voice with which to scream for help.

"My baby is dying!"

The corridor held its breath. Sounds leaked in through the crack under the door. An elevator labored and a wheeled

stretcher squeaked and two nurses giggled something about
IV's. Someone turned a faucet and water whispered through
a pipe like wind through leaves.

Silence again, broken only when the door exploded inward
and two nurses holding a straitjacket stood shouting at her.

"I'm pregnant," she begged them. "I'm losing my child."

One of the nurses kept shouting: who did she think she
was, they had their hands full, she had her nerve destroying
property. The other nurse said, "But, Tessie, there's blood,"
and Tessie said of course there was blood, the woman had a
goddamned nosebleed, she was the one that messed up Ward
9!

"I'd better get the doctor," the other nurse said. She went
out and came back almost immediately with a young man.
He was dark and sharp-featured and his elbows bumped the
doorframe. He sat Barbara on the bed and he looked into her
eyes with a penlight and made her stick out her tongue. He
asked where it hurt.

"Down here." She touched a hand to her abdomen.

"What have you been eating?" He spoke with his head
thrust forward, much too rapidly, like an Indian or Pakistani.

"I'm pregnant," she said. "I don't want to lose the baby."

He looked at her a moment and then he asked the nurses,
"What has she been eating?"

The nurses said she had been eating the same as the other
patients, she had no restrictions on her diet. The doctor took
Barbara's pulse and said the patient must have swallowed poi-
son. His words were clipped and exact and foreign.

Barbara made one last effort to focus her strength and consciousness. "I swear I haven't poisoned myself," she cried.
She gave them her name and telephone and address. "Call
my home, please call my home!"

But she was caught in a whirlpool of orderlies and attendants. They shoved her onto a wheeled stretcher and laced
her down, and the ceiling began racing past overhead, and
absolutely no one at all was listening to her.

On a hill in the park two hundred yards from the harbor
was a bench half hidden behind hedges and bushes. Tate
waited there, unnoticed by lovers and strollers, invisible to
most of the world except the drunks who made hourly rounds
and kept asking him, in polite and incomprehensible Finnish,
for money. He had a clear view of the flower beds and
fresh-mown slopes that dipped down to the quay. Though it

would have been easy for the police or anyone else to take him, it would be hard for them to take him by surprise.

There had been police down on the quay. He had watched them milling around the cruise ship that would cast off, in four minutes, for Leningrad. They had not glanced toward the park or set foot on the hill.

At three minutes to five Tate heard a helicopter. The day was still noon-bright, but the space between now and Theta had shrunk to thirty hours. He could see nothing overhead but dizzying vastnesses of Arctic blue. He scanned the lower arcs of sky. The dome of the Lutheran cathedral rose high and immaculate behind the long colonnades of the President's palace. Tents and stands of the farmers' market clustered about the fountain in the harborside square. The sun had bleached the city white and brought the cracks between cobblestones in far-distant streets into razor-fine focus.

Finally he saw the helicopter, hovering two hundred feet or so above the harbor, darting like a nasty and determined mosquito. It was hard to be certain of its distance: at instants the sun erased it and there was a buzz but no source. He couldn't make out the colors. Blue and white would probably have meant police.

He did not think they had left a guard at the immigration shed on the quay: the same number of policemen had come out as had gone in. But they could have left word, and a word could trap him.

It was a chance he would have to take.

Two minutes before departure time he got up from his bench and gathered up his raincoat and his flight bag and the suitcase he had bought in the Helsinki railway station. The helicopter dipped closer. He descended the hill and crossed the avenue and presented himself at the immigration shed.

He handed his passport and ticket to the Finnish ship's officer. The officer made a careful comparison of passport and ticket with the names on the passenger manifest. A line had been drawn through *Gormley, Edith.* Tate's name had been handwritten beside it. The officer made a checkmark.

The passport traveled on to an emigration officer, who stamped it, and on to another man who went to a phone at the rear of the shed and talked a little Russian, listened to what must have been a great deal of Russian, and finally called Tate.

"What is the purpose of your visit?" He wore a gray suit cut too broad at the shoulder and a black necktie shaped like a ruler. A steel molar glinted in his mouth.

What would the Russian have thought, Tate wondered, if he had answered: *to keep your country and mine from blowing one another up?*

"I'd like to see the French Impressionists in the Hermitage," Tate said.

The Russian handed him his passport and the ship's officer gave him back his ticket. He crossed the asphalt quay to the ship's boarding ramp. Nobody tried to stop him.

He sidestepped stewards and porters and took his raincoat and his luggage to the stern. A family of tourists was chattering French and taking photographs. The winch of a cargo ship unloading Volkswagens hummed. Squawking gulls of uncorrupted white swooped overhead, searching for garbage.

Four minutes behind schedule, the ship's whistle blew three last warnings. Tate saw four policemen and a woman in a green coat hop down the gangplank just before the sailors pulled it in. The ship began moving, drawn by two tugboat guides. Islands drifted past—some so small they surely must have disappeared beneath high tide, one large and high and housing a gleaming yacht club and marina, another a stone fortress that could have held off a Napoleonic navy. For an instant the helicopter hovered overhead, blue and white, then veered toward the shore. White sailboats crisscrossed in the ship's boulevard-broad wake. The city grew smaller, and the tugboats cast the ship loose and turned back.

Tate went inside. The passageways were mobbed with travelers colliding in search of their cabins, their luggage, the bar, the deck. They babbled a half dozen languages but with no stretch at all of the imagination they could have been Americans: there were diet-slim women in colorful print dresses, duchesses of automated kitchens and suburban backyards; children in pigtails and jeans rampaging fearless and greedy up and down the corridors; men cut loose for twenty-one days from the echelons of middle management, skins smooth and sunlamped, stomachs forced slightly out by years of good food and good hard desk work. Their faces were anxious with the habitual expectation of happiness.

Tate observed the confusion a moment, then worked his way down to B deck. Several searching turns took him to dead-end water fountains and bathrooms before a movement of the ship sent him lurching into a door that bore the number on his ticket.

Mr. Gormley had already put his suitcases on the lower

bunk and was attempting to force-feed a film cartridge into a small Japanese camera. "Wondered if you were going to make it," he said.

"So did I." Tate squeezed small enough to shut the door. He hung his raincoat on the hook behind it.

"You don't mind if I take the bottom berth, do you? I've got a trick knee. It's tough for me to climb up and down."

"Of course not," Tate said.

Someone in the passageway shouted, "Here we are, Polly!" and a big blond woman banged into the cabin dragging a little blond woman behind her. She stopped short at the sight of Mr. Gormley. "Oh, I'm sorry."

Mr. Gormley kept sorting his clothes on the bunk. "That's quite all right."

"I'm sorry," she clarified, "but this is *our* cabin." She thrust out two steamer tickets in blue covers and wagged them. "B deck, cabin 103."

Mr. Gromley showed his ticket, and the big woman's jaw dropped.

"That's not possible." The big woman gave her friend a push. "Polly, go get a ship's officer."

Mr. Gormley began putting trousers on hangers.

"I wouldn't unpack any more if I were you," she advised.

Under any other circumstances, the cabin would have struck Tate as a curious prize to squabble over. Spotless to be sure, but tiny.

Mr. Gormley surprised Tate by almost raising a fist to the woman. "Look here, you and your friend are trespassing, and I'll thank you to get out and let us unpack."

"Not on your life." She wore a China-red jacket and white chino slacks and shoes of the same metallic color as her hair. "Polly and I made our reservations January first and we have carbons of the telex to prove it." As she began dredging her enormous red purse, Polly returned with a ship's officer. "*Zdrast*-vicha, grazhda*nin*," the big woman greeted him in what seemed to be fluent and awful Russian. With a cutting sweep of jeweled finger she indicated Tate and Gormley. "*E*ti chela*vy*eki v *na*sha *kom*nata! *Na*sha!"

The officer gave her a hard little smile. "I'm afraid we do not speak Russian."

"Well, maybe you could tell these men to get out of our cabin."

"May I see your tickets please?"

The two women and Tate and Gormley handed over their

tickets. The officer leafed through the two blue booklets and the two red booklets with their different typefaces. "Mr. Gormley, you are no longer traveling with your wife?"

"My wife is sick in Helsinki. I gave her ticket to my friend Mr. Erlandsen."

"May I see your passport, Mr. Erlandsen?"

"Certainly." Tate avoided the stare of the big blonde and gave the officer his passport.

The officer studied the photograph and the pages of visas. "You entered Finland last night?"

"Yes."

"And Denmark yesterday morning?"

"I couldn't get a direct flight." The officer's silence seemed to question the probability of this. "I thought I might as well see some of Copenhagen while I was there."

"Tivoli is very pretty," the officer said.

"I didn't get a chance to see it."

"I see there has been a mistake." The officer's gaze slid slowly off Tate and went, smiling, to the women. "You ladies are on A deck."

"Why, A deck is much better!" Polly cried.

"Just a minute," the big woman said. "Does A deck cost more?"

"Of course not. Please come with me, ladies."

The women followed him. Mr. Gormley closed the door and locked it. His face had turned red and his knuckles bulged white in his fists.

"How is Mrs. Gormley?" Tate asked.

"Just awful, thanks. The hotel doctor gave her penicillin." Mr. Gormley placed his toothbrush, bristles up, in one of the glasses on the shelf above the sink. "That castor oil made her real miserable."

"I'm sorry to hear that."

Mr. Gormley shrugged. "He says she'll be okay in a day or two."

A doctor looked down at Barbara, his hands resting huge and young on the raised railing of the stretcher. "Hello, Betty," he said. His voice was American.

She suspected they had brought her to the operating room. Shafts of air conditioning pierced her. She had only the hospital smock for warmth and it had ripped up one side. Her ankles shivered as though they were floating in ice water. Someone was talking about low hemoglobin.

The doctor wore a gray sweatshirt beneath his smock. She could read the letters *ARTM* and she wondered if he had gone to Dartmouth. He had a student's face. Beyond the operating light, the depth of the ceiling was distant and dark as the universe at night.

"Ever had your stomach pumped, Betty?" the doctor asked. "It's a perfectly benign procedure."

Green-smocked shapes advanced from the shadows to check pulse, heartbeat, pulmonary function. Someone asked if she was comfortable and she wanted to say, *I'm miscarrying, don't bother about me, save the child,* but there were too many hands smothering her face and all she could get out was a helpless mumble.

"That's all right," they told her, "you'll be just fine."

A lab technician wanted blood. Gloved hands made sure she was tied down. Nurses and orderlies and interns and residents swirled around her, eyes grim and competent above their green masks.

A woman tried to put a mask over her nose and mouth and someone screamed, "Get that thing away from her, she o.d.'d!" and the mask was yanked away.

"Will you get the goddamned *pump* in here?" the young doctor shouted.

A door made a swinging sound and wheels squeaked.

"Pulse is too low," Barbara heard. "Let's get this show going before the heart engorges."

A plastic tube went up into her nostril. It jammed where the nosebleed had formed a scab.

A nurse said, "Uh-oh, Doctor, we're stuck," and the tube pushed and wriggled and shoved till the scab broke. Blood began pouring down again, salting Barbara's lip. The tube kept going into her, cold and amber like a translucent vitamin capsule that had been in the refrigerator.

"Atta girl, Betty," someone said. "Good girl."

Her right eye ached and her throat ached as though a sharp bone were being forced down it and the ache went deeper and deeper into her until she lost trace of its exact position. What bothered her most horribly was the eye, to have something cold press on it from behind where she had never felt anything, never known there was a chamber. The eye began crying and the operating lamp became twins.

"Don't tense up," someone snapped, and a sponge was dragged across her mouth. But the cramps kept coming, like kicks aimed at her belly, and the spasms knotted tighter till finally something burst in the lower intestine and she could no longer contain the pain. She tried to scream.

"Jesus Christ, will you look at that!" someone cried.

She felt a hot rush through the vagina and something alive poured out of her and turned cold and damp and dead on her thighs. She kept trying to scream through the vomit and the plastic. The wall of green masks and dismayed eyes crumbled and for an instant the gloved hands forgot to hold her.

She wrenched her head up and blinked the images into focus. The lower half of the operating table was drenched in red, new red, and the red was her.

"Isn't it lovely," Frances Meredith was saying, "to get together like this, just the three of us? Why, it's almost like the old days—so much friendlier than a dinner party where you have to talk to a dozen people and really can't have a genuine conversation."

They were sitting on the flagstone terrace beneath an infinite, cloudless sky, staring across a lawn that dipped to the swimming pool and bathhouse. Frances Meredith had consented to come to Sunday lunch and she had consented to have one martini, provided O'Brien made it himself because he and the man at the Hilton made the only decent martinis in the state of Washington. She had pleasantly refused a refill, and O'Brien had realized that for all the Sunday informality of her chatter she was not about to be caught with her guard down if he should bring up business.

"But communication," she was saying, "the ability to sit down with old friends and say what is really on your mind and to hear what's on theirs—there just isn't very much of that any more." Frances Meredith took a nibble of romaine lettuce. "Or am I just getting grumbling and sensitive with old age?"

"I don't think you're getting sensitive at all," O'Brien said, and when the words were out he realized he had said what he believed instead of what he had intended.

Debbie and Frances Meredith laughed at the amusing mix-up in words. Debbie had had the Swedish girl prepare a salmon mousse and a salad of avocado and orange segments: you could taste the fresh tarragon in the dressing. There were strawberries and a bottle of Dom Pérignon *brut*, with another waiting iced in the pantry. It had been a light brunch, just unorthodox enough for Frances Meredith to feel they had put a little thought into it.

O'Brien explained that what he had meant to say was that in his opinion Frances was not imagining present-day lack of communication: it was a fact.

"But I feel *we* have communication, don't you?" Frances Meredith turned to Debbie.

"I think we have communication," Debbie said.

"Don't you agree, Jack?" Frances Meredith asked. "The three of us have wonderful communication." She had the understanding eyes of a visitor at a hospital bed, and O'Brien realized that so far as Frances Meredith was concerned he was going into surgery and all she intended to do about it was wish him luck.

"Harvey is so independent—just like his granddad." By some dizzying translation, Frances Meredith was talking about her grandchildren again. O'Brien wondered how it was, if she loved her grandson Harvey and thought so much of his classical guitar playing, she had not bothered to find out a damned thing that was happening to him.

"Frances," O'Brien interrupted, "there's a company matter we might as well discuss now."

"Yes, Jack. Only I'd thought this was to be a friendly brunch, not a business lunch."

"If Debbie would excuse us, perhaps we could go to the study for a moment." O'Brien rose and after an instant Frances Meredith patted her lips with her napkin and rose too. He led her through the living room and opened the library door and let her go first.

"You can tell this is a man's room," she said. "One thing I miss about not having Tod is that there really isn't a man's room in the house any more."

There was a scuffling sound at the front door, and glancing back into the hallway O'Brien could see the Swedish girl trying to keep a man in a checkered shirt out of the house.

"What is it, Inger?" O'Brien said.

"I tried to tell him you're having lunch, sir."

O'Brien stared at the overweight man whose beer breath filled a six-foot radius. He was not sure if he recognized him or simply recognized the type.

"Mort Dubrovsky." A big hand waved, demanding to be shaken. "Building C. We talked at the Golden Age Banquet?"

O'Brien thought, but nothing at all came back. "Yes, Mort," he said. "What can I do for you?"

"It's about that Davidine Stokes fuss last week?" The big man looked into the hallway as though it were a cave his eyes had not adjusted to. "If I'm not busting in?"

"We can talk for a moment."

Frances Meredith had wandered back into the hallway.

"Frances, this is Mort Dubrovsky, one of our men from Building C. Mrs. Meredith is the widow of our co-founder."

"How do you do, ma'am. I met your husband once."

Frances Meredith shook the big red hand and watched O'Brien curiously.

"Well, Mort," O'Brien said, "what about Davidine Stokes?"

Mort Dubrovsky thrust out a copy of last year's annual company report. He had circled one of the photographs inside the rear cover. O'Brien recognized Allan Martino's picture.

"I saw Davidine Stokes yesterday." Dubrovsky glanced at Frances Meredith as though she were a dam holding him back. "She was with this guy. They looked very friendly, if you read my meaning."

"I'm sorry, Frances. Would you excuse us?" O'Brien led Mort Dubrovsky into the study and closed the door. "Sit down, Mort. Now tell me exactly what makes you think Mr. Martino and Miss Stokes are friends."

Mort Dubrovsky sat down in a straight-back chair and told O'Brien what had happened. O'Brien thumbed through his leather address book and found Tim Boswell's home number. He dialed the phone and Martha Boswell said her husband was vacuuming the swimming pool and she would call him. When Pacific Aero's vice-president in charge of labor relations came onto the line he sounded short of breath.

"Tim," O'Brien said, "I'd like you to pull the record on Davidine Stokes—everything we've got or can get on her, credit rating, bank account, education, police, the works. And meet me at the club in, say, an hour and a half. Can you do that, Tim?"

"What's the Russian naval base in the Gulf of Finland?" Mr. Gormley stared at the sea. "The secret one."

"They have secret bases at Gogland and Lenissari," Tate said. At first he had been surprised, and now he was growing tired of the old man's encyclopedic questioning. He added, so as not to sound curt, "We'll probably be passing Lenissari in a few hours."

At Gormley's suggestion, they had taken their after-dinner

brandies from the bar out to the foredeck. "What's the big one?" Gormley asked. "They named it for a battleship."

"Kronstadt?"

"When do we pass Kronstadt?"

The hull timbers kept slapping the sea, sending up salt spray that swept the deck in wind-whipped cloudbursts. Both men were getting lightly dewed.

"Not for quite a while," Tate hazarded. "Kronstadt couldn't be more than twenty miles from Leningrad."

"Wonder what they do there that's so damned secret."

Live rock music was audible from the ship's saloon, where passengers had gathered for cards and drinking and dancing. Tate had noticed an almost manic merriment on board, growing all the more frenzied the nearer they got to Russia. His hand automatically tapped the steel rail in time to the music. The face of his watch glowed with the slow fallout of its radium dial. Almost midnight. In western Russia the clocks would be an hour earlier. Twenty-one hours till Theta. In America it would still be midday. He wondered if Barbara could see the sun.

"Hi," someone shouted. "We owe you two fellows an apology." A big shadow and a little one wobbled across the deck, fighting its slope. "Remember us, Polly and Mildred from B deck? At least we thought we were from B deck." The big one clutched the railing and held out a steadying hand to her laggard companion.

"Are you all settled in?" Tate asked.

"Just as comfy as we could be. We even have a porthole." The women had changed for dinner. Polly wore several layers of black that wrapped her like yarn on a bobbin. Mildred was a tower of ormolu, with outsize cornelian highlights sparkling at bodice and fingertips. She smiled at Mr. Gormley and, triggering no response, at Tate. "Do I detect American accents? Polly and I are from the United States too. Mattoon, Illinois? You've probably never heard of it, but if you've ever been to the Champaign-Urbana air terminal, we're an hour's drive from there."

"I hear it's a handsome terminal." Tate watched gulls circle the ship.

"It's very modern. Of course, compared to some of the buildings in Scandinavia it's Victorian, but compared to Scandinavia, what isn't?" Mildred appraised the heavens. Sharply focused points of light jutted through the Baltic night like tips of ice stalactites. "Are you gentlemen traveling alone?"

"We're together," Mr. Gormley stated.

"Polly and I were originally traveling with two girl friends, Annie and Sallie Wentworth? They're from Mattoon too. Sisters. They never married. Well, Annie and Sallie and Polly and I come all the way to Helsinki, Finland, and what do we discover?"

Polly leaned into the conversation, eyebrows pert and mouth ajar as though to relate what they had discovered. Mildred's shoulder edged her out.

"We discover that the shipping line has canceled two of our tickets to Leningrad, just like that, if you please." Mildred snapped her fingers, scaring a gull. "*Apparently* they expected to have one more ship in service, and they overbooked the whole season. The shipping people were very apologetic, but when you come three thousand miles to see Leningrad, you want to see Leningrad. I hear it's the Venice of the North."

Wavering in the moon-bleached dark at horizon level, a thin gray line stretched out to starboard like a bit of Russia that had cast itself adrift.

"They said they could send two of us to Leningrad and two to Tallinn, Estonia. So we drew lots, and Annie and Sallie got Estonia."

"I hope they're enjoying it." Mr. Gormley tossed his brandy down in a swallow.

"Annie and Sallie are a hoot. They'd be able to get a laugh out of a funeral. They're just fun people." Mildred drew a gold cigarette case from her handbag. "But that's why we flew off our handles at you. We thought we'd end up sleeping in the galley if we didn't take a stand!"

"That's quite all right," Tate assured her. "No harm done."

Mildred waved her gold at him. "Smoke?"

"No, thanks."

She turned to Mr. Gormley. "And did I hear you say your wife had picked up some kind of bug, Mr.—ah—?"

"Would you excuse me?" Tate apologized. He couldn't take the women. "I'm a little tired." Mr. Gormley shot him a despairing look.

"Of course," Mildred said. "Pleasant dreams."

As Tate crossed the deck, Mildred chattered on a wavelength audible between thundering waves and screaming rock. "Polly and I have had a bug since Amsterdam. I really think the restaurants serve *canal* water in Amsterdam. Were you and your wife in Amsterdam, Mr.—ah—?"

"Vassar College?" Jack O'Brien was incredulous. Vassar had turned down one of his own nieces because she hadn't made the upper two percentiles of her class in boarding school.

Tim Boswell nodded and said, "Phi Beta Kappa. Harvard Law School."

"This is the same Davidine Stokes that's marching pickets around our gates?"

Tim Boswell took a long swallow of bourbon and nodded.

"Worked eighteen months with Model Cities Program in New York City. Salary seventeen thousand—starting salary?" O'Brien's eye kept tripping on the blunt digital assertions. They were astonishing, but he had no reason to doubt them. Though he didn't ask where the printout had come from, he knew that Tim Boswell's brother-in-law directed the Seattle bureau of the FBI. A year or so ago the FBI had absorbed state and local criminal data systems into a centralized bank at Oskaloosa, Iowa. The Davidine Stokes dossier looked like the sort of thing the agency would be able to churn out with the flick of a button. "Seven months with Illinois State Addictive Drug Control Program—twenty-five thousand?" O'Brien whistled softly.

Tim Boswell set down his glass. "There's money in them thar narcotics."

"This doesn't make sense. From drug work she goes to the public relations department of Standard Oil of New Jersey, where she earns thirty-eight thousand. She must be the highest-paid token black in American industry."

"There could be more to it than tokenism." Tim Boswell jingled his ice cubes. "Fourteen months ago she quit Standard Oil and applied to the Pacific Aero minority hiring program. She trained for three weeks at a salary of ninety-eight dollars and started out on aircraft assembly at a hundred forty-five."

"Transferred to electronics subassembly, bringing her up to a hundred seventy-five," O'Brien read from the printout. "This woman's been getting an executive salary for eight years and she suddenly takes a thirty-thousand-dollar pay cut to work for us. Doesn't make sense."

"She has eight national charge cards with credit limits of four thousand on six of them," Tim Boswell said. "She has close to twenty thousand in her savings account. Three months ago she picked up a hundred seventy-five shares of IBM."

O'Brien's eye dropped to the list of capital assets. "And eighteen hundred shares of us." He glanced toward the golf course. A woman hit a clean, long drive that cleared the lake, and he wondered how many days a week she practiced. "How the hell did we ever hire Davidine Stokes for an assembly line?"

"She's got a black face and she wanted to tighten bolts on a swing-wing bomber jet. We pressed two buttons: dope and prison. Negative on both, hosannas all around, and we were one digit closer to meeting our government quota guidelines."

O'Brien sipped and thought about it. The Chestnut Ridge Country Club was the only place in the world where he could sip and think and not feel guilty for taking his time. The club had originally been the private estate of a Seattle five-and-ten tycoon. The golf course was a copy of the links at St. Andrews in Scotland, and the twenty-odd-room house had been reshaped to accommodate a ballroom, squash courts, an indoor pool, and a pretty decent restaurant. Though he didn't get a chance to use the club as much as he'd have liked, he always found it a vacation to sit on the west terrace and sip a drink and watch golfers on the fifth green.

"Do you remember the day we dropped four points on the New York Exchange and thought we were being flim-flammed?"

"Last March," O'Brien said.

"Miss Stokes bought those eighteen hundred shares that same day. At the bottom. She's made a killing." Tim Boswell had a way of holding his fingers up not quite straight so you couldn't tell how many were meant to be counted. "Consider a few other specifics. She pulls a dozen women off work and stands them up with picket signs. A few hands are shaken, the women go back to the assembly lines. No demands, no concessions. Tempest fugit. Yet that teapot tempest shows up on national prime-time television news and on the wire services, and it shows up as racial friction at Pacific Aero." The fingers made a fist around the almost empty bourbon glass. "And remember, this woman has a background in news management."

O'Brien nodded. "Someone is bankrolling her." He stared out at the putting green, at a woman who'd conscripted her little boy to caddy for her. The child was scarcely as tall as the golf bag but there was something brave in the way he struggled to hold it up. "There's a rumor she's seeing one of our board members," O'Brien said.

"Allan ,Martino." Tim Boswell flipped several folds of printout. "He spends two weekends a month with her."

"Maybe they're in love," O'Brien said. "I've met Davidine Stokes. I can see a man's being attracted."

Tim Boswell gave him an odd glance. "Martino's company—Southern Electronics—they've been expanding. They used some pretty dirty tricks to drive down the stock of an electronics outfit in Utah."

O'Brien sipped his bourbon and said nothing.

"Jack, we're taking a beating on the stock market. We're taking a beating in the press and on TV. We're taking a beating from labor. Now it could be coincidence that all this trouble hits us at once. Or it could be ripple effect. Or it could be part of a concerted attack. Because that's exactly the way Southern Electronics took over Utah Pan-Rad. Hit them on all fronts at once, drove the stock down to rock bottom, panicked the stockholders into selling."

"We're being raided," O'Brien admitted. It hurt to admit it, because he was admitting he'd seen nothing, suspected nothing, done nothing. "For the last six months the raider's been buying out our small stockholders. He's been picking up blocks of stock on the New York Exchange through brokerage houses, holding them in street-name accounts. He's got anywhere from a tenth to a quarter of us. He may not have caused our labor troubles or our cost overruns, but he certainly knows how to exploit them."

Tim Boswell drew closer to the table. "Jack, the raider may have more to do with our cost overruns than you think." He transferred a sheaf of papers from his briefcase to the tabletop. "We're using the same three-inch Halloway rivet on the Sea Condor helicopter and on the Hornet fighter plane. On the Sea Condor it's been costed at eight cents flat; on the Hornet it's been costed at nine point zero eight."

O'Brien squinted at the figures. "What the dickens—?"

"We buy those rivets at a unit price of .0854. Fifty-four hundredths of a cent has been systematically knocked off every rivet in the Condor and added to the Hornet. If it were just rivets I'd say maybe it was a bookkeeping mistake. But exactly the same thing has happened on hydraulic tubing, door rollers, sheet plexi-glass, seats, seat belts . . . every element the two craft have in common. In the last seven months close to forty million dollars has been shifted. Which explains some of Hornet's overruns and Sea Condor's complete lack of them."

O'Brien frowned. "And you think the raider's doing this?"

"I'm not sure. I can see Southern Electronics might want to make Hornet look like a money loser, but why the hell they'd want to make an unsophisticated Marine helicopter look forty million cheaper is beyond me."

"If they're shifting costs," O'Brien said, "they'd have to bury the discrepancy somewhere. They couldn't very well pocket the money, could they?"

"That's the problem, Jack. Someone *has* been pocketing money. Payroll money. Hard to say how much. We'll have to go over every single paycheck PA has issued in the last eighteen months and add up every tenth of a cent to be sure. What it comes down to is that we've been picking the pockets of our own workers and robbing the Navy to pay the Marines. This could blow up in our faces."

"Why didn't the treasurer catch it?"

"Maybe Dev Barker's been too busy looking for outside financing."

"The auditors should have seen it."

"Auditors don't look at overhead as closely as inventory. The thieves could have hidden a lot of discrepancies in overhead. They could have retyped invoices to verify the alterations."

"But auditors should catch a rivet costing eight cents on a helicopter and nine on a fighter plane."

"Well, two of the biggest auditing outfits in the country are under indictment right now for just that kind of slip-up. The fact is, our auditors didn't catch it, and maybe we should consider changing firms."

"Who's the thief?"

"Your controller—Quentin Quinn."

O'Brien shook his head. "How'd you stumble on this, Tim?"

"One of the foremen complained his payroll deductions weren't adding up. I found one of the programmers—a kid Quinn brought from his old outfit—had been systematically looting the payroll. I confronted the kid, and Quentin Quinn popped up on my doorstep. He said if I let the kid off, the kid could shift costs away from Hornet onto Sea Condor and give management a weapon against the Detroit workers. Those Sea Condor figures have always looked a little too rosy and costs were running way over on Hornet. It occurred to me Quinn and his friend might have been doing just the reverse: padding Hornet costs with figures skimmed off Sea Condor—so naturally it would be the easiest thing in the world for them to unpad. I checked, and I was right."

"But the payroll," O'Brien groaned. "Why the hell did they have to steal from the men?"

"My hunch is, the programmer juggled the payroll on his own. He knew if he got caught, Quinn would have to cover for him. Which is exactly what Quinn tried to do."

"I'd like to see what kind of proof you have."

Tim Boswell sighed and opened the briefcase again.

The Last Monday

Wind from the Gulf of Finland blustered across the top deck. On the far side of the harbor a chorus of ships' winches throbbed in rhythms that never quite got together. Tate stared into the Leningrad sky. Soviet gulls streaked squawking across the ice-blue morning. He brought his gaze down to the jumble of ships' smokestacks and funnels, towering in their nearness, and saw the distant glitter of one gold dome and a single blunt thumb of high-rise.

The pier was awash in solitude. It was almost eight o'clock. Fourteen hours and six minutes till Theta. The footsteps of two soldiers clicked hollow and slow on the dock. It seemed to Tate that the Finnish ship was the only living thing at mooring. The liners from Amsterdam and Oslo, the two pleasure craft from Stockholm were still as ghost towns. He watched Russian sailors hurry forward to secure the gangplank. As the first excited passengers began trickling off the ship he turned to go down to his cabin.

When he opened the door of B-103 he found a startled Gormley backed against the bunks, holding something behind him.

"What are you doing with my raincoat?" Tate asked.

"I'm sorry. I thought it was mine. You see, I have one at home exactly like this."

Tate shut the cabin door and reached for the coat. He patted a pocket and found the envelope. The plans were still there.

"Were you looking for these?" Tate asked.

Gormley drew a Wesson .32 revolver from his pocket.

"So you were the backup for the man in Copenhagen." Tate saw how careless, how gullible he had been. The habit of trusting people died hard.

"And you would have ended up in the Baltic last night, General, if those chatterboxes from Illinois hadn't butted in."

"But how did you get cabin reservations? This cruise has been booked up for months."

"Contacts in Finnish security persuaded the shipping line to bump two passengers—friends of the chatterboxes."

"Whose payroll are you on?"

"Free-lance, ever since we moved to Finland. Technically we're retired from Navy Intelligence. But our pensions and Social Security don't quite pay the rent on our little apartment in Kotka. That's a town on the southern coast. Pretty place. From time to time old contacts help us out, toss us odds and ends."

"Then your wife works for them too?"

"Edith is not my wife. She's my sister. She fell from your balcony, trying to get those plans, and she'll probably spend the rest of her life with a hip brace. Now would you please hand them over?"

"You can't fire that gun. The noise would bring the whole ship down on you."

Gormley kept his eyes and gun trained on Tate. He reached sideways for his suitcase, hefted it onto the lower berth, snapped it open, and felt beneath the underclothes. He drew out a silencer, shook it free of the sock that had enclosed it, and fitted it to the barrel. "The plans, General."

Tate moved forward. The gun, grotesquely distended, reacted by waving him to a stop.

"Put them on the bed."

Tate bent down to place the envelope on the lower bunk. Straightening up, he went for Gormley, rushing and low. He would not have expected an old man to move so quickly. The first bullet made a dull kissing sound and missed him wildly. It convulsed the mattress of the upper bunk and left the sheet twitching. The second bullet singed an inch of linoleum from the floor.

Tate grabbed for the elbow and flung the arm off aim and drove his head into Gormley's stomach. The gun clattered from his hand and the floor rang metallic beneath the linoleum. Wheezing, the old man lost his balance, skidded a foot out for buttress. His heel hit the barrel of the silencer, sent it flying with a knock against the door. His hands grabbed air, legs shooting forward. His head slammed into a corner of the sink.

There was a crackling sound that might have been a fistful of celery stalks all snapping at once. Gormley's eyes went wide and stayed wide. For a moment he was absolutely still. Then the feet inched forward in smooth contact with the linoleum and the rest of him followed easily onto the floor like a child coming down a slide in a playground.

Blood came rapidly from a tear at the back of the scalp. Tate felt for a pulse. The heart was still beating. He wound a towel around the head. He dragged the old man by the shoulders to the bunk.

He washed his hands and put the plans back into the raincoat pocket. He slung the coat over his arm and stepped out of the cabin. The Finnish chambermaid, passing with an armload of fresh sheets and a jingling master key, smiled and said, *"Hyvää päivää."*

"The man in 103 has had an accident," Tate said. "You'd better get the ship's doctor." She kept smiling and he doubted she had understood. But there was no time. He took the steps of the stairway two at a leap.

Disembarking passengers had lined up in the A-deck corridor. The chatter was excited and polyglot and he kept catching the word *Hermitage*. A Soviet soldier, wearing a gray uniform that could have been cut from an Army blanket, collected passports at the boarding ramp. He gave each a grim ten-second scrutiny, placed it in a box with alphabetized dividers, and handed back a plastic card with small Cyrillic print.

Tate surrendered his passport, received his plastic card, and joined the flow streaming along the pier toward the immigration shed. There was a second bottleneck as passengers lined up to fill out currency forms and buy rubles. Postcards and souvenirs bore prices in dollars: twenty-five cents for a photograph of the bronze statue of Peter the Great, its colors unbelievably off; three dollars for a pouting eight-inch doll in Ukrainian peasant dress.

Cyrillic Pepsi-Cola cost fifty cents a bottle.

A young Russian woman gave Tate a smile spiked with loathing. She told him he could buy rubles at four for five dollars and would have to declare all foreign currency in his possession.

Tate debated.

When the chambermaid found Gormley, she was almost sure to notify the authorities. He wondered: would it save steps to hand himself over to the police and rely on them to pass the Theta plans to the military? He'd heard of the Soviet police and he'd heard of the way they handled interrogations. He glanced at his wristwatch. He had only sixteen hours, and if he let the police take him there was too great a risk of delay. He would have to find a taxi and somehow communicate to the driver that he wanted to go to a ministry of defense.

He bought twenty dollars' worth of rubles and declared the dollars, kroner, and finnmarks left in his wallet. The woman stamped his currency form, and an unsmiling guard pointed him through a door out into the parking lot.

Five buses waited. Instead of destinations, they bore the names of the languages: *Français, Deutsch, Suomi,* and two *English.* On the other side of an eight-foot fence, three children pressed their noses to the mesh and stared at the foreigners. There was not a single taxi in the parking lot. Two armed soldiers in gray guarded the gate. Traffic was light, and there were no taxis in the street.

Tate saw that one of the English buses was warming up its motor. The bus would get him into the city. There had to be taxis in the city.

He got onto the bus and moved to the rear and took a seat behind two blond heads. They both turned and he recognized Mildred and Polly from Mattoon, Illinois. "Why, good morning." Mildred beamed. "And how are you? Did you get that rest you needed?"

A woman wearing the red armband of Intourist, the Soviet travel agency, stood at the front of the bus and counted passengers.

"Yes, I did, thank you," Tate said.

"And where's your friend Mr. Gormley?"

Through the bus window, Tate saw the chambermaid come running from the immigration shed. The ship's security officer walked rapidly behind her. They had dragged a Soviet soldier with them but did not seem to be making themselves understood. They stopped at the bus door and began shouting Finnish at the Intourist woman. Tate craned an ear. The Intourist woman told them in English that the bus was full and they would have to wait for the next. She pushed them back and the bus door hissed shut.

Tate took a deep breath and sat back in his seat. "Mr. Gormley has come down with some kind of bug," he said.

The chambermaid was stalking the length of the bus, staring up at windows. Tate drew back into shadow too late: she had seen him. The bus gave a forward lurch. It bumped across trolley tracks and veered sharply onto a broad boulevard split down the center by great rifts of park. Thousands of silver birches had powdered the earth and pavement with green pods.

"The city of Leningrad consists of more than one hundred and three artificial islands, resting on millions of oak piles driven forty feet into the Neva's estuary." The Intourist woman spoke into a hand-held microphone. "There are six hundred and twenty-one bridges."

"I bet they're counting the footbridges," Polly said.

Tate stared at the boulevard. There were few parked cars. Traffic moved in shabby, wide-spaced clusters of buses and trucks and bicycles. A solitary pedestrian walked at a stroll. Tate turned in his seat. In the far depth of the avenue's perspective, at the very vanishing point of the cinder-block highrises, a steel speck glittered that might have been the next tour bus.

They came to the river Neva and swung right and slowed at a block of rubble. "Now what in the world are they showing us this garbage for?" Mildred did not bother to whisper.

The Intourist guide said that in the Fascist siege of Leningrad one and a half million citizens had died and the city had endured five million four hundred and fifty thousand rubles' worth of damage, which was equivalent to sixty million dollars. Though the citizens had rebuilt the city brick by brick, they had left this hospital as the Germans left it, a ruin, a monument, a reminder of the perils of Fascism.

Tate looked again at his watch. The second hand had gained on the minute hand. *In thirteen hours and twelve minutes we may all be a monument.*

The bus swerved onto an avenue of granite cubes. Traffic was heavier here, and several of the intersections had streetlights. "This is Nevsky Prospekt," the guide said, "Leningrad's fashionable shopping street."

Tate looked for the Soviet Union's famed prices—color TV's for two thousand dollars, rubber overshoes for twenty, but the bus went too quickly for him to make out any signs in shopwindows besides the familiar American ones: Hertz, Chase Manhattan, American Express. He thought he saw the second bus five intersections behind them, stranded at a red light, but they turned off the avenue before he could be sure.

"We are crossing Zaiachi Bridge to Zaiachi Island," the guide said. The river was wide and the bridge was six lanes broad and windy, with pedestrians clutching at caps and papers and parcels. "We are passing through the triumphal arch

of St. Peter." The bus rumbled beneath a black stone arch
into a cobbled square. High, dark Italianate ramparts enclosed an astonishing number of plane trees. The plane trees
enclosed a church.

"The bastions of the fortress of Peter and Paul are four
hundred feet high. The battlements are sixty-five feet thick.
The cathedral on your right was built by Czar Peter. Its spire
is four hundred feet high."

It seemed strange to Tate that the bastions and the spire
would both be the same height, and he wondered if *four
hundred feet* was the Russian way of saying *tall*.

The bus crossed the river again, passed blocks of columned
granite façades, and slowed at a park. Beds of tulips and li-
lacs circled a statue of a horseman mounted on a rearing
horse. The guide explained that this was the bronze horseman
immortalized by the great poet Alexander Pushkin. "It was
built by Catherine the Great in homage to Czar Peter, the
city's founder. It is thirty-three feet tall. It took four hundred
serfs and fourteen hundred soldiers to transport the granite
base and the statue."

The bus circled the park. Old women sat sunning themselves on benches. In a playground with swings and jungle
gyms and a push-it-yourself carrousel, children chased one
another.

The bus completed its circle and paused at the avenue for
a gap in traffic. The second bus slowed twenty feet from
them and turned into the park. Two blocks along the river,
the bus turned again. "This is Dvortsovaia," the guide said.
"Palace Square. It is twenty vast and breathtaking acres."

Tate stared at Dvortsovaia. Broad gashes of asphalt and tar
scarred the cobblestoned emptiness. Yellow Czarist façades
dwarfed three trucks and a pushcart spaced light-years from
one another. Tate had the impression of silence made visible,
of ghosts of parasols and carriages, ghosts of elegant women
and splendidly groomed horses. All that moved was a shiver-
ing generator, a workman, a chattering pneumatic drill, an
old woman in black carrying a string bag with an egg-shaped
white object in it. In the center of the square, in utter
aloneness, loomed a gigantic stone column.

"The column of Alexander the First, erected to commemorate his defeat of Napoleon in 1812, is the world's biggest
monolith. It is carved out of a single rock. It is one hundred
fifty-five feet high and weighs six hundred tons. It took four
hundred serfs and fourteen hundred soldiers to erect." The

second bus drew into the square behind them. "It is said that when the monolith was being built, the temperature was so cold vodka had to be mixed with the cement instead of water to keep it from freezing."

The passengers laughed.

"To the north you see the Winter Palace, now the Hermitage Museum. We will be stopping here. The Hermitage art collection is one of the world's finest." As the bus rounded the lime-green palace with its peeling white trim, the guide reeled off a list of Rembrandts, Michelangelos, Leonardos, Raphaels, Renoirs, Cézannes, Van Goghs, and Picassos. The bus lurched to a stop and she invited the passengers to disembark.

Tate got off behind Mildred and Polly. There were no taxis. A line of shabbily dressed Russians waiting to get into the museum stood in the sun and dust and stared at the foreigners.

The second bus pulled around the corner of the palace.

Clicking their cameras and laughing and pointing, the tourists swarmed past the Russians, past the colonnade of peeling pillars, past two old men who stood at the entrance taking tickets. The guide shouted at the tourists to form a line. Tate looked back over his shoulder, past the wall of Russian eyes.

The chambermaid and the security officer and the Russian soldier had detached themselves from the second swarm.

Tate huddled deeper into the mob of tourists. The line slowly made its way into the museum. The guide shouted at them to keep together and not get lost. She led them through a gallery of nineteenth-century St. Petersburg ladies: the past smiling out on the unsmiling present. The ladies' pets were the only dogs Tate had seen in the entire city.

The Intourist woman announced that everyone would please turn right and follow her to the twentieth-century French collection. Tate hung back till there was no one behind him. He turned left and found himself in a gallery of Czarist serving spoons, jeweled and dowdy in their undusted cases. He came to a bright vaulted room.

A six-foot glass cube, like an air lock shielding some alien form of life too vulnerable to survive earthly atmosphere, enclosed a silver, jeweled nightingale. The bird was perched on the branch of a six-foot silver tree whose roots ran into a forest of silver toadstools and diamond dewdrops. He wondered if at one time some music-box mechanism in the nightingale had sung for some Czarina's pleasure. It seemed a strange use of technology, to give pleasure. He had never seen anything so strange and needless and baffling.

"Well, you can certainly understand the Russian Revolution!" Mildred stood behind him, her finger accusing the nightingale. "When people are starving, and sick, and unclothed, and the nation's leaders spend *money* on such junk!"

"Why," Polly cried, "it's much worse than *anything* Nixon ever did!"

And much more beautiful, Tate reflected. He thought of an era of pastels and soft scents that perhaps existed only in his head.

The Finnish chambermaid and the ship's security officer came into the gallery. Tate shifted position, keeping the silver tree between him and them. He did a rapid calculation of his distance from the two doors and the Finns' distance from him. He wrapped a fist in his raincoat and slammed it into the nightingale's case. Cracks spider-webbed from the point of impact, and a stuttering alarm broke what must have been fifty years' silence.

"Mr. Erlandsen!" Mildred and Polly cried in not-quite-unison.

The Finns came skidding toward Tate. He tried to keep the nightingale between him and them, but they divided at the case and came at him from both sides. He evaded the chambermaid's pink clutch, but the security officer dove for his legs and caught a foot and brought him slamming down into the floor.

The officer pinned Tate's wrists behind his back. His face was suddenly next to Tate's and his shallow breathing smelled of sausage. The officer barked something in Finnish.

The chambermaid fumbled to loosen her belt. Polly and Mildred stood watching with disbelief spilling down their faces. Tate looked toward the corridor where a bunch of Russian museum-goers kept their distance, and then over at an old toothless custodian in her smock. He shouted the word *Police*, and hoped it was a cognate.

A noose of belt began to bite into his wrists. He wrenched a hand loose and the chambermaid screamed. He swung a fist into the security officer's stomach. The officer staggered back and fell against a case of gold spoons and sent them skittering off their shelves. Before the man could pull himself to his feet Tate bolted for the corridor and plunged through the astonished Russians.

There was not a guard in sight.

He chose the nearer of two doorways and lunged into a gallery of wooden icons and French tourists. The security officer and the chambermaid clawed their way through the crowd that had gathered in amazement behind him. He raced across a gallery in the throes of renovation. His foot slammed into a pail that went screeching across the floor and sent wet plaster flying in glops. He wheeled into another corridor. The security officer came running toward him, the chambermaid puffing behind with her unbelted dress whipping like a ship's spinnaker in a gale. He reversed direction and collided with a man in ill-cut gray who shouted in Russian.

A wooden club came flying at the side of Tate's face.

Something cracked and he was on his knees. There was an instant's lag before the pain riveted his skull. The Finns were screaming at the Russians in Finnish and the Russians screamed back in Russian, and for a moment Tate was the rope in a tug-of-war.

Gray reinforcements came sliding down the corridor, and Russian hands peeled him away from the Finns. His shirt collar was soaked and he tasted blood on his upper lip.

Luckily they understood English upstairs.

"My name is Erlandsen. General Tate Erlandsen, United States Army." He did not say *retired*.

"Come in." The voice added something in Russian, and the guard shut the door. Tate sensed that the shadow was staring at him and not smiling. His eyes were momentarily baffled by the dim room and the glaring window with its view of the Neva.

"General Erlandsen," the shadow said, "it is my duty to tell you that you have committed a criminal offense." Tate's eyes began to cope. A woman sat in half profile at the desk beside the window. A certain neatness of hair and crisp simplicity of dress suggested she was not of the ordinary class of Soviet citizen. "We shall have to turn you over to the police. You may of course contact your embassy."

The possibility of being entrusted to the Soviet police was a question Tate preferred not to consider. The main thing was that he had got this far, to a Soviet official who spoke English and who could possibly be persuaded to help. He could smell disinfectant and his eyes were beginning to make out yellow plaster walls with brown moisture stains of the most abstract Westernized shapes.

"An American submarine-launched missile is going to be

launched at Moscow at six minutes after ten this evening. I've got to speak to the military."

Barbara lay flat on her back. Curtain tracks crisscrossed the ceiling and gray light beat down. The mattress was firm beneath her and her breathing was hoarse. She knew she was approaching the moment when she must decide whether to remain on her back, which ached, or to turn onto her side, which might start to ache.

A lighted clockface on the wall told the time but did not tell day or night or whether she was alive or dead. She could not say if this was a prolongation of the same instant as before or if some nightmare had happened between then and now. Whispers and breathing and tiptoes were everywhere, barely at the threshold of hearing.

A long sound of sighing filled the space around her. She tilted her head and saw a lung machine. There were other beds, ranged in low rows beneath the low ceiling. The room was half bright and rustling and she felt stranded in time.

Surgical uniforms hovered like angels, and it seemed likely she was dead. One uniform said, "Did she go into status?" and the other said, "We caught it in time. The pheno seems to be working."

She managed to open her mouth. "What happened to my baby?" she whispered.

"Betty," they told her, "this is intensive care, no babies here."

"The *Intrepid*," Tate said, "has been sent under a cover mission to the Barents Sea."

A high-fashion, remarkably un-Soviet dark suit exaggerated the interpreter's slenderness. His smooth-shaven face was the color of candle wax and his eyes flickered rapidly behind eight-diopter shields of prescription glass. His tongue had a habit of probing his cheek before he spoke, as though tasting the translation of each phrase in advance.

After the Russian was completed, Tate went on. "The target is the Galosh ABM system surrounding Moscow. The attack will come at 10:06 tonight. The Theta satellite will be in position to abort any response."

Admiral Kiril Buzenko of the Soviet Navy sat heavy and silent behind his desk. His hair was an anarchy of gray curls. His high cheekbones gave his green eyes parapets from which to memorize Tate. He wore a rumpled gray uniform and a lumpy gray shirt. Muscular wrists poked out of too-short sleeves, and blunt fingers toyed with a five-kopek piece. Admiral Buzenko did not look convinced.

"The device was tested last Monday night at Ellsworth Air Force Base," Tate said. "Your own Akula-3 satellite photographed the test." He removed the envelope from his raincoat pocket. Stepping in front of his Russian echo, he slapped it onto Buzenko's desk. The Admiral did not even look at it. His eyes stayed with Tate.

"The missile will be unarmed," Tate said.

The plaster walls had been painted an uneven, scrambled-egg yellow. Gray smudges darkened the area of the light switch, and when the Admiral leaned back in his chair, a brown patch formed an almost perfect halo behind his head. The room's steel furnishings bore speckles, like a razor that needed rinsing. The naked plank floor had been washed, not waxed, to a dead-wood beige.

"The danger is that Moscow, not knowing it is unarmed, will be provoked into a reply."

The air smelled of ammonia, cigarette smoke, sweat. The closed window gave a view of the river Neva, its gray waters pushing silently toward the Baltic. On the far bank, columned façades in pastel pinks and blues seemed remote and uninhabited, a faded and graceful eighteenth-century print.

"I emphasize that this attack is not an act by the American government. It is a mutiny by one man. I've come to you because there is no time, no other way to stop it."

Buzenko growled the first words he had spoken since Tate had been led into the room.

The man in dark flannel smiled. He touched Tate's arm, gently pinching the cloth of the jacket. Tate pulled back. The interpreter's smile came up pleasant but firm as the barrel of a gun. "Admiral Buzenko says you will please take off your clothes."

A contraction wrenched Tate's colon. He obeyed. His eyes moved to Buzenko's impassive, hard-edged face. Buzenko met his stare, saying nothing. Tate sucked in his gut, stood straight as an eighteen-year-old Army inductee. The interpreter looked in his mouth, told him to bend over, and thrust a finger up his anus.

Tate gritted, shut his eyes momentarily against the pain. When he opened them again the interpreter was going through the pockets of his jacket. The man placed wallet, passport, and traveler's checks on the desk. He began searching the raincoat. He took a miniature Japanese camera out of one of the pockets. He passed it to Buzenko, who turned it over in his hand like a jeweler pricing a stone.

Tate stood motionless. His palms were moist and he felt there were electrodes in his armpits. He said, "I don't know how that got there."

Gormley, he realized: Gormley had planted it in his pocket. The bright little marvel of Nipponese miniaturization did a nice silent job of discrediting him.

The Admiral spoke again, and the interpreter said, "You owe the Soviet people two hundred rubles for breaking the glass case in the Hermitage. Would you be kind enough to endorse three hundred ten dollars of your traveler's checks?"

Tate tried to marshal some residue of physical or mental energy. The interpreter held out a pen.

"You may make them payable to the U.S.S.R. Ministry of Fine Arts."

Tate leaned over the desk and signed six fifty-dollar checks and one twenty. The signatures came out hastily and illegible. Buzenko studied the checks as though appraising their negotiability. He did not offer any change. Finally he said something.

"Admiral Buzenko invites you please to come for a little drive in the country."

Tate slipped his watch back onto his wrist. There were only eight hours till Theta. He had crossed the line he could never recross, he had abandoned everything he loved, and the Admiral did not believe him.

Buzenko rose and clumped toward the door. It opened as though it had heard him.

"Has the Admiral understood a word I've said?"

Behind the interpreter's thick lenses, Tate could see blood vessels magnify. "Naturally," the man said. There was an Oxford edge to his voice.

Tate pointed to the envelope on the desk. "Then why is he leaving that behind?"

The interpreter drew a revolver from his inner left pocket. Tate realized that the jacket had been tailored for it and wondered why that fact should surprise him.

The interpreter held the gun at the level of Tate's navel. "Please. There is nothing whatever to worry about. You will dress and come quietly for a drive to the Admiral's country home."

At 8:30 Ā.M., the chief of United States Naval Intelligence sat in a wing chair facing a view of a wooded hill sloping down toward an Arlington parking lot. "Three hours ago," he stated, ruffling the documentation on his knees, "the sonar unit at Lillesand, Norway, detected two Salmon-class Soviet subs passing through the Skagerrak into the North Sea."

The office of the Chief of Naval Operations displayed the three highest badges of Pentagon status: fresh paint, windows with an outside view, and enough space to house ten Army colonels. All brass studs on the leather sofas and chairs were shiny, present and accounted for. The huge cherrywood desk was waxed to a warm reflecting glow, and the cases housing the CNO's four-foot antique models of eighteenth- and nine-teenth-century clippers were so free of dust that their glass edges seemed to be empty wire frames. Ilya Wanamaker glanced twice at his watch. His fingers kept neatening the gray hair at the back of his neck.

"Certain modifications in the craft's noiseprint were noted."

A secretary came noiseless and swift across the unworn, unstained carpet. She placed a penned note on the CNO's desk. He opened it and read the two words *Admiral Gurney*. "Would you excuse me one moment?" he apologized. He rose from his desk and crossed to the anteroom.

Color photographs of submarines from World War II down to the nuclear-fueled present blanketed one wall like gener-ations of a royal family, and an eighteenth-century Chinese screen hid a bank of secure communications equipment as though it were a kitchenette. Admiral Gurney closed both doors. Her usually smooth brow bore a deep vertical crease like the centerfold of a newspaper. "We're in trouble," she said quietly.

"What's happened?"

'General Erlandsen reached Leningrad. He's managed to evade Gormley."

"Jesus Christ."

"From this point on, Admiral, we're winging it."

O'Brien's glance swept the stage. The screen had been set up for the annual light show of movies and slides, and several of the board members had already taken their places at the long table and seemed agreeably resigned to the morning's boredom. The auditorium of the union hall was beginning to fill up with stockholders.

"How are we doing?" O'Brien asked the company secretary.

The secretary had pale, bloodshot eyes defended by extremely thick lenses. "Fifty-three per cent of the proxies have come back marked for management."

The figure was low. "We had 85 per cent last year," O'Brien said.

"A lot of the big holders are voting their stock here today."

It was legal for stockholders to wait for the annual meeting to vote their stock. It still struck O'Brien as unusual. "Which ones?"

"Techno-Mutual, Southern Electronics, Stern Foundation, Frances Meredith, your workers' pension fund. It adds up all told to 27 per cent."

O'Brien tallied management's 53 and the 27. "That leaves 20 per cent unaccounted for."

"About 8 or 9 per cent came in this morning. Small stockholders. A lot of them were mailed last Thursday. Most of them had the same form letter." There was a question mark to the secretary's statement. "They want to put a fellow called Derek Stout on the board instead of Santa."

"Who the hell is Derek Stout?"

"I gather he works for Southern Electronics."

O'Brien glanced down the table. Allan Martino, the man from Southern Electronics, was talking with Quentin Quinn. Quinn looked haggard and unslept. Allan Martino looked suntanned and confident and he was toying with a gold watch chain, very much like a young man who had the world by the nuts. O'Brien reflected that in his day young men went out and built companies and nowadays they went out and tried to steal them. Fashions had changed in other ways too. Nowadays you could wear pink shirts and bell-bottomed trousers and have a black mistress and get ahead anyway. But Allan Martino wasn't going to get one inch further. He might have 8 or 9 per cent of the proxies and he might be holding all the unvoted proxies in the room—but management had 53 per cent.

O'Brien had beaten the raid.

Quentin Quinn patted Allan Martino on the back and hurried toward the wings. O'Brien asked the secretary to excuse him a moment. "Quent," he called, "can I have a word with you?"

Quentin Quinn turned and looked surprised. O'Brien strolled across the stage. He lowered his voice so that they would not be overheard. "Quent, you've been monkeying with the Sea Condor costs. I'd like to know why."

Quentin Quinn was backed up against the wall and he swallowed hard. "You haven't got it straight, Jack. I suggested we could play with the costs a little. Just to help things out in Detroit."

"I've seen the figures. Who the hell do you think you are to expose this company to stockholder suits and cancellation of government contracts?"

"Hold on, Jack. Are you accusing me?"

"Not just accusing you, Quinn. I'm firing you."

Quentin Quinn drew himself up to his full height. He was still two inches shorter than O'Brien. "You fire me and I'll talk and you *will* have a stockholders' suit."

"I'll have a worse suit on my hands if I keep you on."

"You're making a mistake, Jack. No one knows about the Condor costs and no one needs to know." Quentin Quinn looked frightened but he looked sly too. "You keep your mouth shut and I'll keep my mouth shut and Susan Dempsey will keep her mouth shut about how she got that necklace and what happened in New York. Is it a deal?"

The white-jacketed Filipino steward slipped into the dining room carrying a telephone in his left hand and four loops of cord in his right. "Call for you, Admiral." He moved aside a water glass, placed the phone on the table, and stooped to connect the cord to a jack in the baseboard.

Ilya Wanamaker waited till the man had left and closed the door before he lifted the receiver. "Wanamaker," he said. His fork played with a scrap of chicken breast on his plate.

Admiral Anne Gurney, watching him, could think of no more than five men in America who had the guts or the rank to keep the CNO waiting on a dead extension. She saw Wanamaker's eyes snap to attention.

"Yes, sir," he said. After thirty-five seconds he hung up.

They sat alone in a windowed corner of the flag officers' dining room that had been made smaller for them by a red accordion-folded partition. The partition was not soundproof and the room, though it possessed an unfussy naval elegance, was certainly not secure.

"The President," Wanamaker said. "He wants me at the Oval Office immediately."

Admiral Gurney angled her wrist so that she could read the watch face. "It's one o'clock," she reminded.

Their eyes met for an instant.

"I know." The CNO laid down his napkin and rose quickly from the table.

"You're worse than murderers! You make money out of murder!"

People in the auditorium began hissing and booing and telling her to stow it. With a crazy sort of dignity the woman whirled three hundred sixty degrees, facing down the stockholders.

"I lost two sons in Vietnam. They'd be here today if it wasn't for money-hungry maniacs like you. The mothers and fathers sitting in this room investing in this company are a disgrace to God and the human race!"

O'Brien was listening, but he was thinking about Susan Dempsey.

He was thinking about the things they had done on the floor of that hotel room and he was thinking how confused and happy he had been. He didn't believe Susan Dempsey would tell his wife: that was just a threat, a scare tactic. But she had told Quentin Quinn; so it all came down to the same thing, the farce of the pretty young girl and the rich old man. He felt old and used and his mind was not quite on the meeting. He angled his mike head up and leaned forward to answer the stockholder.

"Madam, I'm sincerely sorry about your sons. But let me just point out that very few of the products we manufacture were used in Southeast Asia. In fact, the whole purpose of our products is to prevent war."

"Your products don't prevent a damned thing except *life*. This country's starving because half our money has to go to profiteers like you."

"The government is getting back 48 per cent of every taxable profit dollar earned in aerospace defense. It's getting back up to 50 per cent of every dollar earned by every employee in the industry. It's also taxing the companies and the products that feed into the industry. At the most conservative estimate, sixty-five cents out of every dollar the government spends on aerospace defense goes right back to Washington in the form of taxes. If there's a profiteer in this industry, it's the government of the United States of America."

"You think that makes it right?" she cried. "I don't see the government starving, and I don't see you starving either, but

20 per cent of this country can't afford to eat, they're on food stamps and welfare thanks to you!"

Shouts and jeers clubbed her down. The chairman quickly recognized another stockholder, a tired-looking man with the long hair that had been fashionable among the young in the 1960s.

"I have a question for Mr. O'Brien." The man read from a sheet of typed paper. "According to the published reports of the Department of Defense source selection committee on the Hornet fighter craft, the first 128 planes are estimated to cost 17.8 million dollars per copy. But according to articles published in *Aerospace Weekly* it appears that the cost per copy may go as much as 26 per cent higher. I would like to know: *One*, is an overrun of this magnitude contemplated by management? *Two*, if so, will it be paid for by the DOD either as an allowed overrun or as a cost adjustment in the second run, and if the latter, what will the cost to stockholders be in terms of interest rates? *Three* . . ."

O'Brien rested a hand on the microphone and aimed it down and away. "Damn."

Melvin Culligan gave an alert, chin-up sort of grin and leaned close. "Don't let these junior Ralph Naders get to you. They're full of phony figures and hot air."

"It isn't hot air, Mel."

Melvin Culligan looked at him oddly.

"Two of our employees have been rigging the computer to make Hornet look worse and Sea Condor look a hell of a lot better."

"Come on, Jack." Melvin Culligan seemed astonished not at the crime but at O'Brien. "You're not going to tell the stockholders that."

"When he winds down I'll give him some double-talk—tell him the overruns on Hornet are computer fictions. It's close enough to the truth."

"Jack, don't."

O'Brien considered the advice and he considered the source. Melvin Culligan was the sort of guy who sat back and let things happen to him and that was how he had lost a company. He didn't know a damned thing about Hornet or the rigged computer program and naturally he'd say when you're in trouble, play possum. But O'Brien saw that there was actually very little choice: if he didn't come at least partially clean, he'd be an accessory in the cover-up. Besides,

Pacific Aero had 53 per cent of the proxies. A dose of half-truth wasn't going to spark a stockholder rebellion.

O'Brien angled the microphone again and bent toward it. "The figures you're citing are inaccurate. They're the result of rounding off at the second decimal place. They were based on a cost-forecasting program that wasn't updated to reflect improved performance and cost saving."

"How far are they off?"

"In the aggregate, I'd say they overstate Hornet's costs by a healthy seven-figure sum. Naturally, we're in the process of correcting and rerunning the program."

"What kind of outfit is this if you can't control your computer men?"

O'Brien's throat was raw from answering questions. He took a sip of water. "The personnel responsible for the oversights are in the process of being replaced. You have my assurance that the error will be rectified."

It took thirty seconds for the incredulity to subside, and then Quentin Quinn rose from his seat and apologized to the four people between him and the aisle. He pushed through the door at the rear of the auditorium and found a telephone booth on the level below, just inside the main entrance. He dialed a number and asked for Susan Dempsey. "Go to Mrs. O'Brien and tell her everything."

She sighed. "What good will that do?"

"It'll teach the old bastard what happens to double-crossers."

"And I'll be out of a job."

"O'Brien's going to be out of a job, sweetheart, and you'll have a very cozy job working for the new president."

"It seems awfully mean."

Through the glass wall of the booth Quentin Quinn could see three armed company guards pacing the length of the entrance. "Jesus Christ, I told you to screw the guy, not fall in love with him."

"You know I'm only in love with you, Quent. No one else."

"Then go tell Mrs. O'Brien. Now."

Ilya Wanamaker kept shifting on the upholstered sofa. From time to time he pulled back the cuff of his jacket and stole a glance at his watch. He did not appear to be listening.

In front of the fireplace, beneath the painting of the sea

battle between the *Bonhomme Richard* and the *Serapis*, the director of the Central Intelligence Agency had erected an easel on which to parade a series of color glossies. Graininess betrayed the childish, sticklike diagrams as monstrous blow-ups. The drawings bristled with arrows, just as the accompanying text—illegibly scrawled and incomprehensibly German —snarled with crossouts.

The director of the CIA detailed the odyssey: the plans had been picked up by an operative in Moscow; flown to Copenhagen in a diplomatic pouch; radioed by secure satellite hookup from Copenhagen to CIA headquarters in Langley, Virginia; relayed by secure telephone line to the color Xerox copier in the President's office in the White House.

The physicist explained that a device of the sort described in the plans could be the most potentially destabilizing weapon since the A-bomb. "At present we have no defense against it."

The President sat in his high-backed, black leather swivel chair and did not swivel. "Does the weapon violate any agreement to which the U.S.S.R. is signatory?"

"Technically, I doubt it. But it certainly violates the spirit of all arms limitations negotiations since SALT 1." Despite his years in the United States, the heavyset, gray-haired Secretary of State retained a residual Viennese accent.

"Masers in the sky?" Ilya Wanamaker broke in. "Masers aren't even efficient on the ground. How could you possibly get a maser strong enough to cripple—"

"Ilya, it works." The director of the CIA aimed a weary, overweight frown at the Chief of Naval Operations. "They knocked out the missile in Silo 29 at Ellsworth Air Force Base last Monday night."

"Are you sure of that?"

"No question. The device was disguised as an Akula-3 weather satellite."

"That's as face-saving an explanation as any," Ilya Wanamaker said, "but isn't it a bit more realistic to suppose there was some kind of malfunction in the missile itself?"

"No one's saving anyone's face," the Air Force Chief of Staff asserted. His fingers kept exploring his thinning hairline, as though seeking out the source of an ache. "We found no malfunction, and when we retested the missile it was ready to go."

"Look," Ilya Wanamaker said patiently. "The Navy's been researching masers for twenty years. Outside of amplifying sonar signals, we've found no goddamned use for them at all. They're expensive, they're delicate, and their output is minuscule. How the hell can you believe the Russians would waste their time orbiting these things? Who did you get these plans from?"

"An agent in the Soviet Ministry of Defense," the director of the CIA said.

"Then the Russians are using him. They want us to waste billions on a counterweapon to a weapon that doesn't even exist."

A fan of virginally folded newspapers lay on a drop-leaf table. The director of the CIA toyed with a corner of the Baltimore *Sun.* "As a matter of fact, the Soviets do use this particular agent to feed us a great deal of inaccurate information. But sometimes they let him pass on a genuine tidbit. Keeps him credible."

"What makes you think this tidbit is genuine?" Ilya Wanamaker asked.

"The Silo 29 incident."

"Why in the world, if the Russians had a weapon of this scope, would they give the plans away to us? Just to sustain the credibility of an agent? No chance."

"They're giving away very little," the director of the CIA said. "These are raw, preliminary diagrams. Possibly there are errors in them. They're obviously incomplete. The lead time from these plans to operational capacity would be at least five years."

"It still doesn't make sense to give up any sort of lead."

"It makes excellent diplomatic sense," the Secretary of State said. "The Russians demonstrate the weapon, and then they reveal enough of the plans—but just enough—to explain the demonstration. Without the leaking of these plans, we would think like you, Admiral: that the fault was in the missile . . . and not in the heavens."

"Aside from a one-time shock value," Ilya Wanamaker said, "what is the use of a weapon like this? So far as I can see—if the damned thing really worked—it would put us all out of business. Them *and* us."

"The weapon's main use is psychological. They want us to know what they have, and they want us to know they can use it any time, any place. Even against submarine-launched missiles, Admiral." A slight smile distorted the line of the Secretary of State's lips. "The intention is to paralyze us by serving notice that they possess a paralyzing capability."

"I just can't accept that the Russians possess this capability—that they could have developed it without the CIA's detecting *something*." Ilya Wanamaker made a catcher's mitt of one hand, a baseball of the other. "To have a weapon like this sprung on us, full-grown—frankly, it strains my credulity."

The President adjusted the blotter in its gold-tooled leather holder, the three stacked manila folders bloated with documents. The carved-oak Buchanan desk was laden with telephones: a red, four blacks, an avocado console with a dozen buttons, half of them blinking at this moment. "Tell me, Josh. Do you connect the surfacing of these plans with General Erlandsen's disappearance into the Soviet Union?"

"We see no connection at this moment," the director of the CIA said.

"Tate Erlandsen?" The Army Chief of Staff sounded shocked. "What's he done—defected?"

"He left the United States last Friday and entered the Soviet Union this morning." The director of the CIA shrugged as though it were all minimal. "He's being held by the Russians."

"Why?" asked the Army Chief of Staff.

"They nailed him on a security charge—said he'd been photographing the naval installation at Kronstadt."

"And how does that tie in with Theta?"

"In our opinion it doesn't. Theta is not Erlandsen's field. He's been out of the military for over five years. He lobbies for a defense contractor, but he's no physicist."

"Then why," Ilya Wanamaker asked, "do the Russians want him?"

"We don't know, but as I say, we think that's an unrelated matter."

"It doesn't sound unrelated to me."

"Could you amplify that, Ilya?" the President asked.

"Look at the timing. Erlandsen enters the U.S.S.R. Monday morning, and Monday afternoon an agent radios back these plans. Which, by the way, aren't even in Russian."

"The Russians have a great many German physicists," the director of the CIA said. "Almost as many as we do."

"I still find it very peculiar for an American general to rush into the Soviet Union and get nailed on freshman espionage charges. Erlandsen goes in and these plans come out—one, two: punch, counterpunch. There's got to be a connection."

The door to the tiled corridor, the doors to the offices of the President's personal and engagements secretaries, were shut. The three French windows gave a view of the colonnade, of the rose garden, of a Secret Service agent squinting at the sun. Further across the south lawn, not quite flush with the grass, a stainless-steel helicopter pad glinted like the inlaid lid of a giant deepfreeze.

"Don't you think there's something a little strange about the sequence of events, Josh?" the President asked.

"Granted, there are some shadowy areas surrounding Erlandsen." The director of the CIA made a little pout, as though to suggest that shadows were no stranger than lights. "There's a possible tie-in to the death of a Russian physicist in Copenhagen. A former Naval Intelligence operative apparently attempted suicide in the Helsinki hotel where Erlandsen was staying."

"Excuse me," Ilya Wanamaker cut in, "isn't there a much simpler explanation?"

"I'd like to hear it," the President said.

"Fraud."

"Fraud?" the President asked, and a silence trickled into the Oval Office.

"Look," Ilya Wanamaker said, "all of us in this room are sitting on top of the biggest bureaucracies in the civilized world. Bureaucracies make mistakes. Bureaucracies cover up. Ask yourself *cui bono*—who profits? A new superweapon gets the Air Force off the hook. The missile in Silo 29 aborted because of a Russian superweapon, not because of Air Force incompetence. A new superweapon gets the CIA off the hook: it's an intelligence coup—it helps justify a budget that's come under a lot of congressional fire, and it makes heroes out of our foreign intelligence men. They've been needing a little heroism after all the scandals."

The director of the CIA made a half-strangled sound. "Are you accusing—"

"Josh, I'm not accusing anyone in this room. But if General Erlandsen's company is involved in the manufacture of Minuteman IV, it seems to me that a lot of faces would be saved by churning up a weapon scare. I think it's quite possible General Erlandsen took these plans into Russia solely to leak them back to us—to convince us Russia has this weapon and used it at Silo 29. It would save the jobs of a hell of a lot of people."

"Now see here, Ilya," the director of the CIA exploded. "If

there is one agency that has tried to *counter* irresponsible talk of Soviet leads and missile gaps and superweapons, it's the CIA. Scare stories about Russian strength come out of the *Pentagon* every spring at budget-hearing time—regular as the cherry blossoms."

"I don't see any cherries blossoming today," Ilya Wanamaker said.

"Gentlemen," the President interrupted, "shut up. Now does anyone know what company General Erlandsen lobbies for?"

"He works for Pacific Aero," the Air Force Chief of Staff said.

"And has Pacific Aero been involved in Minuteman?"

"They modified the terminal guidance for Minuteman IV. We've suspended the program temporarily."

"Why have you done that, Brad?"

"When the missile shut down last Monday, it looked as though there was a bug in Pacific Aero's system."

The President studied the faces, one by one, of the six men he had summoned. "Then we've got to consider it: Ilya may have a point."

The cab swung into a drive lined with banked rhododendrons and shaped boxwoods. Light specks pierced the leafy bulk like ore glinting in earth. The bushes proclaimed with more force than an armed guard the privacy of the long slope of lawn and of the white-columned house that stood at its summit.

Susan Dempsey paid the driver his five dollars and a small tip and stood a moment at the paneled door. She lifted the brass knocker and let it drop once. She told the maid that she had phoned and Mrs. O'Brien was expecting her.

From the far dark of the hallway, like a figure emerging from the depth of a painting, she saw a second woman approach, swift and graceful and smiling. They shook hands and the woman asked if Miss Dempsey would like coffee. Yes? Coffee in the living room, Inger.

"You work for my husband, Miss Dempsey?"

"I'm an assistant to Miss Kelly."

They stood in a high room with sofas and rugs the color of milk. Mrs. O'Brien suggested they sit, and they sat on facing armchairs, with a glass tabletop spanning the six feet between them. The maid set silver and translucent china between them and left a hovering scent of cleanliness.

Susan Dempsey glanced at the doorway to make sure they were alone. "Mrs. O'Brien, this is a very hard thing for me to tell you, but I think you should know your husband and I had an affair last week in New York."

Mrs. O'Brien stared at Susan Dempsey a moment. It was very hard to imagine what she might be thinking.

"If you want proof, look at the next bill from Cartier's. Mr. O'Brien gave me a necklace."

"That would be a company expense," Mrs. O'Brien said. "The bill would go to the office. How do you like yours, Miss Dempsey—cream and sugar?"

"Okay."

Mrs. O'Brien put cream and sugar and coffee in a cup and handed it to Susan Dempsey on a saucer. "I can't blame Jack," she said. "You're lovely and you're young."

Susan Dempsey managed to say, "Thank you." She sipped. The cream was real.

"And I can't blame you either. Jack's kind and he's intelligent and he's very successful. And he's nice sex, isn't he? For an older man, I mean. Do you have a young man too, Miss Dempsey?"

Susan Dempsey nodded and didn't see what concern it was of Mrs. O'Brien's.

"You've got to be fair to your young man. May I call you Susan? Your young man may not seem as glamorous as Jack, but I'm sure he will be one day." Mrs. O'Brien had a lovely, relaxed smile and she seemed to know exactly what to do with it.

"I'm not planning to take Mr. O'Brien away from you or anything like that," Susan Dempsey said. "I just thought you ought to know he plays around."

"You're very kind," Mrs. O'Brien said. "But I wouldn't worry. If Jack leaves me, it won't be your fault. Jack does exactly what he wants. All the years we've been married, he's done exactly what he wants. Do you see those two steps by the door?"

Susan Dempsey twisted in her chair and saw two waxed steps leading down into the living room.

"I didn't want those steps. You could break your neck on them. But Jack wanted two steps. So there they are. Or look out the window: you'll see a pond. There was no pond when we bought the property. But Jack said land should have water. He hired a contractor and put in a pond. Jack wanted me, so here I am in his house. I've been in one house or another of his for over twenty-five years. A lot's changed in the last quarter century, Susan, but Jack O'Brien still gets exactly what he wants. And keeps it."

Susan Dempsey was uneasy. Her mother was given to talking of quarter centuries and her grandparents had talked of half centuries.

"You're not even twenty years old, are you?" Mrs. O'Brien asked.

"Twenty-two," Susan Dempsey corrected.

Mrs. O'Brien looked surprised. "I feel we're friends, and I hope you feel that way too. Would you mind if I asked you a personal question?"

"Surely."

"Why do you do that to your mouth? You've got a lovely lip line and you hide it with makeup. Have you got a minute?" Mrs. O'Brien took Susan Dempsey by the hand and led her upstairs. They passed through a blue-and-sapphire bedroom with a king-sized double bed covered in white lace. The bathroom had bright porcelain tiles and a marble shower stall. Bowls of lemon and lavender soap had been placed on a wooden chest with polished brass hinges. There was a domed skylight and you could see treetops and clouds.

Mrs. O'Brien seated Susan Dempsey at a dressing table and told her to use whatever she needed. Susan Dempsey's hands were shaking. She rubbed her lips clean with tissue. She unscrewed the tops of several lipstick cases.

"That one," Mrs. O'Brien suggested. "Now follow the lip line."

Susan Dempsey followed the lip line. She saw two faces in the mirror. The young face looked hard and the older face looked soft.

"Much better," Mrs. O'Brien said. "Why don't you keep that lipstick? I never use it."

"But the case is gold," Susan Dempsey said. Her eyes were burning and her voice was choked.

Mrs. O'Brien's hand touched hers. "I want you to have it. Please. You'd make an old woman very happy."

"The proposal is before us that the present board be re-elected to another term as directors." The chairman of the board paused to pour himself a half tumbler of water. "Do I hear a second?"

Melvin Culligan got to his feet. O'Brien wondered why in the world he couldn't just say "Second" and stay in his seat.

"Mr. Chairman," Melvin Culligan said, "in accordance with bylaw 312-A of the company's constitution, the right of stockholders to nominate candidates to the board of directors, I wish to nominate Derek Stout, of Southern Electronics, in place of Mr. Harold Santa."

O'Brien stared at Melvin Culligan.

For a moment he saw the board table and the auditorium in extremely sharp focus and people seemed to move and react in ridiculously slow motion. His mind began racing like a spool of tape in a computer, taking inventory of every word and smile he had exchanged with Melvin Culligan over the last quarter century, every handshake, every drink, every game of golf.

Melvin Culligan made no effort to avoid O'Brien's gaze. He regarded O'Brien with calm colorless eyes unstained by guilt. In that instant O'Brien understood the strategy. They viewed Santa, the black, as the board member easiest to unseat. Without Santa, O'Brien's strength would fall to five out of twelve board members, and his presidency and polices would be dead.

"May I say a word to the stockholders?" Melvin Culligan asked.

The chairman glanced at O'Brien. It was a helpless shrug of a glance that passed the buck back to the bylaws. "You have two minutes, Mel."

Melvin Culligan took the podium and adjusted the height and angle of the microphone like one who was quite familiar with such things. His voice came out sharp, with consonants that bounced off the balcony. "The record of Derek Stout, who has helped lead Southern Electronics to its present preeminent position, speaks for itself. I believe that Mr. Stout's would be the strong guiding hand that could rescue our company from the disasters engulfing it."

His voice dropped to a more cutting notch. "The record of Mr. Harold Santa also speaks for itself. Mr. Santa has made a reputation—and an enviable income—sitting on the boards of various corporations, lending them an integrated image and invariably voting with management."

The hands of the president of the Pension Fund unlinked from across his pudgy chest and he sprang to his feet. "Mr. Chairman, I protest!"

Melvin Culligan stepped back from the microphone—not quite relinquishing it, but lending the man enough audibility to regret his impulse.

"Mr. Culligan," the Pension Fund president stammered and then plunged, "I speak for the twenty thousand workers of this company who have entrusted me with the management of their pension dollars. I want to express the strongest confidence in the management of Pacific Aero and especially in the qualifications of Mr. Santa."

O'Brien watched Harold Santa playing with a plastic ball-point pen, alternately tapping the nib end to the table and then the tip. Santa's manicured hands contrasted darkly with the white of his cuffs. An emerald cuff link kept winking like a traffic light.

"We are a team," the president of the Pension Fund said. "We are black and white, workers and management together, and I protest any attempt to divide—"

"If," Melvin Culligan cut in, "you have such confidence in management, isn't it strange that as of this very moment, the Pension Fund's stock remains unvoted?"

"The Pension Fund's stock will be voted at this meeting and in support of management."

Melvin Culligan shouted above a wave of applause, "If the Pension Fund supports management, why has it cast the strongest sort of anti-management vote—by dumping two thirds of its stock on the New York Stock Exchange? Isn't it a fact that the stock remains unvoted because you didn't know who the hell the owner would be today?"

The president of the Pension Fund was shouting and Melvin Culligan was shouting and O'Brien would have been shouting too if anger had not gotten him by the throat and choked off his wind. The chairman hammered his gavel on the table and called for one person to talk at a time, please. He pointed out that at the moment Mel Culligan had the floor.

Melvin Culligan was holding a buff-colored envelope. "Mr. Chairman," he said, "I have here a legal instrument empowering me to vote all Pacific Aero shares owned by Rebus International."

O'Brien swallowed and tried very hard to force air into his lungs. Rebus owned 4 and a half per cent of the company. Without Rebus, management's 53 per cent of the proxies fell to 48 and a half.

Melvin Culligan handed the envelope to the chairman. The chairman opened it and glanced at a piece of buff-colored letterhead and offered it to O'Brien.

O'Brien shook his head. He was gazing at his old friend

Melvin Culligan as though from a great distance. And he saw everything, at long last.

He had wracked his brains wondering why an outfit like Southern Electronics, why anyone would want to buy out an aerospace-defense contractor. There was no hope of windfall profits, very little certainty even of profit.

But money wasn't the point. Profit wasn't the point. The Arabs wanted weapons.

They had started by loaning money to the East Coast contractors, taking fighter planes in exchange. The government and the Pentagon had decided, on balance, it was a good, face-saving way out. It kept the industry afloat. The Arabs' millions had been the first shot of morphine, killing the pain of overruns and vanishing profits and underproduction and unemployment, bypassing congressional blockage of funds. The millions had become billions, and the morphine had led by gradual steps to dependence. When the invalid had been reduced to an addict, the Arabs were ready to make their second move: take-over through corporations. They had chosen their target. Pacific Aero.

The shares were openly for sale.

Anyone could buy.

It was free enterprise. People's capitalism.

The American way.

A sick industry, an embarrassed and beleaguered Department of Defense, could only be glad for the helping hand. Any number of American banks and corporations would be delighted to help—for a cut. The Arabs were paying in good American money, oil money. You couldn't get sounder than that. Profits would go up for everyone. Of course, once they had control, the Arabs might demand a bit more of the product for themselves: not just the latest-model fighter planes and radars. Maybe a few of the rockets too. A dozen, a hundred, in time a thousand. They had the plutonium: peaceful plutonium, doled out over the decades of America's bridge building. They probably had contraband plutonium, the missing kilograms skimmed off of AEC plants over the last quarter century. And if the Administration ever succeeded in its plan to hand atomic energy over to private corporations, they'd have commercial thermonuclear warheads, made in the U.S.A.

All they needed was the delivery system, the Minutemen buried in the mideastern sand.

Rebus, as a multinational answerable to no government

and heavily backed by oil money, was in position to spearhead the thrust. Melvin Culligan, already on the board of Pacific Aero, was in position to guide the spear. In retrospect, it all seemed glaringly obvious. Rebus had needed an ally in the Pentagon to open the Trojan gates. They'd bought the Marines with weapons, and Sea Condor had been the convincer. All it had taken to bring the copter in under projected cost was a deal with PA's controller, a promise to Quentin Quinn that if he fixed the figures he'd come out of the takeover with O'Brien's job.

It made sense, shrewd business sense, but at the same time it made no sense at all. "Why?" O'Brien said. "Why have you done this to me, Mel?"

"For God's sake, Jack," Melvin Culligan said, "grow up."

The interpreter handed Buzenko a mahogany box. Buzenko dumped onto the chess table sixteen gold and sixteen silver crusaders inlaid with jewels and enamel. Tate wondered if Fabergé had ever done chessmen for the Czars, and if he had, how in the world Buzenko had been permitted to get hold of them.

Buzenko thrust out two fists. Tate tapped the left fist. It opened to reveal a silver pawn. Buzenko set up the silver crusaders for Tate and then the gold crusaders for himself. He sat back rubbing his hands.

Tate realized that the Admiral could not have believed anything he had said.

Buzenko gestured to him to make his move.

Tate had not played chess since his undergraduate days over a quarter century ago. He advanced his queen's pawn two squares.

Buzenko stared at the chessboard. He spat something guttural at the interpreter. The interpreter left the room. Minutes passed and the interpreter did not come back. It dawned on Tate that there was now absolutely nothing he could say to the Admiral. He had crossed the boundary, abandoned everything, for nothing.

Tate felt a great yearning to sleep. He prayed that Barbara would forgive him, if she was still alive to forgive. He wished Randy could forgive him. He wondered if America would ever forgive him.

Buzenko smiled and hopped his knight over the line of pawns to king's bishop 3.

Tate moved his own knight to king's bishop 3.

"I don't understand . . ." Buzenko edged his king's pawn forward one square. His accent was British. "I don't understand why you took thirty-eight photographs of the naval installation at Kronstadt."

A painted grandfather clock showed phases of a smiling moon and made stiletto-heel ticks. The pendulum bob caught glints from birch logs smoldering in the open fireplace. The room with its raw-wood floors and furniture had the dry, spicy smell of a sauna. Childish drawings dotted the walls and Tate suspected the hand of a Buzenko child. Outside the windows with their apron-filled curtains, afternoon seemed to be filtering through the forest, but the time on the grinning clockface was 9:45.

"You must know it's against the law to photograph strategic installations in Russia." The green eyes brushed Tate's.

Tate slid a pawn forward one square to king's knight 3.

"Over three hundred of Leningrad's 621 bridges are strategic installations. Every year without fail, an American tourist is arrested for taking photographs. They always say the bridges are so pretty, they had no idea they were strategic. But Kronstadt is not pretty, General." Buzenko moved his queen's knight's pawn forward a square.

Tate was suddenly awake, thinking again. Buzenko must have got the warning through. The Admiral was bluffing now, negotiating, but he must have got the warning through. How could he have understood and not got the warning through?

"I didn't photograph Kronstadt," Tate said.

"The camera was found in your raincoat. The film has been fully exposed. Your move."

"An American agent planted the film in the raincoat to discredit me."

"And you Americans accuse us of Byzantine intrigue. General, can you give me a single reason why I should believe anything you've said today?"

"Two reasons." Tate moved his bishop to knight 3. The bishop wore full combat armor, the chain mail meticulously pinpricked, and he carried a ruby-tipped spear. The only Christian note about him was a scarlet enameled cross inlaid into his shield. "Your country and mine."

Buzenko slid his queen's pawn forward a square. His finger hovered in contact with the piece. "You served more than twenty years with the United States Army. You've worked for over five years with the Pacific Aero Corporation and its subsidiaries. Your company builds guidance systems for the new generation of Minuteman ICBMs. You must have a certain familiarity with the device."

"I'm a salesman, Admiral. Not a physicist."

"We're not interested in physics." Buzenko brought the queen's pawn back to its orginal square. "The guidance system relies on the on-board micro-miniaturized computer, yes? And the computer, among other duties, measures the readiness of the missile twenty-four hours a day, yes?" Mirroring Tate's move, Buzenko placed his bishop in knight 2. "We should like to know how many of the present generation of Minutemen now possess the new guidance system. We should like to know the mean time between failure of the on-board computer over its first year since trial installation. We should like to know its downtime."

The corners of the green eyes crinkled.

"General Erlandsen, we are in the same business. We are allies against a common enemy: critics. The critics complain that our countries have stockpiled enough megatonnage to pulverize one another five times over. The critics assume that the missiles work. You and I know otherwise. Even our newest missiles have less than 20 per cent reliability, and we have to compensate with what appears to be 500 per cent overkill. This is the dirty secret of our business. All I'm asking you is: how much less than 20 per cent?"

"Nobody advertises when he's got his nuclear pants down," Tate said. "There's just no way I'd have that sort of information. I'm not cleared for it."

"Yet you answered those questions twelve months ago in testimony in Congress. Your answers were deleted from the published record, but not—I assume—from your memory."

Tate moved a pawn to bishop 4.

Buzenko nudged his queen's pawn forward two squares. His hand rested touching it. "Your position doesn't ring true to me. What is the use of keeping minor military secrets if we are about to be atomized in an all-out nuclear exchange?" He withdrew the pawn. "Let me make a bargain with you, General. You tell me the mean time between failure and the downtime of the computer in the guidance system. I'll make a phone call and see that your Theta plans are passed to a competent authority; and I'll warn the Ministry of Defense to expect an unarmed missile in—" He glanced at the clock. "Thirteen minutes."

"You're playing games with millions of lives, Admiral."

"A very high estimate of your submarine-launched missiles'

accuracy. I believe your own New York *Times* has reported five demonstrations of the new Polaris missiles to congressmen in the last year. Four failed to launch and the fifth was three hundred miles off target." The runway between king and rook was now clear, and Buzenko castled. "Your move, General Erlandsen."

As the Chief of Naval Operations stepped from the West Wing colonnade into the sunlight, his expression was haggard. Too many sixteen-hour days, too many cups of black coffee, and too many high-level shoot-outs like the half hour he had just survived had begun to tell on him. Turning toward the White House parking lot, he walked with the subtly hesitant stride of a man thinking about his retirement pay.

Saluting, a uniformed naval ensign held the door for him. Admiral Anne Gurney sat in the back seat of the Cadillac limousine. The glass partition was raised, and the stereo speakers were turned to a classical radio station.

"Erlandsen managed to get to the Soviet military," Wanamaker said. "He also managed to get the plans to the CIA."

Admiral Gurney stared at him.

"The CIA," Wanamaker said, "believe they've uncovered Soviet Theta plans. They believe the incident at Silo 29 was a demonstration of the Soviet capability."

The limousine edged past a sign warning that the speed limit on White House grounds was five miles per hour.

"Does the President believe the CIA?" Admiral Gurney asked.

Wanamaker nodded. "He believes them."

She looked at her watch. The time was Theta minus eleven. "Then we'd better hurry."

As he passed the bar, O'Brien filled a glass with ice cubes and picked up a bottle of I. W. Harper. He crossed his empty office, stared a moment at the view of the reflecting pool, and dropped into the chair. He poured himself a drink and took a long swallow. He looked around him and seemed to see the rug and the furniture and the ducks and the Pollock for the first time. He had never been comfortable with leather and chrome and glass, he had never enjoyed the Pollock abstract or the patternless mocha rug or the wooden ducks, and it came to him that he would never have to pretend to himself again that they pleased him.

Frances Meredith stepped quietly into the office. "Jack?"

"Yes, Frances?" He was curious how she would say what she had obviously been planning to say for a very long time.

"I'm going to take Melvin Culligan's offer."

He tried to be realistic, which meant trying to pretend that emotions such as shock and hatred and fear didn't exist. The real estate market was way down, but he could probably realize a quarter million on the house. He'd have his pension—suitably managed, fifty thousand a year. They would get a smaller place, with a room for Debbie's Louis Quinze. He'd be able to read books and maybe get good at golf again without feeling guilty about it. They could travel to places they'd loved, like Venice, and places they'd always dreamed about, like India.

They could visit the children. Debbie could scramble eggs.

They would just have to manage.

"I know you love the company, and I do too. But we're old." Frances Meredith wore the fixed smile of a great lady on a charitable five-minute detour through a paraplegic ward. "The day comes when you have to call it a day. It would be a shame to fumble and undo all the good of the past."

Jack O'Brien saw himself in his memory's eye, a man who had helped invent a temperature/airspeed ratio control, who had transmuted the maybe's and if's of dreaming physicists into the solidity of steel, who had served his country and his stockholders and one day had woken up too old to pull the plow any further.

"It can be beautiful not doing anything," Frances Meredith said when it was obvious he wasn't going to answer. "That's why I love roses—it's my way of doing absolutely, unmitigatedly nothing at all."

"Frances," O'Brien said, "what are you planning to do about your grandson?"

Frances Meredith looked politely startled. "Which grandson?"

"The musical one. The guitarist."

"Harvey?" Frances Meredith smiled. "He's very talented."

"He's in a narcotics rehabilitation program in New York City. Argo House. He needs help, Frances. If you haven't retired completely from doing things."

Frances Meredith's mouth was open but no sound was coming out, and O'Brien felt the dizzy exhaustion of putting down an impossibly heavy burden one has carried impossibly far. He looked at Frances Meredith and realized he would never have to hear about her roses or her family or give a damn about her or people like her ever again. He stood. "I might as well get going. Why don't you have a seat? You look the way I felt a minute ago."

She slid into a chair and he nodded toward the bottle.

"Have a drink. It's on the company."

At one minute after three, a man and a woman in raincoats hurried into a stationery store on Thirteenth Street. They rode three flights in an elevator, crossed a fire escape into another building, and knocked on an iron door. A man with a black toupee opened the door, and the Chief of Naval Operations and his aide stepped into the projection room of the Nugget Cinema, a pornographic movie house two blocks from the White House.

The projector, encased in soundproofing that cut its clatter to a sewing-machine hum, took up nine square feet of floor space. The remaining hundred and eleven square feet were Project Theta, D.C. command.

A square-jawed crew-cut man in civilian clothes stood to salute the two admirals, but they motioned him to sit down and carry on.

Except for the radio equipment, the room was almost surgically barren. The window on the south wall had been sealed and plastered. An illuminated map, six feet in diameter, occupied half the north wall. The map showed the land masses and oceans of the world in polar projection, with the North Pole as mathematical center.

A white dot of light was floating downward from the upper left-hand quadrant with its elongated, barely recognizable Australia. Moving no more than one inch a minute, the dot followed a hyperbolic path whose asymptotes crossed in the neighborhood of Novaya Zemlya in the Arctic Ocean. Like a rubber ball bouncing in extremely slow motion, the light bottomed out as it brushed the circle of the 75th longitude. It arced gracefully upward in the direction of Archangel in the Soviet Union.

Four inches beyond Archangel lay a large blue dot marked *Moscow*.

In the Barents Sea, a red light blinked, stationary and persistent.

The crew-cut man sat watching the moving light. At fifteen-second intervals he read its coordinates into the leftmost of the three microphones on his desk. Like an echo delayed seven seconds, the leftmost of the three eight-inch speakers aligned on the desk replied with confirming coordinates.

One clock on the west wall gave local time, four minutes after three; the other clock gave Greenwich Mean Time, 19:04. The tips of their second hands dipped past six and began synchronized swoops up and leftward.

"Start the countdown," the Chief of Naval Operations ordered.

Jack O'Brien stepped from the executive building into the parking lot and stopped to gaze at Pacific Aero. An ocean bed of asphalt supported vessels of massed glass and concrete, a beached fleet whose cargo had once been the strength of the nation. Patches of grass and trees lingered like the preposterous puddles of a long-retreated tide.

He tried to remember what it was he had wanted so long ago when he and his GI partner had leased the shoe factory in St. Louis, what it was he had wanted even longer ago when the mere thought of holding Debbie Brighton's hand had made him dizzy. The only thing he wanted now was to remember what in God's name he had wanted then: it had seemed so real and so near and he had set his life's sights on it, and the years' searching had brought him here to this place, but he didn't know what he had been looking for or if he had even found it.

The chauffeur was standing by the door of the custom-built Lincoln Continental in parking place one. O'Brien asked Sam to take him home and the man touched a finger to his cap. Before O'Brien could get into the back seat, a red Pinto like the one Debbie sometimes used for shopping turned into the lot. The woman at the wheel waved at him, silhouetted against asphalt glare, and O'Brien crossed to the little car and bent down to the open window.

"Miss Kelly phoned," Debbie said. Her eyes were red. "Let's drive somewhere."

"Home," he said. "Please drive me home."

He got into the seat beside her and watched Pacific Aero slide irreversibly past the sealed glass.

"We're going to have to sell the house," he said.

She looked at him and stopped the car, and then she leaned across the seat and kissed him. "You stubborn old idiot," she said, "don't you know I love you?"

"Debbie," he said, "thank you."

Her eyes were moist, almost tearful, and he realized he had not said those two words in that way in thirty years.

In the pornographic cinema two blocks from the White House two images coupled on a screen. The film was silent, and the projectionist had selected for background music a recording of the scherzo from Beethoven's Sixth Symphony. In the audience four men slept and five watched. Only one, a medical-supplies salesman from Wilkes-Barre, Pennsylvania, achieved orgasm.

In the projection room a recorded voice counted downward from the number *six*. When it reached *two*, Ilya Wanamaker's eyes met Anne Gurney's. At *one* an irreversible radio directive blipped out at the speed of light.

The signal was received at the naval transmitting station at Cutler, Maine. It was assumed to be a routine coded command originating from the Pentagon. The message was forwarded by secure low-frequency relay to the fleet ballistic missile submarine USS *Intrepid,* which was testing sonar under the Barents Sea, forty miles from the Russian coast.

The communications officer of the *Intrepid* received the order at 19:05 hours Greenwich Mean Time.

It was carried out sixty seconds later.

The hands of the grandfather clock were outstretched at seven after ten. Its resonant ticks pointed up a twenty-beat silence. Buzenko moved his queen to bishop 4, directly menacing Tate's queen.

The interpreter came stiffly into the room. He spoke rapid Russian with the Admiral. Buzenko pushed back his chair and got up.

"According to your Theta hypothesis, General, we should have been panicked into a nuclear exchange—" Buzenko glanced at the grandfather clock. "One minute ago. Would you excuse me one moment? I have a phone call." He bent over the table and took Tate's queen with his remaining rook. "Your move, General."

Buzenko walked quickly from the room. The interpreter stayed behind.

Tate stared at the chessboard and strained to overhear the phone call. The clock seemed to tick louder. He felt hollow. There was nothing left in him but a flickering dread. *God, let them have believed me, let it have worked, let my wife be*

*alive. They must have believed me, it must have worked, let
her be alive, let us all be alive.*

After a while the interpreter said, "Rook to queen's bishop
1."

"I'm sorry?"

"Rook to queen's bishop 1."

Buzenko appeared in the doorway. He was not smiling and
there was sweat on his face. It took him an eternity to cross
the room. He spoke staccato Russian with the interpreter,
then turned to Tate.

"General Erlandsen," he said, "I'm afraid we've just had
some bad news from Moscow."

Afterwards

Two armed State Department men escorted Tate off the Pan American 747 jetliner. It was night, and Washington's Dulles International Airport was mobbed. Every chair in the waiting area had been taken. Lines stretched out raggedly from the news-stands, the ticket counters, the telephone booths. Travelers jammed the concourse. No one gave the three tired men a glance.

Anne Gurney met them on the lower level. She was wearing her admiral's uniform. "Poor General Erlandsen," she said. "Miles to go before you sleep." She held out a hand but did not seem to care one way or the other when Tate did not take it.

They left the terminal through a side exit. Admiral Gurney gave a sharp little wave. As faltering rain drifted through the low glow of its headlights, a black Cadillac limousine cut straight into the near lane and—whitewalls sighing against asphalt gutter—slowed to a stop at the curb. A crew-cut naval ensign sprang saluting out of the driver's seat and scurried to hold the passenger door.

The State Department men sat in front, and Gurney and Tate arranged themselves in the back seat. The limousine was air-conditioned and the Admiral pushed a button to raise the glass partition.

"You're an expensive man to ransom, General. We have to give them back Savrovski."

"Savrovski?" Tate said.

"He used to coordinate Soviet intelligence in the Los Angeles area."

Tate remembered the name and he remembered Buzenko's coming back from the phone saying that there had been bad news: that an exchange had been arranged, that he and Tate would never finish their chess game or their discussion. "I'm flattered I was worth the price."

"We believe in looking after our own," the Admiral said.

"What makes you think I'm one of your own?"

"Among other things, the caliber of your work."

"Don't you and I work opposite sides of the fence?"

"Not really."

The limousine pulled away from the curb and moved smoothly toward traffic beginning to pile up at the access to the freeway.

"You're very broad-minded."

Admiral Gurney looked at him. "Am I?"

"Didn't any of your killers manage to tell you? I tried to hand your precious Theta to the Russians."

She nodded. "You succeeded. They've got it."

"And you still admire the caliber of my work?"

"Of course. It was the job we picked you for."

"Sharing secrets with the Communists is nothing new," Ilya Wanamaker said. "America has been doing it since World War II."

The security board was lit up solid green: no bugs, no taps, no peeking or eavesdropping lasers. Just the four of them in the Joint Chiefs of Staff Emergency Conference Room: Wanamaker explaining, Tate listening, Gurney half smiling like a Botticelli madonna, and Bailey playing pianissimo piano concertos on the tabletop.

"The first H-bomb," Wanamaker said, "was as big as this room. Teller and von Neumann miniaturized it and made it a deliverable package. Four months later, the Russians made the identical breakthrough, right down to the Texas-made electron lenses. In 1953 the Russians came up with a duplicate of the American lithium bomb—they even duplicated the Du Pont trademark on the casing. It took us three painstaking years to produce the uranium diffusion barrier, and then three yards of it disappeared from Oak Ridge and the Chinese produced it overnight. In 1968, the Russians unveiled an exact copy of the Polaris sub. In each case, Congress was panicked into voting huge allotments to meet the new threat.

"By the time we realized Lee Armstrong was selling weapons information to the Soviets, we had three decades' experience in the fine art of sharing secrets with the enemy. We'd come to realize that sharing secrets is like plowing profits back into a business. If the enemy's technology didn't catch up with ours now and then, Congress would never vote funds for new weapons.

"We kept Armstrong in place. We fed him a stream of obsolescent weapons, and he helped obsolesce them faster by feeding them to the Soviets. Five years ago the Navy began developing Firebird. It was stolen from Asher's Theta device, but it was a legitimate attempt at a solar-power relay. There was nothing secret about it. Asher was an employee of a defense contractor when he thought up Theta and, technically, any patents were ours. Two years ago, for purely experimental reasons, we decided to modify one of the Firebirds into a Theta. That *was* secret.

"Test launches of Minuteman missiles aren't generally announced. But we'd known for some time, through Dr. Bailey, that there would be a test Monday night last week."

Tate's gaze shifted to the man tapping on the conference table.

"It was a chance to test Theta. The device worked. We hadn't intended to let Armstrong have Theta. But you gave it to him, General. Initially, we handled the situation clumsily: tailed him, tailed you, shredded paper, broke into apartments, tried to plug leaks. It was Dr. Bailey who suggested we'd do better to make the best of a bad thing.

"The country is broke and Congress is cutting the military budget to ribbons. Dr. Bailey pointed out that what we need more than anything at this moment is a Soviet breakthrough. Why not give the Russians Theta? We'd still have an edge in lead time. We could convince the CIA that the Russians had developed a new and totally destabilizing weapon, that they had successfully tested it on American soil. Congress would have to loosen the purse strings. All things considered, it began to seem like a damned good idea. And then Lee Armstrong got drunk and killed himself in that car crash.

"That left us with a problem. How were we going to get a copy of the plans into Russian hands? We needed a credible courier. Again, Dr. Bailey had the solution. Who could be more credible to the Russians than a convinced anti-Communist, a retired four-star general, an assistant vice-president of a major aerospace-defense corporation? All we had to do was complete the job Lee Armstrong had begun: we had to make you believe in Theta and we had to make you believe we were about to use it."

"And why the hell did you have to drag my wife into this?"

"Dr. Bailey saw her as the convincer. If Theta was so important to us that we'd kidnap the wife of a four-star general, you'd see we meant business; you'd see you had no choice but to take the plans to the Russians."

"And what if I'd decided Barbara was more important than Theta?"

"Then we'd have a fiscal problem." Ilya Wanamaker smiled. "But you went to Russia. Just as you stood up to those rebels in Panama. You have an ingrained resistance to coercion. You're an old-fashioned American that way. It's part of your psychological makeup."

"And it didn't matter that while you were playing white mouse with me you could have killed my wife?"

Admiral Gurney's eyes caressed Tate as coolly as ice cubes trickling down his skin. She said Mrs. Erlandsen was in a private room at District of Columbia General. "No one has hurt her."

"Then she did a little better than the others. Edith Gormley may never walk again. Asher and Armstrong and Mrs. Benzikoff are dead—not to mention all those poor slobs with pacemakers who happened to be in the way when you threw the switch."

Admiral Gurney raised another barricade of words. She said when Tate missed his return flight from Copenhagen, the agent had realized that the transfer must have fallen through. Naturally he had to keep track. He might have frightened Mrs. Benzikoff, but he certainly had not killed her. When Tate had gone on to Helsinki, the Gormleys had been called in to steer him onto the ship. Mrs. Gormley had tried to heighten the illusion of pursuit by breaking into his hotel room; she had slipped; it was her own fault for embroidering.

"And why did Gormley put microfilm in my pocket?"

By then it was obvious the plans wouldn't get into Russia unless Tate went in too. To minimize State Department suspicion, there had to be a reason for his being holed up with Russian authorities. It seemed easiest to implicate him on espionage charges: the Russians did that sort of thing all the time to Americans.

"You have a knack for dreaming up reasons. Asher died of a reaction to an anesthetic. Armstrong died in a highway accident. I don't suppose you helped the moving finger write either of those death sentences?"

Ilya Wanamaker explained that messing with American citizens was dodgy, especially inside the United States. His eyes neither confessed nor denied: they pleaded the extenuating burdens of leadership.

"And how many Thetas do you have to show for all this conniving and killing?"

Wanamaker shook his head. "None. The prototype self-destructed yesterday at 19:06 GMT. We'll develop the weapon from scratch. We'll still have a five-year lead on the Russians. Assuming they even decide to go with it. The point isn't Theta: it's the money. We had to get funds flowing back into defense research." He seemed to sense a question mark in Tate's gaze, because he went on. "If I were you, I wouldn't bother rushing to the New York *Times*. Technically, you defected to the Russians. You gave them American secrets."

"You don't need to spell it out," Tate said. They had played him like a piano and they had him. They knew it and they knew he knew it.

The room was silent and he felt like a man trying to touch bottom. His feet kept treading water but the bottom wasn't there.

"Let me see my wife," he said.

"Of course you can see her," Wanamaker said. "No one's holding you. And by the way—if we should happen to toss a few Theta contracts Pacific Aero's way—try to act surprised, will you?"

Barbara's room was dark. A nurse was taking her pulse. Tate stayed in the hallway and waited for the nurse to come out. He could see Barbara lying on her side beneath the bed-sheet. She didn't move and she looked dead, but he didn't suppose a nurse would be taking the pulse of a dead person.

The hospital corridor was utterly still. Finally the nurse came to the door and her heels clacked on the tile. She looked at Tate. "May I see her?" he said. "I'm her husband."

"She's still critical," the nurse said. "You mustn't wake her up."

"I only want to look at her."

The nurse left the door open partway for him. It was a private room: there were two chairs and a table and the light in the bathroom had been left on. Tate's eyes took a moment to adjust. He saw Barbara's head with her hair spilling across the pillow. Her body did not move at all under the sheet and he supposed they had given her a pill.

He moved a chair beside the bed and sat and looked at her and thought how close he had come to never seeing her again. Her face was extraordinarily peaceful and he wondered if that was because of the pill.

They pushed a stretcher by in the corridor, and a wheel squeaked and she opened her eyes and seemed to come back from a great distance. She moved a hand toward him.

"Tate," she said. "It's nice to see you." Her voice was hardly more than a whisper but she was smiling.

He leaned his head down and tried not to let her see that something in him wanted very much to cry. He gritted his eyes and blinked and did not cry. "It's nice to see you too," he said.

"You must have been worried," she said.

"I was worried sick."

"Poor Tate. Always having to worry about me." Her face had no color at all but he supposed that could have been the light or the pill or any number of things. "I'm sorry."

"Don't be sorry." He took her hand in both of his. It was cold and he wondered what they'd been doing to her.

"Do you suppose I'll die?" she said. "There was so much blood and clots and tissue. The doctor said sometimes you get that."

"Don't worry about it now," Tate said.

"He said so long as you don't pass fetal tissue the baby's all right. He said the baby's still there." She looked up and a ghost of a smile hovered on her lips. "I don't want to die before the baby comes. Help me not to die, Tate."

He squeezed her hand. There was something in his throat. He couldn't swallow it and it wouldn't come up and he felt very close to letting himself go. He had never cried in front of another person since he'd been a boy and he didn't intend to start now.

"They've made me afraid." Her eyes were bright even in that dark. "I wish I could be brave. I want you to be proud of me. I've been sick for a long time and I'll always be sick but I didn't tell you because it seemed so weak of me."

"You're not weak," he said. "You're stronger than anyone I've ever known."

"They say I'm too old and I could still miscarry and even if the baby's born it's bound to have all sorts of emotional problems. But I want the baby. I want you to have something, something of ours."

"I have you," he said.

She gripped his hand and pressed it hard against her. "Can you stay with me, just till I fall asleep?"

The hospital corridor had a smudged look, like the barrel of a recently fired cannon. Tate saw the old inspector sitting in a chair by the elevator, frowning at a crossword puzzle, and he knew the man had been waiting for him a long while.

"Thanks for finding my wife," he said.

"I almost didn't." The old man folded his newspaper and took off his glasses and blew on the lenses. "They had her in the mental ward."

Tate wasn't sure he had the strength to ask what his wife had been doing in a mental ward.

"Somehow," the old man said, "she managed to telephone your maid. So we knew she was in a ward and we knew they'd used a false name. Luckily they used the same initials." He put his glasses back on and stood and shook his legs as though shaking could get the wrinkles out of his trousers. "The record says she went crazy last Thursday in the National Gallery. She was committed by a patrolman. A doctor signed the papers Saturday. Didn't even look at her."

"How the hell can that happen?" Tate asked.

"Remember the Billy Sol Estes cover-up back in '62? The Department of Agriculture railroaded a secretary into the nut house because she wouldn't let them have her boss's files? This was the same setup. Isn't there a water cooler around here somewhere?" They began strolling, looking for the cooler. "It's a question of law, General. If they'd tried to take her from a private building, the law would have required signatures of two citizens and two doctors. But they took her from a public building. The law's different. All they needed was the patrolman's signature. Anyway, your wife's doing just fine, isn't she?"

"She doesn't look like she's doing just fine."

The water cooler was hiding behind the telephone booth. The inspector filled paper cups for both of them. "She had a pretty rough time. When you're pregnant you can get bleeding and cramps, but the Ilse Koch type guarding her wouldn't believe she was pregnant. Some student doctor who didn't understand English decided she'd been poisoning herself. So they pumped her stomach and she almost lost the baby."

"Almost?" Tate said.

"It was a close call, but they say she's still pregnant and they say that's not necessarily good."

Tate crumpled the empty cup and dropped it into an overflowing wastebasket. "I can see locking her up without a phone—but why the hell did they have to torture her like that?"

"Call that torture?" the inspector said. "It was strictly par for the course. All the kidnappers did was give her a false name and certify her violent insane and dump her in a charity ward. D.C. General took it from there. Your wife got treated the same as any violent insane charity case in an overcrowded understaffed city hospital. She got buried in the shuffle and she got restrained, which is another way of saying they beat her up a little."

"I'll kill them," Tate said.

The inspector looked at him. "I've been digging, General, and I think you've got a chance of nailing a few of the bastards that did this to her."

"How?"

"We've got a witness. An art student was copying a picture in the gallery. He saw what happened and he's nervous, but if you and your wife spoke to him I think he'd be willing to talk. He could corroborate your wife. You'd have a good false arrest and malicious defamation and I'll bet those cowards would pass the buck straight up to the top."

"And the man at the top will scream national security and the courts won't touch it."

"I'm not so sure. You can't have national security without personal security, can you?" The inspector smiled. "I mean, outside of the Soviet Union?"

Tate couldn't help liking the old man. "What's your interest in this, Inspector?"

"Just call me an interested bystander who's going to be sixty-four next week and won't have a damned thing to do but collect his pension. It scares me stiff, General, not having anything to do. I don't suppose you've ever been scared stiff, have you?"

"More and more of the time," Tate said.

"Jack, I honestly thought you knew from the start." Melvin Culligan's manner had been curious all evening—almost ingratiating.

"I never even thought you and Rebus could be behind it," O'Brien admitted. Melvin Culligan had insisted on taking him to dinner and O'Brien had had three bourbons and half a bottle of wine, and there was no reason he couldn't say exactly what he felt. "Everything seemed to point to Southern Electronics. When Allan Martino turned up romancing Davidine Stokes, that convinced me."

"The only reason she bothered with Martino was to keep tabs on Southern Electronics. They *were* trying to take you over, Jack. Only we beat them in the last round."

O'Brien nodded. It made sense in retrospect but it was nice not to have to care. Debbie had not said two words all evening, but she put her hand over his and squeezed.

"I suppose," O'Brien said, "I was getting friendship and business and all sorts of things mixed up that don't have much to do with one another."

"You can't do that, Jack. Especially not nowadays. You have to keep factors in perspective. The market's completely different from when you and I were starting out." Melvin Culligan said the coming market for sophisticated weaponry was the Middle East. There would be petrodollars for research, petrodollars for development, petrodollars for everything from laser-guided bullets to armed satellites, and to hell with Congress—let 'em have social programs.

Debbie had been taking small mouthfuls of lobster, but she put down her fork and looked almost as though she wanted to throw her wine in Melvin Culligan's face. "Mel, I can understand your being excited," she said, "but frankly I think you're being cruel."

For Debbie that was outspoken. After a lifetime of having to smile at boring dinners and bad jokes she was free to say what she thought, and O'Brien realized how much she had bottled up for thirty years.

"Cruel?" Melvin Culligan looked astonished.

"You know what Jack's been through this last week. You once went through it yourself. I just don't see how you could do this to him."

"What the dickens am I doing?"

"You're gloating. You pulled it off and now you're gloating."

"You make me sound like some kind of sneak. Jack, was I ever sneaky with you? Didn't I say you were a damned fool to try to buy up your own stock? Didn't I advise you to go along with the raider?"

O'Brien sighed. "The only thing you didn't tell me, Mel, was that the raider was you."

"I thought I made that pretty clear too."

"I guess not clear enough."

"I'm not supposed to say anything till Rebus had completed the take-over," Melvin Culligan said. "But hell, you didn't think there was ever any question, did you?"

There was a tentative sort of hurt in Melvin Culligan's voice that didn't go with the situation at all and O'Brien looked at him carefully.

"Jack—you didn't think we were going to boot you out, did you?"

O'Brien stared and he saw Debbie staring and Melvin Culligan burst out laughing.

"Jesus Christ, how dumb do you think we are?" Melvin Culligan's laughter was like hiccups and it took almost half a minute for him to bring it under control. "Jack, I couldn't make the offer last week and technically I can't make it now. But within a week or so, I expect to be making you a very, very good offer. I hope you'll stay on. Frankly, if you don't, my ass is in the sling!"

O'Brien realized he ought to have felt very happy at that moment, but all he felt was very numb and much more tired than he had ever been in his life. "That's very handsome of you, Mel," he said. "Very handsome."

Melvin Culligan looked as if he'd discovered something quite extraordinary about O'Brien, like a grandmother in vaudeville or a sixth finger. "You were leading the field from the start, Jack. Oh, we were considering one or two younger men. But when you turned down the ninety million, you had it made. Rebus has been looking for someone with *ethics*. To run the American side. The money was a test. You always knew we wanted you, didn't you, Jack?"

O'Brien wondered what you called it when everything you had ever believed in or fought for went up in smoke and you were left standing unscathed in the ashes.

Maybe you called it relief.

O'Brien's wineglass was shaking in his hand, and Melvin Culligan seemed fascinated with the idea that anyone could have doubted anything so obvious. "Debbie," he asked, "was there any question in your mind?"

Debbie's face went through several gradations of emotion, all carefully controlled. She glanced at O'Brien and she seemed to read something in his eyes. It suddenly struck him that she was not the woman who had just stood up to Melvin Culligan and told him to go to hell; she was the woman she had always been, the little loyal wife, lovely and soft and reliable, and there was something sad about her smile.

"There never was any real question," she said.

"Then why did you let your fool of a husband put up such a fight?"

"I suppose he wanted the best possible price, and the best way to get it was to fight you for it."

It was a good explanation and it made O'Brien seem less of an idiot and he was glad Debbie had thought of it. He realized that he and Debbie and Pacific Aero had been standing at the edge of a very dangerous precipice and they had just crossed it safely. He reached for the wine bottle and refilled their glasses. His hand was still shaking but he was beginning to feel better.

"To the courage to face the next ten years," Melvin Culligan proposed. "It'll be quite a decade for all of us. We'll see major Soviet breakthroughs and we'll see the U.S. defense budget break two hundred billion and we'll see cooperation between American defense companies break down completely. There'll be such a scrambling after contracts you won't know the difference between free enterprise and murder. Two thirds of the companies will go under. It's the end of the golden age. For three decades business has made a killing in defense, and defense has got pretty well murdered by business." Melvin Culligan lifted his glass a little too high. It magnified his eye into something like an octopus's. "Well, it's coming to a choice between free enterprise and survival, and even Americans aren't so brainwashed they'd choose free enterprise. Free enterprise in defense can't beat the Russian threat. Not at today's prices. Free enterprise won't even be able to support a warm production base. If Uncle Sam expects to have a missile to his name, he's going to have to step in and nationalize. You think I'm joking?"

O'Brien did not think he was joking, and Debbie was not smiling.

"I'm dead serious," Melvin Culligan said. "Sure, Rebus is buying in for the weapons. But that's short-term. The big money's going to come when Washington has to buy up the survivors: Pacific Aero and Boeing and maybe Northrup. You're going to see that stock soar. Here's to it."

They drank to the courage to face the next decade.

O'Brien felt uneasy: not because he thought Melvin Culligan's scenario made sense, but because Melvin Culligan seemed to believe it did. "I should phone Washington," O'Brien said. He was happy in a way but he was shaking badly and he needed an excuse to leave the table. "I should tell Tate Erlandsen the news. I haven't spoken to him for over a week. He's probably worried stiff." He excused himself and left Debbie and Melvin Culligan chatting about sports cars. They seemed very friendly and you'd never have guessed that two minutes ago she had said those things to him.

There was a telephone by the hat-check booth, and O'Brien placed a credit-card call. Tate Erlandsen answered and O'Brien apologized for calling at an awkward hour. Tate said the hour wasn't awkward in Washington.

O'Brien told him the company was in the clear. He said that even if Congress swatted down Hornet and Navy sank the entire Air Force, there still wasn't a damned thing to worry about.

"That's very good news," Tate said, and then he added, "I've sent you a letter."

"I'll look forward to getting it," O'Brien said.

"I'm submitting my resignation. I hope this doesn't louse you up."

O'Brien swallowed hard and the sound traveled across the long-distance hookup. "But, Tate, why? The company's never looked better."

"There are things I have to do and I just don't know how much time there's going to be. My wife's pregnant. The doctors say it'll be a difficult pregnancy. I want to be with her."

"I don't see how your being with her can make a pregnancy any less difficult."

"She's bringing a lawsuit and I've just got to be with her."

"Tate, you're many things, but a lawyer you're not."

"The letter explains, Jack. It's better for me to go now."

Another swallow came across the wire and O'Brien sounded rebuffed and hurt. "Well, I'm awfully sorry to lose you."

"Sorry to have to go."

Tate hung up. He stood by the phone a moment, troubled. Something in the living room had changed. He had never liked the room, but tonight, suddenly, it was home.

What has changed? he asked himself.

His eyes sought the detail, the thing that had changed, but there was only a woman sitting at a piano, her hands resting on the highest octave. She had leaned sideways to see around the music rack and to look curiously at him. There was lamplight interlaced with her hair. The pages of "Golliwog's

Cakewalk" spilled from the rack and his eyes memorized the instant: his wife surprised and smiling, her stomach not yet round, her arms suddenly full of music.

"Here," he said, going quickly to her, "let me help."

Big Bestsellers from SIGNET

☐ **LYNDON JOHNSON AND THE AMERICAN DREAM** by Doris Kearns. (#E7609—$2.50)

☐ **THIS IS THE HOUSE** by Deborah Hill. (#J7610—$1.95)

☐ **THE DEMON** by Hubert Selby, Jr. (#J7611—$1.95)

☐ **LORD RIVINGTON'S LADY** by Eileen Jackson. (#W7612—$1.50)

☐ **ROGUE'S MISTRESS** by Constance Gluyas. (#J7533—$1.95)

☐ **SAVAGE EDEN** by Constance Gluyas. (#J7681—$1.95)

☐ **LOVE SONG** by Adam Kennedy. (#E7535—$1.75)

☐ **THE DREAM'S ON ME** by Dotson Rader. (#E7536—$1.75)

☐ **SINATRA** by Earl Wilson. (#E7487—$2.25)

☐ **THE CAPTAIN'S WOMAN** by Mark Logan. (#J7488—$1.95)

☐ **THE WATSONS** by Jane Austen and John Coates. (#J7522—$1.95)

☐ **SANDITON** by Jane Austen and Another Lady. (#J6945—$1.95)

☐ **THE FIRES OF GLENLOCHY** by Constance Heaven. (#E7452—$1.75)

☐ **A PLACE OF STONES** by Constance Heaven. (#W7046—$1.50)

☐ **THE ROCKEFELLERS** by Peter Collier and David Horowitz. (#E7451—$2.75)

THE NEW AMERICAN LIBRARY, INC.,
P.O. Box 999, Bergenfield, New Jersey 07621

Please send me the SIGNET BOOKS I have checked above. I am enclosing $_____(check or money order—no currency or C.O.D.'s). Please include the list price plus 35¢ a copy to cover handling and mailing costs. (Prices and numbers are subject to change without notice.)

Name_____

Address_____

City_____State_____Zip Code_____
Allow at least 4 weeks for delivery

Have You Read These Bestsellers from SIGNET?

☐ **CLANDARA by Evelyn Anthony.** (#E6893—$1.75)

☐ **THE PERSIAN PRICE by Evelyn Anthony.**
(#J7254—$1.95)

☐ **EARTHSOUND by Arthur Herzog.** (#E7255—$1.75)

☐ **THE DEVIL'S OWN by Christopher Nicole.**
(#J7256—$1.95)

☐ **THE GREEK TREASURE by Irving Stone.**
(#E7211—$2.25)

☐ **THE GATES OF HELL by Harrison Salisbury.**
(#E7213—$2.25)

☐ **TERMS OF ENDEARMENT by Larry McMurtry.**
(#J7173—$1.95)

☐ **THE KITCHEN SINK PAPERS by Mike McGrady.**
(#J7212—$1.95)

☐ **ROSE: MY LIFE IN SERVICE by Rosina Harrison.**
(#J7174—$1.95)

☐ **THE FINAL FIRE by Dennis Smith.** (#J7141—$1.95)

☐ **SOME KIND OF HERO by James Kirkwood.**
(#J7142—$1.95)

☐ **THE HOMOSEXUAL MATRIX by C. A. Tripp.**
(#E7172—$2.50)

☐ **CBS: Reflections in a Bloodshot Eye by Robert Metz.**
(#E7115—$2.25)

☐ **'SALEM'S LOT by Stephen King.** (#E8000—$2.25)

☐ **CARRIE by Stephen King.** (#J7280—$1.95)

THE NEW AMERICAN LIBRARY, INC.,
P.O. Box 999, Bergenfield, New Jersey 07621

Please send me the SIGNET BOOKS I have checked above. I am enclosing $_____(check or money order—no currency or C.O.D.'s). Please include the list price plus 35¢ a copy to cover handling and mailing costs. (Prices and numbers are subject to change without notice.)

Name_____

Address_____

City_____State_____Zip Code_____
Allow at least 4 weeks for delivery

Bestsellers from SIGNET You'll Want to Read

☐ **WHERE HAVE YOU GONE JOE DI MAGGIO?** by Maury Allen. (#W6986—$1.50)

☐ **KATE: The Life of Katharine Hepburn** by Charles Higham. (#J6944—$1.95)

☐ **THE DOMINO PRINCIPLE** by Adam Kennedy. (#J7389—$1.95)

☐ **THE SECRET LIST OF HEINRICH ROEHM** by Michael Barak. (#E7352—$1.75)

☐ **ARABESQUE** by Theresa de Kerpely. (#J7424—$1.95)

☐ **PHOENIX ISLAND** by Charlotte Paul. (#J6827—$1.95)

☐ **ALLEGRA** by Clare Darcy. (#E7851—$1.75)

☐ **THE HUSBAND** by Catherine Cookson. (#E7858—$1.75)

☐ **THE LONG CORRIDOR** by Catherine Cookson. (#W6829—$1.50)

☐ **MAGGIE ROWAN** by Catherine Cookson. (#W6745—$1.50)

☐ **THE FREEHOLDER** by Joe David Brown. (#W6952—$1.50)

☐ **LOVING LETTY** by Paul Darcy Boles. (#E6951—$1.75)

☐ **COMING TO LIFE** by Norma Klein. (#W6864—$1.50)

☐ **MIRIAM AT THIRTY-FOUR** by Alan Lelchuk. (#J6793—$1.95)

☐ **DECADES** by Ruth Harris. (#J6705—$1.95)

THE NEW AMERICAN LIBRARY, INC.,
P.O. Box 999, Bergenfield, New Jersey 07621

Please send me the SIGNET BOOKS I have checked above. I am enclosing $_____(check or money order—no currency or C.O.D.'s). Please include the list price plus 35¢ a copy to cover handling and mailing costs. (Prices and numbers are subject to change without notice.)

Name_____

Address_____

City_____State_____Zip Code_____

Allow at least 4 weeks for delivery